Praise for
WINTER TIDES

"One creepy, creepy book ... Blaylock will scare you to death with a minimum of splatter and maximum of tension, Hitchcock-style. I read *Winter Tides* in one long sitting and found my heart couldn't stop racing."

—*Woodland Hills (CA) Daily News*

"Blaylock combines the supernatural with a deep understanding of contemporary California and human nature, producing a book with appeal for both fantasy fans and readers of realistic fiction."

—*Publishers Weekly*

"Vivid descriptions and deft characterizations ... [*Winter Tides*] exposes the underbelly of human nature."

—*Library Journal*

"A wonderful ghost story ... Highly recommended."
—*The Plot Thickens,*
Mysterious Galaxy Newsletter

"A successful novel, dramatic, engaging, and entertaining."

—Jonathan Strahan, *Locus*

Winter Tides

James P. Blaylock

ACE BOOKS, NEW YORK

This book is an Ace original edition,
and has never been previously published.

WINTER TIDES

An Ace Book / published by arrangement with
the author

PRINTING HISTORY
Ace hardcover edition / August 1997
Ace mass-market edition / November 1998

The Penguin Putnam Inc. World Wide Web site address
is http://www.penguinputnam.com

Check out the Ace Science Fiction/Fantasy
newsletter, and much more, at Club PPI!

ISBN: 0-441-00575-6

ACE®
Ace Books are published by The Berkley Publishing
Group, a member of Penguin Putnam Inc.,
375 Hudson Street, New York, NY 10014.
ACE and the "A" design are trademarks
belonging to Charter Communications, Inc.

PRINTED IN THE UNITED STATES OF AMERICA

10 9 8 7 6 5 4 3 2 1

For Viki, John, and Danny

And this time, especially for
Dean and Gerda Koontz
for fifteen years of friendship

With special thanks to
John Accursi, Chris Arena, Loren Blaylock,
Dan Halkyard, Judy and Denny Meyer,
Tim Powers,
Jack Miller and the Huntington Beach
Department of Public Works, and
Sarah Q. Koehler.

1

THE PACIFIC COAST HIGHWAY WINDS ALONG THE VERY edge of California, a narrow asphalt ribbon that marks the western rim of the continent, separating the isolated beach towns and the chaparral-covered hillsides of the Coast Range from eleven thousand miles of Pacific Ocean. Heading south from Crescent City, the Highway swings inland below Eureka, wandering thirty miles from the ocean through redwood groves and mill towns before angling west again above Mendocino and then more or less following the shoreline all the way down into southern California. There are still wild and rocky stretches of coast around San Luis Obispo, and empty coves and bluffs above Santa Barbara, but south of Ventura the Highway plunges into the overpopulated beach cities of Los Angeles and Orange and San Diego counties, past hundreds of thousands of wooden bungalows and stucco apartment houses, past fishing piers and rock jetties and boat harbors and ramshackle main streets lined with fish restaurants and bars and surfboard shops and used bookstores and parking meters. And on any sunny summer afternoon, countless people drive out of the suburbs and cross the Highway, drawn to the uttermost edge of the continent for reasons they can't always define.

In winter, cold north swells move down out of the Arctic in long lines, and the blues and greens of the late summer water turn gray beneath cloudy skies. The unsettled ocean shifts with the rolling swell and darkens with the shadows of moving clouds. Storms hammer the coast, washing precarious sections of the Highway into the ocean and veiling beach cities with curtains of misty rain the same steel-gray cast as the rising swell. The surging tides swamp oceanfront houses in Malibu and Surfside and Newport Beach, and rogue waves slam through wood and concrete piers, ripping pilings out of the ocean floor, shifting heavy rocks in harbor jetties, sweeping countless tons of beach sand away in the longshore currents, ceaselessly changing the contour of the sea bottom.

The beaches themselves are nearly empty of people in winter, especially on stormy days—perhaps only a couple of surfers watching waves break across outside sand bars, or a beachcomber with a metal detector, or someone gathering seashells along the high tide line where the ocean dumps its flotsam of kelp and driftwood and sand dollars and polished stones.

IN THE MIDDLE OF THE CENTURY THERE WERE STILL TRAIN tracks along the ocean side of the Highway through Huntington Beach. A chain-link fence separated the tracks from the fifty yards of sandy shoreline, and onshore winds piled beach sand into ice plant-covered dunes that pressed against the rusty chain link and swept across the edge of the tracks and out onto the Highway, which was narrower back then, with a ragged dirt shoulder along the northern verge. Beyond the shoulder there was a grassy marsh, and beyond that stood, and still stand, the pink and gray cinderblock walls that shelter narrow suburban backyards. By the early 1970s passenger trains had long ago quit running along that part of the coast, and the tracks that followed the Highway had fallen into disrepair. Walking along the tracks at the edge of Huntington Beach State Park, a person could find old rail spikes and other iron debris in the sandy ice plant, or, on a lucky day, a heavy, broad-headed nail with a raised number on it, a thirty or a thirty-six or a forty, recalling the year a particular tie had been sunk in the roadbed.

In the winter there was something lonesome and desolate in the rusty chain link and the blowing sand, in the scattered bits of railroad iron and the deep green ice plant with its feathery pink flowers. There was a natural stillness in the air despite the sound of the cold north swell breaking along the beach and the cries of gulls circling in the sky. And beneath windswept skies it could seem that the ocean was a hundred miles removed from the suburban neighborhoods only a couple of blocks inland, as if the Highway, with its sand-softened verge and its distant vanishing points, was a borderland between the suburbs and the shifting sea. When there was a sizable swell running and the winter sun was low in the sky, a traveler gunning north or south along the Highway could glimpse over the crest of the beach the pale green transparency of a backlit wave as it surged upward over a sandbar and pitched forward with the sound of distant, hollow crashing. . . .

THE WOMAN SITTING BENEATH THE BEACH UMBRELLA WAS a tourist—one of the purest examples of tourist that Dave Quinn had ever seen. She was heavyset, dressed in dark clam-digger pants more reminiscent of 1960 than 1980, and she wore socks and shoes and a broad-brimmed hat with a flower in the hatband. Despite the hat and the umbrella and the cloudy winter sky, she was sunburned pink. Her dark glasses flared up toward her ears in plastic crescents worked with rhinestones. She turned a deck of playing cards over one by one onto her beach blanket, starting a new game of solitaire, and the wind picked up a couple of the cards and flipped them face-side up. She lunged forward, holding her blouse shut at the neck with one hand and pinning the cards to the blanket with the other, and then patiently settled back into the depression in the sand and pulled the rim of the umbrella farther around in front of her to block the wind.

Two slender black-haired girls, clearly twins, maybe twelve or thirteen years old, played in the cold surf, running after the edge of a retreating wave, then screaming with laughter as the next wave chased them back up the beach. They had wandered thirty yards north from where their mother sat on the blanket, and it made Dave edgy to watch them. If they were *his* kids, messing in the surf on a day like this, he would have called them back, and he sure as hell wouldn't be shuffling cards while they played tag with the winter ocean. He watched the rip current running down off the steep beach, roiling up the inside break, cutting its own dangerous channel through the bars.

As long as the girls stayed in shallow water . . .

And anyway, they weren't his kids. He ditched the idea of saying something to their mother. He hated shoving in his opinion when nobody was asking for it.

A couple of tin buckets and shovels lay at the edge of the blanket that the woman had unfurled with tremendous care, and there was a basket with a lid, an actual picnic basket, holding down the windward corner of the blanket. Probably she had cold chicken in the basket, the tourist food of preference. Dave realized that he was starved. He had been out in the water surfing since around six, and it was nearly ten in the morning now. His arms ached from paddling, and the cold water had drained him of energy. What he wanted was breakfast and coffee and a couple hours of sleep before afternoon classes. He looked toward the top of the beach. The concession stands were closed, their windows covered with plywood. Some distance to the south, a half-dozen lifeguard towers sat shuttered and empty, waiting to be repainted. Farther on down, maybe a hundred yards, a couple of surfers had a fire going in a fire pit and sat hunched in front of it, their backs to the wind. A white surfboard with a broken-off nose was shoved up out of the fire pit like the ghost of a rocket, and bright orange flames licked up along the rails of the board, sending a churning cloud of black smoke into the air. The smoke tumbled away in the wind, and Dave could smell the chemical reek of burning fiberglass.

The sky was full of broken-up storm clouds, and the water was brown with sand boiled up from the relentless, wind-chopped swell. The swell was rising, and the surf was deceptively powerful. The bigger set waves broke in long, collapsing walls, one after another across sandbars a hundred yards or more offshore, throwing themselves forward against the force of the outgoing tide, churning up the sandy bottom and scouring out a channel between the bars. The waves re-formed in the channels and then broke a second time near shore with a deep, booming roar that sounded like thunder. The entire surface of the ocean seemed to be moving south because of the longshore current, and with the cloud shadow darkening the water, the ocean was ominous and gray.

Dave watched the twin girls nervously. There was a single surfer out in the water a couple of hundred yards down the beach, lying prone on his surfboard as a broken wave pushed him into shore. About a mile north, the Huntington Beach Pier stretched out into the ocean, and even from that distance Dave could see the surging breakers slamming through the pilings. It was no time to be in the water, especially if you were twelve-year-old tourist girls from Kansas or some damned place. Their mother was half hidden behind her umbrella now, dealing cards again. Relieved, Dave saw that the girls had wandered higher up the beach and seemed to be picking through tossed-up seaweed.

It was time to go. He reached behind his back and grabbed the cord attached to his wetsuit zipper, yanking the suit open and moving his shoulders to loosen it up. The neck of his suit was full of dredged-up sand from when he had gotten worked on his last wave, and there was sand in his hair, too. The wave had pounded him all the way into shore before letting up on him. He peeled the wetsuit off, shivering in the wind, and brushed the sand off his neck and shoulders with the thin old towel that he'd been taking to the beach for the last three or four years. His jeans and a flannel shirt sat in the car, and he wished he had brought them down to the beach. His feet were thawing out, and burned now with an itching, prickly heat. The water was cold, fifty-six or fifty-eight degrees—not headache water, but cold enough to wear you out, to drain you of energy despite a wetsuit.

Winter storms had eroded the beach away steeply, and the swell was rising fast. Broken waves rushed up the beach, leaving parallel trails of sea foam near the dry edge of the sand, then rushed seaward again, driving down the incline and back out into the oncoming swells in a moving surge, the rip current chopping up the surface of the ocean all the way out into the outer break now.

Dave took another look at the twins, who apparently had lost interest in the seaweed and had waded out into shallow water again. They stood in the heavy, receding wave wash, their feet sinking ankle-deep into the soft sand, the water leaping around their legs and splashing them to the knees.

One of the twins pushed the other one, trying to shove her over, and Dave could hear her laughter on the wind, followed by the other one's angry shout as her sister tried to pull her out into deeper water. Their mother looked up from her card game, but the umbrella nearly hid the girls from her view. She leaned forward and waved at them, and the twin who was doing all the pushing and pulling saw her and waved back, and then the woman adjusted her hat lower over her face and returned to the game, letting the kids have fun. The second twin managed to yank herself loose and run up into shallower water while her sister threw a clot of wet sand into her hair, then bent down to scrape up more.

Tossing down his towel, Dave walked back down toward the waterline, watching six big pelicans swoop over the top of a swell, soaring above the waves in a dead-even line, rising and falling as the wave passed beneath them. The twin in the water threw more sand, into her sister's face this time, oblivious to an incoming wave that threw itself forward in a collapsing wall, the white water leaping upward as the wave smashed into the girl's back, knocking her down and washing up the steep beach. She stood up in knee-deep water, but the receding wave rushed back downward, piling up against her legs as she tried to high-step through it, the moving water dragging her backward and off balance. She stumbled sideways, fell, and was buried by another wave.

Dave sprinted along the edge of the surf as she floundered heavily to her feet, coughing water out of her throat. Another wave pushed up out of the deeper water of the inside channel and drove in over the sandbar, throwing itself over in an explosion of white water that seemed to swallow her. Her sister screamed from where she stood on the shore, and Dave ran out into the surf as the drowning girl was swept out into deeper water at high speed now, like a boat carried on a river. She was neck-deep and trying to swim, thrashing her arms desperately and raising her head above the chop as if she wanted to climb into the sky. Her sister waded out into the surf, and Dave yelled at her to stop, but already she was caught up in the rip herself and panicking, trying to make her way in again.

Not two of them, he thought, and instantly he changed course. He would grab the close-in girl first, and then he'd swim after the other one. He couldn't deal with two of them in deep water. He could hear the second girl screaming as he dove through the face of a wave, stood up, and launched himself forward again, diving under another wave that broke in front of him. He swam hard through the turbulence, trying not to lose ground, and when he surfaced a few yards from her he threw himself forward again and grabbed her arm, holding onto her as he tried to stand up. The force of the rip was incredible, and for a moment, before he got his feet set, he was helpless in it, and the weight of the girl nearly pulled him down. Fighting again just to stay where he was, he dragged her close to him and spun her around so that he could get an arm across her chest.

Like a gift from heaven, a wave formed across the inside bar thirty feet out, pitching skyward into a vertical, foam-laced wall of gray-green water. He turned to face the shore, holding onto the girl, and pitched himself forward right before the wave slammed into him. He kicked his feet hard, and the wave picked them up and somersaulted them, dragging Dave across the bottom on his back. He fought to get his feet under him and stand up as the wave receded, tearing at his knees again, trying to pull him back down. He stumbled forward a few steps, climbed the slope, and dumped the girl on the sand. She collapsed forward and gasped for breath, then broke into a fit of coughing and retching as she clambered farther up the beach on her hands and knees.

As Dave turned toward the ocean again, he saw that the woman on the beach was running toward her daughter. The wind snatched her hat off her head and threw it into the air, and she pointed out to sea with a hand full of playing cards. For a moment it looked as if she was going to wade out into the ocean herself. Dave ran straight out into the surf again, waving the woman toward shore and looking for the other twin, who was simply gone now. When he was waist-deep he kicked himself high over a breaking wave and spotted her—impossibly far out. Waves broke on either side of her, but the rip itself was a churning current through the surf, holding the waves off and throwing up its own backward-breaking chop.

Dave dove through the face of another wave and came up swimming, angling into the center of the rip. He rose over an unbroken swell and found her again. She was still thrashing around, holding her head above water and looking straight up into the sky, sucking in air. The sun had disappeared behind the clouds, and the wind chop slapped into his face. When he looked for her again, kicking hard to hold himself above the chop, he couldn't find her, and for a moment he was certain she'd gone down. He swam forward hard, knowing that she was at least twenty yards farther out. If she *had* gone under, he might never locate her. . . .

A swell rolled beneath him, and he kicked himself out of the water again, thrusting himself into the air. He saw her then and started swimming hard again, glancing back over his shoulder toward the beach. The mother and sister stood on the sand watching, already a good distance north. Dave was nearly dead even with the smoke from the burning surfboard, so the rip was broad as hell, and the current seemed to be moving them hard to the south even as the rip was dragging them out.

He felt the hostility of the ocean then, the cold water, the chop that splashed him so constantly in the face that he could hardly get a breath. A wave hammered down over a sandbar ahead and to the right, a dark wall of cloud-shadowed ocean that broke in a roaring avalanche of wind-blown whitewater. For the first time the thought came to him that he might be in trouble, and he felt a sudden hollow fear in his chest that he mentally backed away from. Panic could drown him, and it would certainly drown the girl, if she hadn't already gone down. Ahead of him loomed another mountain of moving water, and he swam toward it, the wave passing beneath him, and as he rose over the swell he saw her again, surprisingly close, lying on her back, sculling with her arms and kicking her feet frantically.

He swam toward her, dog-paddling as much as swimming, angling around behind her and trying to stay out of sight. The last thing he needed was for her to go nuts when she saw him and try to climb up onto his head. Coming up behind her, he slipped his left hand across her shoulder and under her right arm, tightening his grip and levering his hip under her before she had a chance to move.

Instantly wild with surprise, she tried to heave herself upright, throwing both arms out and beating the water with her fists.

"It's all right," Dave shouted, hanging onto her and holding her steady. "You're okay now." She fought for another moment, out of a panicked excitement, and he treaded water hard, keeping them both well up out of the chop. The sound of the breaking waves seemed weirdly distant to him now, as if the backs of the swells blocked the noise of the breaking surf. The rip, which had slowed down in the deeper water, was dissipating, and Dave started sidestroking south. If he could get entirely free of the rip, he could haul her back inside the surf line, where the waves would push them into shore. The surf would kick the hell out of them, but what other choice did he have? They rose over a swell, and he scanned the beach for a lifeguard Jeep. There was nothing—just the smoke from the fire well to the north, dwindled down almost to nothing now. A couple of tiny dark figures, the mother and sister, kept pace with them on the beach.

Get help, he thought. There was a phone by the concession stands. The mother wasn't thinking. It wasn't her day to think. And she trusted him, too. She had faith in him.

"What's your name?" he asked the girl. That was the longest sentence he could phrase right now. He didn't have the breath for anything more.

She didn't answer, but held up her wrist. He saw that she wore a bracelet of white beads with red letters on them, spelling out the name Elinor. There were two extra beads, a red diamond on one side, a red heart on the other.

"Where you from?" He continued with the sidestroke. They didn't seem to be moving out to sea any longer, but it was hard to tell if the rip had dropped them or was still holding on. He didn't seem to be making any progress, though, just swimming in place.

"Haddington," she said after a moment, as if she had finally made the decision to speak to him.

"Haddington to Huntington," he said. "That's kind of funny." He swallowed a mouthful of water and coughed it back out. "Where's that?" he asked after he got his voice back. He changed course, stroking straight in toward shore now. He had to try to get in again, rip or no rip, before he wore out.

"Scotland."

"Scotland?" His right arm felt like rubber, and he was suddenly aware that he was cold, really cold. He scissored his legs, pushing the two of them forward another couple of feet, and felt the muscle in his left calf tightening up. He couldn't afford a cramp, not if he couldn't use his arms to swim with. She didn't have any kind of Scottish accent, and he had the notion that she was lying to him, although how she could find the energy to make up lies at a time like this . . .

He dropped her then. She slipped out of his grasp and went under, and he caught her under the arms as she fought to get her head out of the water. He threw his arm across her chest again, leaned back, and started swimming. "Sorry," he gasped.

Now she was breathing hard, again, quick and shallow with fear. "We're all right," he told her, but he knew they weren't. "Haddington's near the ocean?"

He felt her nod.

"Good beaches?"

She didn't respond now.

"I've got to switch arms," Dave said to her, treading water again. "You can just relax. I won't let you go." Without waiting for an answer, he rolled beneath her, sliding his right arm across her chest and loosening his left, getting his right hip under her and starting to swim again. His sidestroke was nearly worthless on his left side, but his right arm was done for, at least for a little while. In a minute he would switch back. He looked back over his shoulder toward the shore, watching the backs of the waves form in the distance and listening to the sound of their breaking, which was a continuous roar now. He thought about his wetsuit lying on the beach next to his surfboard, and about not wanting to give the twins' mother any advice, even though he had known damned well he should have.

It was almost funny. He had been too gutless to say anything to their mother, and now he was out in the middle of the ocean trying to save her child, and both of them, he and the child, were going to drown.

If they were my kids . . .

"So that was your twin sister?"

"No."

"No?"

"She's not my sister."

"She looks like your sister."

It was work to talk. Too much work to play games, and the girl was obviously lying, which must have taken some effort, some thought. Her matter-of-fact voice was irritating. The tone struck him as weird, almost hateful, as if she was purposefully insulting him.

His stroke was sloppy, and he was kicking rubber-legged. He concentrated on evening it out, and at the same time he wondered if he should give it up and just tread water. He could tread water for another hour—although not with the girl hanging onto his back. . . .

They would get a lifeguard boat out to them long before that.

"She's my cousin," the girl said after a moment. She had relaxed a little now, letting him carry her weight, and she stared at the sky, as if watching the moving clouds. "She's always wanted to look like me," she said. "But she was burned. There was a fire. Her face is ugly, and her hair was burned off."

"Her hair?"

"That's a wig. She cries at night because she's ugly. I lie there and listen to her cry. I was trying to drown her to make her stop."

She said this almost cheerfully, talking to the sky, chatting away now, and Dave nearly dropped her in surprise. Her words sounded alien, as gray and cold as the ocean, as if she were talking about killing a bug. And now he was certain that she was telling the truth now, about wanting to drown her sister, and Dave remembered her trying to haul the other girl out into the ocean, into the rip. He felt the irrational urge to drop her just to wake her up—let her kick and thrash for a moment, until her attitude adjusted.

And if he dropped her now he could save himself. . . .

He drew back from the picture in his mind.

He could feel the dull ache of the half-relaxed cramp in his calf, and he was careful not to straighten his ankle too far and bring it on, and yet the bent ankle took the power out of his kick. He watched the ocean now for signs of an approaching wave. They'd made some progress, and a big enough swell might pick them up.

The girl was silent now. He swam on silently, too. He smelled salt spray then, and saw that a wave was breaking to the north of them, well in shore.

"Some day I'll kill her. That's why you have to save me."

"Why don't you just keep quiet?" he said, and he felt her giggle.

Suddenly he was swept with fatigue, and he quit swimming and started to tread water, holding onto her with one arm and sculling with the other. He was shivering with cold, and his arms and legs were so weak that he had to keep up a constant kicking to stay above the surface. A half hour of this was impossible. Ten minutes was impossible.

We aren't going to make it. . . .

He forced the thought away and said, "Here we go," then started swimming again, letting his head rest on the surface of the ocean, as if he were swimming in a pool. Almost immediately he gasped in a throatful of salt water and jackknifed reflexively forward at the waist, coughing the water back out, holding on tight to the twin. He treaded water hard again, gasping in air. He kicked his feet harder, propelling them forward, trying to smooth things out, to get some glide, some forward momentum, but the power in his legs was gone, and he couldn't keep it up. His muscles were on fire, and yet he was shivering with cold. He worked to keep his head up out of the chop, but it seemed as if he was settling deeper with each tired stroke, barely making any progress at all, simply kicking himself higher in the water, bobbing like some kind of dying thing, struggling just to stay above it now.

Alone, I could make it.

The thought came to him out of nowhere, as if his mind as well as his body had decided to betray him. If he held onto the girl, they would both drown. It was as easy as that. They rose to the top of a swell. The nearly deserted beach was incredibly distant. The mother stood there, still watching. Probably she thought they were all right, that everything was under control. He kept up the tired stroke, getting nowhere now. Surely the girl knew it.

He envisioned simply letting go—the twin sinking away into the green depths, as easy as falling asleep, and he forced his mind to focus. He was treading water again with a weak scissors kick. His sidestroke was gone. They bobbed up and down, his kick quickening as it got weaker. The ocean was empty out in the vast distances, just the small shape of a ship standing still way off on the horizon. How far from shore were they? A hundred yards?

He was going to drop her. He knew now with utter certainty that soon, very soon, he wouldn't be given a choice. When the time came, it wouldn't be his to decide.

She stared into his eyes, as if reading his mind, her own face a mask of terror now, her brassy attitude swept away. She kicked her feet with a wild ineffectiveness, thrashing against his legs, gripping his arms, and making small noises in her throat.

Don't do it, he told himself, kicking his legs machinelike, marking time. He was shivering, his shoulders numb from cold and fatigue. As if she knew he was fading, she was suddenly energized by fear, and she let go with her right hand long enough to clutch at his neck, to try to pull herself higher out of the water. He fought to control her, pushing her away at arm's length, the wild thought entering his head that she was stronger than he was by now, and that she would drag him under and drown him. *I might have to drown her to save myself.*

Another immense swell rolled through, and he nearly sank beneath it. It was powerful, pulling off the ocean bottom, dragging them several useless feet toward shore. Feeling the energy in the wave, he kicked harder, edging them up out of the chop and over the top of the swell. He looked back down into the wave's trough, surprised at the sheer size of the wave. Seconds later it broke, an avalanche of white water smashing skyward, twice the height of the wave itself, vertical ribbons of water shooting up and falling in long arcs. Farther out into the ocean another shadowy swell moved toward them, rising up out of deep water and obscuring the sky.

"Breathe," he said. "Deep. Really deep."

How many waves in the set? The approaching wave was big—bigger than the one that had just rolled through. If there were waves beyond it, they'd be immense. He steadied himself in the water, his fatigue momentarily gone, his heart racing with fear-fueled adrenaline. He could hear the girl gasping in lungfuls of air. With her hanging on, he'd never dive deep enough to get under it.

The first of the swells steepened, pushing skyward, blotting out any view of the ocean behind it. Fifty feet away from them it started to feather at the crest, the wind tearing at the wave as it rushed forward, the wave's face nearly vertical now, defying gravity and inertia, a heavy tangle of kelp visible just beneath its green surface.

"Hold your breath!" he said, yanking the twin next to him and taking one last deep breath himself. He tried to surface dive, pushing her down beneath him. He kept his eyes open, kicking his feet hard, fighting for some depth. The water was full of a deafening roar as the wave pounded down, releasing whirling tornadoes of fine bubbles like columns in a watery cathedral. The girl's hair swirled in front of his eyes, and he got a brief glimpse of her pale face, her eyes wide and staring as the churning water swept across them. With a suddenness that astonished him, he was pulled up and back like a piece of driftwood. Her wrist slipped through his hand, and his fingers closed over the bracelet, which he dragged from her wrist as the wave cartwheeled him around and then slammed him downward, pounding him off the ocean floor and tumbling him toward shore. The girl was simply gone from his grasp, vanished.

Something brushed his leg—the girl? Kelp? He flailed

outward with his hand, touched something solid, but instantly it was gone, and the wave slammed him against the bottom a second time, dragging him across a sandbar on his back, then flipping him head over heels and rushing him forward again. He tried to force himself to relax, but his lungs felt as if they'd imploded, and in a sudden panic he clawed his way upward, deluged by swirling foam. His head broke the surface, and he threw it back and sucked in air, fighting his way clear of the churning white water until he could kick himself around again and look out to sea. The water was empty, the girl gone.

Let her go? The unwelcome question settled in his mind.

She had slipped away so *easily* . . . He forced the thought away, slipped her bracelet over his own wrist, and dove beneath the surface, opening his eyes to see through the churning bubbles into the green darkness. But almost at once he was out of breath, and he kicked his way toward the sunlight again as the third wave in the set bore down on him, breaking hard forty feet farther out, an avalanche of moving white water. He hyperventilated, dove again, stroking for the bottom, and the wave blasted into him, pushing him toward shore. He let himself go limp, not struggling this time, and the wave dragged him like a rag doll, tumbling him over and over, letting up on him when it moved into the deeper water of a channel. He surfaced, treading water tiredly, looking futilely around for some sign of the girl again, watching another wave break far outside. Two lifeguard boats floated outside the breaking waves now, too late to do any good. He waited out the incoming wave, hyperventilating again, and then dove beneath it, finding the bottom and letting the wave pass above him.

When he surfaced he realized it was raining. The sky was solid with clouds, and the wind whipped the rain into his face and swept it across the surface of the ocean in flurries. Perhaps the girl had been swept in to shore. With any luck she had been. He had to believe she had been. Another wave rolled through, smaller than the others but still breaking outside of where he swam tiredly toward shore. He let the white water pick him up and carry him. When the wave dropped him he kept swimming, a tired, mechanical crawl stroke with no kick. He heard a voice and looked up to see a lifeguard reaching out with a red float. Dave grabbed it and hung onto it.

"Where's the girl?" The lifeguard's hurried question came to him from a vague distance, as if he were just waking up out of an anesthetic. A broken wave struck them, and he let go of the float, letting the wave churn past. He gestured tiredly toward the open ocean. "I'm okay," he said, and started to swim again, letting the waves push him, surprised moments later when his toes dragged against the sandy bottom and he stumbled to his feet in shallow water. Up on the beach a yellow lifeguard Jeep was just pulling even with the crest of the sand. When he was up onto the beach, he sat down and looked out over the ocean, letting the rain hit him, shivering with the cold. There were hands under his arms, helping him up, and he was suddenly sick and faint, and he knew, without anyone having to tell him, that the girl was lost.

Tides

2

THE NIGHT WAS QUIET—HAUNTINGLY QUIET, AS IF THE fog dampened the sound of her footsteps along with other nighttime noises. The bars and cafes along Main Street were closed, and there was little traffic. Anne could smell the fog on the air along with something else—dirty oil, she decided, although there weren't too many wells still operating in the downtown neighborhoods, and the oil-soaked vacant lots that had once made up most of the acreage in the city were covered with apartments and condominiums now. The redeveloped downtown was a different place from the run-down beach city she remembered from her childhood visits, and although it was probably safer now—fewer bikers and bad alleys and bars—she wasn't sure she liked the change. Probably it was just nostalgia. Up in Canada, when she had talked about moving south, people had warned her against walking at night in southern California, and now she couldn't help but listen to the silences between her own footsteps, half expecting the slow tread of someone following, someone hidden by the night and the fog.

She had been in town only a few days, and she was entirely friendless. It was a perfectly loony place for her to have moved to, especially because she didn't meet people easily. She stopped now at the edge of the Pacific Coast Highway and waited for the signal to change, trying to see through the fog to the foot of the pier and the stairs to the beach. The headlights of a northbound car appeared, and the car braked at the yellow light. She heard music from inside the closed-up car, and it took her a moment to recognize the tune—a pepped-up version of ''Pearl on the Half Shell'' that sounded strangely at odds with the foggy, motionless night. The ''Walk'' sign blinked on, and she stepped off the curb, reaching the other side just as the light changed again. The ghostly car accelerated slowly away, the sound of the jittery music disappearing along with the car's taillights.

It was nearly midnight, and the pier was closed, barricaded by a high metal gate. That was disappointing. Anne hadn't thought that the pier would be closed. She looked around her at the foggy darkness, and a rash idea entered her head. Suddenly she felt a little like a criminal, which, it occurred to her now, she was very nearly about to become—and not for the first time, either. Once, when she was about eight, she and her sister had climbed over the fence at the agricultural college and fed apples to the cows, despite written warnings to stay out. No one had caught them, and a week later they had risked another cow feeding, the success of which had clearly set her on a criminal path that had, these many years later, led her to the foot of this closed-up pier. What next? Tearing the tags off mattresses? Jaywalking? Murder?

She swung her leg over the top bar of the waist-high railing and climbed out onto the edge of the pier, where she sidestepped down past the gate. She looked below, down at the nearly invisible beach and the descending concrete stairs, then climbed back over the railing again, walking farther out onto the deserted pier in order to distance herself from the gate. She stopped at the railing when she knew she was invisible from the street, and peered down into the gloom. She had a picture in her mind of the ocean late at night: the moonlight on pier pilings, the ghostly waves rushing up out of the darkness, the empty beach, the shimmer of lights on the water up the curving coast.

She could hear the ocean sighing on the wet sand below the pier. And there was the sound of waves breaking somewhere out in the fog, which swirled around her now, the mists opening and closing like windows and doors. For a moment she got a glimpse of the beach below—the closed-up concession stands, a lonely towel left on the damp sand, a couple of oil drum trash cans. Then the fog closed in again, and she heard the heavy boom of a breaking wave as the pier shuddered from the impact.

She walked slowly through the mists, past the darkened lifeguard tower. The pier lamps glowed like moons overhead, but their light was mostly consumed by the fog, and very little of it reached the ground. At the end of the pier, the fog was dense enough so that she didn't see the railing ahead of her until she was almost upon it. She put her hands on the cold metal, which was beaded with moisture, and looked down into the gray darkness. She imagined the ocean below, the shifting of the dark currents, the waves rolling in, the terror of falling over the railing, of finding herself in the cold ocean on a lightless night, the entire coast shrouded in fog. . . .

There was a sound like something moving behind her—like the scrape of feet on concrete—but almost as soon as she heard it, it stopped. She looked hard into the mists around her, at the dark stationary shapes of a trash can, a low bench, a lamppost. Nothing moved. She listened, holding her breath, but couldn't hear anything now, just the muted crashing of waves from farther in toward shore. The relative silence seemed to suggest something purposeful—someone hiding, perhaps, just out of sight in the fog.

And as if suddenly clairvoyant, she was aware of a presence in the night air around her, an unsettling change in the atmosphere, as if the very fog was stained with distilled emotion, with the long-ago fearful ghost of resentful loneliness and hateful despair conjured by the fog and the ocean and the sound of breaking waves.

It was time to go. She moved away from the railing, keeping to the middle of the pier, looking around her as she walked. She could see no one, but as soon as her own shoe soles scraped on the concrete pier, she was abruptly certain that someone was keeping pace with her, matching their own footfalls to her own. She stopped, and the sound stopped. Then she stepped forward again and was struck by this same illusion—probably a trick of the fog, an echo. She walked faster, the mist closing in around her so that she was completely enshrouded now. Dim objects loomed up along the edges of the pier—two ghostly telescopes on metal swivels, a tiny wooden building, a long sink for cleaning fish.

She stopped again and listened.

For a moment she could hear the footfalls, even though she herself was dead still. They didn't sound like an echo. They were clear and unhurried, like someone strolling, scuffing their shoes on concrete. The sound was strangely loud, but then almost at once seemed to evaporate, fading away in the fog, and again there was a lingering silence. Still she could see no one, only the pale fog swirling up around the pier railings like languid spirits.

She hurried forward now. There were fifty yards or more between her and the gate, but the Coast Highway with its traffic lights and street lamps was still invisible ahead of her. She could see only the dim railing on either side of the pier, and, on her right, the lifeguard tower looming up again out of the fog, the lamplight glowing on the wide, angled-out windows.

Then she saw something—movement, at the edge of the tower.

She was certain that someone had just that moment stepped out of sight behind it, between the tower and the railing on a little outthrust section of pier. She had got just a glimpse of red—a flannel shirt? A cloth coat? She looked back again, her heart pounding, as she angled toward the opposite railing, ready to run, suppressing the urge to scream.

There—she saw it again: someone standing still, facing her but half hidden by the corner of the wall, just a shadow in the fog that swirled across the pier, the shadow growing more and then less distinct. She felt suddenly dizzy, and she gripped the cold handrail to steady herself, unsure whether it was the fog that obscured the waiting figure, or the fog that made it visible, like a film slide projected on mist. And now it vanished altogether as the ocean breeze momentarily swept the fog clear, and then almost instantly the mists billowed in off the ocean again, and the figure materialized within it, closer now, as if she had stepped forward five or six paces and stopped, waiting for another gust of sea wind to hide it again.

The sound of footsteps resumed, preternaturally loud, as if echoing down a corridor. Anne found herself running through the dreamlike fog, hearing the footsteps behind her louder even than the pounding of her own feet. She swung herself over the railing again, edged her way past the gate, and vaulted the railing back onto the pier where, after a quick backward glance, she headed straight across the Highway, ignoring the red light, not looking back down the empty sidewalk again until she was halfway up the block. A shadow in a doorway impelled her toward the curb, and when she realized that it was a man drinking out of a bottle in a paper bag, she almost sighed with relief. She slowed down now to catch her breath. There were no longer any footsteps. The night was quiet and still, but she hurried on up Main to Orange Street anyway, fumbling for her keys in her jeans pocket. Her hands shook as she unlocked the street door of her apartment, stepped through and locked it behind her, and then ascended the stairs through the empty building toward her flat on the second floor.

3

THE HIGH, RECTANGULAR BUILDING THAT WAS THE EARL of Gloucester, a theatre props and sets company, was built back in 1927 as a feed and fertilizer warehouse. It took up most of the length of the block near the corner of 6th and Walnut Streets in Huntington Beach, about a hundred yards from the Coast Highway and another hundred yards west from Main Street. Its faded clapboard siding had been painted blue sometime in the 1970s, and the wooden windows were trimmed with white moldings that the ocean air had slowly repainted a shade of lichen gray over the years. At one time a lean-to boardwalk porch had stood along the 6th Street side of the warehouse, but most of it had been torn down and replaced with a more practical concrete loading dock. In front of the business entrance there was still a section of the old porch that ran on back to the end of the building. Two acres of weedy vacant lot separated the warehouse from the highway, and at the top of the lot stood one of the few working oil wells left in the downtown. It was fenced with rusted chain link and sagging barbed wire.

The warehouse itself was a relic of Huntington's sleepier past, weathered by salt air and wind and shaded by a pair of enormous eucalyptus trees that dropped bark and leaves and seeds onto the roof. Jolene, the Earl's secretary, had recently computerized the inventory and the books. That and the new loading dock were the company's concessions to the modern world. The Earl himself, Earl Dalton, still typed his letters on an ancient Royal typewriter that had been used as a prop in Hollywood films before he had bought it at auction. Inside the warehouse the smell of the wet sawdust from unseasoned fir was heavy in the air, along with the smell of dust and resin and the musty hay bales stacked against the warehouse wall near the loading dock.

Working alone in the early morning, Dave Quinn shot one-by-four frames together to build palace walls for a production of *King Lear* that would be staged at the Earl's own Ocean Theatre next door to the warehouse. Next he would glue polystyrene sheets to these frames, and then a sets artist—who hadn't started to work yet—would etch the polystyrene and airbrush mossy-looking stones onto it. Then they could move the sections of crenelated castle wall into the theatre itself and fasten them together to build the facade of the Duke of Albany's palace.

But if the sets artist didn't appear soon, like today, Dave would have to move most of his set pieces into the shop in back to make room for more immediate work, which was already cluttering up the area in front of the loading dock door. A theatre company out in Westminster was staging *Oklahoma!*, and the Earl's was delivering set and prop pieces: hay bales and a Doe-C-Doe Wagon, two horses, thirty feet of split rail corral fence, and six barrels big enough for actors to dance on. Dave had built the fence himself. The Earl himself had gotten the barrels from a Kentucky distillery, and they still smelled like whisky and charcoal. The wagon, a sort of open buckboard, was already gray with weather and age when they'd gotten it out of a Minnesota barn. Dave had replaced half a dozen of its spokes along with the wagon's seat, sandblasted the new wood, and grayed it with rottenstone and beeswax. The effect was pretty good. You could pick out the new wood if you were looking close and paying attention, but from theater seats the wagon was an authentic period piece.

He set down the power staple gun now, and the air compressor chugged for a moment and then fell silent. He could hear in the distance the low rumble of waves breaking through the concrete pilings of the Huntington Beach Pier. The swell had risen during the night, a late-season north swell with tides high enough to worry beachfront homeowners. In 1988 the old pier had been destroyed by a spectacular wave that had broken across the end of it, over a quarter mile out to sea, dwarfing the pier's twenty-foot light stanchions and sweeping away the flimsy bait shops and cafes and rest rooms, snapping concrete pilings and wrenching apart iron railings that had withstood countless ocean storms since the pier had been restored and reinforced in 1931. Now, as the end of the century drew near, the newly rebuilt pier, with its angled pilings heavily moored in the sea bottom, was engineered to withstand an even heavier swell. . . .

He walked to the stairs and climbed the wooden steps toward the vast loft that made up the second floor of the Earl of Gloucester. Built on a frame of heavy timbers, the loft occupied maybe a quarter of the open ceiling space in the warehouse, and it was built high enough off the concrete floor to store stage sets and props underneath, including the front section of a Spanish galleon. The ship's bowsprit and carved mermaid were angled back as if the galleon were tossing on a stormy sea, and the sea itself was attached to the underside of the ship—painted plywood waves mounted on tracks so that the waves moved back and forth, one in front of the other. There was nautical debris stacked around the galleon—open treasure chests, masts, oars, crab and lobster traps, and sections of an old barnacle-encrusted wharf. Fishing nets hung with seashells and glass floats were strung from the floor joists of the loft above.

The loft itself was mostly offices along a balcony with a wooden railing. The old offices looked like sets themselves, like something off a sound stage—office cubicles from *It's a Wonderful Life* or *Farewell My Lovely*. The walls were paneled with vertical wooden boards and battens, painted gloss white, and the doors had brass knobs and ripple glass windows. At either end of the balcony there were palm tree tikis standing on top of the railings. They were comical tikis, with long noses and blubbery lips and undersized arms folded across their bellies. One of the tikis wore a garish aloha shirt and a straw hat, and it bent down over the floor below, watching like a sentinel, secured precariously to the post at the end of the balcony by a wide leather belt. Tikis had been the rage in the early sixties, but they'd gone so far out of style by now that they'd nearly disappeared off the fashion map. Earl Dalton, who had established the company in 1951, predicted a tiki comeback and was "displaying the tikis to advantage," as he put it. The Earl's had an economy Hawaiian package, with a bamboo bridge, giant clamshells, an outrigger canoe, torches, and a backdrop painted with palm trees and a moonlit ocean— everything you'd need for a luau except the hula dancers and beach sand, both of which could be obtained for a fee. The tikis were a bonus if you rented the whole package.

The sound of his feet echoed on the wooden floorboards, and he stopped for a moment and stood on the balcony next to the tiki in the shirt. The sound of the ocean was louder now, and he could see through the bank of west-facing windows that the fog was thinner than he had thought. From where he stood he could look out over the rooftops toward the pier, where a long gray wall of water rushed through the pilings, seeming almost to scrape the bottom of the pier before throwing itself forward, the lip of the wave striking the ocean and exploding skyward in a fury of violent white water that surged in a ten-foot wall toward the beach. Dave heard the staccato boom of its breaking then, a crack nearly like thunder. . . .

•   •   •

LESLIE COLLIER AND HIS FIVE-YEAR-OLD GRANDDAUGHTER Jenny appeared now on the path through the vacant lot. The path led to the Supreme Doughnut Shop, which sat a hundred yards away from the Earl of Gloucester on the edge of the Highway. Collier, an old friend of the Earl's, rented the two-bedroom bungalow behind the Ocean Theatre. The Earl owned the bungalow and the theater both, and he paid Collier a small salary to keep the theater in operation, even though it hadn't earned a penny in years. The comedy improv on Friday nights drew a big beach crowd, but that was about it. *King Lear* would play to half an audience, which didn't matter to the Earl, who could afford Collier's salary and wrote off the bungalow rental as a business expense. Nothing having to do with money mattered to the Earl. What did matter was that the show went up on schedule, and that the little out-of-time world he had invented on the corner of 6th and Walnut Streets spun along in its course without interruption or complication.

The two of them stopped at the edge of the lot, and Collier, balancing his coffee cup in front of him, did a little sideways shuffle, back and forth like Soupy Sales, the sunlit fog swirling around him. Jenny tried it herself, getting it about half right, and then Collier showed her again. Dave could hear the sound of Jenny's laughter, and he watched as the two set out again, disappearing beyond the corner of the warehouse.

DAVE WATCHED AS ANOTHER WAVE SLAMMED THROUGH the pier, and it occurred to him that no matter how much concrete they poured into holes in the sea bottom, no matter how many engineers calculated figures and assessed the potential energy in a breaking wave, one day a swell would come in out of the Pacific that would sweep it all away like it was nothing at all.

4

EDMUND DALTON'S VIDEO CAMERA EQUIPMENT WASN'T professional quality, but it did the job, and most of his film work was better than the average in the "industry," as he liked to call it. His artistic sensibilities made up for a lot, and his last film had a couple of subtle touches that he was really very proud of. It was a shame that he couldn't talk about them to anyone, but he had never found anyone worthy of sharing his secrets. The camera had a wide-angle lens, and it picked up images in a moderately dark room. It stood on its tripod in the corner of what, for a Huntington Beach condo, was a large bedroom. The far wall of the bedroom was blank and white, clear of furniture, pictures, or anything else. The carpeted floor at the empty end of the room was covered with heavy plastic, and the plastic was covered with more carpet. He adjusted the angle of the camera one last time, set the remote control on the nightstand by his bed, and walked up the hall past the bathroom, which doubled as a photo lab for developing black-and-white prints. There was only a single window in the bathroom, which could be blacked out in a moment with a pull-down shade. On the long counter, past the double sinks, sat an enlarger and chemical trays.

The second bedroom, what he liked to call the library, stood at the far end of the hall. There were custom-built wooden shelves along one wall of the room, decorated with crown moldings and turned posts and brass fixtures, the shelves holding books and videocassettes and statuary. The bottom shelf of the unit was six inches off the floor, its bottom edge hidden by molding. He removed a bronze buffalo from one of the bottom shelves now, got his fingers in behind the shelf, and pushed a hidden spring latch. The back edge of the shelf bumped up so that he could get his hands on it and lift it out of its depression. There was an open area beneath, with a couple of dozen videocassettes lying on edge, all of them encased in plastic boxes, which were slid into bags containing stuffed manila envelopes. He considered the titles, smiling with amusement—*Mary Poppins*, *Pollyana*, *Pippi Longstocking*, *Snow White*, *Cinderella*. . . . Finally he picked out *Pippi Longstocking*, took it out of its case, and plugged it into the VHS machine beneath the big-screen television. He settled down in his chair and sorted through photos from the envelope while the film ran through ten minutes of blank tape.

THERE WAS A GIRL WHO FREQUENTLY HITCHHIKED ON THE Highway in the morning, usually from the Sunset Beach area down toward Huntington. Edmund had seen her a half-dozen times. Inevitably she wore tight short-shorts and a tie-dyed t-shirt and carried a bag on a shoulder strap. She wore calf-high fringed leather boots, too, like a hippie. It was hard to tell how old she was without slowing down to look, which up until now he hadn't done. But despite the sixties getup, she had the obvious look of a young prostitute.

He spotted her this morning on the south side of the Highway at Goldenwest Street, and he pulled over to the curb, tapping his horn. He ran the passenger side window down, watching her in the rearview mirror as she ran toward the car. He expected her to solicit him right through the window, but instead she pulled the door open and climbed in, tossing her shoulder bag to the floor.

"Thanks," she said.

"Sure." He glanced at her. She was older than he'd thought she was, and she had the pale, thin look of a druggie. Still, she could pass for sixteen in the right light and makeup. He fought down a nervous thrill, his imagination already running. . . .

"Where you going?" she asked him.

"South," he said. "How about you?"

"South's fine."

They drove along in silence for a few moments.

"Nice car," she said.

"Thanks. It gets me around."

"Shit. *It gets you around?*"

"You don't like it, you shouldn't have accepted the ride." He smiled at her, as if he were kidding, but that kind of disrespect from a lowlife ticked him off.

"Whoa," she said. "Don't go off on me. I didn't say I didn't like it. Do you want a date?"

"A what?" The question caught him by surprise, and at first he didn't quite know what she meant. He realized then that she smelled like marijuana smoke and patchouli. The smell irritated the hell out of him, just because of what it meant about her lifestyle. He'd have to make her take a shower if things worked out—which they would.

"A date. You know. Do you want somebody?"

He looked at her again, harder now. She was built pretty well, for a skinny girl, and she had a hungry look in her eyes, as if there was nothing about her that money couldn't buy. With the right coaching, though, she could look hippie-innocent enough. And he could do her hair up in braids, too, like his old friend Pippi. He ran names through his head. Cinderella? Not hardly. Sleeping Beauty? He might be able to do something with that.

"I might want a date," he said. "How about we stop by my place?"

"Fine with me," she said, settling back in the seat.

He nodded and turned left at the corner, heading up toward his condo. He had half expected *her* to suggest a place, which he wouldn't have agreed to, since he didn't actually want a date, not in the way she meant it. Anyway, he needed his camera equipment and the rest of his tools. On the other hand, right now he had to behave like a perfect gentleman, because he wanted her to be willing, up to a point. He wondered what he'd give her to make her willing *beyond* that point. Sometimes the promise of money only took them so far. Pills would take them farther. But there were other times when he had resorted to unfriendlier forms of persuasion, which itself could be very nearly an art form. He didn't want bruises, although he found a certain look of raw fear to be pleasing, and he was becoming a master at generating that fear simply by particularly graphic threats concerning what *might* happen without a little bit of co-operation. By then, of course, if their mouths were taped shut, and they'd already been separated from their clothing and their pitiful dignity, they were generally open to suggestion.

And then there had been times when he had been forced into an act of particularly persuasive violence, which was regrettable only because of the money it had cost him in the end. Buying silence turned out to be more expensive than he would have thought. The film that had resulted from that experience, however, was first rate, and he almost hoped that his highway hippie might need some of the same persuading before they were through. He looked her over again, and she stared back at him.

"Can you do me a favor?" he asked when he pulled into the long driveway that led to the parking garages.

"I guess. What kind of favor?"

"Duck."

She hunched down without asking why, and he heard her giggle from where she crouched on the floorboards. "Why don't you just flip the neighbors off?" she asked. "I can't believe how some people let other people manipulate them."

"Neither can I," he said, punching the garage door opener and swinging around into the dark garage. "Neither can I."

✺5✺

ANNE'S SISTER ELINOR HAD ONCE KILLED SOMETHING IN their uncle's shop near the Royal Oak Cemetery on Vancouver Island, on the outskirts of Victoria. It was a small animal, probably a rat. She might have gotten it dead out of a trap and *pretended* to have killed it, but Anne didn't think so. Her sister had been entirely capable of killing a rat or a mouse, or even a cat. It had been during summer holiday, a rainy July afternoon. Anne could picture it perfectly, every detail of her uncle's house and yard, the rain, the dark line of trees beyond the wall, her sister's precise pose where she sat in the shop in a kitchen chair, her back straight, stitching seams into one of the grotesque dolls that she fashioned out of nylon stockings. . . .

Elinor's dolls had become increasingly strange in the six months that she had been making them. She spent her time on almost nothing else—stuffing the nylon with cotton and then bunching and stitching the nylon into more and more lifelike representations of human figures. The anatomical proportions were purposefully, often grotesquely, wrong, the eyes offset, the mouths leering or pouting, the bodily parts so shockingly rendered that Elinor hid them from her mother along with the copies of magazines that provided her with models and inspiration. Elinor was a prodigy, and Anne had always been envious of her sister's talent and offended by it at the same time. Anne's own talent had been slower to develop, something that no longer bothered her as it had when she was younger. And now that she was older she knew that Elinor's dolls were evidence of grossly disturbed sensibilities, but at eleven years old her sister both frightened and fascinated her.

At the back door of her uncle's farmhouse there was a path that wound around the side of an old garage and into a barnyard walled with stone. The barn itself had been converted to a shop. It was small—a couple of tool-filled stalls, some open space with machinery, a wood loft, a generator. There was always the smell of petrol and wood chips, and on that day, she recalled, there was also the smell of the damp wool of her sweater, still wet from earlier in the morning when she and Elinor had been out walking in the rain. Their uncle had been a boatbuilder by trade, living in Vancouver, but when Anne and Elinor were girls he had already retired from it and moved to the island, where he had started building cabinetry, more as a pastime than an occupation. The family had always had money, and owned hundreds of acres of timberland up near the top of the island.

Anne had walked down the path through the backyard early that afternoon, carrying an umbrella, although the rain had mostly stopped. The house lay empty and quiet behind her because her uncle and aunt had gone into town for the day. She had been looking for Elinor after having spent three hours reading in her upstairs bedroom. She and her sister were just ten years old. The day before had been their birthday.

Anne smelled the stench of burning fur before she saw what it was that had been lit on fire. An open stone ring, like a cistern, lay just ahead of her, an open incinerator where her uncle burned wood chips and scraps, and the smoke drifting up out of it was heavy with the smell of burnt bone and hair. The drizzle had put the fire nearly out, and it was only smoldering now, and Anne didn't recognize the scraps of ash-smeared red fabric as her birthday coat until she was next to it.

Most of the coat was burned despite the rain, and her sister told her matter-of-factly, some time later, that she had doused it with petrol before lighting it on fire. The rat, or whatever it was, lay across the charred remains of the coat in the center of the stone ring, burned down to a thing of hair and bone and leathery flesh. Sickened, Anne had turned away, looking for Elinor and seeing her through the open door of the shop, sitting on the wooden chair, putting the final stitches into the face of a doll whose eyes were shut, as if in sleep, but whose mouth was open in a silent scream. As Anne watched her, her sister yanked the thread tight in the seam, her lips set in a slight smile as if she took a subtle pleasure in her work. She didn't look up, didn't acknowledge Anne's presence.

By the time their uncle and aunt had returned later that afternoon, the coat and the rat were gone. Elinor had taken them into the woods near the lake and hidden them, and then the next day Anne and Elinor had left for home. In order to protect her sister—or herself, she realized much later—Anne had told her uncle and aunt that she had already packed the coat, and that she didn't want to unpack it to wear it home, despite the bad weather. And then later, when the coat was clearly missing, Elinor told their mother that Anne had taken it off during their morning walk and had left it absentmindedly by the roadside, the two of them going home without it. When they had remembered and run back for it, the coat had been gone. Somebody had walked off with it. Elinor had felt bad for her sister, who had been absolutely crushed by losing the coat, and simply *couldn't* have told their uncle and aunt.

Anne had kept silent about the lie. Countless times since, she had wondered why. Perhaps it was fear that her mother would think that *she* was lying and that Elinor was telling the truth. Perhaps it was fear of Elinor. It had been one of a hundred exasperating lies that Anne had put up with in order to coexist with her sister. Her mother, as usual, had believed Elinor entirely. There was no reason she shouldn't have. Elinor's story made sense. Elinor had been brilliant at making up hateful stories that made good sense. If Anne had told her mother the truth, her mother wouldn't have believed it. Later that same night, after Elinor had lied to their mother and Elinor and Anne had gone to bed, Elinor had explained to her in detail about killing the rat.

Some time later, after Elinor was gone, Anne had looked for the things that Elinor had kept hidden. The dolls and the magazines were gone. Their mother, apparently, had found them, although in the years after, even when Anne was an adult, there was no mention of any of it. And it wasn't until after her mother's death that Anne found the boxes that contained the dolls, packed away with the half-dozen paintings that Elinor the prodigy had finished in the span of her short life.

6

OVER THE YEARS THE DREAM REAPPEARED IN THE LATE winter, as if it were compelled by the irresistible force of the turning seasons. And ever since Dave had moved back to Huntington Beach, he dreamed even more often about the ocean. Sometimes, on particularly quiet nights, when there was heavy surf and an onshore wind, he could hear the distant breaking of the waves from his house near the park, and he had noticed that the closer he came to sleep, the louder and more insistent was the noise of the breaking waves, as if it were the waves themselves that swept away conscious thought, and submerged his mind beneath their silent green swell.

Unlike most of his dreams, though, there was nothing strange about the logic of this dream, and nearly nothing had changed in it over the past fifteen years. It almost never involved him actually trying to save the girl from drowning. Instead, he was alone in the ocean, swimming over the tops of increasingly bigger waves. He would scan the empty winter beach with a feeling of growing dread, the sky clouded by smoke rising out of the sand as if from a sub-terranean chimney, the whole world utterly still and silent except for the moving ocean and the moving smoke. A wave would crest in front of him, and in sudden fear he would dive underwater and swim toward the ocean bottom, into the green darkness, listening for the noise of the wave's breaking and waiting for the inevitable shock when the turbulence hit him. What looked like swirling seaweed, like surge-washed eelgrass and kelp, would suddenly appear before him, and for one fleeting moment he would see the girl's face in the weeds, ghost pale, her eyes open and staring, and he would feel her brush against him as the ocean dragged her downward to her death.

Often he would wake up afraid to move, with the sound of the dream ocean sighing in his ears like the beating of a vast heart. He would lie there waiting, certain that something was pending, that something immensely terrible was about to be revealed. And then he would realize that it had already been revealed to him, whatever it was, that it lay waiting in some crevice of his mind, ready to germinate and bloom again like the seed of an alien flower.

WHEN HE AWOKE ON THE FRONT PORCH, DAVE FOUND that he was gripping the cold metal arms of the front porch chair as if something had tried to yank him out of it. He relaxed his grip, leaning back, shrugging the stiffness out of his shoulders. There was the smell of gardenia blossoms on the night air and the sound of a moth fluttering against the lamp globe on the porch ceiling. The fog was heavy out on the yard and street. He sat forward, realizing that he must have been asleep for some time. He was cold despite his jacket, and the book he had been reading lay open on his lap.

As ever, in his mind the last fragments of the dream fell away as the tide of sleep receded, but now he found himself still listening to a sound that came to him from out of the foggy night, like brush strokes on a drum skin at first, or like the soft pacing of someone dragging their shoe soles out on the wet sidewalk, and he knew that he had been listening to the pacing even in his dream, mixed up in the sound of the ocean and breaking waves. His heart raced with the realization, and he was instantly filled again with the certainty that something was pending, that something was about to be revealed to him.

And then, as if she had in that moment appeared from within a veil of fog, a woman stood looking at him on the front walk, her features unfocused in the murk so that she seemed almost faceless, her dark amorphous clothing misty beneath the streetlamp. Her hair was long and black. Momentarily her features nearly coalesced in the heavy mist, and he was struck with the feeling of vague recognition, but then a window seemed to open in the fog, and just as quickly as she had appeared, she disappeared. He heard the footfalls scraping again on the wet sidewalk, but even they sounded dreamlike, as regular as a heartbeat, and abruptly they fell away, and the night was silent around him.

He got up from the chair and descended the concrete porch steps to the front walk, and it seemed to him that there was cool air rising from the concrete like an upwelling of ocean water drawn to the surface by a passing wave. He smelled smoke on the wet night air, just a trace of it that lingered for a moment on the lanquid breeze and then was gone. The sidewalk and the street were empty. The streetlamps cast misty circles of yellow light on the curb and the grassy parkway. Moisture from the telephone lines dripped slowly onto the driveway, and now that he was out from under the shelter of the porch, he could hear waves breaking along the distant beach.

To satisfy an uneasy curiosity, he walked toward the corner. The neighboring houses were dark, their porches and driveways empty. He crossed the street at the end of the block and continued on, heading down toward the ocean, which was six blocks away. It seemed to him that she must have disappeared in this direction, although he couldn't quite say why, since she had merely vanished from where she had stood, and might just as easily have ascended into the clouds.

The entire episode began to seem unreal to him, and it dawned on him that she might simply have been a waking hallucination, a trailing remnant of his dream. He turned around and headed home, realizing that he was merely chasing phantoms. It was time for bed—past time. His house loomed into view, the living room light shining out onto the porch. Through the screen door he could see his coffee cup on the table next to the couch. A folded-open copy of *Fine Woodworking* magazine lay on the floor along with the disassembled parts of an old wooden carpenter's plane that he was restoring. He climbed the steps, picked his book up from the chair, and went inside the house, where he shut the door and bolted it. For a few more moments he peered out through the blinds, listening to the quiet night and watching the foggy, empty street.

He walked to the library table that sat against the back wall of the room, opened the single drawer, and reached far into the back of it, in among a scattering of old photographs, finding the beaded bracelet that he had kept in the years since Elinor's drowning. He couldn't say why he hadn't given it back to the drowned girl's mother, to Elinor's mother, that morning on the beach. He simply hadn't. The moment had never come. He hadn't been able to face her. He had slipped away, crossing the Highway to where his car was parked on the dirt shoulder near the boatyard, the bracelet in the pocket of his trunks. He looked at it now, the ivory-white beads with blocky red letters spelling out her name, a heart and a diamond on either side. The rest of the bracelet was elastic string, which had lost its stretch in the intervening years.

After a moment he slipped it back into the drawer, losing it once again among the photographs.

7

RIGHT NOW NOTARY AND TAX PREP OPERATED OUT OF AN aging strip mall on Beach Boulevard near Talbert. There was a Laundromat next door and a liquor store next to that, which was also a *carnicería* that sold *asada* and *carnitas* tacos to go, and which cashed paychecks and did a limited pawn business. The counter in the liquor store was shielded by bulletproof glass, and the doors and windows were covered with a sliding wrought iron gate after two in the morning. The Laundromat was open all night.

Ray Mifflin sat at the office desk reading a *People* magazine and drinking coffee out of a Styrofoam cup. He could hear a muffled churning from beyond the wall, a washing machine chugging away in the Laundromat. From time to time he glanced out the window, waiting for his client to show—a Mr. Edmund Dalton of Huntington Beach, son of a very rich man. Dalton was fifteen minutes late. Ray didn't normally open until ten, although he was usually in the office a couple hours early. This was ridiculous, though. This morning he had pulled in shortly after dawn for an appointment with a man who was too busy to wait for business hours. Ray had just turned sixty, and he was damned if he would put up with being treated like a fool by some rich young punk.

He was tired, but it was only lately that he had realized it. He *looked* tired. His hair was thin. Rogaine treatments hadn't done a thing for him. Neither had diet pills. He was sedentary, his back was a wreck, and he was simply goddamn weary of the whole thing. He missed his breakfast, too. When he got up early like this, he always felt starved within a half hour, and this morning he craved a Hostess apple pie, which, of course, he couldn't put his hands on because the damned liquor store didn't open until eight, when the vagrants sleeping on the Laundromat chairs woke up hungry.

He was charging his early-morning customer a hundred dollars to notarize a quitclaim deed, but at this moment the pie was more attractive to him than the money was, and if the man didn't show up in another ten minutes he was going to hang the be-back-soon clock on the door and head down to the all-night market.

This whole transaction smelled wrong anyway: the rush to get it done, the early-hours appointment, the money. . . .

Ray had notarized another deed for the man barely a month ago, and that one had smelled a little high, too, although it was true that he wouldn't have thought more than twice about last month's work if it weren't for this second one. There was nothing really out of the ordinary about the

deed that he had notarized last month. It involved an old
guy, pretty much on the ropes, quitclaiming a piece of property to his son, getting out from under some of his assets
before he dropped dead and the estate got caught up in
probate and taxes. There was something about the son,
though, that Ray didn't like—he was way too anxious and
smug. You'd think that if the old man was giving you a
gift-wrapped piece of Newport Beach you'd be a little bit
deferential, a little grateful. But this had been hurry-up-and-
get-it-done, and when the deed was signed, the son had
called the old man a cab, given him some folding money
out in the parking lot, and drove away by himself in a
Mercedes. The old man had hit the liquor store for a pint
of bourbon while he was waiting for the cab.

On the other hand, it wasn't any of Ray's concern. If
you ask too many questions about another man's business,
it becomes your business, and pretty soon you're wading
through mud and you don't have any galoshes. And besides, there were lots of ungrateful sons out there, and lots
of fathers who boozed it up.

There was a knock on the door now, and whoever was
standing outside leaned hard enough against it that the dead
bolt clanked against the frame. Ray got up and looked out
past the curtain. When he saw it was Dalton, he unlocked
the door and let him in. "Take a seat," he said, motioning
at one of the two office chairs opposite the desk.

Dalton looked far too fresh and pressed for this early in
the morning, and the sight of him made Ray feel even more
tired than he already felt. He also felt powerless, dressed
in yesterday's limp shirt and a pair of slacks that should
have gone to the cleaners last week. Dalton wore a suit and
tie, and his shirt had a monogram on the pocket, a stylized
D. He wore his clothes easily, too, as if he was born to
model shirts. He was slightly taller than Ray, who was five-
ten, and he had a medium build. There was a lot about him
that was medium—a lot of restraint, a magazine image. He
looked a little like Frank Sinatra in his prime, but with
wavier hair and a tan that must have come out of a tanning
salon, given the time of the year. Women probably found
him handsome.

Ray rubbed the top of his head and sat down heavily in his own chair. "Cup of coffee?"

"No, thanks. I don't drink coffee."

"My coffee's no good anyway," Ray said. "I usually chase it with Rolaids."

"Why do you drink it, then?" Dalton was apparently serious. He had no sense of humor at all, despite his smile.

"Force of habit," Ray said. "What have you got?"

"Same as last time. Nothing complicated. This won't be the last one, either."

"Where's your father, out in the car?"

Dalton shook his head. "He's not too well, I'm afraid. I believe I mentioned that they were going to do bypass surgery on him?"

"Yeah, I remember."

"Unfortunately they couldn't, not in the shape he was in. So they put him on a diet and exercise regimen, which was completely worthless. He's weaker than ever. You saw what he looked like last month."

Ray nodded. Last month the old man had looked like a street drunk wearing somebody else's clothes.

"I'm pretty sure that there's something more wrong with him. His stomach problems get worse every day. He can't eat. My guess is it's cancer, but I'll be damned if I want them to run the tests on him. What's the use? If they find out it's cancer, what are they going to do—chemo therapy? Not in the shape he's in. I'm just trying to keep him comfortable now. He might hang on six months, or he might go tomorrow."

"He's insured?"

"With Kaiser Permanente."

Ray clicked his tongue.

"They've taken good care of him. The HMO is the wave of the future. But when a man's dying of heart disease, cancer doesn't interest him all that much. He's got a big enough fight as it is."

"And that's why he wants to get rid of these properties?"

"That's exactly it," Dalton said. "He's clearing the decks, I guess. It's sad, but it's practical."

"Well, it's not all *that* practical. We've got a small problem."

"What's that? I've got his signature here on the deed."

"Even so," Ray said, "we need him, too."

"Well, we're not going to get him. I'm not exaggerating about his condition. It would kill him to have to deal with this now. You've already met him. What's the sudden interest in his personal appearance?"

Ray held his hands out helplessly. His instincts had been right. There was a problem here. And now his instincts told him that it was a problem that was bigger than a hundred bucks.

"It's the law, Mr. Dalton." The only thing to do for the moment was to stonewall him—shift the blame to the government. Hell, there were other notaries around. Let him go hose somebody else if he didn't want to play ball.

Dalton looked at him for a moment, as if considering Ray's objection. "What's that picture on the wall there?" he asked suddenly, pointing at a framed photo.

"That's the Mifflin hacienda. Belonged to my folks." The photo was of a U-shaped ranch-style house with a wide verandah and shuttered windows. The blue of the ocean was visible beyond the dry scrub that surrounded the house. There was a terra-cotta and tile fountain in front with a sporty-looking old car parked beside it.

"And now the place is yours?" Dalton asked him.

"It sure as hell is, whenever I can find the time to get down there."

"It was your birthright, your inheritance?"

"I guess you could put it that way. It's only about four hours away, too. Outside a little village called Punta Rioja—just below Ensenada." Ray instantly regretted saying this. He was talking too much, getting too familiar with a man he didn't know. That was against the rules.

"That's how you learned the language, then?"

"That's right."

"It's come in handy for you, too."

"There's a big Hispanic population up here. They pay taxes."

"That's good to hear. They need help, and they come to

Ray Mifflin. I bet they need all *kinds* of help.''

"I'm not sure I follow you."

Dalton shook his head, as if what he'd said wasn't important anyway. He waved his papers in the air. "Well, you've got *your* little hacienda already. I guess you understand what I'm talking about here."

"Yes, sir," Ray said. "And so will your father. All we need is his signature, like I said."

"You've seen the signature before, though. It's not as if this thing doesn't have a history. I mean, this isn't the first of these. And as I said before, you've already met my father."

"Well, the county doesn't have as much respect for history as you and I do, Mr. Dalton. Legally, either your father's got to be here or else you've got to have two witnesses to attest to the fact that this is his signature."

"Are you implying that you don't believe this is his signature?" He laid the papers on the desktop and gestured at them.

"*Hell*, no," Ray told him. "But this isn't about what *I* believe. This is about what's legal and illegal. I'd love to do you a favor, Mr. Dalton, but I've got a career on the line here, and I'm afraid I've got to follow the rules."

Dalton shrugged and sat back in his seat. "I guess maybe we can get an ambulance to transport him. I don't like it, though. I can't imagine that's what the law had in mind."

"Like I said, how about a couple of witnesses to the signature? That ought to be easy enough. Either that or I could run on out to Huntington Beach with you. I'd have to charge you my hourly plus travel, but if that's the only way to work it . . ." He held his hands out and shrugged. "What is it, anyway? Another quitclaim deed? Not that it's any of my business, aside from the signature question."

"That's it. Quitclaim deed again. Real estate. I've still got to get his estate under control before the tax man gets hold of it. I already feel like a vulture, you know, grabbing these deeds like this. But the government doesn't let you do anything else. And like I said, I don't want to bother my father with this. There's no use for the two of us to go pushing into his sickroom and shoving a pen into his hand.

He's my father, for God's sake. He deserves a little bit of respect.''

''I sympathize with that. That's my attitude, too. But we're all legislated into hard corners, Mr. Dalton. Why don't you round up those witnesses and come back in during regular hours?'' Ray stood up and held his hand out. If Dalton shook it and left, then to hell with the hundred bucks or anything else. He wouldn't be back.

Dalton didn't get up, though. He sat in the chair and looked Ray in the face, as if he were studying something out. ''I appreciate your position,'' he said finally. ''And call me Edmund, for God's sake. We're all friends here.''

''I'm glad you understand,'' Ray said. ''You're a businessman yourself. My advice is to make all this legal and aboveboard. Neither one of us needs some county official down here asking questions.'' Ray had a gut feeling now: Dalton was going to make him an offer. Either Ray could act indignant or he could take it. He made up his mind then. He'd act indignant first; then he'd take the offer if it held up.

Dalton sat there silently again, studying his fingernails, which appeared to Ray to have been manicured. Last month's deed had transferred title to a lot that must have been worth a couple hundred thousand, and this one on the desk now was something of the same kind. The guy could afford a manicure. A hundred bucks! Ray laughed out loud, cutting it off short and shaking his head.

''Something's funny,'' Dalton said.

''I just remembered something I heard on the radio once, that's all.''

''Go ahead.'' Dalton tossed his head. ''Let's hear it.''

''Well, I don't know. It was funny as hell at the time—a few years back, when Jimmy Hoffa disappeared.''

Dalton nodded. ''I hear he's buried under the goalposts at some football stadium. What's the joke?''

''Well, what I read was that there were all kinds of ransom notes that came in. Hundreds of them, all bogus, apparently.''

''I bet there were.''

''One of them was really rich, considering it was Hoffa.''

"What'd it say?" Dalton had a big grin now, as if he was ready for a good laugh.

"It said—this is what I heard—'We've got Hoffa. Put five hundred dollars in a paper sack and . . .' " Ray waved his hand in a little whirlwind gesture and waited for Dalton's reaction.

"And what?"

"I forget. Put it under a bush or something."

"Five hundred?" Dalton appeared to be mystified, maybe doubtful. "That's all they asked for?"

"That's what's funny. That's it. That's the joke. It was because it was Hoffa, see. If it was somebody else—JFK or somebody—the joke wouldn't make any sense." Either the man was dense, or he was playing dumb because he was catching on. "The idea was that Hoffa was only *worth* five hundred bucks. . . ."

Dalton sat back in the chair again, all the anticipation gone out of his face. The joke had fallen flat on him. "You laugh easy. I admire that."

"Well, in a world like this, you pretty much have to."

"Business down a little bit? What else do you do here? You can't make a living stamping papers."

"Income tax. Investment counseling."

"In*vest*ments?"

Ray nodded.

"That's *good*. You're a wise man, Ray. You could fool anyone with an office like this. Anyone with any sense would bet you'd never made a successful investment in your life. I guess that's a lowball approach to the game." He looked around, taking in the metal file cabinets, the stained carpeting, the desk against the back wall piled high with overfull file folders, the Mr. Coffee machine surrounded with plastic spoons and empty Cremora packets and used Styrofoam cups. "Now let me see if I've figured out what you're driving at with this Hoffa joke, Ray. Basically, to begin with, you think that I don't want to round up any witnesses because the signature's a fake. Am I right so far?"

"I didn't say it was a fake."

"Wait, wait . . . No offense. I'm just organizing things

here. You figure the signature's a fake, and so you tell me this Hoffa story, making fun of five hundred bucks in a bag. That's the punch line, isn't it? My hundred dollars is the same kind of thing. That's the joke.''

Ray nodded slowly. ''That's the punch line,'' he said carefully, watching Dalton's eyes, which were still full of sincerity.

''Well, you're right.''

''About what?''

''About the signature. It's a complete fake. I forged it.''

''I'D BE CAREFUL WHO I TOLD THAT TO, ED.'' RAY TRIED not to let his surprise show. *Forged* it. He was suddenly certain that coming in early this morning had been a good idea after all. He was going to make a profit.

''Edmund.''

''I'm sorry?''

''Edmund. I prefer my full name. And believe me, I *am* careful. I'm unbelievably careful. I'm telling you because I think you'll see reason. Here's my problem. My father's got a little bit of Alzheimer's along with the rest. You don't know from day to day what he's going to say or do.''

''My mother had it,'' Ray said. This was true about his mother, although probably it wasn't true about Dalton's father.

''You know what I'm talking about then. About a year ago, before he got bad, we talked about the estate problem and figured the whole thing out—what we had to do to put things in order.''

''That's smart,'' Ray told him. ''Don't get sentimental. Get it right *before* he dies.''

"Exactly. I guess I mean to say that my father worked hard all his life, Ray. He took a sack lunch to work. Oil field work, with his hands. He had a little luck and got in on the ground floor with a few wells in Huntington Beach, back when your property deed included mineral rights. When the real estate boom started up in the late sixties, he did *real* damned well with the money he'd put away. He isn't any kind of Howard Hughes, but he made his profit. And it's my idea that he *earned* his money, Ray, through intelligence and hard work."

"I won't argue with that."

"Well, the government will argue with it. They don't care *who* earned it. They'll eat a piece out of his assets that would choke men like us, and they won't even taste it."

Ray shrugged. "The army'll buy another five-hundred-dollar toilet brush."

"*That's* what disgusts my father. And even though I didn't earn that money like he did, it disgusts me too."

"I bet it does."

"My father can remember a time when a man kept what he earned. That was his incentive to work harder."

"*Hell* of an incentive."

"Well, back when we talked it out a year ago, the upshot was that he decided to quitclaim it to me, a little at a time. He had his pride, and he didn't want to be insolvent. But he didn't need all of it. The quitclaim was painless—simple signature. No lawyer to deal with. Minimal paperwork. Way easier than a trust or something like that."

"That's right. All you need's a notary," Ray said.

"We should have gone on and done it right away, but we didn't, and I didn't push it, because it was too much like pushing my father into the grave, if you know what I mean."

"Absolutely," Ray said. "That's what I was talking about. We get sentimental. Nobody wants to act like a damn vulture. And now it's too late. The Alzheimer's screwed things up, is what you're telling me. The cancer . . . You didn't work fast enough, and now it looks like you're stuck."

"You've got it. That's the whole truth."

"I sympathize entirely, Edmund, but my hands are tied here. The law's a simple thing in this case."

"Simple is just the word, isn't it?"

"That's right."

"Five hundred dollars in a paper bag! That's a riot. Jimmy Hoffa!" Dalton shook his head, his eyes full of amusement.

"I laughed like hell when I heard it."

"I'll bet you did. So tell me. What do you want?"

"For what?"

"For notarizing these deeds. I think I mentioned that this wouldn't be the last one. My father did very well, Ray. Very well."

"I seem to recall your having said that you were the only heir?"

"Sole heir, thank God."

"Well, one way or another I guess I'm not interested. I've spent my whole life keeping out of trouble."

"And drinking bad coffee out of dirty cups while you run up pathetic little 1040's for Mexican aliens. *Se habla español*, eh? You can talk the talk. Very profitable talk. What do you get for that, about forty bucks a pop?"

"It's an honest living, Mr. Dalton."

"I'd pay five percent to a good man."

"That's generous."

"It beats a hundred bucks."

"Yes indeed it does. It's a tempting offer."

"Look at this deed for a moment. This piece of property is out in Fountain Valley. A good-sized vacant lot down near Brookhurst and Ellis. It was assessed last year at three hundred K. Five percent of that is fifteen thousand dollars, Ray. I'm talking cash here. Nobody on earth has to know that you took a dime. That's a hell of a commission for inking up that little rubber pad."

"You wouldn't be paying for ink, Mr. Dalton. We both know that."

"That's very true. I'm paying for your expertise, and I'm asking you to involve yourself in fraud, legally speaking. Ethically speaking, of course, there's no fraud involved. And where's the risk? As long as my father's alive, nobody

knows whether he signed the deed or not. *He's* not going
to cause us any trouble. If there's no injured party, then
there's no real problem, is there?''

"No, I guess there's not. Unless these deeds call attention to themselves.''

"This is the *county*, Ray. Nobody pays attention. People
who pay attention work someplace else.'' Dalton gestured
with both hands, as if what he said stood to reason . . .
which it did. "So, what do you think? Half the money up
front? Right now? Call it seventy-five hundred? Give me
six months to unload the property, and I'll pay you the rest.
If I can't sell it, I'll pay you anyway. If it sells for more
than the assessed value, I'll throw in a percentage. And I'll
tell you what. Here's a fail-safe. If you want out, or if you
come up short for money at any time, I'll cash you out at
half of the second payment, so that you don't have to wait
the full six months. So for early retirement you get seventy-
five percent of the total cash value. How's that sound?''

"Like three-quarters of a pie.''

"Look,'' Dalton said, "all I want is a man that's solid
and committed.''

"Sounds like maybe you want a lawyer.''

"To hell with lawyers. Speaking of lawyers, did you hear
that they're using them as laboratory animals now?''

"Is that right?''

"There's some things rats just won't do.'' Dalton winked
and grinned big, and Ray laughed out loud. "I don't trust
lawyers. They cost too much, they're slippery bastards. I
just don't need a lawyer. Do *you* think I need a lawyer?''

"I guess not. Not if you're careful.''

"*That's* what I want. Just what you said. A *careful*
man.''

Ray shrugged.

"And I'm fairly certain you're a careful man, Ray. Do
you know why I say that?''

"I guess I don't.''

"Because a mutual friend of mine told me something
about you, Ray. He told me that you've got a soft spot for
Mexicans. He told me that back in the old days, if I wanted
to bring in a truckload of illegals, I'd want to talk to Ray

Mifflin first. Ray Mifflin would know when it was safe, this guy said. Ray Mifflin had contacts in the INS. He had the inside word on the checkpoint down the Highway south of San Clemente. Kick fifty bucks a head back in Ray's direction, and you'd bring your people through.'' He sat staring at Ray, grinning faintly.

"Your friend's full of baloney,'' Ray told him.

"That's just what I said to him. I didn't believe a word of it. I didn't believe what he told me about the drugs, either, about how they'd offer a discount to the *mojadas* if they'd carry a little bundle of white powder across the border. *Some*body turned a profit on that scam, I guess. I'm relieved to find out it wasn't you, Ray. Obviously the idea's just too fantastic. And anyway, it's ancient history. A couple of years ancient, anyway. You're not a CPA, are you, Ray?''

"Nope.''

"Somehow I didn't think so. Tell me, then; what the hell do you have to lose? Five percent is good money. No smuggling, no sweat, just a pen with ink in it. It could be your ticket out of this dump. And from my perspective, it's a hell of a lot less than I'd pay a lawyer. No insult intended.''

Ray nodded. His head buzzed. He could guess who Dalton's big-mouth friend was. Ray was being threatened, of course. Still, this was *way* better money than he had anticipated, which was a red flag if there ever was one. He thought about the other little pissant deals he'd cut recently—a hundred here, a fifty there. There had been a hell of a lot more money smuggling illegals, money on every conceivable end. Even the owners of garment shops in L.A. would pay you for employees. That deal had gotten too hot and complicated, though—partly because of the dope connection—and he had dropped it. He wasn't going to do serious jail time for a few more bucks.

"This is the tip of the iceberg, Ray. My father holds the deed to acreage down on the cliffs in Dana Point that's worth so much it's almost criminal. As long as he stays alive, we're both on the gravy train. If he dies . . .'' Dalton shrugged. "Then it's too damned late, isn't it? For you, anyway. *I'll* still do all right. How old are you, Ray?''

"Fifty-six," Ray said, making up his mind.

"And you're still living on coffee and junk food. Maybe it's time to take a little chance."

"Maybe it is," Ray said.

9

ANNE AWOKE IN THE SEMIDARKNESS OF A SHUTTERED room, and for a moment she didn't remember where she was. It was her own chenille bedspread, with its pink and blue flowers, but the room itself was disorientingly strange: it was too small, and the windows were wrong, and there were boxes stacked in the corners. . . .

Then the sleep drained away and she remembered. She had been in the apartment for four nights now—sooner or later it should start feeling like home. On Monday she had looked at the place and impulsively signed a rental agreement, and on Tuesday she had moved in. The landlord, Mr. Hedgepeth, was incredibly fat and had wheezed going up the stairs into the apartment and then had to sit down and catch up with himself before he could show her through the other three rooms. He had carried a stick that he pointed at things with—the view of the ocean out the living room windows, the old Catalina tiles over the bathroom sink, the walk-in closet with red cedar cabinets built in and a window for ventilation.

There was a connecting door in the closet, too, which was locked tight, and which opened into the law office that she shared a closet wall with. Mr. Hedgepeth had the key. He offered to put a lock on her side of the door, too. It wouldn't be a problem, just a hasp and a little Master lock. She could keep the key to that one if she wanted to. She had the idea that someday, if she stayed there, she would rent the law office, too, which had a pair of good skylights. She could open up the connecting door and use the office as a studio. But here she was already thinking years ahead. What was there for her here, except an obliging landlord and a funky old apartment with charm?

Mr. Hedgepeth had offered to carpet the painted wooden floor, which was clean but foot-worn, but she had talked him into leaving it. He had told her then that she could go ahead and splatter paint on it, because the whole thing would either have to be carpeted or repainted next time anyway, so it didn't matter. His wife had painted pictures, he had said, before she died, and he welcomed an artist into the place, as long as she didn't have some kind of artistic temperament. Anne had assured him that she didn't, that her temperament was inartistic, nearly boring.

She flopped back down onto the bed now and stared at the ceiling. How far was she from home? Fifteen hundred miles? Two thousand by the Coast Highway, with all its twists and turns? She hoped it was far enough.

The drive south from Victoria had taken her a long damned time—lots of Sleepy 8 motels and farmhouse B and B's. In Port Angeles she had driven west and then south on 101 instead of east to Highway 5, and so instead of a two- or three-day run down into southern California, she had spent eighteen days on the Highway, stopping at likely-seeming galleries and walking on foggy, driftwood-littered beaches. She had set a hundred-mile-a-day limit—no more than a couple hours or so on the road—and some-where above Eureka, when she was about halfway done with the journey, she had considered slowing down even more.

Someone had told her once that if you set out to cross a street, making each step half the distance to the opposite curb, you would never reach your destination, but would be walking across that street eternally. The same thing could be said for traveling: if you worked it right, taking your time, you could drive south on the Highway forever, with your shadow racing along the rocky edge of the road and the gray Pacific shifting and crashing on the rocks far below. . . .

. . . Except that her stuff had been due to arrive in Huntington Beach at the Bekins storage warehouse on the first of April, and she was uncomfortable letting it sit there, especially the paintings. And, even more to the point, something had happened when she had crossed the Golden Gate into San Francisco. It had begun to feel to her almost as if the car were rolling downhill toward an inevitable destination, as if she were some sort of sea creature that had come unmoored from its rock and was adrift on an outgoing tide, swept on a current toward some farther shore. And maybe this was it—this apartment she had rented from Mr. Hedgepeth. Maybe this was her destiny.

Feeling suddenly lonely, she sat up and pulled the curtains open. Judging from the noise and the traffic outside, it was late in the morning. There was still fog in the air, but the spring sun shone faintly through it, and within another hour or two it would burn off. The street outside was lined with old houses, mostly wooden bungalows with big front porches and cracked sidewalks. There were camphor trees along the curb, and the branches arched entirely over the street. It was worth living there for the trees alone, although that hadn't been what had drawn her to Huntington Beach. There had been plenty of trees in Victoria.

What *had* drawn her here? she wondered suddenly. She wasn't sure that she believed in tides and destiny. Why not Laguna Beach? It would have been simple to have Bekins truck her stuff farther down the Highway. She had looked at three nice apartments in Laguna, including one with a studio that had better light than this apartment in Huntington. Rents weren't all that much higher in Laguna, and six of her paintings were hung in Potter's Gallery on Oak Street. It didn't make any sense, her driving twenty miles back up the coast to find a place to live. Of course she had also found a day job at the Earl of Gloucester, the old theater props warehouse here in town, but considering what it paid, she would have made more waitressing in Laguna, which was packed with upscale restaurants. On the other hand, the job at the props warehouse looked like potential fun, and now that her mother was no longer living, she didn't need the money anyway. That hadn't sunk in yet; neither of those things, her money or her mother's death, seemed quite real to her.

And any college psychology student would have an opinion on what she was doing in Huntington Beach. She looked into the dresser mirror, which stood against the wall at the end of the bed. Her long dark hair was a fright, pushed around by sleep. In the dim light of the bedroom it looked jet black, although in the sunlight there were shades of auburn in it. Yesterday she had turned twenty-eight years old, and she had celebrated alone, eating a burger and fries at the Longboarder and then bringing a slice of cake home to her room. She had only eaten half of the cake before her walk on the pier. There was something about eating her birthday cake alone that had ruined her appetite.

And yet right now she didn't feel half as dismal as she had the right to feel, and even the loneliness that she had felt a few minutes ago had evaporated almost instantly. She had been in the apartment for only four nights, but somehow this morning, despite waking up stupid, she finally felt moved in. What she had seen last night on the pier, or thought she had seen, had been nothing but a trick of foggy lamplight and runaway imagination, a fragment of a bad dream that had followed her south from home. And of course, speaking of lamplight, there hadn't been nearly enough of it for her to have seen colors. Red would merely have looked dark gray.

Actually, the leftover cake sounded good to her right now. There was nothing wrong with cake for breakfast. Marie Antoinette had recommended it. Of course the food police had cut her head off afterward, but that just made her a martyr to the cause of starting the day with dessert. She climbed out of bed and went into the living room, which doubled as a studio. It was a big room—nearly twenty by forty—in a building that was mostly office space. Hers was the only actual apartment in the building. Her front door opened onto a long interior corridor some ten feet wide and with five other doors similar to hers, most of which led into one-room offices. At the top end of the corridor was a bathroom shared by the rest of the tenants—

two fairly pitiful law firms (bankruptcy and divorce) and a
record company called Doctor Slim. The other two offices
were empty, and, because she could afford it, she had
briefly considered renting one of them to use as a studio,
except that the living room in this apartment was nicer—
big windows looking down toward Main Street on the east
and south sides both, and she didn't have to cross the hall
to work. Outside, there were stairs from the bottom end of
the corridor down to the street, where there was a door that
was kept locked after business hours—officially five
o'clock. Mr. Hedgepeth had warned her against leaving the
street door unlocked. He made random checks, he said, at
all hours, and it was written into the rental agreement that
failing to lock the street door, as well as keeping pets, was
cause for eviction.

She unlocked the chain lock and the dead bolt and
opened the front door now, looking out into the corridor.
The old building was silent, musty-smelling, and dim. Today she would switch the low-wattage bulbs in the overhead lamps to something bigger. Mr. Hedgepeth could
charge her another couple of bucks a month if he wanted
to. It was Saturday, her first weekend day in the building,
and so, as far as she knew, none of the offices were open.
The place was hers on the weekend. She could bowl in the
corridor if she wanted to.

She closed the door again and moved to the other side
of the living room, where she opened two windows to let
in the morning air. Then she looked for the paper plate with
the other half of her cake on it. The plate was gone, disappeared from the table it had sat on next to the stuffed
chair. She glanced around the room, looking for the cake,
which, she told herself, she must have moved somewhere
else absentmindedly. But she was certain that she simply
hadn't put it anyplace else; she remembered distinctly
having left it on the table. Was it still on the table when
she'd gotten home from the pier late last night? She
couldn't remember. She hadn't been in any mood to be
thinking about cake. But the door had been bolted while
she was gone; that much she remembered.

⊰ 10 ⊱

DAVE HEADED DOWNSTAIRS NOW, OUT THE SIDE DOOR AND around the back of the warehouse, where he found Collier on the side porch of the bungalow, drinking his doughnut shop coffee that he had decanted into a ceramic mug. There was the sound of a television from inside the house—Sesame Street characters singing about the neighborhood. Jenny was a Sesame Street regular, still young enough at five years old to think she was living in some remote corner of it. With any luck she'd have a couple more years of thinking so before the world changed her mind for her.

Jenny's parents had died three years ago in a car wreck. She had been two at the time that Collier had gotten custody of her, and he was the only father she remembered. His son had owned a condominium in Anaheim, which had gone to Jenny, except that it turned out to be worth less than her parents had paid for it. Stuck in the middle of a decaying neighborhood, half the condos in the complex were empty, the owners disappeared. Collier had paid the mortgage with his son's bank account, thinking at first to hold onto the condo as Jenny's legacy, but with each month that passed, the account shrank and so did the value of the condo, and after five thousand dollars had evaporated that way, Collier had done the same thing that all the other tenants were doing—he gave it back to the bank by simply walking away.

There was some money left in Jenny's account—money that Collier wouldn't touch. It wouldn't change his life in any way he cared about, but some day, he had told Dave, it might change hers.

Collier had pulled his chair over to the edge of the porch,

and he sprinkled water onto his garden over the top of the
porch railing. He had onions and sugar cane going, along
with a half dozen tomato vines in cages. He nodded at Dave
and gestured with the hose, nearly squirting him down.

"You should have hollered," he said. "I'd have bought
you a cup of coffee."

"I've had enough," Dave told him.

"Well, sit down. You work too much. I see that light
come on at dawn and go out at nine or ten at night. A
person would think you owned the place. Either that or
you're trying to avoid something."

"I like work."

"That doesn't make it healthy. Work can be a disease
just like anything else. You find more workaholics than any
other kind of holic."

Dave sat down on a painted metal chair and looked out
into the foggy morning. Across the little patch of grass that
was the bungalow's lawn, the back of the Ocean Theater
rose three tall stories, its rear windows hung with heavy
black drapery to keep out the sun during matinees. It was
built of the same redwood clapboard as the Earl's, but it
was considerably older, with arched, Gothic-style windows
and lot of interior woodwork that gave it atmosphere. It
had fairly recently been painted white on the outside, and
from a distance it looked good, but the window putty was
falling out, and the old rear porch and most of the sills had
been worked over hard by termites and weather. Casey, the
Earl's younger son, had applied to put it on the Historic
Register, which might save it from the wrecking ball, in
the event that Casey's older brother Edmund gained control
of the business and the property.

"How's the Duke's palace?" Collier asked.

"Coming along. We get a new artist today. She's supposed to be pretty good. How's old Parsons doing with
Lear?"

"Good enough, when he's sober. He's about got it
down."

"How is he when he's not sober?"

"He's a ball of fire out on the heath, but he can't keep

the monologues straight. If Lear was a drunk, nobody could touch Parsons in the role.''

"Touch up the script," Dave said. "*Make* Lear a drunk. Shakespeare's dead. He couldn't care less.''

Collier looked at him but didn't say anything, as if he was thinking the idea over. "That's a hell of a concept," he said finally.

"I was kidding.''

"No, I like it. If Shakespeare would have thought of it, he'd have used it. Damn, this is a *good* idea. We modernize the whole shebang, or else we just mix things the hell up. Eclectic costuming. Anachronistic props. We make Lear a drunk, like you said. He keeps sending the Fool down to the corner for a pint, which he's hiding from his daughters. Cordelia starts looking around and finds bottles everywhere—in the book cases, the toilet tank, under the beds. She calls him on it, and he gets mad, and the other sisters take his side and get him liquored up so bad that the whole damned kingdom starts to fall apart. He starts having the DT's out on the heath. Probably the Fool's been taking a nip himself, and that's why he talks like such a damned lunatic. . . .'' He nodded at Dave. "I'm telling you, this is *good*— King Lear for the nineties.'' He stood up then and crimped the hose in order to stop the flow of water. He unscrewed the sprinkler from the end and set it on the floor of the porch, then leaned out over the balcony and took a long drink out of the nozzle. "Hose water?'' he asked, waving the hose in Dave's direction.

Dave shook his head. "I ought to get back to work, get something done before the boss shows up.''

"The Earl getting in today?'' He stepped down off the porch and turned off the spigot.

"I meant Edmund.''

"*Edmund*,'' Collier said flatly. "If this was a fair world, they'd grind that bastard up and use him for chum.''

"I won't argue with that.'' Dave followed him down onto the lawn, and the two of them stood at the edge of the garden.

Collier bent over and pinched the bottom growth off the tomato vines. "You know what he was telling me yesterday? They're going to tear down the bungalow.''

"Not a chance.''

"Big chance, apparently. They'll sell the back two acres here to the city. Municipal parking. They'd make enough money to subsidize our rent somewhere else. That's his word—*subsidize*. Translated, it means that Jenny and I are out on the street. Eviction. Hell, I don't have any income besides what I get from the Earl—nothing except Social Security. What good is a subsidized rent to me? I've been living here rent-free for ten years. I'm grateful for it, too, but I've got into the habit of it now. I don't know what we'd do if we had to move out. Another hundred a month would break me. I don't care too much myself, but Jenny's got to have a decent place to live. Damned Social Services is already yapping at me about Jenny.''

"That can't be any kind of big problem. You've got plenty of friends on your side. They're probably just doing some kind of routine checks.''

"I think some bastard's been calling in stories, making stuff up.''

"Who?''

"Ed, that's who. He wants us the hell out of here because he's a greedy punk.''

"You won't be evicted,'' Dave said. "It just won't happen. You know the Earl. He won't even talk about it. He'll just put it off forever. I think he's philosophically opposed to municipal parking.''

"Yeah, I *do* know the Earl. He nearly dropped dead from that triple bypass last year. If he dies on us, the bastard son ascends to the throne. He doesn't have any philosophy except for money.''

"He ascends to the throne along with his brother.''

"Well, God bless his brother. He's always been my favorite. Hell, I'm Casey's *god*father. It pains me to say that he's drunk most of his backbone away, if you follow me. Don't get me wrong. I'd jump in front of a train to save him. But I don't think he's got a lot of fight in him. I think his brother could take him in a cold second.''

"He'd surprise you.''

"I truly hope so.''

The screen door banged shut, and Jenny came down the porch steps drinking a Dr. Pepper.

"It's too early for that," Collier said to her. "What about milk?"

"It's sick," she said, and she put a finger halfway down her throat to indicate that she was gagged by the idea.

"Well, I don't want you drinking sodas, not this early in the morning. With lunch it's okay sometimes, but not with breakfast."

"I'm finished," she said. "See?" She turned the can over, dribbling the last few drops out onto the lawn. "Can I have a 'nother one?"

"No," Collier said. "You can't even have this one." She giggled at Dave, who gave her a hard look in order to support Collier. Whatever wisdom there was in the no-soda-in-the-morning attitude was completely lost on her.

"Give us Cordelia," Collier said to her.

Jenny shook her head and looked at the ground.

"Just a little bit of Cordelia."

She shook her head again.

"What? Nothing?"

"Nothing," she said.

"Nothing will come of nothing," Collier said to her, grimacing in a theatrical rage.

"Unhappy that I am," Jenny said, "I cannot . . . I can't . . ."

"I cannot heave my heart into my mouth," Collier reminded her.

"My heart in my mouth," Jenny said, grinning widely now. She skipped away, circling around the yard, spinning to make herself dizzy.

"She's a natural," Collier said, watching her happily. Suddenly he laughed out loud, as if he'd just thought of something funny. "So the Fool walks up to Lear, see, and Lear's been on an all-night bender. He can't even see straight. And the Fool says . . ."

The front end of a car appeared in the parking lot just then, pulling up alongside the theatre and stopping, and its appearance utterly interrupted Collier, who watched the car uneasily. A woman got out, wearing a dress and carrying a notebook.

"*Now* what?" Collier said. The woman looked around her as if she were assessing the general condition of things.

"Real estate agent," Dave said.

"Social Services! Jesus." Collier took the empty can from Jenny, tilted it up to his mouth, and pretended to drink from it. "Why don't you run on inside?" he said to his granddaughter. "Put on a clean t-shirt. And put on shoes, too."

"Why?"

"Because."

"Because why?"

"Because this is Aunt Betty, and she likes it when little girls look nice."

"Who's Aunt Betty?"

"Aunt Betty Crocker. Now go on in and put on a clean shirt. Whatever one you want."

Jenny turned and ran up the steps. The screen door slammed again.

The woman crossed the asphalt at the back of the theater, heading toward them. She was a fairly tall woman, with an upright carriage and a way of walking that made it look as if she'd had a few years of ballet. It would have been years ago, though, because she looked about sixty-five, her hair gray.

"Social Services agent," Collier said. "Her name is Mrs. Nyles. I've had the pleasure once before. Somebody called something in again, I guess. Goddamned Edmund . . ."

"You want me to stick around?"

"No, you go on. I'll fill you in if it's anything." Collier shook his head tiredly.

Dave walked back toward the Earl's. This was none of his business unless Collier wanted to make it his business. The Earl had already told him that someone had turned Collier in for child neglect, although Dave hadn't known that Social Services was making an issue of it. This woman was probably a caseworker. The child-neglect allegation was way out of line—probably Collier was right about it being Edmund who had made the call. Jenny led a strange life for a kid, though, spending nearly as much time in the old theatre as she spent at home, dressing in costumes out of the basement wardrobe, climbing up and down the ladders to the backstage balconies like a monkey. She could disappear for half an afternoon in among the litter of stage props and equipment stored beneath the stage. A week ago she disappeared entirely, and the police were notified. Casey had found her across the Highway, digging for sand crabs beneath the pier, dressed like a street beggar out of the Arabian Nights. That incident alone might have stirred up Social Services. As for Collier, Dave was certain he was doing the best he knew how, and Jenny always seemed to him to be a happy enough child.

He looked back as he rounded the corner of the warehouse. Jenny was back outside, barefoot, but dressed in a frilly sort of Easter dress now, her hair completely wild, as if she had blow-dried it with a fan. Collier stood talking to the social worker while Jenny turned multiple cartwheels across the lawn.

⚜ 11 ⚜

CLEARLY ANNE WASN'T THINKING RIGHT. SHE MUST HAVE put the cake away. This was silly. . . . She walked into the kitchen and opened the refrigerator, the obvious spot. There was no cake, and nothing on the counter, either. She went into the bedroom and looked around—at the dresser, the dressing table, the bedside stand. She looked into the trash can in the bathroom. Hell. She knew damned well that she'd left the cake in the living room. She'd even felt guilty about it—first about eating it and then about not putting it away.

Who else had a key? Mr. Hedgepeth, certainly. But

somehow the idea of fat old Mr. Hedgepeth breaking in last night for the purpose of eating her birthday cake was too preposterous. Had he eaten the paper plate, too? She sat down on the end of the bed, trying to think things through. When she had gone out into the corridor a few minutes ago, the lock on the door had been bolted, and the chain lock in place. So nobody had sneaked in during the night while she was asleep. . . .

She wondered abruptly whether Mr. Hedgepeth changed the door locks between tenants, and her smile disappeared. Suddenly she felt vulnerable living alone in the old building. The little chain lock was nothing. Anybody with a key could kick the door open in a second. Even without a key, it wouldn't take much. She walked out into the living room and looked again at the table. And now she saw it—the paper plate with the cake on it had fallen to the floor behind the table itself, and from where she had stood a moment ago it had been hidden by the edge of the chair. She stood for a moment staring at it. Somehow it had fallen cake side down, and then had apparently slid several inches across the floor, leaving a trail of frosting.

She went into the kitchen after paper towels, her late-night walk on the pier returning to her memory. In her mind she saw the slash of cranberry red again, slipping into invisibility behind the tower and the fog. . . .

Cut it out. She was getting morbid. Somehow she had knocked the cake off the damned table without knowing it, probably when she had stood up. Being cake, it hadn't made a big clatter. There was no great mystery. Mr. Hedgepeth wasn't involved. He hadn't sneaked in and flung the cake to the floor. She bent over and wiped up the line of chocolate frosting. Then, as an experiment, she laid the fallen plate and cake so that it sat slightly off the edge of the table and bumped the table leg. The cake was immovable. It sat there as heavily as if it were made of iron. She scooted it farther off the edge and bumped it again, and then caught it when the plate fell. Clearly she hadn't paid any attention when she'd set it down last night. And of course when the cake was fresh, the frosting had been soft enough for the whole thing to have slid when it hit the floor.

There was no reason to believe that something had pushed it another fourteen or fifteen inches across the floor-boards. . . .

She recalled the figure on the pier last night. . . . ''I don't believe in you,'' she said out loud. But then she was immediately certain that what she didn't believe in was herself.

She threw the paper towels into the trash, then wiped up the floor again with a wet towel before mopping it dry. Case closed. So much for having cake for breakfast. She found some grapes in the refrigerator and then went back out into the living room. Most of her paintings were still wrapped from shipping, and they were stacked against the walls three and four deep. Six of them were going up to a gallery in Carmel—all of them seascapes. The rest of the paintings would clutter the flat up for who knew how long. Probably she should rent one of the empty rooms across the hall simply for storage.

She looked at the painting on the easel near the window. There was nothing romantic about the subject matter except the sky, which she was painting in the style of Turner. *Steal from the best*, she thought. She didn't like what she had done with the pier. The pilings looked gangly, somehow, even though the proportions were technically about right— as if the pier were some sort of Ichabod Crane caterpillar walking up out of the sea. . . .

She noticed something now—what appeared to be a smudge of brown paint, perhaps, against the green-gray ocean. She bent over and looked more closely at it, just a fingerpaint smear of dried stuff against the still-wet oil. Immediately it occurred to her what it was, although there was no plausible explanation for how it had gotten there, and immediately she rejected the idea. She sniffed at it, but the linseed smell of the paint masked the smell of anything else. Finally she took a palette knife, carefully scraped the smudge off, and then wiped the knife clean with one of the paper towels. What the smudge had looked like to her was chocolate frosting. Whatever it was, she hadn't put it there.

Elinor, she thought, unable to help herself. But then she forced the thought out of her mind, in case thinking about it made it true.

WHEN HE HEARD A CAR DOOR SLAM, DAVE SET HIS EMPTY coffee cup down and stepped to the window in order to look out into the lot. It was Edmund's Mercedes, and the man himself was taking something out of the trunk. He shut the trunk lid and then activated the alarm system with the remote button on his key chain. Edmund was thirty-four, with a business degree from Whittier College. He was a racquetball hound who had enough leisure to play every day as well as put in an hour at the gym working out. He golfed, too, twice a week, and got his hair trimmed once a week, and still had time for business lunches and meetings, although whom he met with, Dave couldn't say; probably the meetings had something to do with the bets he made on the golf and the racquetball. They sure as hell didn't have anything to do with the Earl of Gloucester. He had an easy smile and an easy way of wearing his expensive clothes, and although Dave had a hunch that he spent a lot of evenings alone, he didn't have to, since women had fallen all over him for as long as Dave had known him, which was over twenty years now. They never lingered, though.

The smile and the clothes and the expensive cars were all parts of an essentially vacant package, at least as far as Dave was concerned. Dave had never heard Edmund say anything at all that wasn't calculated. He didn't have conversations like other people did, never mentioned the weather, the ocean, traffic—no small talk at all. Here he was, working in what had to be one of the strangest and most colorful buildings on the coast, and yet he seemed no more affected by it than if he'd been working at a grommet factory. Probably he simply hated all of it, and would have been just as happy if it had been a grommet factory. It was within his power to understand a grommet factory, but the Earl of Gloucester was beyond him.

Dave realized that he was in a lousy mood—which he might as well blame on Edmund, as long as he was working him over anyway. He wondered if there wasn't a little bit of jealousy in his dislike for the man, which had intensified over the last year or so. He thought about it for a moment, but he couldn't find any. Jealous of what? The truth was, Dave had never really been able to see beneath Edmund's surface.

Earl Dalton, Edmund's father, was a multimillionaire on paper—dozens of properties in a half-dozen Orange County beach cities. The lot that the Earl of Gloucester sat on was easily worth more than the business itself was worth, and the adjacent lot, the old theatre, and Collier's bungalow would have been bulldozed ten years ago and sold for apartments if it was up to Edmund. It wasn't up to Edmund, though, and that was a relentless irritation to him. What he had apparently told Collier about tearing down the bungalow had to be wishful thinking, meant largely to cause the old man grief.

Edmund walked toward the door now, carrying a laptop computer in a leather case, and he seemed to Dave to be smiling about something, as if he had just recalled the punch line of a fairly funny joke. He swung the door open and walked in, looking around suspiciously and pulling his key out of the already unlocked dead bolt. When he saw Dave, his face fell into its usual mixture of gravity and indifference.

"You're early," he said flatly, as if he didn't like it.

"I like to work when it's quiet," Dave said. "I'm always early. What drags you out of bed at this hour?"

"Same thing. I like the quiet. And the kind of work you do makes too much noise, so consider yourself finished for a couple of hours. What is all this crap?'' He gestured at the litter of casters and door skins and lumber.

"King Lear.''

"*More?* What the hell have we spent on this one?''

"On materials?''

"On materials.''

"A little under three thousand so far.''

"So far? That's completely insane.''

"Completely. And of course we need more. God knows how much before it's through. It hasn't been painted yet, either. There's no telling what the art will cost. You might have to sell your Mercedes before it's over.''

"And there's your hourly, I guess,'' Edmund said back to him. "You like that overtime, don't you, Dave? A few extra bucks at the end of the week? The eagle flies a little bit higher when he's got a couple of extra quarters in him, eh? This week he might clear the damned phone lines. Oh! That's right. You're not in this for money. You don't clock in when you work on Collier's plays, do you? You and my old man, giving something back to the community. Looking out for everybody else's welfare but your own.'' He clucked his tongue and shook his head, as if he could barely fathom it. "That sure is charitable. The world of the theater is indebted. Another loser production trods the boards. Now why don't you close up shop and run along till ten? I've got paperwork to do, and I don't want to listen to that damned saw. Take a two-hour hike. Freshen up a little. Grab an omelet.''

"You're the boss. Or at least you're one of the boss's sons. That counts for something.''

"It's the difference between us.''

"It's one of them.''

"It's the Grand Canyon, my man.'' Without waiting for a reply, Edmund turned around and walked to the stairs, heading up toward his office. Dave waited until he had gone inside and closed the door, and then he switched on the chop saw again and started cutting out lumber for frames, deliberately sawing off a half-inch at a time so that he would have to make about twenty cuts before a piece was short enough. He considered putting a dull blade in the saw so that it would whine louder. Clearly he should have said something that would count as the last word, but, as usual, he hadn't been able to think of anything. Making a lot of noise with the saw was a childish comeback, but at least it was immediate and effective.

Two years ago he had been employed by an advertising agency in Irvine, but the work didn't suit him; all it did was make some sham sense out of the years he had put into college. What he was doing working at the Earl's he couldn't say, except that it *did* suit him, at least right now—except, of course, that he had to put up with Edmund. The job paid the rent on his house downtown, and, with his own key to the door, he could come and go as he pleased, working alone until midnight or coming in at four in the morning, whatever seemed right. And he was attracted to the dusty, museumlike atmosphere of the warehouse, to the pure gaudy clutter of stuff in the farthest corners of the old building, to the mice that appeared and disappeared among the lumber of props late in the evening, to the sound of winter rain on the metal roof, and to the ten thousand shadows cast by a hundred hanging lamps.

Also, the Earl himself had no problem with Dave working on his own projects when he wasn't building something for Collier or for the company. This morning Dave had brought the chop saw out front by the door instead of assembling the frames back in the shop at the rear of the building, just because the frames were big—fourteen by six feet—and the shop was too cluttered. There were industrial-quality power tools in the shop—a big planer, a horizontal mortiser, a twelve-inch radial arm saw, drill presses, band saws, a lathe, an old green-painted table saw that was nearly as big and heavy as an automobile. Dave had half completed a replication of two mission-style Morris chairs, and this evening, if he could finish enough of Collier's sets during the day, he would steam-bend the slats for the chair backs.

Working at the Earl's hardly qualified as a job at all from Dave's point of view. Maybe someday things would change, although for the Earl himself things never had, at least not for the last forty-five years, and each added prop, like an added jewel in a kaleidoscope, had thrown a new pattern of shadows on the walls and floor, and the old warehouse had accreted a more complicated and unfathomable magic as the years had fallen away.

Tired of irritating Edmund, Dave pushed the wood forward to the pencil line and depressed the switch in the handle, making the last cut. The saw wound down, and Dave stood up, taking a step back and laying the wood onto the pile with the rest. There was a crash directly behind him just then, and he leaped forward, kicking the saw table and staggering into the lumber pile. He turned around and saw that the tiki in the Hawaiian shirt had fallen off the balcony, hit the floor, and knocked through one of the panels of the Duke of Albany's palace, smashing it to pieces. Edmund stood at the railing, looking both sorrowful and surprised.

"My *God*," Edmund said. "The damn tiki fell right over the edge. I think its belt was rotten. I tried to stop it, but I just couldn't. It didn't hurt anything, did it? Tiki all right?"

"Tiki's fine," Dave said flatly, his heart still hammering in his chest. He picked up a scrap of painted Styrofoam, rejected the urge to throw it, and tossed it back onto the floor instead.

"Uh-oh. It didn't damage your work, did it?" Edmund bent over the railing now, as if to get a better look at the smashed facade. "What *was* that thing? Nothing important, was it?"

"About two hundred dollars worth of castle," Dave said evenly.

"And all that work, too! Well, I knew something like this was going to happen. The only thing I can say is that it's lucky you weren't standing any closer. That tiki would have crushed your skull, falling like that. To hell with the castle. I couldn't stand it if one of my employees got hurt. Our workmen's comp would go through the roof." He snorted with laughter, walked back into his office, and shut the door.

Various options ran through Dave's head: going up there and throwing Edmund over the balcony railing, putting a

carborundum blade in the Skil saw and chopping pieces out
of Edmund's Mercedes . . .

He looked out at the car in the lot, picturing the car
destroyed, and just then Casey's old Chevy pickup truck
pulled in, driving up to within an inch of Edmund's car
before stopping. Dave walked outside and motioned for him
to stay in the car. He opened the door and got in on the
passenger side. "Just go ahead and drive," he said.

CASEY BACKED OUT ONTO 6TH STREET AND HEADED
slowly down toward the Highway, craning his neck to see
the ocean. "Breakfast?"

"Yeah."

"Doughnut?"

"Absolutely. I need a little more self-abasement." Dave
laughed derisively, and Casey gave him a look of mock
astonishment.

"That laugh tells me a lot about you, believe it or not.
And the first thing it tells me is that you've been fighting
with Edmund again, despite what I told you."

To whatever degree such a thing is possible in human
beings, Casey was his brother's day-and-night opposite. He
wore a white peasant shirt with the sleeves rolled up, a pair
of old Levis, and hippie sandals, like an escapee from the
late sixties. The shirt had flowers and vines embroidered
on the front—the work of his girlfriend Nancy, who taught
in a Montessori school in Seal Beach. Casey's shoulders
and chest were muscled from twenty years of surfing, and
his hair was uncut and scraggly, as if he hadn't washed the
salt out of it after yesterday's session. Although he didn't
eat meat or white bread, his usual breakfast was the top

end of a six-pack, and, if he could find a restaurant open, Mexican food. He pulled around onto the Highway and directly into the parking lot of the Supreme Doughnuts, where he cut the engine.

"So what's wrong?" he asked. "You've got some kind of vibe here."

"I've got a hell of a vibe," Dave said, looking straight out through the window. "If you hadn't shown up, I'd be burying your brother in the vacant lot about now. I might yet."

Casey shook his head, no longer joking around. "You shouldn't let him get to you. He's not worth it."

"He could get to the Pope."

"The Pope wouldn't care. He wouldn't lower himself that far, and neither should you. Personally, I've got a lifetime of dealing with Edmund, and with me it's just water off a duck. I learned that years ago."

"You *learned* it."

"Just like you'd learn anything. You've got to understand that he's a game-player. Just don't play with him. Life's not about winning and losing, you know. That kind of thinking is toxic."

"Spare me, okay? You know as well as I do that dealing with people like your brother can eat you up."

"Me? I won't *let* it eat me up."

"You're human."

"That's why I don't have to let it eat me up. When you're human you can throw it out. If you're a gorilla you've got to beat on your chest and make noises. I choose not to be a gorilla, that's all."

"You mean you can *talk* it out. Emote."

"No. I mean *throw* it out. Close your eyes and picture the wind blowing it away. Watch it get small like a kite rising in the sky. Pretty soon you lose sight of it. You cut the string, and it's just gone. Most of the time it doesn't come back."

"Where'd you read that?"

"I made it up."

"It sounds like something out of a low-rent self-help book."

"Who cares what it sounds like? Just do it."

"I can't just *do* it. Now you sound like a shoe commercial."

"Sure you can. You just don't know it yet. And forget what I sound like. This isn't easy, trying to talk sense to you. You're slippery as hell, man. You're like a fish. Every time the talk gets serious, you crack a joke and change the subject. I tell you the truth here, and you talk about shoe commercials. *Listen* to me, for God's sake."

"I think your brother tried to kill me with the tiki. How's that for a joke?"

"What the hell are you talking about?"

"I'm not making this up. He unbelted the damned tiki and shoved it off the railing. Nearly hit me in the head."

"How close?"

"A couple of feet. My back was turned."

"That's his idea of fun again," Casey said uneasily. "That's part of the game. You see, from his point of view, the ball's in your court now. He's waiting for you to pick it up and knock the hell out of it. But don't do it. Just let it lie there. Make *him* pick it up. Pretty soon he'll get tired of it."

"Edmund's games are getting a little too vicious. I think part of him—a big part of him—wanted like hell to drop that tiki right on my head. He was playing around with the idea."

"Playing. That's the key word here."

"I think so too. And I think that half the monsters you read about in the newspapers started out *playing* with the idea of doing what they did. They toyed with the idea, getting closer and closer, getting used to the concept."

"You know I don't want to be giving you any advice, Dave."

"I know. So go ahead and give me some more advice, now that I know you don't want to."

"Well, my advice is that you don't let Edmund take you along on his bad trip. You know what I'm talking about? There's something you've got to understand about people like my brother—and this is true for any kind of crazy person. You've got to get it out of your mind that you can deal with him by pulling him up to your level, you know? You can't smarten him up. You can't make him see reason. What he'll do is drag you down to *his* level, and that's a cold and lonely place, man. There's nothing much happening when you've only got yourself for company. I'm not big on pity, but Edmund's kind of a pitiful case when you look hard at him. He actually thinks it's important that people call him Edmund instead of Ed. He's got his degree in business, but there isn't any business he really knows anything about. It's a generic degree, and he knows it. He's had a couple of years of martial arts, and he thinks he's Kung Fu. He shoots mediocre golf. He's all haircut and Italian shirts and tanning salons. He's all surface. And he's *always* been that way, and that's partly why he's so full of anger. And now look at you; you're full of it too, and you don't have any kind of excuse, except that he poisoned you with it. Am I right? It's all directed at him, isn't it? I know it is. I've been there." He opened the truck door and slid out now, and Dave got out too.

"Okay, you're right about that, at least partly," Dave said to him. And it was true. Dave had been baiting him with the saw, cutting up ten thousand little bitty pieces of wood in order to drive Edmund crazy, in order to *show* him. But ignoring Edmund was impossible unless you were some sort of Zen master. Or unless you drank a case a day, maybe, which was Casey's patented method of tolerating the world.

They bought doughnuts and went back out, sitting on the hood of the pickup while they watched the waves break on the north side of the pier.

"Outside," Casey said, pointing at a set rolling in off the horizon. The fog had mostly burned off, and the morning ocean was glassy and bottle green. There was only a handful of surfers out, and one of them drifted over a small wave, spotted the incoming set, and paddled furiously out to sea. In a moment all of them were stroking hard, trying to make it over the top of the first wave of the set before they were buried by it.

"Big swell," Dave said.

"Biggest in a couple of years, anyway. Are we on it?

It's still early.'' He looked at his watch. ''What do you say?''

''Maybe you're on it. I'm maybe a little out of shape for a swell like this.'' Dave watched the ocean intently, avoiding Casey's glance.

''Right. Try a different excuse. That one's pathetic.''

''I don't have a board, remember?''

''So you say. I've got a feeling you've got something hidden up in the rafters. Anyway, I've got one. I've got that seven-ten Windansea that I bought from Bill sitting right there in my garage along with my own. That's plenty of board for this swell.'' Usually Casey didn't push it, but would accept Dave's excuse and back off. This morning he seemed to want to make an issue of it. ''Why don't we just run down to your place and grab your wetsuit?''

''I sold it, too.''

''When?''

''Last year. Garage sale. Twenty-five bucks. I bought a set of chisels with the money.''

''That sounds like a lie, bro.''

Dave shrugged. ''It's all the same. We've been through this before, Case. Nothing's changed. And anyway, the swell's too big. I'm not up for it. You know how long it's been. I haven't been wet for years.''

''Hell, I haven't been *dry* for years. But I'm stone sober this morning. Never drink before you surf, eh? That's worse than drinking and driving. And what do you mean, *wet*? You've been in the shower, haven't you? You're halfway out to the lineup every morning when you turn on the faucet. You've been working on a comeback and you don't even know it.''

''This is no kind of swell for a comeback.''

''We'll go down the coast and check it out. It'll be cleaner down south.''

''Actually, I've got these sets to finish for Collier. He's starting to worry.''

''Collier's like my old man; he doesn't worry. It's not in him to worry. This afternoon's soon enough for Collier's sets. Besides, we interviewed that new artist. She starts any time now. She'll knock these sets out in two days. Her stuff's good—too good for us, really, but this is what she wants to do, she says, so we're going to give her a try. She's a knockout, man." Casey squinted at Dave and nodded his head to underscore this last statement.

"I'll take your word for it."

"If it wasn't for Nancy . . ."

"If it wasn't for Nancy you'd be the biggest derelict in H.B."

"I won't argue. Now listen. Here's the plan. First things first. We grab the boards, rent you a suit, and go. I can't believe we're wasting a swell like this. What are we, old?"

"We're busy. At least I am. Hell, I'm old, too." He listened to the sounds of the morning—the traffic, a radio playing inside the Java Hut next door, laughter from three surfers out on the street throwing pieces of doughnut at each other. All of it together masked the sound of the ocean.

"Throw it out, Dave." Casey said this quietly, and then the two of them sat in silence for a moment while they watched an incoming wave.

"It's not that easy for me."

"It wasn't your fault. We've been through this before, haven't we? Didn't we discuss this once or twice?"

Dave was silent.

"Nancy and I were talking about this last night. If you were blind or had polio or something, then I wouldn't open my mouth about it. But what you're carrying around happened fifteen years ago. You're holding onto it like a suitcase."

"It's not that easy."

"You're repeating yourself."

"It's not that easy."

"Don't push me, man. The more you stonewall me, the more I'm going to speak the truth. When you broke up with Kelly it was over kids, as I recall. She wanted kids and you didn't."

"I'd be a lousy father."

"Now *that's* almost funny. You're a *shrewd* judge of character."

"Hard to say."

"I think it's easy to say, and I'm going to say it. You didn't drown that little girl, Dave. You tried like hell to save her. I *know* you did, because I myself *am* a shrewd judge of character. You have been purely screwed up since, whether you want to admit it or not. And if I weren't your best friend, I wouldn't be saying what I'm saying."

"Who says I don't want to admit it? You think I'm not familiar with being screwed up? I've been thinking hard about it for a *long* time. Here's something else I know. We're living in a world in which children drown, man, and there's not a damned thing we can do to save them. If she had been my own kid, I'd be a hell of a lot crazier than I am. I'm never going to find out how crazy."

"But she wasn't your kid, and you didn't let her drown. So quit beating yourself up."

After a moment Dave said, "How about you? You and Nancy have been together for a few years. Where's your family? What's your excuse, as long as we're speaking the truth?"

"I'm a drunk."

The silence was heavy for a moment. "Then throw it the hell out," Dave said finally. "Take your own advice."

"I'm working on it."

"Yeah, well, so am I," Dave said. "And right now I ought to be working on Collier's sets. In another hour I'm on company time."

"*Company time*," Casey said, letting the phrase hang there. He looked at the half of a doughnut that he'd been holding in his hand for the last ten minutes and then lobbed it into the trash can by the door. "Morning's wearing on. In another couple of hours it'll be blown out."

"I can't help that," Dave said.

·14·

ONE OF THE EARL'S STAKE-BED TRUCKS WAS PARKED AT the dock now, with the wagon and the fence rails loaded. The warehouse door was open wide, and the hay bales had been shoved out into the sunlight where they waited for loading. Dave could see Edmund talking to someone just inside—a woman who was standing in the shadows—and Dave found himself staring at her, trying to make out her features.

He turned away to watch Casey's truck pull out of the lot and turn up toward the Highway. There was a slight onshore wind now, and the air carried on it the smell of the ocean, and for a regretful moment Dave recalled the cold feel of the water sluicing down the back of his wetsuit in the early morning, the sun just coming up, the dawn quiet except for the sounds of the waves and the gulls.

Dave had been twenty-two when he had let the girl drown, and in the years before that he and Casey had surfed a hundred breaks between the Oregon border and Puerto Escondido. There were dozens of times when the ocean had let them down, and they had found it calm and flat, but had suited up and paddled out anyway, just to get wet, and sat around watching the horizon, talking about whatever was in the air. Their conversation at the doughnut shop this morning made him feel old, and, what was worse, it made him feel like he'd been living in a closet for the last fifteen years.

He heard the woman's laugh from inside the warehouse, and he turned around to look. She stood inside the doorway—probably the new sets artist, the woman who could give Nancy a run for her money. Casey had understated her looks. For a fleeting moment she seemed oddly familiar to him, but he couldn't say quite why, and right then she said something to Edmund, and the two of them moved out of the doorway and disappeared into the shadows inside the warehouse. Dave was struck with curiosity and apprehension both, as if somehow he had been set up for a blind date with this woman—which of course was pure, stupid, wishful thinking.

Heading inside, he picked up the broken pieces of the Duke's palace and considered the possibility of patching it back together and retouching it with paint. But the tiki had smashed too much of it to dust and fragments, and so he took the pieces out to the Dumpster and tossed them in. Then he picked up the tiki, levered it over his shoulder, and hauled it back up to the top of the stairs, where he set it down heavily on the balcony. The tiki's belt was nowhere to be seen, neither down on the floor nor up on the balcony. Obviously Edmund had gotten rid of it. The side of the tiki's forehead had been dented by the fall, and after thinking about it for a moment, Dave headed back downstairs to his toolbox and took out his three-pound sledgehammer. Back upstairs he straddled the tiki, judged the angle, and then pounded the tiki on the head with a two-handed blow, denting the opposite side of its cranium to make its head symmetrical again.

"What exactly are you doing?" It was Edmund's voice, full of fake cheerfulness, and Dave looked up to see him and the woman standing at the bottom of the stairs. Apparently Edmund had been showing her around.

"Tiki repair," Dave said, but it was the woman whom he was looking at when he said it.

"I'm Anne Morris," she said, climbing the stairs. Edmund followed along behind her. She stepped up onto the threshold and held out her hand. She looked at Dave for what seemed to him to be a moment too long, as if she were thinking about something, and once again Dave was struck with something about her—her gypsy hair, perhaps, which was dark and full.

Dave shook her hand awkwardly, suddenly feeling like a fool for staring back at her. "Dave Quinn," he said. "I'm glad to meet you. You weren't out walking, were you, a couple of nights ago, late? I *know* I've seen you somewhere before."

"I don't think I was," she said. "Out walking where?"

"Up by the park?"

"No," she said. "I guess not."

"Nice try, Dave," Edmund said. "That line's been in mothballs so long it smells like camphor." He laughed pleasantly, to show that he was kidding. "Dave is the all-around handyman and gopher here at the Earl of Gloucester," Edmund said to Anne. "I don't know what we'd do without him." And then to Dave he said, "Strap it up there a little tighter this time, okay? We don't want a replay of this morning's little problem, do we?"

Throw it out, Dave told himself.

Edmund winked hard, like an old uncle handing out sage advice, and then put his hand against Anne's back and guided her past Dave and into his office.

⇛ 15 ⇚

EDMUND CLOSED THE DOOR AND MOTIONED TO A CHAIR on the opposite side of his desk. Anne sat down, looking around at the scant furniture. Besides the desk and two chairs, there was nothing in the room but a file cabinet. There were no pictures on the wall, not even swap meet–quality prints. There was a plastic plant on top of the file cabinet, the leaves of which appeared to be scrupulously clean. The desktop was empty of real books, although there were half a dozen computer manuals to go along with a new Power Mac, as well as three copies of *GQ*, fanned out neatly. Beside the computer lay a stack of CD-ROMs in jewel cases, filed in a wooden box with a hinged glass lid.

"Here's a couple of forms for you to fill out, Anne."
He smiled at her. "You don't mind if I call you Anne?"

"Not at all."

"We're a first-name sort of company."

"Good."

"I hope Dave didn't bother you . . . ?" Edmund nodded
at the door.

"No, he didn't bother me. He seemed harmless."

"I *hope* so." He looked at her meaningfully, then started
shuffling papers, laying out IRS forms and the other paperwork. Anne wondered what he meant with his "I hope
so." Obviously the two men had a problem with each other.

"To tell you the truth, Dave is an old friend of my
brother's. He used to have a lot of potential—degree from
a good university, a solid job in advertising. Something
happened to him, though. He went off the rails somewhere."

"That's a shame."

"*Hell* of a shame. He's my brother's best friend, like I
said. I've known him for years." He shook his head seriously. "When he was what you'd call in between jobs, my
father offered him work here, and he's been around ever
since. He's got a laid-back work ethic, I guess you'd call
it. A lot of ex-surfers are like that. He just kind of comes
and goes. I don't know what he'd be up to if it weren't for
my father. If you run a company of this size long enough,
you learn a lot about what I call the virtually unemployable,
although I don't mean to say that he's gotten entirely to
that point yet. Anyway, there's a small percentage of people
who simply cannot work. They're neurotic, they're drunks,
they're drug addicts, they're chronically lazy, they have no
sense of time. Such people essentially have to be taken care
of. That's all we can do. And it's our philosophy here at
the company that they're better taken care of by the private
sector than by the government. I don't know if this sort of
thing is common up in Canada, but in southern California
a number of large and very successful corporations make
it a habit, for example, to hire victims of Down syndrome.
They make very good employees once they find their
niche."

"So I've heard," Anne said. "Which category does ... is his name Dave?" Dalton nodded. "Which category does Dave fall into? I'm simply curious. Certainly he doesn't have Down syndrome?"

"No, no, no. Of course he doesn't." He sat back in his chair now and looked at the ceiling as if he were working something out. "You know, it would almost be better if he did. There'd be a certain degree of predictability, at least. You could work with him without ..." He bit his lip and squinted. "This is rather a private matter, of course, and I'm already out on a limb here, simply having brought it up with someone who's not a confidential employee. On the other hand, I think that an attractive woman like you has the right to know about any ... peculiarities in the personalities of her fellow workers."

"Honestly," Anne said, "it was just idle curiosity. I shouldn't have asked. It's not my business."

"On the contrary, it might well *become* your business. You wanted a category? How about 'emotionally damaged'?" He widened his eyes when he said this, in a way that made it look as if it hurt just a little bit.

"That's a common enough category."

"I suppose it is. I don't know all the details of the case— nobody does, really, except Dave—but some years back he was involved in the drowning of an adolescent girl."

For a moment Anne was speechless. "That's terrible," she said finally. "How many years ago?"

"I don't know, really. A few."

She nodded. A few ... "How old was the girl?"

"Fourteen, something like that. Maybe fifteen. All I can tell you is that the details were a little bit murky. My brother will tell you that Dave was a hero, trying to save this girl's life, and that's pretty much been the prevailing story. And maybe it's true. I don't know for sure that it's not. There was some evidence, though, that there was a ... relationship. What the hell can I call it?" He waved his hands helplessly. "Let's just say there might have been something between them." He gave her an arch look now. "Put it this way: she was *far* too young for Dave to have had a legitimate interest in her, if in fact he *did* have an interest in her. I don't want to be a rumormonger here.''

"So you're telling me he knew her?"

Edmund shrugged and raised his eyebrows. "That's the way it looked, although that's not the official story."

"So he's what? A murderer? A child molester?"

"Oh, God, no. I don't mean that. There was no real *proof*. He was never even charged with a crime. Let's just say that the *papers* implied that there was more to the drowning than meets the eye. I guess that makes it public knowledge, and there's no reason for me to be so hesitant here, but I can't really say any more than that. There's a certain protocol that I've got to follow as an employer. . . ."

"Of course there is."

"Well, I'm sorry to bore you with all of this downbeat talk. I'm a little out of line, and I apologize. And I hate like hell to be running Dave down, because we try to be as supportive as we can be around here. But you'll be working with him fairly closely, and if it weren't for that, I wouldn't have brought the subject up. We had a little bit of difficulty with falling objects today, Dave and I did, and I'm afraid I'm a little sensitive about the safety of our employees, myself included. There's no way I want to start wearing a football helmet around here. On the other hand, you're getting tired of hearing me run down a man you don't even know. *I'm* getting a little bit tired of it. He's an old family friend, as I said, and I want to give him the benefit of every doubt. But I've got a business to run here, too.''

"I guess that's the truth."

"Sometimes it's a hard truth. There are elements of running a business that just aren't very pleasant."

"I don't doubt it."

"You be careful, then. If his behavior is out of line in any way, report it to me. I'll hold what you tell me in the strictest confidence.''

"Well, thank you for the advice, Mr. Dalton. I'll keep it in mind.''

"Edmund,'' he said to her, smiling again. "You call me Edmund, and I'll call you Anne. Now, you've already met my brother Casey. You won't see him around much. He's another surfer, only he never got over it. Never really grew up. I guess you don't have to when you can use your father as a banker. Everybody calls my father the Earl, by the way, like a title. His name actually *is* Earl, but almost nobody calls him plain Earl. It's always *the* Earl. He'll be back in town this afternoon. You'll know who he is when you see him. I think I can guarantee that. I guess you could say he's a character.''

Dalton shook his head fondly, as if recalling something humorous about his father, and it occurred to Anne that he looked all right when he smiled. She saw then that his nails were manicured, which had always struck her as weird in a man. . . .

But so what? She liked a manicure now and then herself. There was something luxurious and relaxing about it that was no doubt equally luxurious to a man. And it was possible that the clothes and the grooming were simply part of the uniform of the successful southern California businessman in the late twentieth century. The Earl of Gloucester was eccentric, to say the least, and Edmund's stark office might easily be something like a calm in a storm instead of a lack of imagination. He was a little heavy-handed with his warnings about Dave, but then if all of this about Dave was true, then probably she *should* know it. Living alone as she did in an often empty building, she was an easy target.

On the other hand, quite possibly this was all a simple case of office politics that had gotten out of hand, and she was seeing only the surface of something here, some long-standing feud. She had learned more than once in the past to avoid taking sides.

She worked at the last of the forms now, filling in all the blanks. She collected the finished forms, tapped them straight against the top of the desk, and handed them to Edmund, who smiled happily at her.

"I think we've made a very good choice in you," he said, putting his hand briefly on her shoulder.

"I'll try to keep you thinking that way." She smiled back at him.

"I'm absolutely certain you will," he said.

16

IN A LITTLE STREET OFF HILLSIDE AVENUE IN VICTORIA, British Columbia, was a narrow and musty bookshop that Anne found during the last summer she lived at home. She was eighteen, and in September she would move to Seattle to attend the University of Washington. But in that last carefree summer she made an effort to spend time with her mother, who went into town on business on Monday and Wednesday afternoons. Anne had four or five hours to herself in Victoria, which were never quite enough. She sat on the benches along Government Street and sketched boats in the harbor and views of the Parliament Building and the Empress Hotel and the flower-hung streetlamps against a cloud-drift sky. And if she had time, she walked up Hillside to the bookshop, the end store in a row of picturesque old buildings that had been built a century earlier.

The bookshop was three stories high and no more than twenty feet wide. There were dusty windows facing the streets on the front and side of the shop, but they were shaded by adjacent storefronts and half hidden by books shelved on the deep sills. Even on a sunny summer afternoon, it seemed to be perpetual evening in the store.

On the top floor, with its exposed roof rafters and water-stained wooden beams, were art books and prints that had been priced so many years ago that she nearly always found something to take home with her. Open wooden stairs with a rickety railing ascended the back wall of the shop, the stair treads worn from use and partly hidden by stacks of unshelved books. The tilted floors were covered with a heavy old flowered linoleum in chalky blues and pinks and yellows that had clearly been meant to modernize the shop fifty years earlier. Now only the dim ghosts of the flowers were visible in the center of the aisles, and patches of linoleum had crumbled away altogether to reveal scattered islands of pine floorboard.

Late one afternoon in August, Anne browsed alone through the books upstairs, listening idly to the sound of rain on the roof. A summer storm lingered over the harbor, and the rain hammered against the shingles and drove against the windowpanes. Because of the dreary weather, it was more than usually dark in the shop, and except for the rain it was quiet, with no other customers and with the old owner dozing in his chair downstairs.

Vaguely it dawned on her that she was listening to the rain on the roof almost in the way she would listen to distant music. The drumming had a monotonous quality to it, as if the rain were falling in a repeated pattern of drops. She listened more intently, idly turning the pages of an old book, and it began to sound to her almost as if someone were walking on the shingles overhead, marching in place, the sound of their footfalls having become one with the rain, and, it seemed to her now, with the beating of her own heart.

At this same moment it seemed to her that she was utterly alone in the shop, that the owner had gone out, perhaps closed the place up, having forgotten that she was up there. The idea sent a thrill of fear through her, and abruptly she knew that she wasn't alone at all, that someone else was in the room, upstairs, right now. How they had come unseen up the stairs, she couldn't say, but they had. She stood very still, listening. The room had rapidly grown cool, and the light glowing from the several ceiling lamps had dimmed away to a vague coppery glow. Quietly she shelved the book that she had just taken down and slowly turned toward the stairs, suddenly anxious to leave. And right then, in the narrow space between the eye-level books in front of her and the shelf above them, she saw something move, just a quick glimpse of red cloth—someone in the aisle against the far wall of the room.

Still she heard nothing except the rain. She stepped toward the top of the stairs, around the edge of the shelves, and peered down the center aisle. It was empty. She *knew* someone was there. The certainty of it had intensified, and along with it was a growing atmosphere of vague menace. There was the faint stench of burning on the air, too, distant and muted as if carried on the wind, and she felt a crawling sensation, a fingernails-on-a-chalkboard sensation. She looked down the stairs, but they were empty. There was no sound at all from below. The rain drummed on the roof, and the odd footsteplike shuffling continued almost hypnotically, the sound ghostly and insubstantial, as if someone were walking along paved paths at the edge of her imagination, at the edge of her memory.

"Hello?" she said. Her voice was small, but she couldn't bring herself to speak louder. There was no answer. She walked slowly along the stair railing toward the inner wall of the shop, edging past the books to see down the third aisle. Nothing. No one was there. The middle aisle was still empty. No one had been there at all. No one *could* have been there. She turned now, back toward the top of the stairs, glancing at the window. . . .

. . . And in the dusty glass she saw the reflection of someone standing, a pale face, a girl's face, staring straight at her through unfocused eyes. Rainwater ran in rivulets down the outside of the panes, and the reflected red coat and pale features of the girl in the window seemed to shift with the moving water, so that the reflection had the illusion of repeated movement, like the same few frames of a film played over and over again. The smell of burning heightened then, and the sound of the rain was indistinguishable from the sound of what was now clearly feet treading on the old linoleum floor. She knew abruptly and without doubt that the girl in the window was Elinor, her hands repeating the same twisting and pulling motions, the unmistakable mime-like movements of someone sewing, pulling a needle and thread through an imaginary piece of cloth.

The reflection vanished on the instant. The smell of burning was intense now—the burnt rat and cloth smell of the rain-dampened incinerator on her uncle's farm—and the sound of footsteps filled her head. Anne bolted down the stairs, hanging onto the railing. She turned at the second-floor landing and looked back, and there was a red blur of movement and the sound of a deep human sigh, and just then something pushed her hard on the back. She screamed and fell forward, grabbing for the handrail, spinning around and falling into the books stacked along the wall. Her hand lost its hold on the rail, and she felt herself tumbling downward in an avalanche of books, and abruptly she landed at the base of the stairs, sitting up, the books heaped around her.

The old man who owned the shop was halfway across the room by then, a look of surprised concern on his face, putting his hand out to help her up. She pulled herself to her feet and ran without speaking, down the center aisle of the shop, out the door and into the rain, not realizing until she was two blocks down Hillside that she had left her umbrella behind. She slowed down to catch her breath. The afternoon smelled like rain and ocean wind now—the smell of burning lingering only in her mind—and the rain pattered on the sidewalk and street without any suggestion of the sound of footsteps. Still she didn't look behind her, fearful of the shapes and colors that she might see in the gray weather, and it wasn't until she was safely seated on one of the benches in the pub beneath the Empress Hotel that she felt a momentary shame for having made a shambles of the old man's books and having run out of the shop without a word.

It had been Elinor's image reflected in the rainwater and window glass. Anne carried the ghost of her sister with her; or perhaps Elinor's ghost trailed after her, clinging to her as if by some static electricity of the spirit. What part of that ghost was Elinor? She comprised some remnant of distilled emotion, some sensory recollection of the things of the world, of smells and colors and objects. . . .

Anne could still feel the pressure of unseen hands on her back, and yet she remembered tripping on the books, putting her foot on them and slipping. It was more reasonable to think that she had fallen because of her careless hurry to get out of the room.

In Elinor's lifetime, Anne had never felt that mental oneness with her sister that other identical twins sometimes reported—no simultaneous thoughts; no strange parallel tastes. Aside from their artistic talent, the two of them had been as dissimilar as night and day.

⊰ 17 ⊱

EDMUND HAD FALLEN ASLEEP WITH HIS HEAD ON HIS DESK. It was past seven in the evening now, foggy and silent outside, and except for Edmund the Earl's was empty of people. He jerked upright in his chair now and looked around, suddenly wide awake. For a minute he sat blinking at the back wall of the office, disoriented, his heart racing, trying to define what had awakened him. The interior of the warehouse was dim beyond the office windows—just a couple of the night lamps on. His apprehension drained slowly away, but he was unable to shake the sensation that somebody was, or had been, lurking somewhere nearby.

He rotated his neck and flexed his shoulders to loosen up. There was a television going, the noise no doubt coming from Collier's house, and he heard a shrill shriek of laughter from a child. The old man was half deaf, and he kept his windows open in any kind of weather so that everyone in downtown Huntington Beach got to listen in to his nightly rounds with *I Love Lucy* and other dusty old repeats. Edmund wasn't in the mood for calling in a complaint to the police, although yesterday he had called Social Services to report that Collier's granddaughter had a bruise on her cheek, as if she'd been hit. She didn't, but what the hell did that matter? They'd still be full of suspicion, and probably they'd make Collier *deny* that he beat the little girl, which would wreck the old man's week.

He rubbed his face, trying to wake up. Two nearly sleepless nights had exhausted him, but ever since he had met Anne his mind had been active at night, and this morning he had awakened even more tired than when he had gone to bed. He had been *visited* in the night—by the girl of his dreams, literally speaking. His dreams had been over-whelmingly sensual, with such a real-time, waking quality to them that he had felt more drugged than asleep.

In his mind he had always carried with him the image of the perfect woman, what he liked to think of as his silent partner. Over the years she had seemed to look vaguely like a dozen women, made up out of elements of the less perfect specimens he had known—the women who had starred in his films, a couple he had known in school, a waitress, a girl from his neighborhood who had often been neglectful about pulling down the shades at night. . . .

Now his dream woman had a face, a form, a name. She looked identical to Anne. He called her the Night Girl. Anne, clearly, was the Day Girl.

He realized now that he had simply been waiting for Anne's arrival for years, and that he had been waiting even more avidly for the arrival of the Night Girl. She was cer-tainly not Anne herself, this woman whom he summoned at night. He knew that absolutely. What she was, he couldn't say. Perhaps she was a succubus, a being conjured up from beyond this world—a demon, if that's how you wanted to look at it. But Edmund didn't look at it that way. Edmund didn't believe in demons. If he had to classify himself, he would call himself a pagan, and what he be-lieved—what he had learned from his study of magic—was that good and evil, devils and angels, were an invention of Johnny-come-latelies, and that the spirits of darkness and the spirits of light were simple entities, like apes and fish, neither good nor bad, although they could certainly be use-ful.

The woman in his mind had simply been waiting pa-tiently for a persona, like an empty vessel waiting to be filled. It had been Edmund who had seen how perfectly Anne filled that vessel. It had been Edmund who made the two of them one.

There had been something in Anne's story about moving

south from Canada that had started him thinking. She had told him that she seemed to have been drawn here, almost inevitably, although clearly she had no idea why. Well, *he* had an idea, and soon he would tell her what it was. *He* had drawn her here. It was as simple as that. There was a magnetism between the two of them, a deep connection, a psychic bond that he had felt upon first meeting her. It was partly sexual—yes, indeed it was—and partly artistic. But all in all it was too powerful a bond to define easily. He could sense that Anne the Day Girl was at least partly opposing it, which was exactly as it should be. It clearly meant that she felt it too, a passion that *had* to be disconcerting to her, because it was so deep. There had been instant recognition on a level that couldn't be admitted, not all at once. And Edmund had always believed that quick personal familiarity was cheap, nearly always a sign of a shallow mind. If Anne had reacted too quickly to him, if she had come onto him, he would have been deeply disappointed in her; she wouldn't have been the Day Girl after all.

He heard footsteps now, and he stopped dead still to listen. From outside? Someone in the building? The footsteps continued, neither diminishing nor growing louder. It sounded exactly as if someone were walking below, pacing up and down on the floor beneath the balcony, although that would be impossible, given the clutter of junk down there. He stood up and walked to the office door, swinging it open silently a couple of inches and looking out. There was no one in sight. He stepped out onto the balcony, darting a glance over the railing. Pieces of Collier's foam castle littered the floor below. Now that he was out of the office and in the vastness of the warehouse itself, it sounded to him as if the footsteps had receded into the distance somewhere—perhaps out in the parking lot. The sound faded before he'd gotten halfway down the stairs, where he paused for a moment and listened, waiting for them to start up again.

Out of nowhere he recalled suddenly that the Earl had given Anne permission to store paintings inside one of the disused storage rooms.

Had she? Edmund had been out most of the day.

He walked to the storage room door, turned the knob, and swung the door open, immediately spotting the shadow of the paintings, which were stacked against the wall. There were a couple of cardboard boxes of stuff, too, which must also be Anne's. He stepped inside and waved his hand around the dark room until he found the pull string to the ceiling light. Even with the light on, the room was dim. He sorted through one of the boxes, which was filled mostly with old clothes, a child's clothes, apparently, along with a couple of pieces of embroidery and a red, knee-length felt coat. There were moth holes in the coat, and it smelled musty, as if from long years of storage. He shoved it back into its box along with the embroidery, then closed up the lid again, putting the box back where it had lain against the wall.

Whatever was stored in the other box lay wrapped in tissue. He carefully unwrapped a soft object, which turned out to be a female doll apparently stitched up out of nylon stockings. The stitching at first appeared to be erratic, completely careless, but then he saw that there was an effect to it, that it had clearly been purposeful. The doll had an unsettling organic quality to it, and the stuffed nylon was fleshy, almost suggesting tumors, disease. The stitched-on eyes appeared at first to be comical, but then he saw that if anything they were the opposite of comical; they were astonishingly, morbidly sexual, full of languid desire. The doll's lips were stitched in red, its mouth slightly open. It was clothed in loose, removable garments, and he probed its nylon flesh with his fingers to check for anatomical accuracy. He was rewarded. This was brilliantly done, seriously done. If ever there were a voodoo doll worthy of the name, he had found it here among Anne's effects. There was a unique sickness here that he could only admire, a perverse carnality that excited him. The doll even felt warm to the touch, as if it generated its own heat. He unwrapped two more, a male and then another female, lifting their robes to peek underneath. His mind raced with suggestions—what he might do with them!

And to think that Anne had made them! He had known,

of course, that she had a deeper element to her, the Night
Girl element, but he had never guessed its extent. The male
doll had oversized sexual organs. It was even circumcised!
He checked deeper in the box, discovering that it contained
a dozen or more dolls, a regular orgy of them, each of them
wrapped carefully in tissue. Anne had taken her dollmaking
damned seriously. And yet she had hidden them here, in
these cardboard boxes. He wondered what else she had to
hide.

He turned to the paintings, all of them framed, wrapped
with heavy brown parcel paper and taped shut with masking
tape. He hurried out into the warehouse, his imagination
wild with anticipation, and found a razor knife and a roll
of tape the same width as the tape that secured the parcel
paper. He sorted through the paintings, picking one out at
random. Carefully he slit the old tape, right at the seam
where the paper was folded across the top. He pulled the
paper back and eased the painting two-thirds of the way
out of it, laying it flat on the floor beneath the ceiling lamp.
It was a landscape painting, dark and dim, with twisted
trees and a gray sky. As with the dolls, his first thought
was that it was simply ugly, but as he studied it, once again
he saw that it wasn't, that it was eerily accurate in a nightmarish sort of way—full of the dark suggestion of moving
shadows, of secret fleshy things. . . .

The limbs of the trees were delicately rendered, spidery
and distinct, but the trunks were deformed with bulbous
appendages and growths that called to mind the stark carnality and deformity of the dolls. Dim light shone through
the trees from behind, as if somewhere back in the woods
a diffused yellow light glowed—firelight.

He knew that fire. He had seen that fire himself.

The knowledge that Anne had seen it too was simply
thrilling. And that she could depict it so clearly, with all
its magical suggestion. . . . Here and there in the woods a
band of dim yellow streaked out from between the trunks
of the trees, illuminating what at first looked like dead
leaves. He bent over, squinting at the picture, and saw that
the leaves were cunningly painted to suggest other organic
forms—the carapaces of beetles, leggy spiders, crabs, crick-

etlike scuttling creatures out at night at the fringe of a dead woods. Several of them suggested human faces, with blank eyes and slack, open mouths.

He sat back on his haunches and drew a breath. He had never seen anything like this. Clearly he had misjudged Anne, and misjudged her badly.

But then he knew that he hadn't misjudged her at all. Quite the contrary. This *confirmed* nearly everything that he had suspected: Anne the Day Girl was wholesomeness personified. She was the girl next door: radiant, sunshine, spring and flowers. But the dolls and these nightmarish paintings were something else again. They revealed a side of her that she kept carefully hidden from the day—her deepest, secret desires and fears.

What did *Anne* imagine was going on back there in those dead woods, around that hidden fire?

Someday soon, when the time was right, he would put the question to her, draw her out, reveal that he knew her on this darker level, that he admired it, that he comprehended it, that it touched him in places that were difficult to speak of except to someone with a common soul, someone who was willing to expose hidden passions. Yes, he *knew* her now.

He was suddenly aware of the sound of footsteps again, as if someone were walking along the path behind the warehouse now, scuffing their feet on the hard-packed soil. He stood silently, listening. Collier? The footsteps continued, monotonously repetitive, someone walking heavily in place, just outside. He stepped to the tilted-open window and looked out through the dusty glass, but he could see nothing outside except the fog, which pushed up against the wall of the warehouse with an almost perceptible pressure. The footsteps sounded slightly more distant to him—not as if they'd moved away, but as if perhaps they'd always been distant, out in the parking lot, perhaps, and he'd been fooled by the acoustics of the foggy night. And then the sound stopped abruptly, and the night was silent again.

He turned back to the painting, stooping to examine the boles of the trees, and right then he felt something behind him—cool air, a hovering presence, as if someone were standing silently, regarding his back. He stood up slowly, his breathing shallow, and turned around to face the open window. Tendrils of fog wisped through the hardware cloth screen, and the misty air seemed to him to be suggestively shaded, as if the fog itself were adrift around the contours of a human face, the face of someone peering straight through the window. He drew back involuntarily and put up his hands, but the illusion vanished. Clearly there was nobody there, nothing, no sign of movement.

It had been his imagination, perhaps, enflamed by the painting perhaps, seeing things in the breeze-blown fog.

He breathed deeply and worked the tension out of his shoulders and neck. Clearly he had been spooked by the dolls and the paintings, which was a testimony to their raw power. Abruptly, the footsteps started up again, a slow tread that might easily be someone in the parking lot after all. His Mercedes was parked out there. He wouldn't put it past Dave to key his car or do some other damned cowardly thing because of the tiki trouble. He nearly laughed out loud as he hurried back through the warehouse, recalling the shocked look on Dave's face. If only he'd had his camera to record it!

He looked out through the window next to the front door. Through the fog he could see the ghostly shape of his Mercedes. He switched on the light over the loading ramp and stepped out into the cool night. He could smell the fog, feel its dampness, and now he could hear the low sound of surf booming in the distance. He realized that he didn't have any kind of weapon, and he ducked back inside and picked up a pry bar from Dave's toolbox, then went back out again. He stood for a moment, watching and listening, hefting the pry bar, full of the sensation that someone was lurking nearby, hidden by the fog.

Off to the right, standing at the edge of the empty lot, was the black insect shape of the oil well and the vague shadow of chain link. He could see a telephone pole along the street, and the wall of the warehouse rising behind him. Suddenly the footfalls sounded again, loudly now, as if from all around him at once, the sound echoing off the high wooden wall of the warehouse. He saw a movement in the fog near the back corner of the lot, near where the oil well stood nearly hidden in the murk. He gripped the pry bar and glanced behind him, ready to slide back in through the open door and lock it. . . .

And then a misty shadow separated itself from the rectilinear darkness of the oil well and chain link and moved toward him through the mist—just a dim shape in the darkness, the footsteps closer, more insistent. The fog swirled around the moving figure. He was struck with the uncanny notion that it was the Night Girl, that she had come to him out here, in the open, shrouded by fog. He was thrilled with the sudden dangerous idea of leading her out into the dark privacy of the weedy lot. . . .

He stepped forward, overwhelmed with eagerness as the dark form materialized more solidly in the mist.

It wasn't the Night Girl, though, not unless she had taken on a different form—the form of a girl now, literally speaking. He dropped the pry bar into the gravel behind him and licked his lips, waiting for her to come closer. The idea that she *might* be the Night Girl transformed into some other shape appealed to him. And why shouldn't she be? It had been he himself who had summoned her in the first place, who had endowed her with Anne's figure, with Anne's face, and with Anne's persona. Some hidden desire from his subconscious mind could have called up a different image now—younger, absolutely innocent, naive.

The girl stood absolutely still, her hair and clothing unruffled by the night wind, the dense fog sharpening her features rather than veiling them, as if she were a creature spun out of darkness and mist.

He took another step toward her, holding out his hand, his heart racing. He had to do his part, approach her as insistently as she approached him. She gazed back at him, though, as if she were completely blind, as if she sensed him but couldn't see him. A sudden breeze off the ocean blew through the fog, which swirled and lifted around them. The oil well out in the lot appeared out of the mist, its sagging chain-link fence surrounded with high weeds. In that moment the girl's image flickered in the patchy fog, and she was gone.

Edmund stood staring at the place she had been, but he was looking at the murky lights of the doughnut shop on the corner now. Feeling exposed, he turned back toward the warehouse, spotting Collier out on his front porch, leaning against the railing, smoking a pipe. His front door stood open, and light from the television glowed through the open door. Certain that Collier hadn't seen him, Edmund hurried on beyond the corner of the building, where he stood waiting in the darkness, wondering if the girl would return.

There was the sudden howl of brakes out on the Highway, a long screech, a car thudding into something, another screech, and then the sound of the car smashing into a building. There was the immediate blare of a horn and the simultaneous sound of glass breaking. Collier came down off his porch, and Edmund moved back out of sight, watching as the shadowy figure of the old man hurried toward the corner, compelled to see the wreck. And Jenny wasn't with him, either, so he had left the girl home alone. That would be another one for Social Services, although Edmund might find somebody else to phone in the complaint, since he'd been working that angle pretty hard lately.

The wind died down now, the fog drifted back in, and Edmund was once again alone in a sea of gray. He reentered the warehouse, shut the door behind him, and returned to the storage room, where he carefully slid the painting back into its paper casing, cut a new strip of masking tape, and resealed the package. He set it back among the others, then stood looking at the unpacked dolls. He realized right then that he coveted the dolls. He had rarely encountered anything that stirred him so deeply. There was a good chance that Anne wouldn't pay any attention at all to the closed-up boxes. Taking a few of them wasn't any kind of a risk. And anyway, later on he could pull the boxes open, toss the contents around, and report that someone had broken into the room and torn things up.

How many? He decided to take four, at least for the moment. The number simply seemed right to him—three of the females and one of the males. What he would do with them he couldn't say, but he had faith that something would be revealed to him, perhaps in the sanctuary of his bedroom.

There was the sound of voices beyond the open window now—little-girl voices. He stepped to the window again and looked out, but could see nothing. He headed back out through the warehouse again, carrying one of the male dolls with him. The vague idea of showing it to someone drifted into his mind like the fog through the window. Of course, if he showed it to Jenny or to the girl in the fog, he wouldn't uncover its sexual organs; he wanted simply . . .

. . . He wanted simply to gauge the doll's immediate effect on a perfectly naive audience. He hurried out the door again, through the murk along the edge of the vacant lot, making out the lights of the bungalow, the misty porch lamp, watching out for the girls. He saw no one, heard no voices, but he had the distinct impression that he wasn't alone in the night, that someone waited nearby, watching him. He could feel those staring, vacant eyes. . . .

He saw the boxy shadow of Collier's old International Harvester parked near the edge of the lot. Nearby lay a tumble of trash and old wooden pallets that Collier had recently cleared out of the rear of the old theatre, and which would probably lie there until doomsday, given the half-assed way Collier went about his business. . . .

He caught the sound of footsteps on the night air suddenly, and he stopped and squinted into the gloom. There was movement ahead of him now—a growing, darkening shadow beyond the pile of debris, as if someone were approaching, or as if the fog itself were growing more solid and substantial. The figure of the little girl he had seen earlier stood before him, still half obscured by mists. He glanced around to make sure he was alone.

"Hello," he said, stepping forward, holding the doll out in front of him. The doll's body heat was more intense than ever, as if it were playing a hot-and-cold game, and Edmund were getting closer to some as yet undefined goal. The aptness of this notion emboldened him, and he smiled and nodded at her. The girl said nothing, just stood and stared at him, her eyes vacant. He reached his free hand forward and crooked a finger at her. "Do you want to see the dolly?'' he whispered, tilting his head with sincerity . . .

. . . And at that moment the doll burst into flames in his hand. Gasping with surprise, he dropped it on the asphalt and kicked it away. The burning doll flew beneath the chassis of Collier's Harvester, instantly igniting the oil-slick pavement beneath the old truck. Edmund stepped back away from it, watching in disbelief as it burned, the stuffed nylon blazing with a ferocious white heat. The doll's eyes stared straight at him, its arms curling upward so that it seemed to clutch at its own chest as its flimsy cloth robe burned away.

When Edmund glanced up, the girl was gone. He looked wildly around, realizing now that flames were licking the undercarriage of the truck, and already he could smell burning rubber from one of the tires. He glanced at the door of the bungalow, watching out for Collier, who was probably down at the doughnut shop still, trying to cadge a free cup of coffee.

Impulsively, he stepped across to the trash pile, slid one of the wooden pallets free of the pile, swung it around, and crammed it under the bumper of the truck. He grabbed another one, tilted it against the back edge of the first one, and kicked at it, jamming it under there, dancing back out of the way of the fire when it leaped out along the dry wood and ran up the back end of the trunk, the old orange paint bubbling and scorching.

Edmund turned and ran back along the side of the building, into the warehouse and up to his office, where he unlocked his filing cabinet and pulled out three or four issues of the most salacious pornographic magazine he owned. Quickly he picked out a couple of choice issues that he didn't care much about any more, and then ran downstairs again, stopping long enough by the loading dock door to dial 911 and breathlessly report the fire. He dashed out again, running back around the building to where the truck burned spectacularly, smoke billowing up into the fog. Right then a big stuffed-animal alligator in the back seat burst into flames, and the rear window broke in a clatter of glass. Edmund pitched the magazines onto the floor in the rear of the truck, then ran across the lawn and unrolled the garden hose. He cranked the spigot on, spraying water toward the truck, hauling the hose around behind it and directing the water in through the shattered rear window to soak down the magazines. He could hear a siren in the distance now, the siren's whine drowned out by a sudden shouting as Collier lumbered into view, back from the doughnut shop and the wreck. Lit by the front porch lamp, the look on his face was worth a fortune.

⊰ 18 ⊱

DAVE CROSSED WALNUT STREET, HEADING BACK TO THE warehouse and carrying takeout Chinese from Mr. Lucky. Everyone else had gone home long ago, and the Earl of Gloucester was mostly dark, the depths of the warehouse lit only by the night lamps in the ceiling—a half-dozen incandescent globes that cast a dim yellow glow through the skylights, which seemed to float in the lowering fog like hovering alien vessels. He walked down 6th Street to take a look behind the warehouse, straining to see through the fog, and then back around the front to check the theatre parking lot. There was no reason to think that last night's arsonist would be back tonight, but there was no use being careless.

Collier's truck had been uninsured, of course. Dave had offered to loan him the money to buy something else, just to get him around, but Collier had told him that right now there was no place he wanted to go. He could walk to the market and the doughnut shop. What else did he need? Social Services, of course, would think that maybe Jenny needed more than the market and the doughnut shop, and although Dave didn't point this out to Collier, this morning he had driven his own car over, parked it in the theatre lot, and given Collier a set of keys. Dave walked to work anyway; he could as easily walk down and fetch his car if he needed it, and in the meantime Collier would have access to a car.

He crossed the dark parking lot and let himself in at the door, then took the cardboard food containers out of the bag and set them on the little plywood table that served the warehouse personnel as a writing desk for invoice work. In the silence he could hear the scratching of mice in the newspaper bin by the door, and a cricket started up somewhere back in the darkness under the balcony. He opened the little container of white rice and scooped out a forkful, then bent over and flicked it back behind the paper bin. A white mouse darted out of sight beneath the bin, and Dave watched in silence for a moment as the mouse poked its nose out of the shadows, then walked stealthily toward the rice. Was the mouse surprised that food had fallen out of the sky again? Did Dave share the blame for the sad state of mouse astronomy?

He opened the container of kung pao chicken and looked inside, happy to see that there were a half-dozen red peppers showing. He found the wooden chopsticks inside the bag, rubber-banded to a fork and a napkin, and slipped them out of their paper cover in order to break them apart. He stopped then, listening. There were footsteps out in the lot, the slow crunching of gravel—just a couple of steps and then a pause, as if someone were hesitating outside.

There were more footsteps, and he stepped to the door and flipped on the parking lot light, which turned the fog a milky white. Someone stood in the lot, fifteen feet from the door, just a black shadow in the mist. Whoever it was took a step forward, bending sideways at the waist as if peering hard toward where Dave stood in the doorway. He could hear labored breathing, and he could see that it was a man now, an old man with tousled gray hair, dressed in a shabby suit coat. For a moment Dave thought it was the Earl, dead drunk, maybe. But it wasn't. It could be last night's arsonist, of course, or some completely new threat, but all in all the old man didn't look very threatening. It was more likely that he wanted spare change. "You looking for someone?" Dave asked.

"Yeah, I'm looking for someone." The man's voice was shot, obviously graveled from years of cigarettes and living on the street. He stepped toward the door now, walking with a limp. Dave recognized him. He'd seen the man around town. Probably homeless, living in the jungle in Central Park.

"You're not looking for me?"

"That other asshole."

"That other asshole's not here," Dave said. "Maybe I can help you with something."

"Not very damn likely. That bastard *owes* me. You wouldn't know anything about it."

"I guess I don't," Dave said, suddenly interested. "Can I help? *Who* is it, exactly, that you're looking for?"

"I don't know his name. I knew it, but I forgot. He was a suit. I saw him come out of here this afternoon. I'll know him when I see him again."

"He won't be in till tomorrow morning." A "suit." Clearly he meant Edmund. The term didn't even remotely describe anyone else who worked for the Earl.

"Tomorrow's fine. How about I wait inside?" He nodded at the open door.

"I've got to lock up and go home in about an hour."

"That's good. You do that."

"Look, you can't stay inside. I'm sorry. Maybe I can give you a ride somewhere."

"Sure you're sorry. Everybody's sorry. But there's a man I want to talk to, and I'm going to talk to him. We'll see who's sorry then."

"What's he look like?"

"Looks like an asshole, like I said. Drives a Mar-cedes. Carries a briefcase."

"I know who you mean," Dave said.

"You *know* him?"

"My boss."

"I figured he was *some*body's boss. He's sure as hell not *mine* though, whatever he might *think*."

"You're lucky."

"Damn straight. You tell him something for me?"

"Sure I will," Dave said. "Whatever you want. Tell me what to say and I'll give it to him word for word." He remembered the Chinese food then. "You want something to eat? Come on in."

"Depends on what it is." The old man stepped inside the warehouse and looked around, as if he couldn't quite believe what he saw.

"Kung pao chicken from the Chinese restaurant over on Eighth Street." Dave went over to the containers of food and picked up the chicken. "Sorry I don't have a plate," he said.

"You got a fork? I don't eat with sticks." The man had a slight stoop, and his left hand moved in the pill-rolling tremor common to Parkinson's patients. "You got anything to drink?"

"I had an iced tea somewhere."

"I know that. I mean a *drink*."

"Sorry. There's a water cooler upstairs."

"I'm not that thirsty."

He worked away at the chicken in silence for another moment, then said, "I'm Red Mayhew."

"Dave Quinn."

"And what's this asshole's name?"

"Edmund Dalton," Dave said. "Did you do some work for him, or what?"

"*Or what's* more like it. That's right, *Dalton*—I forgot. I drove up Beach Boulevard with him and simulated his father for some cheap notary north of Talbert. Killed over two hours. Afterwards he gave me a twenty and left me to pay for the cab. Cost me half of it to get back down here. I was damned if I was going to walk. I walk too damn much already."

"So you ended up with ten bucks for all that work?"

"I should have asked for more money up front, but I figured that a man driving a car like that wouldn't be so damn cheap. I admit I was stupid, but I'm goddamned if it don't piss me off anyway."

"I don't blame you. You simulated his father?"

"You're damn straight I did. I signed the man's name.

He couldn't have got just anyone to do it, either—not somebody that looked like the picture on the driver's license.''

"And you want to ask him for more money?''

"That's why I'm here. I ended up with ten bucks, minus refreshments, and half my day down the drain. Don't get me wrong, if I didn't need the money, I wouldn't ask. But I do need it. I've got some debts.'' He put the chicken carton down, picked up a napkin, and wiped his face. "Maybe you could loan me five? I'll pay you back after I talk to your friend.''

"He's not my friend,'' Dave said, taking out his wallet. He pulled out a five-dollar bill and handed it over. "He won't give you any more money. That's a cold fact.''

"He live around here?''

"Seaview Condominiums up on Seventeenth.'' Immediately he wished he hadn't said anything. Not that he wanted to protect Edmund, but it might easily turn out badly for the old man. Edmund wouldn't wait ten seconds to call the police . . . unless the police were a threat to him, because of having the old man "simulate his father.'' In any case, it was better if Mayhew got used to the ten dollars and didn't push for more. "How much do you figure he owes you?''

"Hell, I don't know. Twice what he paid me. If I would have got back here with thirty bucks, I wouldn't bother the man. I'd be happy.''

Dave thought it over for a long minute. "I wouldn't think about asking him for any more money,'' he said. "I happen to think he's dangerous. He's also cheap as hell, as you already know. You don't want a fight over this, and you sure don't want the police involved. So here's what I'll do. I'll give you another twenty right now, and then you don't have to bother with him. That's thirty-five you'll make, not counting the cab money.''

"You don't owe me anything, son.''

"It doesn't hurt me a bit. And if I can find a way to get it back out of Dalton, I'll get it back.'' Dave found another twenty in his wallet, gave it to the old man, and then walked out through the door with him, into the lot.

"I'll pay this back," Mayhew said. He shook his head. "That goddamn punk."

"Take my word for it," Dave said. "You don't want to bother Dalton for any more money."

"The day I can't handle a punk like that . . ."

"Well, what I mean is it's pointless."

"He's a king hell cheapskate," Mayhew said.

"The absolute king."

"Well, he cheated the wrong man this time."

"I'm glad I could take care of the problem, then," Dave said uneasily. Somehow this wasn't sinking in. When the old man walked away, it was west up 6th Street. Dave watched him until he disappeared in the fog, and then went inside to eat what was left of the cold food.

19

THERE WAS ONLY ONE NOTARY ON BEACH NORTH OF TAL-bert, at least for six blocks or so. Dave drove up and down three times, pulling into strip malls back off the highway to check small offices hidden by fast-food restaurants, parked trucks, and vendors set up along the boulevard. Unless Red Mayhew had remembered it wrong, Right Now Notary had to be the place. There was a Laundromat and a liquor store next door to the notary, and Dave pulled into a slot midway between the two of them and shut off the engine.

He had thought about Mayhew last night for a while before he'd gotten to sleep, and had concluded a couple of things. First, he wasn't going to say anything at all to Edmund about the old man coming past the Earl's. By itself, it wasn't worth anything—there was no ammunition in it. In fact, it would strike Edmund as hilarious, Dave's giving him twenty-five bucks. Second, any way Dave looked at it, Edmund had hired old Mayhew in order to pull off some kind of scam. What was it?

Last night, some time past eleven, Dave had waked up a notary friend of his who lived in Santa Ana in order to ask her what she thought. "Fake quitclaim signature," she had told him. She hadn't even had to think about it. Edmund, she'd said, had probably been transferring some kind of property—a car or a piece of real estate—and Mayhew had acted the part of the owner of the property, because the real owner didn't know anything about it.

Dave got out of the car now, looking at the front of the liquor store, which was apparently barred at night with a sliding wrought iron gate. Graffiti had been sprayed through the half-closed gate onto the stucco behind it, and the writing on the wall had a sort of waffle effect to it now that the gate was fully closed. The entire strip center needed help. Someone had emptied an ashtray onto the weathered asphalt of the parking lot, and the little painted brick planters along the fronts of the three stores were choked with overgrown Bermuda grass and liquor store trash. He walked up past the Laundromat, still unable to work out anything good to say to the notary. He wouldn't get anywhere making vague threats or allegations. There was a good possibility that the notary didn't even realize he had been scammed. If he was involved in the scam himself, then why would Edmund bring in Mayhew to fool him? Maybe he would take Dave's information as a favor.

Through the plate glass window of the office, Dave could see a man hunched over a desk, working at a pile of forms with a pencil and a calculator. He was probably fifty-something, bald on top, and his short-sleeved white dress shirt had ink stains on the pocket. The aluminum door frame scraped on the linoleum floor when Dave pushed it open, and a buzzer went off briefly. The man looked up, nodded, and gestured at an empty office chair.

"What can I do you for?" he asked.

"Notary information," Dave said, sitting down. There were diplomas and certificates hanging on the wall in dime-store frames, and the place smelled like old ashtrays and overcooked coffee.

"Go ahead. First five minutes free."

"It's not a complicated question. Just hypothetical."

"That's the best kind. The answer doesn't make a damn bit of difference."

"Let's say a person wants to get a quitclaim deed notarized."

"Let's say he does."

"But the owner of the property, whatever it is, can't sign the deed."

"Why can't he sign the deed?" The man set his pencil down and leaned back in his chair.

"He's dead, say."

"What's he doing owning property if he's dead? Acreage in heaven?"

"He just died yesterday. Family's in the middle of squaring away his estate, and he dies on them before they can get all the papers signed, and now the property's going to be hung up in probate."

"And they want to fake the date and the signature and have it notarized?"

"Yeah."

"That's fraud, hypothetically speaking."

"But it's done, isn't it?"

"Everything's done, if you find the right person to do it."

Dave stared at him for a moment, looking as dead serious as he could. *What the hell . . .* he thought, and he asked, "Are you the right person?"

The man looked at him, frowning and apparently puzzled. "Am I the right person to what? To commit fraud?"

"Hypothetically," Dave said weakly. *What a mistake . . .*

"That's a hell of a question, Mr.—what was your name again?"

"Jones," Dave said without thinking.

"Jones what?"

"Jim . . . Jim Jones." He knew at once what he had said. The charade was over, whatever it had been. He wouldn't recover from that kind of stupidity.

"Well, I'll be damned. I'm Ray Mifflin, Mr. Jones." He broke into a smile, knocked a cigarette out of a pack of Marlboros and lit it with a throwaway lighter, then sucked down a big lungful of smoke and blew it toward the ceiling. He hunched forward now, looked around warily, and said, "I heard you were dead down in South America somewhere."

Dave thought about pretending that the name had been a joke, but decided to try to brass it out instead. "It's a fairly common name," he said.

Mifflin stared at him, grinning faintly. "I bet it *is* a common name. You must get a little tired of the jokes when the Kool-Aid comes out of the cupboard." He leaned forward again, picked up his pencil, and punched calculator buttons with the eraser.

"Look . . ." Dave started to say.

"Why don't you just tell me what you want, son?" Mifflin swiveled around in his chair and poured himself a cup of coffee, then rocked back and waited. "You can keep it as hypothetical as you want to."

"I believe you've done some business recently with a man named Edmund Dalton," Dave said. "I'm not going to tell you how I know this, but I have reason to believe that the quit claim deed you notarized for him had a false signature on it and that the old man who claimed to be his father was not his father."

"Hypothetically speaking?"

"Entirely hypothetical."

"And you're offended by this hypothetical crime?"

"Actually, I don't see much wrong with backdating a document. I don't have any problem with forgery, either, if the alternative's a worse crime."

"That's very philosophical of you."

"It's just that in this case there are complications."

"What complications are those, Mr. Jones?"

"Well . . . I can tell you that there's a good chance that Mr. Dalton probably doesn't have any legitimate claim to any property owned by his father."

"And how would you know? Just a hunch?"

"His brother might have something to say about the disposition of their father's property."

"He might, if he has a brother."

"He's got a brother."

Mifflin stubbed out the cigarette in an ashtray, and then sat and stared at the wall for a moment, obviously thinking things through. "Coffee, Mr. Jones?"

"No, thanks."

"Look, I don't mean to pry, but what the hell are you doing here? You're not any kind of county official. You're certainly no kind of cop. Let me make a calculated guess. You're a disgruntled employee. You overheard somebody say something, or else you snooped around in somebody's computer files and came up with some intriguing dirt."

"Not exactly."

"But something like that. So I ask myself, again, what the hell you're doing here. You don't want to screw *me*, because you don't know me. So you must be looking to screw this hypothetical what's-his-name."

"Neither one," Dave said, although he realized that what Mifflin said was true. What *else* was he intending to do?

"Okay, then you're going to shake this man down. I don't suppose you want to cut me in?"

"I'm not shaking anybody down."

"Well . . . I believe you. You don't seem like the type. But then I don't get it. What is this, a friendly warning?"

"Not even that. A clarification, maybe."

"A clarification. Well, I appreciate it. I'll tell you what. If, hypothetically, I *was* involved in the kind of thing you're talking about, I'd surely want to know. Because it could mean serious trouble for me. I hope you understand that."

"It's easy enough to understand."

"So I thank you for the clarification. And I'll just say one more thing. If you're thinking of taking it any further than this, be *very* careful and very sure of yourself. This sort of accusation wouldn't be taken lightly by anybody involved, including the authorities. Given what you tell me, there's a father out there who would have to testify against his son, which he probably wouldn't do. There's a brother who would have to testify against his brother. There's an old man out there somewhere who's forged a signature and who sure as hell didn't know what kind of can of worms he was opening up, either for himself or for everyone else. And there's a hypothetical notary who would have to convince powerful people that he was duped. And if he couldn't convince people that he was duped, then . . .'' The man spread his hands out and shrugged. ''You understand what I'm talking about?''

''I didn't mean to toss around allegations,'' Dave said. ''Obviously I didn't have a very clear view of this whole thing.''

''This kind of thing is often way more complicated than it would appear to be to the man on the street.''

''I guess you're right,'' Dave said. ''Just in case it gets any more complicated, take my phone number.'' He wrote his home number on a Post-it pad that sat on the desk. ''You never know,'' he said.

''*That's* true.'' Mifflin picked up the note, folded it in half, and slipped it into his pocket protector with his pens. ''I thank you for coming in, actually. It's been enlightening.'' He put his hand out, and Dave shook it. ''Pull the door shut when you go out, will you? It sticks on the floor.''

Dave went out through the door and headed for his car, feeling defeated somehow. At the same time, he was absolutely certain that he had hit the nail on the head. Edmund was stealing property from the Earl, which meant he was stealing from Casey. At least Mifflin knew that now. If he was the honest man that he seemed to be, he would get out from under it. There was something about his reaction, though, that had been a little too casual, a little too light. That didn't incriminate him, but it was curious.

❧ 20 ❧

THE FOG SWEPT ACROSS THE BLUFFS IN WAVES, SO THAT the highway appeared and disappeared in front of Anne's Saturn like film going in and out of focus. At times it was so thick and gray that it threw the glare from the headlights back against the windshield, and she braked steadily, forced to creep along, watching the white line that defined the edge of the lane and the nearly invisible darkness of the undergrowth along the ocean side of the road. The message from Jane Potter on the answering machine made the trip worthwhile, fog or no fog—or at least it would if she got into downtown Laguna alive. A man had bought six of her paintings late that afternoon—everything of hers that was hanging in the gallery. Jane had offered to discount them a thousand dollars because he was taking all five, but he had told her—a little haughtily, according to Jane—that he didn't buy things on discount. And that was perfectly all right with Anne. Give the man his pride. Probably he didn't clip coupons either.

He had wanted to meet the artist, he'd said, and that was why Anne was driving out there at eight in the evening on a foggy night. She had four more wrapped paintings in the trunk, and Jane seemed to think that there was the ghost of a chance that he would want those, too, when he saw them. That struck Anne as a little bit excessive. *Ob*sessive was maybe a better word for it. She must seem a little anxious, though, throwing herself and her paintings into the car that very evening. She could hardly *not* come, though, under the circumstances. And since she had to haul more paintings out there anyway . . .

The fog cleared suddenly, and for a moment the hillside

ahead of her shone with lights, and there were more lights
out on the cliffs away off to her right. She accelerated,
driving past the off ramp to Scotchman's Cove and into
civilization. The highway was nearly empty through north
Laguna, and the fog held off until she turned up Broadway.
Then the night was ghostly gray again, and she drove
slowly down Beach Street, across Forest, and into the public parking garage. It was damp in the concrete structure,
and the night was hushed enough so that the sound of the
key turning in the trunk lock was oddly loud.

She was reminded suddenly of her foggy, late-night stroll
on the pier, and was vividly aware of the sound of her shoe
soles on the concrete. Despite herself, she listened for answering footsteps, and darted uneasy glances into the dark
recesses of the nearly empty garage. Hastily, she got two
of the smaller canvases out of the trunk and then slammed
the lid, hurrying up the alley toward the corner. Potter's
Gallery lay across Oak Street on the corner of the highway.
Its south and west walls were glass, and Anne saw him
standing in the middle of the front room, gesturing and
laughing. Jane Potter stood next to him. Both of them held
flutes of champagne. Anne stopped at the curb and stood
there for a moment, thinking about turning around. She
could put the paintings back into the trunk, find a phone
booth, and explain that it was just too foggy to make the
drive. . . .

The man in the gallery was Edmund Dalton.

Was he the mysterious art lover who had bought five of
her paintings? Of course he was. He had to be. This afternoon he had bought her a cup of coffee, and while they
were drinking it he had asked too many questions about
her paintings and where he could have a look at them. He
must have made a beeline for Laguna Beach. The whole
thing was curious, too curious, and would probably become
tiresome.

She made a quick decision to see this through, and set
out again, across the street and up the sidewalk. If he
wanted to buy her paintings, let him. Clearly he already
had. It was Jane's business whom she sold paintings to.
And although Anne could certainly make use of the fog

excuse and simply go home, what good would it do in the long run? She would see the man face to face tomorrow anyway; she might as well get it over tonight. And besides, maybe he was innocent of anything. Maybe he actually *liked* her paintings. She backed in through the door, cradling the paintings in her arms. If it *was* a ploy, then he had spent four thousand dollars in an effort to pick her up. It was nearly funny. And, she realized, it was nearly flattering.

He bowed graciously, waving the champagne glass. "Surprise," he said, and widened his eyes at her.

"This is ... astonishing," she said, handing Jane the new paintings.

"You two know each other, then?" Jane set the paintings carefully on the floor, tilting them against the now-empty wall where Anne's paintings had hung.

"Yes, indeed. We've met," Edmund told her. And then to Anne he said, "Champagne?"

"What the heck."

"Let me." Edmund pulled a bottle out of a stainless steel champagne bucket nearly brimming with ice and water. "Domaine Chandon," he told her, wrapping the bottle in a towel and slowly filling a flute.

"Mr. Dalton brought the champagne," Jane said, winking at Anne.

Edmund handed her the glass, raised his own, and said, "To art."

The two women raised their own glasses, and the three of them drank. Edmund held his glass to the light and looked through it. "That's *good* color," he said. Anne nodded. Probably he was right. "This champagne is *very* good. It's hand-riddled, actually, in the Napa Valley."

"Is it?" she asked, smiling with appreciation. Actually she had no real idea what that meant, but she was abruptly determined not to ask.

"It's uncanny, Anne. When we had our little chat about art, there was something about your sensibilities that were so consistent with my own, that I *knew*, I positively *knew*, that I would love your paintings. I was just telling Jane how ordinary I find these." He pointed at an impressionistic sort of landscape done in oils—a sweep of beach coastline, springtime colors, lots of palms and flowers. Anne recognized the Hotel Laguna and the curve of Main Beach with its lifeguard tower and boardwalk. Actually the painting was very nicely done.

"I kind of like it," she said.

Jane blinked hard at her from where she stood, behind Edmund now, as if to tell her to be more agreeable, and Anne wondered if she would be blinking just as hard if somebody with a fat wallet was bad-mouthing a painting of her own.

"I guess what I meant was that it was so *ordinary*," Dalton said, repeating himself. "Don't you think? This is the sort of thing you see everywhere. Your paintings, though . . ." He shook his head, as if he couldn't find the words to describe them.

"Maybe if you'd spent much time on Vancouver Island, my subjects would look fairly ordinary too."

"I can't imagine finding your paintings ordinary in any sense, Anne. There's something in them, in the shadows, maybe, that speaks volumes about you."

"Really? In the shadows?"

"Absolutely. I wonder if sometimes you let the shadows carry you away . . . ?"

"I almost never let anything carry me away."

"Now why don't I believe you?" Edmund asked, smiling widely.

Anne shrugged. Whatever he was implying was so obscure that she couldn't think of anything to say.

"Well, this is exciting," Jane said innocently. "I'm astonished that you two know each other. It's almost like something out of a fairy tale, isn't it?"

Edmund nodded enthusiastically. "More than you can guess," he said. "What have you brought for me, Anne?"

"Just a couple of things to hang in the blank spots."

"Can I see them?"

Jane was already cutting the heavy string and tearing off the quilted paper. The paintings were similar to the five that Edmund had already bought, only smaller—coastal landscapes under a wild sky. The two that Anne had left in the trunk were twice the size, and were better, but somehow she didn't want to bring them in at all now. Edmund's enthusiasm was having some sort of equal and opposite reaction in her. The more he wanted to buy, the less she wanted to sell. It was the odd implication in his voice, as if she were selling herself rather than the paintings.

And his opinion of the painting on the wall was screwy. It was really very good—technically better than her own. And when she had talked to Edmund briefly about art, she hadn't gotten the idea that he had any sensibilities at all. He had known that van Gogh had cut his ear off, but when she mentioned Turner—one of her own personal saints—the reference was utterly lost on him. That in itself was nothing—almost nobody gave any real damn for old dead artists—but it argued that he wasn't any kind of art enthusiast, which right now he was clearly pretending to be.

"Surely this can't be all you've brought?" he said, his voice full of disappointment.

"I'm afraid it is," she told him.

"I was rather hoping you'd fill the trunk and back seat," Jane said. "We've got room for eight canvases at least, especially considering the size of these."

"I couldn't make up my mind, actually." Anne shrugged. "And I was a little rushed. By the time I'd eaten dinner, the fog was getting heavier, and I was worried about the drive out here, especially since I had to detour past the Art Supply Warehouse to pick up canvas and . . . I don't know—a bunch of stuff. So I needed room in the car, and there was no way that I was going to get out there to buy anything tomorrow or the next day, now that I'm employed." She grinned at Edmund again, realizing that she'd been talking a little breathlessly, reeling off a string of half-baked excuses.

"I fully understand," he said. "Although I'll tell you right now that in no way must your job get in the way of your art. If anything, it ought to *facilitate* your art. And if you ever need time off, even at a moment's notice, you only have to say the word."

"Well, I certainly appreciate that," Anne said.

"I value artistic inspiration more highly than you can imagine."

"It's good to hear that."

"And so I'm not just talking about your having to make a quick trip down to the store for supplies. I'm talking about the urge to paint. If you wake up in the morning and you're struck with inspiration, then *paint*."

"Well . . ." She tried to look enthusiastic. When she woke up in the morning, she was generally struck with the urge for coffee. She had mostly gotten over the idea of inspiration years ago.

"I absolutely mean it. Just dial my number and leave a message. But I warn you, sometime I'd like to watch you paint. I won't make any noise. I'll just sit in a chair in the corner and watch you work. I want to share in the *power* of your inspiration."

"Honestly," Anne said to him, "I can't imagine working with anyone watching."

"I'd be quiet as a mouse."

"Even so . . ." She shook her head. Share in the power of her inspiration . . . ?

"Perhaps when we've gotten to know each other better. Say, I'll tell you what. What I *would* like to do is stop by your studio and have a look at the paintings that you didn't bring along tonight. It's crazy for me to be running back and forth to Laguna Beach when you've got canvases right down the street from the Earl's."

The request stunned her for a moment. It was impossible, at least right now. It was entirely logical, of course, except that his motives were wrong. Somehow she was absolutely certain of it. And anyway, she hardly knew him. "I'm afraid that Potter's is my sole agent." She shrugged, as if there was nothing she could do about it. Jane, thank God, seemed to catch on.

"Maybe you can run a few more down here later in the week," she said. "I want to repaint the wall first anyway. We could have them up by Sunday afternoon."

Edmund didn't look at her, but spoke to Anne instead. "I'll happily pay the gallery's commission."

"It's not only that," Anne told him. "All of them are

wrapped, and ... You know what? I just don't want to. This probably seems fairly weird to you, but I like to *paint* in my studio; I don't like the idea of *showing* the paintings there. It mixes the money end of things with the creative end, and that just has the wrong flavor to it. Does that make sense?"

"I *totally* respect that," he said.

"Good. And now, I'm afraid, I've got to go."

"That's a wise idea," Edmund said to her. "The fog's socked in along the bluffs. Drive slowly. Do you want to caravan?"

"I'm not going home that way," Anne lied. "I'm going up through the canyon."

"That's smart. There's bound to be less fog, and you can grab the 405 back down into Huntington Beach. I ought to go that way too."

"Actually, I'm going to visit a friend in Irvine."

"Ah." Edmund nodded his head. "I fully understand," he said.

Again she found the statement impossible to respond to, so she set down her champagne glass and abruptly headed for the door, relieved to see that the fog had dispersed for the moment, although it might easily still be bad once she was out of town again. "See you soon," she said to Jane, and pushed out through the door.

Edmund was instantly beside her, striding along toward the corner. "I'll walk you to your car," he said. "It's late."

"Thanks."

They turned the corner and went across the street and down the steps into the parking garage. "Is that you?" Edmund asked, nodding at the Saturn.

"That's me."

"That's a very reasonable car."

"I like the name, I guess. That's about as spacey as I get."

"I don't know about that," he said. "I have the feeling there's more to Anne Morris than meets the eye."

"There's more to anybody than meets the eye," she said.

"*That's* the truth. Hey, do you ever travel?"

"I've traveled some," she said, trying to sound noncommittal.

"Well, I've got a trip planned to Mexico, to a resort below San Felipe. Beautiful ocean down there. Really, it's fabulous."

"I bet it is," she said. "It sounds wonderful."

"It's a place called Club Mex—all the amenities. You name it, you've got it. They know me down there. This will be something like my eighth trip. I slip away as often as I can, out from under things, if you know what I mean."

"I certainly do," she said. "And I've got to slip away right now myself."

"You'd like Club Mex. I think I could guarantee that."

"I'm sure I would." She unlocked her car door and started to climb in.

"Oh, oh," he said, smiling broadly at her.

"What?"

"Someone's apparently broken into your car."

Surprised by this, she looked into the back seat. There was no sign of anyone having broken in.

"All your supplies," he said. "The canvas and all. From what was that place? The Art Supply Warehouse? I thought you said it pretty much filled up the interior."

Instantly she regretted the lie. "I meant it filled up the trunk."

"Ah. I guess you did say the trunk. Well, drive safely. Watch the fog."

She climbed into the car, waved once at him, started the engine, and backed out of the space. When the Saturn bumped down onto the street, she glanced into the rearview mirror and he was still standing there, still smiling. She beeped the horn once, just to be friendly, and then turned up toward Laguna Canyon Road. As soon as she rounded the curve in the road, she doubled back down Broadway and headed home again along the coast.

❧ 21 ❧

Edmund's wild drive through Laguna Canyon had been nothing but a waste of time and gasoline. By the time he had driven a mile north of El Toro Road he realized that she had betrayed him, unless she had driven her Saturn like a race car driver. He had gotten back into Huntington Beach at nearly eleven o'clock, and found her car parked on the street near her apartment. Her light was off, the street door locked. She was cagey—he had to give her that—but given a little time, she would come around. She wasn't a *complete* fool, after all. Her response irritated him, though. He had to admit that. He had hoped for more out of her.

He lay in bed now beneath light covers. On the bedside table lay the doll that he had found in Anne's box. There was an urn for the burning of incense, too, along with a half-dozen books on magic—three of which he had paid *very* good money for only two months ago—the kind of books that weren't for public consumption, that circulated within certain small and secret circles of knowledgeable people. It had taken him ten years of searching to find his way into one such circle, and another five years to outgrow it, to rise above it. His interest in black magic dated from when he was an adolescent, and he had managed to put together a good library over the years, although accumulating his books had been a matter of constantly rejecting the books that he had outgrown, and he knew that at some future date he would need only one or two books, although those would cost him many times the value of the rest of his library.

The most esoteric and useful of the books on the bedside table was relatively new, and was titled simply *Demonol-*

ogy: Exorcism and Incantation. What was wonderful about it was that it was equally useful to the priest or the magician—a cookbook of magical recipes without the usual screwball archaic language that appeared in so many of the books that *pretended* to be profound. Unlike what many people thought, fancy language wasn't a door. The door was in your mind, and you found it by patient investigation. He opened to the chapter on incubi and succubi, although he had read them so many times that he knew most of the passages by heart. He found that reading was a good way to begin the focusing process, and he read for ten minutes now without pause, without thought, letting the words form the pictures in his mind that they seemed to want to form. It wasn't his duty to promote the process with thinking; it was his duty to open his mind.

He closed the book, put it aside, and set a lamp oil candle in the ceramic urn. He lit the wick and watched the yellow flame spring up, settling down and burning evenly in the still room. He turned the rheostat down to dim the lights, folded his legs in the lotus position, took three deep breaths, glanced at his watch, held the last lungful of air, and centered his hand over the flame. He shut his eyes and pictured a faraway place, his mind fleeing away into a darkness lit only by a distant fire. He felt the sensation of flying through cool dark spaces, and the fire in the distance drew closer and closer until he could see the deep shadow of the woods that encircled the fire. Tonight he pictured it more clearly than he had ever pictured it before—the boles of the stunted trees, the priapic suggestion of their upthrust limbs, the tumorous shapes of the roots pushing up out of the mold-covered soil. He was abruptly and thrillingly aware that he was picturing the place in Anne's painting, and at this same moment he felt the pain of his burning hand and jerked it away from the flame, sucking in a breath simultaneously. He threw his head back and breathed heavily for another few moments, and then glanced at his watch.

Nearly two and half minutes—a good ten seconds less than last night. It had been the consciousness of Anne's painting that had tripped him. But it had also been Anne's painting that allowed him to see the place as clearly as he

had seen it. He looked at his hand and found that there was
a blister dead center in the palm. Next time he would try
to hold it even closer to the flame. According to what he
had read, there was a meditative point at which one's flesh
was impervious to fire and where one lost the desperate
desire to breathe. Reaching that point was a step along a
path that included, even farther along, the ability to levitate,
followed by the ability to fly. And along with flying, the
ability to reach that place in the deep woods where the fire
burned, that place inhabited only by people of deep pagan
knowledge and desire.

Now, starting with his feet, he tensed every muscle group
in his body, one after another, for a slow five-count, van-
quishing anger and futility from his mind. He pictured the
fire in the woods again, stared at the flames, watched them
dance, his muscles relaxing. For a time his mind darted
around, but he drew it back to the fire, and then on the
center of darkness that lay hidden within the flame, until
his thoughts narrowed like sunlight through a lens, and the
world around him became a vast darkness.

Only when he had abolished all thought did he allow her
face to come into his mind. He held its image, feeling the
rise and fall of his chest, breathing her into himself. . . .

He heard a dog bark then, and with the harsh sound of
the barking her face vanished, his muscles tensed, his anger
washed over him like a tide. He cursed, full of a terrible
and immediate urge to kill the dog, and right then there
was a tremendous knocking at the front door. Immediately
the doorbell rang, and then the knocking started back up.
Suppressing the desire to scream, he climbed out of bed,
stormed across the room to the closet, and found his bathrobe. Unless the building was on fire, whoever was knocking would be a sorry bastard in a moment. He went out
into the living room, looking at the shadow beyond the
window in the front door. The pounding continued.

"Hold the *hell* on!" he yelled, tying his robe shut. He
ran his fingers through his hair to smooth it out, unbolted
the door, and swung it open. Red Mayhew stood there, his
face drooping with alcoholic stupidity. He stank to high
heaven. Without pausing another instant Dalton swung the

door shut and threw the bolt, and immediately Mayhew stabbed away at the bell again. Halfway across the room, Dalton turned around and retraced his steps. Clearly he had to deal with this, and deal with it now. He opened the door again. Mayhew glared at him, swaying precariously on the threshold.

"Get the hell out of here," Dalton told him evenly. He looked past him, down the walkway, which was overhung with fog-shadowed shrubbery. Thank God there was no one in sight.

"I want what's mine," Mayhew said thickly.

"You'll get what's yours, you drunk piece of shit," Dalton said. "I'll give you five seconds to disappear. If you're still here, I'll drag you inside, put a weapon in your hand, beat you senseless, and call the cops. Do you understand me? I'll have you jailed if you're still alive."

"You little puke . . ."

"Four seconds."

"Call a cop? I'll call a cop! Tell them I simulated your father? Mr. goddamn big stuff. Eh? You pay me a *fair* wage, or I'll run you right the hell in, you little scumbag pervert, with your goddamn car and whatever the hell . . ." Mayhew lost his train of thought, but he made furious slashing motions with his hand now. The force of it threw him off balance, and he stumbled into a forest of sword ferns alongside the porch, going down on one knee.

Shit! There was the sound of someone coming now, and Dalton bent over and grabbed the old man by the arm.

"Come on, old-timer," Edmund said out loud, yanking Mayhew to his feet. The man on the path, a stranger, nodded at him, but didn't seem to want to stop and help, thank God. "Homeless, I think," Edmund told him. "Found him sleeping on the porch. I'm going to run him down to the shelter."

The man nodded and kept right on going, not wanting to get involved. Mayhew swayed there uneasily, then raised his head and glared at Dalton again. "Little piece of crap like you . . ."

"That's right," Edmund whispered at him. "I think this

has gone far enough, Mr. Mayhew. Am I to understand that you've come after money?''

''Damn straight I did.'' Mention of the word ''money'' seemed to sober him. ''What you owe me.''

''I have no problem with that. I just wish you had asked for more when we transacted our business. But that's behind us now. Will fifty dollars make us even?''

Mayhew stared at him, as if he were thinking this through.

''Fifty dollars it is, then, Mr. Mayhew. Wait here.'' He went inside, bolting the door behind him to keep the old man from following him. Hurriedly he found his wallet, took out a fifty, went back out through the living room, and opened the door again. The bell rang when he was almost there, and he yanked it open to find Mayhew staring, his nose nearly pressed against the little wooden posts across the window. ''Patience is a virtue, Mr. Mayhew,'' Dalton told him, holding the fifty up in front of his face with both hands. ''Keep it safe now. Here.'' He tucked it into the old man's coat pocket and patted it. ''Are you with me, Mr. Mayhew? Shall I ask for a receipt?''

Mayhew swatted his hand away and backed off a step, taking the bill out of his pocket and looking hard at it. He nodded. ''We're . . . square,'' he said. ''This and the money from that other fellow.''

''What fellow would that be, Mr. Mayhew?''

''Down at Sixth Street. The one who sent me down here.''

''At my place of business?''

''Damn right, your place of business. Don't think I don't know who you are, either.'' He put the money into his pants pocket and looked up and down the walk.

''I see. I know you too, Mr. Mayhew. Can I tell you something, a little secret between the two of us?''

Mayhew squinted at him.

''If you ever come back here, if you confront me in public under any circumstances whatsoever, if you talk again to any of my employees, I'll have your tongue cut out. Do you understand me?''

''Under*stand* . . . ?''

"Listen!" Dalton grabbed the lapels of his coat, pulling the old man's face close. "I'll have your tongue cut out. With a scissors. Do you understand me? You'll vomit on your own blood, but you'll live, Mr. Mayhew, you'll live. I hope I've made myself clear."

There was a satisfying look of horror on Mayhew's face now, and the old man tried to pull away from him. He looked around wildly, clearly wanting to get the hell out of there now, and just for good measure Dalton pushed him over backward, into the sword ferns again. Mayhew scrabbled through the shrubbery, crawling back out onto the walk, breathing hoarsely. He held both hands out in front of him, as if to ward Dalton off, and Dalton jerked both of his own hands into the air and thrust his tongue out, scissoring his fingers together and making a gagging sound in his throat. Crouching and looking back, Mayhew stumbled away down the walk. In a moment he was gone in the fog.

Wearily, Dalton went back inside and bolted the door again. All in all he felt better now, exorcised. The horror on Mayhew's face was bracing. If Mayhew talked to the police, they wouldn't believe a word of what he said. On the other hand, Dalton wasn't anxious for the old man to talk to the police or anyone else. And apparently he had already talked to someone. . . . It would have been after hours, and that, of course, meant Dave, who probably thought it was funny as hell to send the old man down here, drunk on his ass, to raise Cain. What to do about it, though? Nothing tonight.

BEHIND CLOSED EYES, EDMUND PICTURED THE SPIRIT DOOR in the white wall of the bedroom, a door that had existence only in the lonely, late-night quiet of his brooding half-sleep. Firelight seemed to flicker on the wall, illuminating the door, which drifted silently open, as if a languid breeze had whispered against it. He heard the sound of its whispering echo in the infinite windy darkness beyond. For a long time as he lay there staring at it, that darkness that had been a door was merely a vague black rectangle, depthless, its edges ghostly and almost imperceptible. The wind from beyond the door ruffled the darkness as if it were a curtain, and the darkness gained dimension until it seemed to him that he could see deep within it, as into a vast, empty, night-filled room. Something moved there, a gray wisp rising like smoke entrapped in an invisible bottle, spinning in slow circles.

He felt languid and easy as he lay there, and he imagined that his eyelids were windows, that he was gazing out through panes of glass at the landscape of the darkened room and at the carefully empty, white-painted wall beyond. He breathed evenly, staring at the long blank surface of it, at the curling smoke, and he thought of her again, pictured her, brought her back into his mind. He had discovered that summoning her was a simple act of will, and the very thought of it thrilled him, hinted at a power he had only begun to make use of, spoke to him of potential ecstasies. . . .

The smoky haze beyond the door formed itself into her shape, her image drawn from the deep pool of longing and desire that lay within him. Slowly he opened his eyes, forming her name in his mind. There was a dim light through the bedroom window, barely illuminating the room, just a wash of curtain-filtered lamplight that shone across the several paintings tilted against the wall. His eyes could see the outline of her face and the contour of her unclothed body among the dim shadows of the bedroom furniture. He saw her again in the darkness-obscured landscapes of the paintings, in the drape of the window curtains, in the casual slump of his bathrobe on the chair in the corner of the room.

His eyes fixed on the empty white wall, and what had seemed to be a vertical shadow cast by lamplight through the window now revealed itself to be the spirit door itself. There was a ghostly, smoky movement in the darkness beyond it, a sibilant whispering, and then, framed by the doorway, her shadow stirred against the deeper shadow of the darkness, and she separated from it, moving him across a vast distance, like a figure flitting toward him through the landscape of a dream.

He pushed himself slowly up onto his elbows, hearing the rustling of sheets, the creaking and shifting of the bed.

He felt the woman's presence like a breath of cool air. He whispered her name, and the Night Girl stood before him, black hair, moth-pale flesh, eyes like moonlight. He breathed her scent and closed his eyes, and then, without the bed having shifted again, without his knowing the precise moment that she had come to him, she lay beside him, cool against his heated flesh, the night perfectly silent, the black hollow in the wall wavering like a misty curtain.

22

"I GUESS THEY THINK IT WAS JENNY THAT STARTED THE fire," the Earl said to Dave. He spooned sugar into his coffee and then beat at the bottom of the mug with the spoon instead of stirring it. The cup held about a pint, and had a picture of Morro Rock on it. The Earl looked tired to Dave, his face pale, his shoulders slumped. He wore paisley suspenders and a bow tie, and his hair was slicked back with some sort of oily, rose-smelling hair tonic. He was a short man, only about five-five with the build of Tweedledee. "Looks like she squirted those pallets down with charcoal lighter from Collier's shed and put a match to it."

"I don't believe it," Dave said. "Jenny just wouldn't do that."

The Earl shrugged. "Neither do I. Anybody might have started it. Those pallets and trash have been piled up there for three weeks or more. The problem is that Jenny doesn't deny it."

"She admitted to starting it?"

"No, she still says her *friend* started it. They were playing with matches outside. Collier was down at the doughnut shop looking at the wreck."

"He left her home alone?"

"Looks like. Only for a few minutes, I guess. He heard the crash at the corner and went down there to see if he could help. Apparently he didn't figure it could hurt much, leaving her alone for a couple of minutes."

"Neither do I. What about this friend? Has somebody checked Jenny's story out?"

The Earl sat down in his office chair and swiveled slowly back and forth. "The friend's imaginary." His usual cheerfulness was utterly absent this morning, and he ran his hand tiredly through his hair. Dave looked at the picture of the Earl's wife, framed on the desk. She was blonde, her hair done up like Greta Garbo, and she was looking ethereally off into space. The Earl had married her in '46, after he and Collier had gotten out of the army. She'd died in childbirth in '55, and the Earl had never remarried.

"Who says the friend's imaginary?" Dave asked.

"Collier himself. He got home just as the fire department was pulling in. It was Jenny who told them about the friend, how she started the fire. Jenny couldn't say how. Apparently the fire had got going pretty good when Edmund saw it. By the time he called the department, it was too late to save Collier's truck. That's where the pallets were—shoved under the rear bumper."

"And they think Jenny pushed these pallets under the truck and lit them on fire? She burned her grandfather's truck on purpose, in other words?"

"Nobody's *saying* that, exactly, but it's implied."

"If that's what they're implying, then they're full of baloney."

"I hear you. You're aware of this thing with Collier and Social Services?"

"Yeah. How serious are they?"

"Very serious, with this fire. And Collier's got this bee in his bonnet about it. He thinks there's someone calling them up, making up stories. And now this kind of thing . . ." The Earl shook his head sadly. "And you heard about the magazines?"

Dave shook his head.

"Apparently the investigating officer found a couple of

skin magazines in the back of the Harvester, half burned
up from the fire.''

"What kind of magazines? *Playboy* or something?"

"*Or something* is right. Pretty filthy stuff, as I understand
it. Cops confiscated them. At least that's what Edmund tells
me. Said he hadn't ever seen anything like them."

"These magazines were *that* bad, and Collier had them
lying around in the open, loose in the back of the truck?"

"That's where they were when the fire department got
there. You can see the problem with all this Social Services
trouble."

"Collier says the magazines aren't his?"

"Of course he says that. Collier dismissed the whole
damned thing. Said he didn't care where they'd come from
and didn't give a damn. He told the cop that he was seventy
years old and could care less about dirty magazines. Apparently the cop even got a good laugh out of it when
Collier put it to him that way. It was the cop's idea that
maybe the magazines were stashed there by neighborhood
kids, you know. That old heap of Collier's has been sitting
there for a couple of months with bad brakes. Probably
that's just what happened. As I see it, though, a man hates
to be put in the position of having to deny something like
that, doesn't he? One way or another he loses. Like Edmund said, though, they can't be used as any sort of evidence of anything, because of how they were found—
without a warrant or anything."

"I suppose they went into the police report, though."

"I suppose they did, along with Collier saying they
weren't his."

The Earl poured himself another cup of coffee, and there
was the rattling sound of the big door sliding open and the
truck backing up to the loading ramp. A radio started up
abruptly—a salsa station, too loud at first, but then turned
down, and someone shouted a question in Spanish. Dave
caught the words *barril* and *caballo*, and there was the
sound of the *Oklahoma* props being loaded onto the flatbed.

"Those pallets were piled up by the side of the building,
fifteen feet from the car," Dave said to the Earl. "They're

pretty heavy. I'm surprised anyone thought that Jenny could even move them."

"Well, like I told you, there were two of them—her and her imaginary friend. I guess the friend did all the lifting." The Earl laughed humorlessly. "Anyway, she says she doesn't know about moving the pallets. She got scared and ran inside. Hell," he said, "it'll all blow over."

"I hope it does, for Collier's sake as well as Jenny's."

"We've been here since fifty-four, and nothing like that's *ever* happened. Never any real trouble. Hardly an argument." He shook his head. "But I don't believe that little girl started that fire, no matter how many imaginary friends she's got."

"What does Edmund think about it?" Dave asked. "He was there for the whole thing?"

"Edmund was working late, smelled the smoke. Apparently he'd seen Jenny standing out there, near where the fire broke out, maybe five minutes earlier. He tried like hell to save Collier's truck, but it was too late."

"Well," Dave said, "that's a dirty shame." He tried to keep the skepticism out of his voice, but there were a couple of things about this that he didn't believe. Given that it wasn't Jenny who started the fire—and he'd bet a shiny new dime that it wasn't—then it was an arsonist. But an arsonist who wanted to do what? Burn Collier's International Harvester, a truck that was worth about two hundred dollars soaking wet? Collier didn't have any enemies ... except one.

Edmund started the fire himself. Dave knew this with utter certainty. He understood that the idea was crazy, that he *wanted* to think that Edmund was up to something shabby like this. Casey would warn him about that kind of thinking, and probably Casey would be right. And certainly there was no use telling the Earl that his older son was a creep and a liar. The Earl couldn't see it. He *wouldn't* see it. And even if he could be made to see it, he would deny it just as easily and surely as if he were brushing away a fly. He denied the termites in the windowsills, the leaky skylights, the money draining through the floorboards of the old Ocean Theatre. The Earl didn't want "pollution."

He didn't want the outside world. The Earl of Gloucester was his fortress. It kept the outside out and the inside in. That's why this kind of thing hit him so hard. One thing was true, though: he'd bounce back just as hard.

"Collier's been a little bit worried about a couple of other things lately, too," Dave said. "He didn't need this."

"What else is he worried about? He hasn't said anything to me about any other worries."

"He thinks you're going to sell the bungalow out from under him. Sell the property to the city."

"*That* old hogwash. He's been on that tack for years now. He's worried he's going to be out in the street in his old age, living in an alley. Collier's a worrier. Always has been. That's why he's so damned cheerful and full of crap all the time. It's a cover. I told him that bungalow was his as long as he cared to stay there. And now that he's got Jenny, he'd be smart to stay there until she's grown. He can't do any better than he's doing right here."

"That's just what he thinks. He's worried that if he loses the place, they'll take Jenny away. Put her in a foster home."

"To hell with that. If birds crapped rocks, we'd *all* have to wear helmets."

"There's more truth than poetry in that," Dave said.

EDMUND WAS AWAKENED BY THE TELEPHONE RINGING, dimly aware that it had been ringing for a long time. There was sunlight through the windows, the fog already burned off, so it must be late morning. He groped for the phone, but it wasn't where it was supposed to be, and he pushed himself up onto his elbow, focusing his eyes as pain lanced across his forehead. His mouth was parched, and he could taste something faintly perfumey, as if he'd been chewing rose petals. He was naked and cold, had been sleeping without covers. The two blankets and bedspread were folded and piled where he'd left them, but the top sheet was torn and rumpled and moist, as if he had sweated with a fever all night. He licked his lips. The phone continued to ring. He spotted it on the floor, next to where he had moved the bedside table last night so that all of it would be out of his line of vision. He bent over and picked it up.

"Yeah," he said, the word sticking in his throat. He looked for his water glass, but it was knocked over and lay broken on the floor.

"Dalton?"

"Yeah. Wait a second." He recognized Ray Mifflin's voice. He covered the mouthpiece with his hand and cleared his throat, suddenly recalling last night—the door in the wall, bits and pieces of what had followed—but all of it only vaguely, like recalling a dream. The pain in his forehead was a dull throbbing now, like a hangover headache. He looked at the east wall, but there was no door now, just the clean expanse of freshly painted white.

And yet he could tell *exactly* where the door had opened, could very nearly see a line of shadow there like a hairline scar, like the edge of the dark side of the moon against the darker blackness of space.

He realized suddenly that he was holding the phone to his face, that he had forgotten about the call. "Yeah, Ray. Sorry."

"The phone must've rung twenty times."

"I was asleep."

"Well, I hope you're awake now. It seems that we've got a little problem."

"You sound miffed, Mr. Mifflin." Edmund snickered, but Ray didn't laugh. "Seriously, what's the trouble?" He worked his shoulders and neck to loosen up.

"It seems as if there's a gentleman who's interested in our transactions."

"A gentleman? That wouldn't be my pseudo father, would it?" He had half expected this after Mayhew's capers last night. Threatening the man was useless. He should never have used Mayhew in the first place.

"If you mean that homeless man you brought in the first time, no, I don't. This guy's fairly young. Thirties, maybe. He introduced himself as Jim Jones, which of course isn't his name."

"Jones?"

"That's the name of that minister who killed all those people in Guyana with poison grapeade. A few years back? C'mon. *Edmund*. You've got to remember that one."

"*That's* who he pretended to be? That cultist?" Edmund smashed his eyes shut and rubbed his forehead, trying to grasp this, but it was simply too insane. He looked at the bedsheet again, but he couldn't remember tearing it up. Things had happened last night that . . .

"No, damn it. He didn't pretend to be *that* Jim Jones."

Edmund looked at the telephone receiver in disbelief. "Look, Ray. What the hell are you telling me here? I'm *way* off the beam."

"I'm telling you it was a *phony name*, the first one that came into his head."

"So was he some kind of agent? What? These guys must carry I.D. You didn't say anything to this clown, did you? Did he have a subpoena?"

"He didn't work for the county or for any other agency, Edmund. I'm not sure who he was, but I suspect he's one of your employees, getting cute."

"Christ. Of course he was. Fairly tall? Brown hair?"

"Yeah. Looked a little like Jimmy Stewart, but with more muscle, and a different voice, of course."

"Yeah, I know him. Christ."

"He's up to some damn thing. I couldn't read him, but he was obviously snooping around. I got him to back off, but I wanted to let you know. We don't want trouble."

"He's not trouble, Ray. He's nothing. He's a nonentity. Don't let him worry you."

"He tells me you've got a brother."

"Yes, indeed," Ray said, without any hesitation. A lie wouldn't do here. The jig was clearly already up with Mifflin, not that it mattered.

"Well, that's not nothing, is it? Looks to me like we've got trouble one way or another. I don't need lies, Edmund. I don't need to wake up one morning and have some clown from the county handing me my head in a box."

"Unlax, Ray. To hell with my brother."

"That's two people we've got to say to hell with—this Jimmy Stewart character and your brother. Yesterday the coast was clear. Today there's some kind of invasion. Next thing it'll be your sister and your cousin."

"There is no sister, Ray, and I'm telling you not to worry about it. My brother's a beach bum. He renounced money ten years ago."

"Nobody renounces money. Look, if it's all the same to you, I'm going to cash out."

"What are you talking about, 'cash out'?"

There was a long silence, and then, speaking very evenly, Mifflin said, "It was our agreement that I could take an early retirement—those were *your* words—if I ever wanted out. You agreed to pay me half the money you owed me for the commission."

"Hell, of *course* I remember that. But what I said is that I'd advance you the money if you were short. And I'm happy to do that. What do you need? New car?"

"I need to put this behind me."

"You mean out *altogether*? *Out* out?"

"That's the ticket."

"Hold on just a second, Ray, let me explain a couple of things. First, my brother doesn't give a rat's ass about any of this. He's a hippie. Second, he doesn't have *any* idea what kind of properties our old man has. My brother doesn't soil his mind with business. He literally *doesn't know*. I'm the one who keeps that end of things straight, and I've been keeping it straight for nearly twenty years. If he wanted to see the books, I could show him the books, and I guarantee you he wouldn't have a clue."

"This is not making me any more secure. Keeping two sets of books is like writing all your secrets out in a diary and then leaving it on the shelf. You cook your own damn goose."

"I didn't say two sets of books, Ray. I said that he

doesn't know from books. And one way or another, what's he going to do to me if he does find out? Press charges? Why? To gain what? And as far as he'd know, *you'd* be innocent. I would have swindled you, too. What would *I* do, point the finger at you? Why? What earthly good would it do me? It's you who's got me over a barrel, Ray. Not the other way around.''

''Still, there's precautions to take, Edmund. And if I don't know the whole story, I can't take the precautions, can I? I've got a career, for Christ's sake.''

''I swear on my mother's grave that from now on, you'll *know* the whole story. That's all I've got—one hippie, beach bum brother. He gives most of his money away as it is. I've got no sisters, no aunts and uncles, no cousins, nobody else.''

''I hope you can understand that I can't take a chance.''

''Well, it seems to me that you already took one. And so far you've made out pretty damned well.''

''What about this employee of yours?''

''He's no threat to either of us. What did you say to him?''

''Nothing. He's got nothing.''

''Then that's what he's got. You want to know the whole story? I'll tell you the whole story. He's a friend of my brother's. Long-time, nosy, worthless friend. The worst-case scenario is this: let's say he finds out something—which he won't, of course—but let's say he does, and he goes to my brother. He tells him that bad brother Edmund has cashed out some of the old man's property. What does Casey do about it?''

''Who's that?''

''That's my brother. Casey's my brother. What's he going to do about it? Call a cop? I don't think so. And besides, I'm his *brother*, for God's sake. I pretty much raised him. Maybe, if he really shows some backbone, he'll ask for his half of the money, which, of course, I can hand over as soon as the bank opens, since I'm holding onto it for him anyway.''

''What do you mean, 'holding onto it'?''

''What I said. What did you think, that I was taking *his*

half, too?'' Edmund rolled his eyes and held the telephone out at arm's length, gaping at it theatrically. ''Ray. My man. I'm not that stupid. There'd be hell to pay down the line if I stole from him. His money's sitting safe in the bank. Another six-month C.D. every time our ship comes in. As an investment counselor, you'll tell me that the interest is crap on a C.D., but it's insured, anyway—it's safe, it's easy, he can cash it out quick if he wants to. I'll be happy as hell to show you the paperwork.'' This was brilliant. He should have thought of it straight off, but it had taken his brain a few minutes to get up to power. ''If you honestly think we ought to move his money into some other kind of account . . .''

''So you're telling me that you're only taking half this money?''

''Only the money that's due me when the old man dies. I thought we went over all this. I'm not greedy, Ray; I'm impatient. Technically that's a crime, I guess. But like I said, inheritance tax is a crime too. Probate's a crime. And by the way, your commission's coming out of my half. I'll tell you this, though. If property values drop any farther, and selling these lots now turns out to have been a good idea, then brother Casey's going to ante up half your commission. I'm not passing myself off as a saint here, but I'm not stealing from my brother, either.'' He waited for Mifflin's response.

''Okay, then. I wish you would have told me this before Jimmy Stewart walked in.''

Edmund nearly laughed out loud. Mifflin had bought the farm—hook, line, and sinker. Maybe he had overestimated the man. ''If I would have told you I had a brother, Ray, you wouldn't have touched this at any price. You were petrified as it was. Am I right?''

''Yeah, I guess you're right. I wouldn't have touched it.''

''But now you've touched it and you've made half a year's income already, with more on the way. Don't worry, be happy.''

''I'm happy.''

''Good. Because I already managed to move that first

piece of real estate, that one out in Fountain Valley. You've got a check coming as soon as it clears escrow. Best I could do was thirty days." All this was a lie too, but maybe it would help keep Ray quiet.

He glanced at the five paintings tilted against the wall and noticed that one had been defaced—the paint scaled off all over the carpet. He bent over and squinted at it, not quite comprehending. There was something hovering at the edge of his mind, though, like a dream that he was nearly at the point of remembering.

It was the largest and most expensive of the paintings—a storm over a peninsula of land that was covered with wind-swept trees, the ocean beyond, the sky a riot of clouds. A patch of that sky had been rasped clean of paint.

"What? I'm sorry, Ray. Someone's at the door. Hold on!" he yelled at no one, half covering the receiver.

"I said I hope that's the last of these little surprises," Ray said.

Edmund controlled his temper. "That's all I've got to offer in the surprise category. Are we clear, then?"

"Yeah."

"Then I'll hang up and get the door. Nice to hear from you, Ray." He hung up the phone and got down onto his hands and knees to look more closely at the painting. A jagged shard from the broken water glass lay behind the canvas, paint scrapings clinging to the edge. Beside it lay a small tweezers, and the sight of it recalled the memory that had eluded him.

He had broken the water glass himself, rapping it against the doorjamb. He could remember the feel of her hand on his shoulder, tracing patterns on his back, the closeness of her body as she hovered behind him, her urgent presence, the murky compulsion of the act of defacing the painting.

And now he recalled all of it clearly, the long night restored from where its memory had lain in shadow. He got up off the floor and sat on the bed again. He realized that his hands were trembling, and he crossed his arms in front of him to keep them still. He felt momentarily feverish and nauseated, claustrophobic, playing the night through in his mind, frame by languid frame, the urgent hours of darkness wearing on, a memory of gray daylight through the window. Another thrill of recollection swept through him, pushing up into his throat, down into his loins. He licked his lips again, and the memory sharpened, a picture coming suddenly into focus: him crouching before the painting, holding the round body of a spider in the palm of his hand like a tiny black moon. He had removed its legs, plucked them off, laughing out loud, enjoying it immensely, rolling the hairlike legs smoothly between his fingers, his senses wildly acute, feeling the tiny joints popping apart, silky, exquisite explosions beneath his fingertips, the black fragments falling lightly atop the moist white sheet. . . .

He walked to the window now and opened the blinds with a trembling hand, then closed them immediately, the sunlight nearly blinding him. He knelt on the carpet and peered under the bed. A flashlight lay on the floor near the head end. He had a memory of crawling on his belly in the dust, his back scraping the ribs of the bed frame as he searched along the edge of the carpet and on the wooden legs of the bed frame, hunting things for her. And he could recall the pleasure of the two of them mashing the fat little bodies of spiders and silverfish and dead flies, daubing the brown ooze onto the canvas.

He had summoned her, yes, but it was she who had possessed him last night, and he had been willingly possessed. It was a marriage, deeper, perhaps, than any conventional marriage could ever be. Dark fear on the one hand, desire on the other—the realm of Nightland, of the imagination loosened from its black iron restraints. He fetched the flashlight out from beneath the bed and clicked it off, even though the battery was long dead, and then examined the ruined painting again, peering at it closely. Tiny fragments of spiders' legs adhered to the canvas like nonsense hieroglyphics in that pale area where the sky had been scraped clean. The act of gluing them in place with saliva mixed with the mashed insects had occupied what seemed to him now to have been an eternity. He had knelt there working at it, carefully plucking up a fragment of insect from the sheet, laying it on the canvas, utterly consumed by an artistic passion that wasn't his alone, but was mingled with

hers. He knew now that his efforts had been stimulated by
his memory of the Night Girl's painting, and he admired
the tiny delicate renderings on the scraped-clean patch of
canvas. He could recall all of it now with perfect clarity:
the absolute cunning rightness of a tiny smear of insect
paste, the perfect angle of intersecting legs . . .

In a sudden flash of insight he understood that the spirit
door was nothing more nor less than a blank canvas, black
instead of white, and that with his own passion he had
created something profound. His blood was still warm with
that passion, and he longed for the darkness again and for
the return of the Night Girl.

Anne's painting, the Day Girl's painting, was a dead loss
from the point of view of anyone who didn't understand
what had happened to it, how it had been changed, and he
wondered if Anne herself could ever really understand it,
unless her own persona had been consumed by that same
passion. Anne was fettered by convention, by her waking
reins on the energies that obviously lay seething within her.
He understood those energies well now, and he would help
her find them if only she would let him, and together they
would find a way to share it, by day as well as by night.

24

WELL, AS OF TODAY, ANNE WAS A WORKING GIRL. SHE
stood at the window thinking about this, looking down at
Main Street. The morning was foggy again, although there
was sunlight behind the fog, and she had the feeling that
the weather would clear up and the day would be perfect.
Already she wanted to ditch work and simply wander
around—down to the pier, maybe down to Central Park,
which Mr. Hedgepeth had told her was wooded and worth

seeing. Apparently there was a duck pond and hiking trails. A walk on the beach wouldn't be a bad thing, either. There were sure to be seashells.

She almost laughed out loud. Here she was working when she didn't even have to, mixing herself into Edmund and Dave's troubles as if she needed some of that commodity in her life.

Dave . . . He *was* rather attractive. She rubbed the lace curtains between her fingers, recalling his eyes, his cheekbones. He had a good face—nice to paint. He was handsome enough, but maybe more pleasant than handsome. He reminded her of someone, too. He looked something like photographs of her father, although that wasn't entirely it. There was someone else. . . . Maybe that was what caused the immediate attraction, which wasn't at all her style. She usually needed six months to warm up to a man. Dave was a few years older than she was, too, but that sort of thing didn't bother her at all. And she preferred the awkward type. He had clearly been embarrassed just saying hello.

Edmund, on the other hand, was a little too glib and a little too sure of himself, and she distrusted both of those things. Any man who was too happy with himself was certain to be mistaken, at least about that. At the university she'd had two different flings, but both of the men had wanted more than she had been willing to give them— although who she was holding out for she couldn't quite say, and she was beginning to feel a little bit too much like an old maid. Spending her birthday alone hadn't helped.

She turned away from the window, picking up her airbrush and paints and putting them in a wooden tackle box and setting the box by the door. It was early, but she decided to head on down to the Earl of Gloucester anyway, if only to check in. She went into the kitchen, rinsed her cereal bowl and spoon, put away the Shredded Wheat, and drank the last half inch of cooled-off tea in her mug. She looked into the mirror over the kitchen sink and put on lipstick, a darker red than she usually wore. It looked flashy, but she felt a little flashy this morning. And right then she decided to change her blouse, too, maybe put on something that was a little less baggy, something that showed off her figure....

Was she really going to make a move on Dave? Good God, she didn't even *know* him. And rumor had it that he had a shaky past, that he was a pervert and a murderer, that he dropped things on people's heads. Of course it was Edmund who was the rumor mill, and the more she saw of Edmund, the more he had begun to remind her of her sister Elinor. The similarity had nothing to do with his appearance; it was simply that he had the eyes and the facial expressions of a potential liar: the sometimes fraudulent smile, the too-serious tone, the self-promotion at the expense of someone else. There was an egocentricity that was like a high wall around him, protecting him from something, keeping something out. Maybe, as with Elinor, hiding something from the world. All his doubts about Dave had begun to sound pretty purely defensive—maybe worse.

So she would make up her own mind about the mysterious Dave. In her bedroom, she slipped into a mohair sweater, gave her hair one more toss, and was ready to go out. At the front door she looked around the apartment one last time, still thinking about Elinor, thinking about the birthday cake frosting smeared across her painting.

"Leave my stuff alone," she said out loud. Then she picked up the tackle box and went out through the open door into the empty corridor, shutting the door and locking the dead bolt behind her.

25

THE ROUTE DOWN PECAN TO MAIN, BACK UP ORANGE Street to Goldenwest, and then up to Palm and around the corner to his apartment was a little under three miles. Edmund used to run farther, but over the last week or so he had gotten into the habit of jogging past Anne's apartment in the morning, which distracted him from merely physical exercise. He wanted to become familiar with her habits, and he had learned that she was often out of her apartment as early as eight. In fact, it was only 8:15 now, and she was already at work, prostituting her art on behalf of the great Leslie Collier and his asinine play.

Edmund looped around onto Main, running easily, not even breaking a sweat in the cool ocean air. The fog still drifted through town, heavy enough to dull people's perceptions of the day starting up around them. He knew for a fact that the other tenants in Anne's building wouldn't be in until at least ten. It would be *easy* to drop in this morning, just for a moment, and have a look around. . . . The idea filled him with a thrill of fear and excitement. This morning? Right now?

Last night, late, he had dropped by just for a moment. He had gone up the back stairs and left a little something hidden there—an act that was either a step along the way or a purely pointless waste of time. It was his choice. All he had to do was clear away the cobwebs of fear and indecision. Paying the building a visit this morning was inevitable, when he opened his eyes and really looked. Otherwise, why was he circling the block? *Something* was going on here, and as long as he kept moving, he was resisting it.

An alley ran behind her apartment building, between Pecan and Orange, and without missing a stride he turned up the alley. When Main Street fell away behind him, he stopped running to catch his breath. There was nothing but silence around him now, silence and the hovering fog. The alley separated the back yards of houses on Pecan from the backyards of houses on Orange, and although there were a couple of garages that fronted the alley, they were closed up tight. The other end of the alley was lost in mist. He walked slowly back toward Main until he drew even with the rear of Anne's building. Behind it, above the patch of dirt that separated the building from a broken-down shed, were old wooden stairs going up to a disused second-floor balcony filled with junk furniture and broken cardboard boxes. A door opened onto the balcony, but the door was locked with a hasp and an old rusted lock, and the glass window in the door was barred.

Taking one last quick look around, Edmund strode to the base of the stairs, which was closed off by a low gate built of wood and chicken wire. He braced himself on the post at the base of the stairs and easily vaulted the gate. It would have been equally easy to tear the chicken wire away from the rusted staples that held it in place, but he didn't want anything about the gate or the fence to change in the slightest. If the landlord was satisfied with his locks and his chicken wire, it was a good idea to keep him that way.

He hurried up the steps and onto the porch, where a section of wall hid him from the alley, and raised the seat cushion from a weather-wrecked easy chair. Bolt cutters lay underneath the cushion, just where he had left them, full of potential. He fitted them over the lock, leaned into the handles, and clipped the bar of the lock as close to the body of the thing as he could. When the lock was closed up, it would still appear to be locked from down below, and it might be weeks or months before someone discovered that it wasn't locked at all. He took it off the hasp, shoved the lock and the bolt cutters under the seat cushion, and tried the door. When it swung open, he stepped inside, shutting the door behind him.

He found himself in an old service porch with a water heater and a half-dozen wall shelves stacked with paint cans and boxes of nails and screws and odds and ends of handyman junk. Another door lay beyond, this one unlocked. He opened it a couple of inches and peered through the crack, into the central hallway of the building. There were two doors to his immediate right; one stood half open, revealing a restroom beyond. The other had a sign painted on the window—Bob Slattery, Attorney. On the left stood another door, this one called "Dr. Slim," a name that meant nothing to him. The door to Anne's apartment lay halfway down the hall on the right.

He anticipated some sort of inspiration. If he gave it a chance, the old building itself would suggest something to him; some oddly situated window would allow him access to a secret room, or a door would have been left unlocked, or he would find that the rooms were connected by an attic crawl space. There was always *something* significant; you only had to open yourself to its possibilities. He walked down the hallway to the end, trying the doors, and then followed the stairs down to the bottom landing, where he looked out through the glass at the street. The shadow of a pedestrian passed in front of the window, and on impulse he stepped back. Downstairs were three more doors, all of them locked. He could sense that there was nothing for him there. The key to the puzzle lay upstairs somewhere.

He found it at the lawyer's office, which was locked with an old brass exterior lock with an angled bolt. Evidently the lawyer had nothing of value inside, because a twelve-year-old could get past such a lock. He slipped a polished metal mirror out of his waist pack and threw the bolt, then opened the door and stepped inside. The office was poverty-stricken—worse than Ray Mifflin's chickenshit office. Clearly the lawyer was some kind of white trash bankruptcy shyster. The blinds were drawn across the windows, and at first in the dim light through the dirty skylights he saw nothing interesting. He roamed around, poking into drawers and files, vaguely looking for photographs, maybe flesh magazines. There were good odds that a lawyer of this caliber kept some fancy reading material around to break up the monotony of his dull day.

But there was nothing that was worth a damn. It looked as if he were wasting his time. Still, the easy lock *had* to mean something. It was clearly an invitation, specifically to him. . . .

He looked at the closet then. He opened the closet door and peeked inside, pulling a light chain that hung beneath a bare ceiling bulb. It was a fairly shallow walk-in closet, nearly empty, just a couple of shelves of cardboard boxes and in-out files. There was a door in the back, though, locked with a padlock, half hidden by a couple of coats that hung from a piece of closet rod.

Bingo! His hunches had paid off. The door *had* to lead into Anne's apartment. There was light shining on the other side of the door, just a dim light, but it meant a view of some part of Anne's hidden life!

He crouched on the closet floor and crawled on his hands and knees beneath the coats, where he slid his mirror through the half-inch gap under the door. He held onto the mirror with the tips of his fingers, moving it around, cocking his head to get the right view of it. For a moment he could see nothing but dim smudges, and he put his eye nearly against it in order to see more. The inside of a closet sprang into view. He could see clothing, boxes, an open door. Beyond the door there was something . . .

The bottom of a bed frame! It was her bedroom light that was on! He oriented himself now, edging the mirror along slowly to increase the size of the view. He could see that the hem of her bedspread edged the corner of the bed frame neatly. So she had made her bed! Typical of Anne the Day Girl. In a dizzying moment the thought came to him that perhaps she had returned home from work, that she was in the apartment right now, bustling around, cleaning things up!

He waited, crouched on his hands and knees, his cheek nearly pressed to the edge of the metal mirror, waiting for her to appear, for her feet to pad into view. Nothing moved, though. There was no sound, no one stirring around. He listened hard for any sound at all from behind the door, but there was perfect silence. Of course she had simply left the light on by mistake.

Disappointed, he crawled back out of the closet and stood up, returning the mirror to his waist pack and then checking his watch. It was after nine now—still too early for the building to be waking up, but getting dangerously close. He would have to hurry. He stepped across to the door, opened it, and peered out into the empty hall. Leaving the door open, he went out through the service porch again, onto the rear balcony. Already the fog was burning off, and there was a breeze in the air, blowing offshore. In another few minutes it would be clear, and he would be running a good chance of being seen, which would compromise his ability to come and go. People pay too much attention to a man lurking around. Next time maybe he would wear a uniform, a generic gas company-type uniform. . . .

He slipped the bolt cutters out from under the seat cushion and went back in, closing the door after himself again. Inside the closet again he studied the lock, considering what he was about to do. It was a common enough Master lock, clean and new, probably put on the door when Anne took the apartment. If he cut it, he could get into Anne's apartment this one time, and, unless he made noise, he could linger there nearly as long as he wanted this morning, even if the lawyer showed up for work.

If the lawyer saw that the lock had been cut, though, this avenue would be forever closed to him. The lawyer would shout for the landlord, who would call the police. He stood thinking, weighing his options.

Hurriedly, he left the lawyer's office again and went back outside. He set the back-door lock carefully into position and ditched the bolt cutters under the seat cushion again before heading down the stairs. Within moments he was jogging up the alley again, his mind working out a plan that had almost infinite potential. In twenty minutes the hardware store downtown would open. He would buy his own lock. Tomorrow morning it would be a simple thing to slip back in and replace the lock that was on there now.

Then he *would hold the key to the back door of Anne's closet!*

God, how beautiful that image was—how poetic! It was simply a perfect metaphor, and it had been given to him out of nowhere. Once again he had come into this situation empty-handed, mapless, trusting to intuition, to the raw possibilities of art, and he had found the answers to all his questions simply waiting for him.

Now he could come and go as he pleased! His imagination worked on the idea, picturing what he might see, what he might find out about her. And to think that he had almost cut the lock off here and now and wasted a golden opportunity, all because he was acting like a kid who wanted his candy right now. He whooped with sudden laughter. As he had always been taught, if he waited like a good little boy, very soon he would have all the candy he could desire.

⇥ 26 ⇤

FROM WHERE HE STOOD IN THE EARL'S OFFICE, DAVE
heard footsteps on the stairs. It was Collier coming up,
looking happy enough despite the fire.

"What's the word?" The Earl asked him.

"The word is that the angel of Social Services doesn't
buy this fire explanation either. She hefted one of those
pallets. No way she thinks Jenny had anything to do with
moving them under the truck."

"This is the woman I saw the other morning?" Dave
asked.

"The very one. Mrs. Lydia Nyles," Collier told him.
"She can look down her glasses at you, I'll tell you that.
Very skeptical sort of woman. I told her that skepticism
wasn't healthy, but I don't think she gave a damn."

"Be careful what you say to these people," the Earl said.
"Don't go talking like a crazy man. They take this stuff
seriously."

"You're damned right they do. If someone calls in a
report, she's got to investigate it. And if she thought I was
mistreating Jenny and she *didn't* take it seriously, I'd have
a few things to say to her. Lydia Nyles is okay, though,
when you get past the skepticism. Jenny likes her, and
that's what counts. Jenny's a shrewd judge. I've got a good
eye myself. Mrs. Nyles is deep, very deep, but her heart's
right." He winked at Dave and then squinted out the window at the distant ocean. "Yes, indeed. She's not a bad-
looking woman, either, when it comes right down to it. She
says she used to act a little bit out at South Coast Rep.
Directed a couple of plays out in Westminster for the children's theatre."

"She's sympathetic to this whole thing, then?" the Earl asked.

"Very. I'm thinking about offering her a part in *Lear*."

"Is there a part for a woman of that age?"

"Nothing at all, except for Mrs. deShane's part. I'd have to invent something," Collier said.

"She might see it as some sort of conflict of interest . . ." Dave started to say.

"Did you tell the Earl about the changes in the *Lear* plot?"

"No," Dave said. "Not yet."

"*Some*body better tell me," the Earl said. "I go away for a couple of days and you two rewrite Shakespeare on me?"

"Just a couple of modifications," Collier said. "Most of the dialogue and the blocking will still work. I've been up half the night working on the revised script, and I've got some ideas for sets and props that we'd better get a jump on. I think we'll change the way the public understands Shakespeare." He nodded profoundly at the Earl, and then, before he could say anything more, there was a shuffling downstairs, and he glanced out through the open door of the office to see who it was. "Company," he said.

It was Anne, coming into work early and carrying a wooden tackle box and a long metal ruler. The Earl got up out of his chair and stepped out of the office and onto the balcony, smiling like he'd just won the lottery. "Up here!" he shouted. "Have you met Anne?" he asked Dave.

"Yeah, briefly."

"Well, you better meet her again. Pay attention this time." He nodded and elbowed Collier in the ribs. "Take my advice on this one," he said to Dave, but before the Earl could give him whatever advice he was supposed to take, she reached the top of the balcony and nodded a good morning, smiling at Dave.

"I'm early," she said. "I wanted to get my bearings a little bit."

Dave tried to read something into her smile. Was it directed particularly at him? He wondered abruptly what Edmund had said to poison her against him. She had an easy way of carrying herself, a sureness about her, that made his chances seem slim. . . .

His chances of what? he wondered. So far he hadn't even managed a simple good morning—only his trademark idiot grin. "We're just starting to talk about Collier's play," Dave said. "So you're right on time."

"That's right," the Earl told her. "Since you'll be working on his sets, you ought to hear what he's got in mind. We've got *King Lear* in the works, which is high-toned theatre for a beach city like ours, but then we're high-toned people, and we've got a higher calling. This is Leslie Collier, by the way, and this young man is Dave Quinn, my right-hand man."

"Most people just call me Collier," Collier told her, bowing at the waist.

"Anne and I have already met," Dave said unnecessarily to the Earl, and he grinned at her again. Out of the corner of his eye he saw Collier nudge the Earl's foot with his own, and he realized that he must be blushing, betrayed by the blood in his own veins.

"Did you get your stuff moved in downstairs?" the Earl asked her.

"All of it. Thanks again."

"Our pleasure," the Earl said. "Anne needed some storage room for a bunch of paintings," he said to Dave and Collier, "so I had her move them in downstairs, in one of the empty closets by the shop. George and Luis chucked out a lot of that old cardboard crap that we had stored down there in order to make room for it."

"Paintings? Really?" Dave nodded in appreciation, wondering if he ought to ask to see them, or whether that was out of line.

"It's just old stuff," Anne said hastily. "Call it family heirlooms. I don't want to throw it all out, mostly for sentimental reasons, but it's not worth renting storage space, either."

"We've got storage space to burn," the Earl said. And then to Collier he said, "So tell us about the play. We'll make this a de facto story conference. Coffee?" He gestured toward the nearly full pot, but nobody wanted any.

Collier told the Earl and Anne about the play, about making Lear a drunk, his kingdom a shambles because he couldn't leave the bottle alone. The Earl watched Collier attentively, nodding here and there, taking him seriously from the start, objecting to nothing until Collier was done.

"The king'll have to sober up by the end of the play," the Earl said finally. "We've got to have some sympathy for him sooner or later, and no one's got any sympathy for a character who stays drunk past a point."

"I was thinking he'd have to be raving drunk on the heath," Collier told him. "Probably he's having the DT's out there. God knows *what* he sees in the storm clouds, but I've got a couple of knockout ideas—which, by the way, I've got to ask Dave about. And now that we've got an artist, I can ask her too. What I want is three enormous copper baby faces, perfectly spherical, one to represent each of the three daughters. Hammered copper, although we can probably get that effect with copper-colored Rustoleum and black paint."

"I can cut the faces out of door skins," Dave said. "How big did you want them?"

"Call 'em eight feet across," Collier said.

Dave nodded. "We can check out the price of copper foil, but the paint would be worlds cheaper."

"Easy to make it look hammered," Anne said.

"Good," Collier said. "And don't we have about a million rubber snakes around here someplace? We need 'em for the DT's."

"Sure we've got snakes," the Earl said. "Every damned variety. But why stop with the snakes? There's a couple of dozen stuffed alligators in a box somewhere."

"I don't know about the alligators," Collier said doubtfully.

"What the hell's wrong with them?" The Earl poured himself another cup of coffee. "A reptile's a reptile."

"They're a little too much, maybe. There's such a thing as subtlety."

"Fair enough," the Earl said. "It's your play. If you don't want any alligators, so be it. Although I think the public likes an alligator. And alligators or no alligators, I still say that nobody's going to give a damn that the poor king's been mightily abused—not if he's still drunk, they're not.''

"Hold the hell on, damn it. By the end the man's sober. You've got to picture it. Drenched by rain and beat sense-less by the elements, he staggers back into town, except it's too damned late. They've got Cordelia, and they've already hung her. The old king's terrible to see, very wrathful, but a king's wrath doesn't cut any mustard with the Fates. Let him rage. She's as dead as an oyster.''

"I hate the hell out of that,'' the Earl said. "I can't bear that scene and never could. Why don't we save Cordelia?''

"Okay,'' Collier said, nodding slowly. "Let's say we save the girl. Have it your way. It's got to be good, though; it's got to be an improvement over the original.'' He thought for a moment, furrowing up his forehead, and then said, "How about if she's saved by angels? We fly 'em in like in the old Greek plays, in a basket out of the clouds.''

"We've got no time to set up the flying apparatus. And besides, I think you ought to give the old king a chance to do the right thing, and not leave it up to angels. That's bad form—*deus ex machina*. Let your man solve his own prob-lems or else go down trying. What do you say, Dave?''

"Sure,'' Dave said. "I can do without the angels.''

"Okay, then,'' Collier said, "how about a truckload of potted plants out on the stage? Fake plants on collapsible stems. They hang the girl, see, and the plants wither and die, and then the door bangs open and it's Lear and the fool and whoever else you want, loaded for bear. There's a hell of a swordfight, death left and right, about a gallon of blood pumped out onto the stage, the fog machine work-ing hard, cannon fire, big old blunderbuss pistols reeling out of the wings and shooting out sparks. And then when the smoke clears, there lies the girl, apparently dead. The old man reads out the usual speeches, but when he kisses Cordelia on the forehead, up she comes, large as life.''

"Like in Snow White,'' Anne said. She looked ready to burst out laughing, and Dave was full of a sudden joy. He took a chance and winked at her.

"*Just* like Snow White,'' Collier said. "Except of course

it's the old king, and not a prince. And anyway, right then all those dead plants spring up straight, flowers blooming up all over the stage. I want hundreds of them, all opening up, and bam! into the curtain call. It'll be miraculous.''

"It'll fetch the house down," the Earl said. "Except I don't know about the pistols. That was pretty early for pistols, wasn't it? What do you two think? Can we stand anachronism?''

"I like the pistols," Dave said. "We're not crazy for historical accuracy here anyway, are we?''

"I'm wondering about an elephant," Collier said. "We could run in a Hannibal subplot." He looked at the Earl, who shook his head.

"Stage wouldn't hold up, unless you're talking a plywood elephant.''

"I was just kidding," Collier said. "To hell with the elephant. What about the title, though? I'd like to meddle with the title so that the public's not misled.''

"Why don't we call it *The Travesty of King Lear*?'' Dave said, the idea coming to him out of nowhere.

There was a moment of silence, and both Collier and the Earl looked at him hard, as if trying to figure out whether he was serious or making a joke. "That's *good*," Collier said finally. "I really think that's good. But it has a little too much of the alligator in it, if you follow me.''

"Alligator?'' Dave asked.

"I mean to say that it lacks a certain subtlety. I don't mean to say it's not brilliant. Of course it's brilliant. I'm just not sure it's *right*." He looked at his watch then. "Good God almighty," he said, "it's nearly nine.''

"Is that all?'' the Earl asked. "Sun's barely up. Don't be in such a dad-blamed hurry all the time, you'll work my employees stupid. Dave, why don't you and Anne run on up to the corner and buy yourselves a cup of coffee and a cinnamon roll? I'm out of here this afternoon, by the way, and I'm giving Jolene the day off. Once the trucks get loaded, you'll have the place pretty much to yourselves, so you can really spread out. Right now I want you to take an hour to talk strategy. Develop a working rapport. Then you can come back and do some *real* work.''

"I could use a cup of coffee," Anne said. She stepped out onto the balcony ahead of Dave.

The Earl put his hand on Dave's shoulder and whispered, "*Talk* to the girl, for God's sake. Turn on the old charm." Dave followed Anne down the stairs and out onto the loading dock, where the Earl, having followed them, pressed a ten-dollar bill into his hand. "On the house," he said.

⊰ 27 ⊱

EDMUND CAME OUT THROUGH THE FRONT DOOR OF THE Ace Hardware on Main. Now that the fog had cleared away, the day was irritatingly bright with sunshine. He realized he was completely worn out. Usually a little exercise gave him an extra jolt of energy, but this morning it had simply crushed him. He had put in another full night, and he felt almost fluish with fatigue and headache now, and with the dusky memories of what once, years ago, might have seemed to him to be shameful. Shame, he had long ago discovered, was just another hang-up. But despite his exhaustion, he longed for the return of evening and the dark urges that accompanied it.

He had found a lock that was identical to the one that hung on the connecting door in the lawyer's closet. Anne's landlord had probably bought his at the same store. The need to replace the existing lock was urgent in him. It had become a part of what he had finally begun to see as *the whole picture*—finished and framed and hanging on the wall. That kind of thinking was dangerous, of course. Because of his appreciation of inspiration and of sudden artistic passion, he was hesitant to imagine it too clearly. An artist had to be open to change. And as each element in the work became clear, they suggested other elements that had to be accepted and clarified, or else rejected. A piece wasn't finished until it was finished. And you couldn't rush it.

Knowing all that didn't make him any less anxious to switch the locks, and his mind skipped on ahead as it had a dozen times already, imagining himself slipping into her closet, perhaps as she lay sleeping. He pictured the darkness, the line of light past the edge of the closet door, the smell of her clothing, the musty wooden smell of the closet. He listened to the sounds of her apartment, beyond the closet wall, peering through the door at her bed, the sheets and blankets pushed around. There was the sound of water running, and when it didn't stop, he knew it was the shower. She was in the bathroom, not ten feet from where he stood in the darkness. He opened the closet door, peered out into the room, and located the door of the bathroom, which, in the privacy of her solitary existence, she had left open. Steam clouded the lit bathroom. There was the sound of the water shutting off, of a shower door clicking open, movement in the foggy mirror. . . .

He came to himself, standing on the sidewalk outside the hardware store, realizing with a shudder that he had drifted off. His mouth had been open, and he wiped his chin and looked around. No one was staring at him. Recalling his daydream, he licked his lips and then slipped the lock into his waist pack. It wouldn't hurt to check the street door of Anne's apartment, just to see if any of the tenants had come in yet.

He crossed the street, looking down toward the pier. People crowded the sidewalk tables a block down in front of Starbucks, swilling coffee. He stopped dead on the sidewalk. Unbelievably, Dave and Anne sat at one of the tables, talking like old friends. Here was a surprise. This wasn't in the picture two minutes ago. It was more like a hole in the picture, or a splash of bad color that had to be painted out.

He started up the sidewalk toward them, suddenly overcome with a furious anger. Anne clearly wasn't the problem here. Dave was the problem—the meddling, ignorant . . . His thoughts were suddenly scattered and staticky, and his head pounded violently. He grasped his forehead and leaned against the wall of a building. His vision was black along the edges, and he forced himself to breathe regularly, in through his mouth, out through his nose. *Control*, he told himself. *Anger is your enemy*.

After a minute he regained his composure, and when he did, he abruptly understood that Dave, too, had a part in the piece. Perhaps a brief part. But to forget that now, to fly off the handle and make a scene on the street, might ruin what was beginning to look like a masterpiece.

Without looking back, he turned around and headed north on Main again. Obviously it would be far better if Anne didn't see him. If ever there was a time when it was best to be subtle, now was that time. Sunlight shone on the windows of Anne's apartment. He tried the downstairs door, but it was still locked, and immediately he stepped down onto the sidewalk again and walked toward the alley. In the time it took him to get to the back of the building, he had made up his mind. His clearheadedness and insight had returned to him, along with a faith in himself. Quickly he looked around. Seeing no one in the alley, he vaulted the gate again and ascended the stairs.

⊰ 28 ⊱

"IT'S HARD TO BELIEVE HE'S SERIOUS," ANNE SAID. SHE and Dave sat in the sunlight at a streetside table in front of Starbucks. The morning was clear, and it was almost hot in the sun, even though it was early. There was no fog, and the wind had turned around offshore and was blowing light and warm, like a trade wind. "Not that I've got anything against copper baby faces, but they're not what I expected, exactly."

"I'm a little surprised myself," Dave said. "Collier's

come up with some stretchers, but this takes the cake.
Maybe it'll work, though.''

"How successful is the theatre? It *can't* make much
money, can it?''

"Money? It's a flat-out loser as far as money's concerned. It's the Earl's hobby, like owning a bunch of classic
cars that you can't really drive anywhere. The thing is, it's
a safe bet that *any* staging of *King Lear* will lose money,
so they might as well lose it colorfully. That's what the
Earl meant with his comment about the alligators. They
won't save anything by being timid.''

"In for a penny, in for a pound.''

"That's the first principle with Collier and the Earl.''

"Can they *afford* to lose money all the time?''

"The Earl can. He can afford to do anything he wants.
That's what he's been doing ever since his wife died nearly
forty years ago. Collier doesn't have a dime, so he's *got*
nothing to lose. They make a great team.''

"So why do I have a hard time fitting Edmund into this
picture?'' She looked at his face, as if gauging his reaction
to her mention of Edmund.

"He's kind of a square peg, I guess,'' Dave said carefully. "Square peg'' wasn't the first phrase that came into
his mind, and other more colorful phrases followed, but this
was no time to look like he held a grudge.

"Will he put up with it? With Mr. Collier's play?''

"Who? Edmund?''

She nodded.

"What can Edmund do? It's the Earl's business.''

"I got the impression . . .''

"That Edmund was the man.'' Dave shrugged. "Edmund's just Edmund. He wears a suit, he shoots golf, he
signs the paychecks. . . .''

"I've played a little golf in my time.''

"Yeah, and I've worn a suit.'' Dave smiled at her. "Edmund's not my favorite subject, to tell you the truth, and I
don't want to sit around and bad-mouth the man. It's bad
for the digestion.''

"Sorry,'' she said. "I just don't quite know what to think
of him.''

"Neither do a lot of people. Personally, I try *not* to think of him."

"I don't think he's trustworthy," she said. "But maybe you already know that."

The statement filled him with a sudden joy. She already didn't like Edmund. She saw straight through him. "I've known Edmund for twenty years," he said, "and if there was ever a moment in those twenty years when he was what you'd call trustworthy, I must have been out of town." It was a careful thing to say, given the possibilities. He wouldn't have had any trouble listing Edmund's crimes, and never mind the shady deal with the notary, the threats against Collier, or the thing with the tiki earlier in the week. He could have gone on for an hour about dozens of petty, treacherous little incidents over the years. But he was sick of Edmund, and he was determined to take Casey's advice and turn the other cheek, if only to look the other way. The problem was, you could turn the other cheek if an insult was directed against you, but you couldn't if it was directed against your neighbor—Collier in this instance, or Casey.

"Well, watch out for him. I don't think he has your best interests at heart."

For a moment he considered asking her what she meant, but to hell with it. He nodded instead, and said, "Thanks. I'll watch out for him."

"He told me earlier that someone had been looking through the boxes that the Earl had let me store in one of the back rooms."

"Maybe somebody has."

"I think he was implying that it was you, although he didn't come right out and say so."

"Edmund hardly ever comes right out and says anything. One way or another, *I* didn't look through the boxes."

"I didn't think you had."

"Thanks."

She looked radiant in the sunlight, with her dark hair and her flannel shirt with the sleeves rolled up. As far as he could tell, she wasn't wearing any makeup, although he wasn't any kind of expert, and it was possible that she was just good with it. She caught his eye, and he glanced away, down Main Street toward the pier. Twice already he had caught himself staring at her, and her noticing it embarrassed the hell out of him. The sidewalks were jumping with people in the nice weather, eating breakfast in the cafes and walking down toward the pier. A shaggy-haired surfer hauled a sign out of the Windansea shop advertising a wet suit sale, and the sign reminded Dave that he had lied to Casey. He hadn't sold his wet suit. It was lying around in the garage somewhere. But it was hopelessly out of date now, and he seemed to remember that there was a hole in one of the knees. . . .

The breeze ruffled the back of his hair, reminding him of the smell of the ocean when you were out in the water on an offshore day, the way the spindrift blew back over the crest, the way the wave held up, glowing with green sunlight. It had been a long time since he had been a part of that; a lot of water had rolled past under the pier. Ten years ago he had been married for all of fourteen months. The marriage had worked for about half that time, and then had gone off the rails. Kelly was a teacher—solid, cheerful, smart. She danced. He didn't dance. She sat and drank coffee in the morning and read magazines. On weekends she could kill hours that way, when she had hours to kill. She wanted company when she was killing time, but he hadn't been good company. He hadn't ever been able to sit around without being edgy, especially early in the day, and it was only recently, looking back, that he realized that somewhere along the line he had become a slave to production, to work, whatever you wanted to call it. Two minutes out of bed in the morning and he was moving, as if he were running to keep up with something, or to outdistance something. When Kelly had wanted children and he hadn't, she had said to him, "Who did you think you were marrying?" After the breakup she had married another teacher, had three kids, and the last time he'd seen her, she had seemed perfectly happy.

He stole another glance at Anne now, and saw that she was staring into her coffee cup. She looked troubled, somehow, and she looked up at him briefly, almost curiously, and quickly looked away again.

"Reading the coffee grounds?"

"Uh-huh," she said. "I'm bilingual that way—English and coffee grounds."

"What do they say?"

"I can't tell you," she said. "Not yet. And anyway, everything changes if you tell. That's why the stuff that psychics come up with never works. They always tell you what they see, and then everything changes, and they're wrong."

"Are you sure?"

"Entirely. I'm completely convinced. So what you have to do is ask me in about five years, and I'll tell you if I was right or not."

"I don't know if I can wait five years."

She looked at him for a moment, as if she were trying to read something into the statement. "You're in a hurry?" she asked. Clearly she was serious.

He shrugged. "I was just thinking about time passing—the things I might have done, but I didn't. The way things might have worked out." He tapped the tabletop with his spoon and tried to look as if he were only half serious.

"That kind of thinking seems like a trap to me."

"Maybe because what *you've* done amounts to something you're happy with. What you've accomplished is hanging on a wall for everyone to see, including yourself. There must be some satisfaction in that."

She shrugged. "Whatever I've got hanging on the wall isn't as good as it should be. I'm never satisfied, except maybe for a couple of months. And it certainly doesn't make you any happier day to day because you paint pictures. You can't seriously believe that a painter is happier on any given day than a plumber is."

"No, but a plumber might wish he was a painter. A painter doesn't wish he was anything but a painter. Admit it. When's the last time you sat around wishing you were a plumber or a bookkeeper or a real estate agent?"

"You're right as far as it goes, except none of that has anything to do with happiness. Believe me. I've known a *lot* of miserable painters. Good ones, too. And that sort of wishing is a disease, I think—wishing for what you might

have had if things had been different. Things are never
different. They can't ever be. They're just what they are.
Anyway, we've drifted way off the subject. You were talking about the way things might have been, which is a type
of regret that's simply a condition of life. It's better to laugh
at it. You're alive, aren't you? You're working this weird
job, the sun's shining, the coffee's good. What do you
want, egg in your beer?''

"I want a double espresso for the road," he said. "What
do you want?"

"A quarter for the telescope out on the pier. Would the
Earl put up with that?"

"The Earl would recommend it," Dave said.

THE OCEAN WAS WINTER GREEN, GLASSY AND CLEAR, AND
Catalina Island floated on the horizon as if it lay a couple
of miles offshore instead of twenty-six. Up the coast the
Palos Verdes Peninsula stood out sharply against the blue
sky, marking the southern edge of the South Bay beaches,
and in the east the Balboa and Newport piers were so
clearly defined that Dave could nearly count their pilings.
The swell had calmed down, and the waves were slanting
through in long, clean lines, sets of six or eight, lacy sheets
of spray blowing back over the crests and into the faces of
surfers climbing and dropping on the long green walls. Sunlight sparkled on the water, and the ocean was full of sail-
boats, twenty or thirty of them working their way down
from the direction of Belmont Shores or Alamitos Bay,
coming around to catch the offshores, their spinnakers billowing out in the wind.

When the telescopes clicked off, they walked out toward
the end of the pier, where a half-dozen fishermen hunched
at the railing, watching their lines lift and fall with the
passing swell. Finally they stood looking into the deep water at the end of the pier, and Dave took two pennies out
of his pocket and handed one to Anne. Making a wish, he
dropped his in, watching for its tiny splash and then following its course for another moment as it sank. Anne
turned around, flipped hers over her shoulder, and together
they walked back to the Earl's shortly after ten. Edmund

wasn't in, but neither of them mentioned it, and the late start they'd gotten made it hard to start at all. The warm weather made the morning slow and drowsy, with shafts of sunlight through the windows and skylights. Dave started cutting out the baby heads, and Anne sketched big-cheeked faces onto a pad of heavy paper. At noon the truck left for Westminster with the *Oklahoma!* props, and wouldn't be back until near closing, and as the clatter of the departing truck faded in the distance, the warehouse grew hushed, the afternoon stillness broken only by the clicking of paint rollers in roller pans and the remote sound of the Earl's jukebox upstairs, Doris Day singing "Sentimental Journey."

They ate lunch back in among the palm trees and fishing nets under the balcony while the paint dried, and Dave told her about how he had rebuilt the prow of the Spanish galleon, and how Casey had engineered the gear mechanism that worked the painted ocean waves along her side. Dust motes drifted in the sunshine that shone through the dusty windows, and the afternoon stretched on, drowsy and slow, while they worked at the baby faces, Dave with cans of copper spray paint, and Anne with a chunky-tipped Marks-a-lot pen. The light in the Earl's grew dim finally, and Dave was surprised to find that it was nearly six, nearly time to close up, and just as he thought it, he heard the sound of the old Ford truck hammering around the corner from the Highway, laboring through second gear.

That was it. The day was over. So now what? Dave wondered. Go home? Sit around and read a book? Cadge another dinner from Casey and Nancy? He watched Anne put her pens back into her tackle box, and just then the Earl walked out of his office door, looking frazzled from a long nap. He surveyed the darkening warehouse, caught sight of Dave sweeping up, and jerked his head toward the catwalk stairs, then stepped back into his office and shut the door.

"Let's go upstairs and watch the sunset," Dave said to Anne abruptly.

"Upstairs?"

"Follow me." He headed up onto the balcony, past the Earl's office, and around onto the stairs that angled up toward the roof. Anne followed him out onto the catwalk, where they stood looking west through the high window, over the rooftop of Collier's bungalow and across the highway where the sun hung impossibly large and orange above the ocean, cloud drift stained a smoky red stretching away on either side of it. The sun seemed to pick up speed as it fell into the sea, its edge rippling against the evening horizon.

Dave realized that she had her hand on his shoulder, probably in order to steady herself, and so he stood there watching until the sun disappeared and the ocean changed from green to gray in the twilight.

⊰ 29 ⊱

EDMUND WORE THE KEY AROUND HIS NECK ON A CHAIN, as if it were an identification tag. The lawyer's car was gone from the lot at five, and the downstairs door was locked. It hadn't taken sixty seconds to get in through the rear door, slip the lock on the law office, and gain access to Anne's apartment through the connecting door, which banged to a stop against the clothes rod in her closet, but left plenty of space to squeeze through. He had brought the stolen male doll with him. He didn't quite know why, but he had the notion that he would use it somehow, perhaps as a reminder that Anne's private world wasn't entirely private; that someone knew—and admired—her secrets.

He stood well away from the window and pulled on a pair of throwaway surgical gloves. He had to take advantage of the last of the afternoon sunlight. He didn't dare light a lamp, and he would have to be careful with the Mini Maglite he'd brought, so that nobody saw it from the street. At any moment, of course, Anne herself might show up, so he had fastened the chain lock inside the door, which would prevent her from getting in. The ensuing confusion would give him enough time to get back out into the law office in order to hide. Probably she would go back downstairs again to call the landlord, and then he could slip out the back and be gone. Her finding the locked door might lead to unfortunate discoveries, but it was better than his being surprised, especially this early in the game.

He was fairly sure that somewhere in the apartment he would find evidence of Anne the Night Girl—a painting, perhaps another one of the dolls, a suggestive article of clothing. . . . The bed had been made with a certain amount of care, with a half-dozen throw pillows leaning against the headboard. Unnecessarily making the bed was typical of the Day Girl, an obsession with things being *nice* in some childish sense of the word. He found a collection of ceramic dogs on one of the bookcase shelves, all of them dusted, perfectly arranged. They were cheaply made, dime-store items, really. He was momentarily surprised at Anne's taste, but of course this was the Day Girl again, probably full of nostalgia for childhood trinkets. He picked one out, a dachshund, slipped it into his pocket, and then went on to the dresser.

In her dresser he found nothing interesting beyond predictable items of lingerie. He stood looking at these for a moment, feeling the fabric between his fingers, waiting for inspiration. But nothing came to him. He wasn't a thief. If what he found suggested nothing to him, then he would take nothing. The three paintings that were unwrapped and leaning against the wall of the bedroom were the same sort of thing that he already owned, nature paintings, mainly— beautifully done, but without the depths of the Night Girl's work. There were other paintings that were wrapped in paper, but he didn't dare open them. He could sense that they were more of the same, that Anne had hidden her most profound pieces; most likely she had hidden them from herself.

Leaving the doll on the bed, he wandered into her bathroom now, where he looked inside the shower, smelling the soap and the shampoo, picturing the door opening, her stepping out onto the shaggy pink rug, reaching for the towel.

. . . The medicine chest was uninteresting, just some head-ache remedies, antacid, cold and flu medicine. He looked for birth control pills, but couldn't find any. One of the cabinet drawers held various articles of feminine hygiene, which he examined and put carefully away again. He went back out into her bedroom and lay down on the double bed, running his hands over the bedspread. He moved the throw pillows aside and pulled the bedspread down over the pil-low that he imagined Anne slept on, the soft, pale field of her dreams. It smelled like fabric softener. He put his own head down, listening to the quiet evening through the open window.

He pictured a twilight landscape, himself standing at the edge of a woods, leaves drifting from the trees. He was aware of his own nakedness, and in his dream his own body was mingled with the body of the doll that lay near him on the bed. Instead of embarrassment, his nakedness and his newfound anatomy felt right to him. He saw something shifting back in among the trees, a clearing, firelight. There was movement around the fire, shadows of restless figures in strange postures. In the dream he moved toward them, motivated by intense sexual urgency, feeling the nearness of the Night Girl in the surrounding darkness. And into his mind drifted the utter certainty that in this dream he was crossing a threshold, moving through a borderland from day into true night, and he was overwhelmed with a combina-tion of nameless dread and animal desire as a beastlike shadow separated itself from the other shadows cast by the firelight and moved toward him through the darkness of the woods. . . .

He lurched awake, bathed in sweat, his heart pounding, uncertain exactly where he was. His hands were sticky in his surgical gloves, and he gaped at the doll on the bed beside him.

Voices! That's what had awakened him. Out in the hall-way! He scrambled to his feet, looking around wildly. No, they were on the street below. It sounded like Anne's voice. He ducked below the level of the windowsill and peered out at the sidewalk. It *was* Anne, accompanied by Dave, angling arm in arm across the street toward the building.

Dave was laughing like a moron, the damned . . .

Edmund fought down his sudden anger, yanking the spread up over the pillows now and hastily pulling it straight. He rearranged the throw pillows, hearing the street door slam shut downstairs, then muffled voices again, inside the building now. Picking up the doll, he turned to the open closet door. In a moment he'd be gone. . . .

And then, in a rush of wild emotion, he remembered the chain lock on the door. He hurried through the bedroom and into the living room, hearing them out in the hallway now. Carefully, knowing that they were only a foot away, just on the other side of the door, he slid the chain latch through its slide, then noiselessly extended the chain itself so that it wouldn't rattle or knock. At the same moment that he heard Anne's key slide into the dead bolt, he turned back toward the bedroom, moving as noiselessly as he could, thankful now that the two of them were chattering away. From the darkness of the bedroom he heard the bolt click, heard the door hinges squeak open, and he watched through the crack in the bedroom door as the light switched on in the living room.

"WHEN I WAS THIRTEEN I GOT AN EASEL FROM MY UNCLE and aunt who lived in Scotland," Anne said. "I have these two wonderful uncles, you know—identical twins. One of them moved to Vancouver Island back in the 1930s, which was where my mother was living at the time, when she was about five. Uncle Johnny was twenty, and the other uncle, Billy, stayed in Scotland, in a little village called Haddington, which is near Edinburgh, just a few miles from the North Sea. We used to go for the summer, six weeks at a time, and this one summer my uncle and aunt gave me an easel, like I said, that my uncle had made out of hawthorne. It had all these wonderful copper hinges and pins to hold it together when you set it up, and you could take out the pins and collapse the whole thing so that it looked like a bundle of sticks. My aunt sewed an immense bag for my paints and canvases, with little pockets and cubbyholes and with the face of a Scotty dog embroidered on the front. I could unbutton the whole thing and lay it out flat on the ground like a picnic cloth.

"Unless it rained, every morning was the same. I ate oatmeal and made my bed up, fixed a box lunch, and then went out walking, carrying the easel and bag down a rocky path through the hills to this rushy little spring-fed lake in the glen. It was called Muck Pond, and it was very weedy, although the water was quite clear and beautiful. It was cold even in the summer, with the wind off the sea, and the sky was usually full of enormous clouds that had blown down out of Scandinavia. The hills were green, unbelievably green, and there were these shaggy sheep that roamed the hillsides. I was always a little afraid of the sheep, but I don't think I would be today. They were wonderful to paint, because they would stand there forever just looking at you. Along the edge of the lake there was a woods that my aunt and uncle called a park, but they were very dark and wild, so I never went into them alone. If you followed the path far enough, it led through the woods and down along the lower end of the lake, where there was a cottage owned by a little old woman named Mrs. MacNutt—I swear, that was her name—who kept about a dozen cats and who we saw sometimes in town. A couple of times she had come out of the woods in the afternoon and had stopped to tell me about her cats, which was all right, except I really didn't want to talk with anyone. Aside from Mrs. MacNutt, though, it was the most lonesome place you can imagine, and I almost never saw another human being there . . . except this once."

"My God!" Dave said, grabbing his forehead. "You saw a *human being*?"

"Just shut up and listen. You want some more of this chicken, by the way?"

"No, thanks," Dave said. It was Mr. Lucky again—more kung pao chicken and fried dumplings. She poured tea into his cup out of a ceramic teapot that was a cobalt blue cube with a bamboo handle. "Go on," he said, watching the pink glow of a neon light cast on the wall of the building across the street.

"Well, one afternoon I stayed late, and it was getting on toward suppertime. I was standing about fifty yards above the pond, and there was a storm coming up, and the clouds were wild and black. I noticed some movement out of the corner of my eye, down at the edge of the woods. I don't know what—just something moving, something red, as if a person in a red coat, say, had stepped out of the woods and then directly back in, or had hidden herself behind a rock. When I looked, there was nothing, but for a little while after that I had this creepy feeling that someone was there, watching me. Of course it occurred to me that it was old Mrs. MacNutt, and I half expected her to reappear in order to tell me about the cats or to warn me about the storm, but she didn't.

"Anyway, gusts of wind were blowing the grass flat in long, billowing waves, so that everything—the grass, the sky, the surface of the pond, the trees in the woods—was alive with movement, and the air was full of the wind moaning and with the rustle and shiver of the grass and bushes. I was *very* romantic at the time, very susceptible to all this, and I completely forgot that somebody might still be lurking in the woods. I had about finished the painting, and the weather was so spectacular that I just couldn't leave. I had to be home before dark anyway, so I kept hoping that it wouldn't start raining and ruin my canvas and that I could have another ten minutes. What happened was that I left the canvas on the easel and ran down to the edge of the pond. I don't know how long I was there, probably about five minutes, looking at the reflection of the clouds on the lake and the green color of the rushes and the way the fallen leaves swept out over the edge of the water. When I turned around and walked back up, I saw that my easel had fallen down, and naturally I thought that the wind had blown it over. The canvas was lying there

paint side up, but there was a long scar across it, as if it
had scraped across one of the crossbraces of the easel when
it had fallen.

"It hadn't, though. There was paint on the easel, but only
where you'd expect it to be. Lying on the ground, though,
as if someone had dropped it, was a broken stick, a little
piece of a tree branch, and the broken end of the stick was
clotted with paint."

"So someone deliberately scraped your painting while
you were down at the pond?" Dave asked. "I bet it was
Mrs. Nutt. You didn't give a damn about her cats, so she
sabotaged your painting. You can tell a lot about people
from their names."

"Mrs. *Mac*Nutt. And, no, it wasn't her. I saw who it
was."

"A malicious sheep?"

"A girl. Probably thirteen. I guessed she was thirteen."

"You saw her?"

"Yes. I had set the easel back up and put the canvas on
it before I saw the stick lying on the ground. It took me a
minute to figure out what had happened, because it was just
too strange, but as soon as I knew that someone had scraped
the painting, I started shoving everything away, back in my
bag, and collapsing the easel. I was looking around all the
time, watching for them, and right then it started to rain,
enormous drops. The wind was picking up, blowing the
grass flat, and the rain was sweeping through nearly sideways. It had gotten suddenly dark, too, because of the
clouds, and I was crying, hauling all this stuff up the path,
which was running with water. I looked back down toward
the pond, and it was just wild with the rain beating it, and
the rushes were tossing in the wind, and the trees along the
edge were just a shadow behind the curtain of rain. But
right there, at the edge of the woods, where the path entered
the darkness, she was standing there again. She wasn't
moving now. She seemed to be watching me, although her
face was turned slightly away. She wore a red coat, just as
I'd thought, although in the darkness and the rain, that was
the only color you could see in the landscape. Everything
else was gray and black. It looked as if someone had col-

ored in a little red patch on a black-and-white postcard.''

"A red coat? You're sure?"

Anne nodded. "Why, what's wrong with that?"

"Nothing. I was just thinking about something. What did she look like besides the coat? Dark hair?"

"In fact, yes. Dark hair and a red coat. Why are you asking this?"

"I don't know, really. You finish your story, and then we'll get on to mine, to what happened to me the other night. I think you might find it interesting. Anyway, what did you do?"

"I screamed and ran, carrying all my stuff. The path curved up through some rocks, and I lost sight of the pond and the woods, and when I came out of the rocks again, where I could see, she was gone. My uncle was coming along the path, and he grabbed my easel and bag and took me home, although I carried the canvas, which was a complete wreck. I ended up throwing it away."

"Did you tell anybody what happened? About the girl in the red coat?"

"No. I couldn't."

"What do you mean, you *couldn't*?"

"I couldn't because the girl in the red coat was my sister."

"Your sister?"

"I recognized the coat. She was a long way off, but I knew it was her. I had felt it when I saw her at first, but I *knew* it when I saw her the second time. I don't mean I knew it in any rational way; I just knew it, intuitively."

"Then that was even more reason to say something about it—not that I normally approve of ratting people out, but that was dangerously creepy behavior. Or—let me guess—she was paying you back for something you'd done to her."

Anne stared at him for a moment and then said, "My sister had been dead for a little over two years."

He nodded at her. "That's . . . a complicating factor."

"And it wasn't the first time I'd seen her, and not the last time, either. Now, tell me: what happened to you the other night?"

ᚱ31ᚱ

EDMUND KNELT IN THE DARK CLOSET, STRAINING TO HEAR
the conversation that filtered back from the living room. He
caught evocative snatches of it, but it was maddeningly
incomplete. It didn't sound like love talk to him, although
he told himself that it didn't matter one way or another. If
Anne was attracted to a loser like Dave, it was merely impulses of the Day Girl in her; it was superficial. He knew
he could find a way to brush it aside. He could see one of
them move briefly past the edge of the door, and he strained
to see more. He didn't dare open the door any wider. If
only Anne were alone in the apartment!

Her fascination with Dave hinted at a level of superfi-
ciality that rather surprised and disappointed him. The
Night Girl demonstrated such an incredible depth of perception that it was nearly unthinkable that the two, the Day
Girl and the Night Girl, should be so distantly related in
sensibilities. He had thought that there would be evidence
of Anne's dual nature when he examined her personal effects, but there was absolutely none. Instead of two sides
of the same coin, they appeared to be two different coins
altogether, and this struck him as being almost pathological,
perhaps evidence of a severely split personality. He certainly didn't want to involve himself with a nutcase.

For long minutes there was nothing more to be seen beyond the door. His legs cramped up, and he moved around
the closet to loosen up. Somehow he was *compelled* to stay,
even though his spying on them was not only fruitless, but
it made him mad. Several times he made up his mind to
go, but each of those times he lingered, waiting for something. It dawned on him now that he had lost control. He

wasn't steering the car any longer; it wasn't his foot on the accelerator. He had become passive. Probably it was at least partly anger—the same anger that he'd felt earlier when he'd seen Dave and Anne together drinking coffee. Anger and loss of control weren't conducive to his art; they were weaknesses.

He told himself this, but he didn't leave. He crouched in front of the door again. Their voices were low, like flies buzzing, as if they were baiting him. Probably he wasn't *meant* to accomplish anything tonight. And he certainly wouldn't have anything to do with Anne when she was polluted with Dave's persona. He wasn't interested in being the next in line. Tomorrow, perhaps, some of tonight's pollution would drain away, and she'd be more approachable, more worth approaching.

He stood up again and examined the dark space around him with his flashlight. There were a couple of boxes on the floor, but they contained nothing interesting, just some clothing and a box with a few pieces of costume jewelry. He looked at it blankly, waiting for it to suggest something, but it was all junk—rhinestone pins and gaudy necklaces and a cheap pocket watch with a train engine etched into the hinged cover.

He was struck with the desire to create something right here, something for Anne—a simple piece that would startle and shock her, edge her mind out of the rut it had fallen into under Dave's tired influence. What he wanted here was a simple tableau—an artistic arrangement that would disarrange her! Suddenly happy with his own brilliance, he took a moment to pull his gloves on again before bending down and folding back the lid of one of the boxes. He bent his doll in the middle and set it so that it reclined in a bed of Anne's clothing, looking straight back at him so that it would seem to be looking into Anne's own eyes when she discovered it.

He arranged the doll's robe so that it was less discreet, more truthful. It would remind Anne that somewhere within her lay obsessions and desires that she couldn't continue to deny. He felt its flesh for signs of living heat, but the doll was cool to the touch. If it ignited in the closet . . . Well, then it ignited in the closet. He couldn't help that. It would simply be a *fait accompli*. He wasn't going to start second-guessing his instincts now. That was the death of an artist.

He concentrated on his task, letting his mind run, and almost immediately it settled on the pocket watch in with the costume jewelry. He dug out the watch, wound it up, and set it to the correct time. Carefully he lay the watch between the doll's legs. It was perfect. It hid a small part of the doll's nakedness, so it made the whole tableau more subtle, superficially less indecent. And yet the watch and its placement suggested hidden things. Time was running, the watch seemed to say. Soon something would come to pass, something that was long *meant* to come to pass. . . .

Anne's imagination would *have* to react to something as potent as this. She would see her own art in a startlingly new way: the artist rediscovering her own passions! The Day Girl and the Night Girl, face to face.

He stood for another moment looking at the tableau, shining his flashlight on it, spotlighting it. He knew that leaving this token was a fairly chancy move; it would probably change things irrevocably. But perhaps it was time to change things irrevocably.

He closed the closet door softly when he left.

⇥ 32 ⇤

DAVE STOOD AT THE WINDOW, WATCHING THE TRAFFIC ON Main Street. The night was clear and warm with the winds. He heard her teapot whistle, and a minute later Anne brought him a cup of tea and sat down again.

"Was that what you saw in the coffee grounds today?" he asked, not turning away from the window.

"Actually, it was. Except I saw it in your face. Simple

recognition, I guess. All along you've looked familiar to me.''

''After fifteen years? You've got a good memory.''

''There are some things you don't forget. Some faces stay in your memory, and you carry them around for the rest of your life. Sometimes because you're afraid of them, and sometimes because . . . because you're not, I guess. You haven't changed that much. And besides, you've always been a kind of ideal, you know.''

''Don't stretch things *too* far. . . .''

''No, I mean it. You've always been a kind of guardian angel. And I used to imagine that you'd reappear some day.''

Dave was silent. It was almost funny. This wasn't at all what he had wanted. It was far *more*, in a way: the woman you've gone crazy for admits that she'd been waiting for you to appear for years, except that it turns out that you'd let her sister drown, her twin sister. He wasn't anybody's guardian angel, and he didn't at all want to be. What he wanted was something else entirely.

''Edmund had told me about it anyway, told me about you, that is. About a little girl drowning on the beach, and your being involved, and it screwing things up for you.''

''*Edmund* told you about it?''

''Basically. He was way off base with the details, and he left out the part about your saving me, so at the time I didn't think he was talking about the same incident. He even had the date wrong. And of course it was too farfetched to think there was any connection.''

''Out of all the gin joints . . .''

''That's what I thought. But then when we were drinking coffee this afternoon, and you were staring toward the ocean, it was simply obvious. Starkly obvious. I'm telling you, you haven't changed.''

''You have.''

''I was thirteen. You do a lot of changing between thirteen and twenty-eight.''

There was a silence now. It seemed to Dave that he had spent all day long building a card house, and that it had just fallen—a little like finding out that the woman you're in love with is your long-lost sister. Worse, perhaps, since there might be a certain joy in finding your sister. "Look," he said to her, "I've got to take off."

"Why? It's just after ten."

"I'm a little tired, I guess. I don't know."

"You don't have to go."

He shrugged.

"Well, can I ask you one thing? And if you don't want to answer me, that's all right."

"You want to know what happened with Elinor? Why she drowned?"

"That wasn't exactly what I had in mind."

"Because what happened was that I was in big trouble swimming around out there. I was cold and I was tired, and suddenly I started thinking of dropping her. Just letting her go and saving myself. I wasn't *considering* it, you know. It wasn't as if the question had come up, and I was debating it in my mind. It's that it occurred to me that I *would* drop her, if I had to. A part of me, somewhere down inside, wanted to drop her. I wasn't strong enough to help myself."

"You mean to help yourself and her too?"

"Yes and no. I mean that if I couldn't help both of us, I wasn't strong enough to drown for her sake."

"For *her* sake? Let me get this straight. It seems to me that if you had drowned, so would she. Obviously she couldn't save herself. How is that drowning for her sake?"

"I can't answer that, although I've tried to a couple of times."

She stared at the floor for a moment and then asked, "*Did* you drop her? Let go of her? Don't tell me if you don't want to."

"No," he said after a moment. "I didn't have a chance to. A wave washed over us. She got swept away."

"Then how do you know you would have?" she asked quietly.

He shook his head. "At the time it just didn't matter. I lost her. She drowned. I don't even know when it happened exactly. I was tired out, we were tumbling around in the wave, and all of a sudden I wasn't holding on to her anymore. I saw her face for a moment, her hair, the color of her swimsuit, but she was gone so *fast*.''

''I'm sorry.''

''To hell with it. It was nearly fifteen years ago, like you said. That's what Casey's always telling me: 'You're a man now. Pull up your pants and get on with your life.' ''

''Well, I won't tell you that.''

''You might as well; it's true. Anyway, was that the question you wanted to ask?''

''No, it wasn't. Not even close. What I wanted to ask was why you left that day on the beach. Why you just disappeared. We gave the lifeguards about ten minutes' worth of information, and by that time you were long gone. My mother wanted to thank you, you know. Years later, when she died, she still wanted to thank you. And I'm not saying that because I think you should have stuck around and chatted. I guess I know now why you couldn't have. I only want you to know that my mother was never anything but grateful that you saved me, and that you tried to save Elinor. I wish you could have known that back then.''

Dave stood up and looked out the window again. He put his hands in his pockets and stared at the neon across the street. ''Thanks for telling me that.''

''You're welcome. You know, it's almost funny. Both of us have been carrying Elinor's ghost around with us, haven't we? I absolutely hated her. I haven't told you about that yet. I was glad she drowned. That's bad, isn't it?''

''I can't answer that. She was a strange kid, though. We talked a little bit when we were out there, and all I can tell you about it is that she was full of some kind of weird anger. Worse than anger. She would have been hard to like. I quit liking her as soon as she started talking.''

''I can imagine. You didn't have to like her, though. You were a stranger. I was her sister. Her *twin* sister. We were supposed to share everything, you know, like you read about. We were supposed to think alike, pull pranks on our teachers.''

''But you didn't think alike?''

''Never. And anyway, when I said I was glad she had drowned, I meant it. When you were out there saving her,

I was hoping that you wouldn't. Then when you didn't, it was like the biggest relief you could imagine.''

''And you never blamed yourself for thinking that?''

''I *always* blamed myself, at least for thinking it. But I didn't ever really believe that she drowned because of me. And you can't really believe that she drowned because of you, either.''

He shrugged. ''What I believe is that I don't know what I would have done in the next five minutes if that wave hadn't pulled Elinor out of my hands.''

''Who cares? It didn't happen, Dave. You didn't fail. You only found out that it's possible to fail. And if that's the first time you found that out, then you must have led a sheltered life. And you can't argue with what I'm saying, either. I'm right. You're wrong.''

''Okay, so I'm wrong. Don't beat me up with it.''

''I might just beat you senseless if you don't quit moping around.''

''All right, all right. No more moping. We'll move on. You know, there was one thing that I haven't told you. She was wearing a bracelet, with her name on it—beads with letters spelling out Elinor.''

''I had one too. We made them at a fair, at a bead booth, I guess when we were ten or eleven.''

''When the wave pulled her away, I ended up holding the bracelet. I kept it. I was going to give it to your mother, but I didn't. I couldn't.''

''We already worked through that one.''

''I know we did. I kept the bracelet, though, for some reason. Strange kind of souvenir, I guess. What I was thinking, though, is that there was something about her wearing it that made me like her a little bit, something that reminded me that she was a child, I guess. I don't know . . . maybe that just made it worse when she drowned.''

''So what did you do with it?''

''I kept it. It's hidden in a drawer, where I'll never see it unless I look for it. If you want it, you can have it.''

She shook her head. ''I kept a few things too, and I don't really want *them* either. My advice is to throw it into the ocean. Get rid of it.''

They sat without speaking until Dave asked, "So you think it was Elinor that you saw on the pier?"

"Why not?" Anne said. "You don't believe in ghosts?"

"I can believe in damned near anything right now. Sure. Ghosts—why not? I should have expected this after you told me you read coffee grounds. And you're telling me that it was Elinor that I saw on the sidewalk the other night?"

"From the way you described it—what it sounded like, what it smelled like. It's nearly always the same."

"Even though I didn't see her clearly, I *know* she looked just like you. Dead ringer."

"A couple of times I've seen her . . . her adult reflection in a window. I think it's me, but then she fades away, and there's no reflection at all, and I realize there never had been—not a reflection of me, anyway."

"What's she after?"

"I don't know. Maybe she wants something from us."

"Maybe we want something from her," Dave said.

"Maybe we do." They sat in silence for a moment, and then Anne asked, "How about you? What do you want right now? More tea? Cold dumpling, maybe?"

"I've had it," Dave said. He turned to the window again, watching the headlights on Main Street. "I better take off."

"I'll see you tomorrow, then?"

"Yeah. You'll see me tomorrow. I'm sorry if I turned out to be bad company this evening."

"I don't think you're bad company at all. I think that I've waited fifteen years to tell you what I thought. Now I don't think I said it very well."

She let the subject drop, and after another moment of silence and of staring out the window, Dave turned around to look at her and found that she was crying. He closed his eyes, tried to speak, and couldn't again.

"Sorry," she said, standing up and stepping toward him. And then, before he could react, she leaned forward and kissed him softly on the cheek. She walked across and opened the door, and he walked out into the corridor. "See you in the morning."

"I'll be there," he said.

"Wait," she said and turned around, disappearing toward the kitchen. In a moment she was back. She handed him a key. "Street door," she said. "At least you can get up to my apartment now." She smiled at him, winked, and shut the door.

He left, down the stairs and out the door to the street, turning right at the corner and heading home, the heaviness of the last half hour having fallen away with Anne's wink. He nearly felt like whistling, but right then he realized that he hadn't even asked her for her phone number, and for a second he was tempted to go back up and get it.

He heard a car start up around the corner behind him, and the car's headlights switched on and illuminated the brick wall across the street when it swung around and started to accelerate. It slowed, though, when it drew abreast of him. He glanced over to see how many people were in it, ready to sprint back up to Main Street. He just wasn't up to any crap. But the only person in the car was the driver, and as soon as Dave focused on him, he sped up, turning left at the corner a block up and heading down toward the Highway.

The car was Edmund's Mercedes.

⇥33⇤

"I'm not listening," Casey told him. "You can go ahead and talk, but I'm watching *Jeopardy*, so I'm not paying attention to anything you say. They've got South Pacific islands as a category, and I'm nailing it."

"You don't have a choice, Case. I'm not joking around now. I've got something serious to say, and I'd just as soon not say it over the phone. I was thinking of coming over.

And how the hell are you watching *Jeopardy*? It's eleven-thirty.''

"The marvels of videotape. I don't watch TV until late. Nancy won't watch it at all, so I wait until she goes to bed.''

"Well, I've got something I want to talk about.''

"How serious is it?''

"Very.''

"Can you turn it into a *Jeopardy* answer?''

"Look . . .''

"Then you can't come over. I never talk serious this late at night. Okay, wait, wait . . . Man! *Fiji*, for God's sake. I can't believe how lame these people are. If I was on there tonight, I'd tear it up. South Pacific islands and basketball on the same damned slate. None of these bozos knew *any*thing about the Celtics back in the Larry Bird days.''

"Don't put me off, Case. Am I coming over or not?''

"What for?''

"Because your brother . . .''

Casey began knocking against the phone now with some sort of metal object and whistling tunelessly. "I'm not listening,'' he said, breaking in on all the noisemaking. He wasn't drunk, either. He was perfectly sharp and coherent.

There was sudden silence. Dave could hear the *Jeopardy* music in the background. "Your brother . . .'' he started to say again. The knocking started up along with the whistling. Dave waited it out.

"You want to talk?'' Casey said finally.

"Yeah, I want to talk.''

"Then we'll talk on the beach. In fact, it's funny you called, because I'd already made up my mind that you were going out tomorrow morning. That's the plan. No bullshit. Tomorrow the elusive Dave gets wet. The swell's faded, but it's still good, probably better than it's been, if it's shape you want instead of size. I'm bringing that board I bought from Bill. You'll love it. You get your goddamn wetsuit off the back fence. You might want to bring it into the house if you want it dry.''

"What the hell are you talking about? What wetsuit?''

"Whoa! Don't bother to lie to me and tell me you sold

it at a yard sale. I broke into your lousy garage this afternoon and found it. It's not hip any more, but it'll keep you
warm. The zippers work. The seams are tight except for
the knee's a little ragged. I hosed the sawdust off and hung
it over your back fence, over by the lemon tree. You're
ready to ride, bro.''

"I don't know . . ."

"Of course you don't. That's why I'm calling the shots.
I was going to make it a surprise attack, but now that
you've called, you might as well check it out right now.
Here's the game plan: I'm knocking at your door at half
past five. You with me so far?"

"Go on," Dave said.

"All right. If you're not ready to go, I'm coming in after
you. And you know what? I'll break the front window if I
have to, Dave. I'll punch a fucking hole right through it.
Try me if you think I won't. Our little talk at the doughnut
shop riled me up, man. I got home *pissed* off. I decided
that you talk too much these days. You know why you talk
so much? Because talking kills time. Talking makes mountains out of molehills. Pretty soon you don't know the difference. You make a big scene out of nothing, and you lose
track of what's really worth dealing with—you know what
I mean? Talking's like snow; it covers things up so that
you can't make out their shape any more. You're whistling
in the dark, Dave, and it's time you shut the hell up and
faced your fears. So I'm going to cut you a deal. I'll listen
to you talk one more time if I can see you surf. And I mean
tomorrow morning.''

Dave sat for a moment in stunned silence. Everything
Casey said was true, of course. There was no way to deny
any of it.

"I don't want silence, Dave. I want your word on it right
now. Either tell me yes or hang up and wait for the glass
to break. We've got Double Jeopardy coming up here.''

"Five-thirty," Dave said. He almost followed it up with
something sentimental about the value of Casey's friendship, but he stopped himself. He didn't trust himself to say
anything more.

"Hey, Dave."

"Yeah."

"I'm on the wagon. I don't know how long it'll last, but I've got a few hours sober now. I'm sitting here drinking diet Cokes. I'm not telling Nancy anything about it. She'll figure it out soon enough. You're the one who started it off. That's probably why I was so mad when I got home."

"Good for me."

"I owe you. And I'm going to kick your ass if you don't have coffee going at five-thirty. Did you write that down?"

"I wrote it down."

"Good. Sweet dreams." He hung up the phone then. Dave listened until he heard the dial tone, and then hung his phone up and turned on the television, somehow thinking for one crazy moment that he could catch the rest of *Jeopardy*.

34

AT DAWN THE AIR WAS STILL AND THE OCEAN WAS glassy, the dark waves rolling up out of the depths and breaking on the outer sandbars, long waves that lined up for fifty or sixty yards, the breaking section running smoothly down the clean wall, hissing shoreward, re-forming, and breaking again inside in a small-size, quick-speed replica of the outside break. The moon still hung in the western sky, and in the east the horizon was layered with pink and gray that died into the blue darkness of night. Overhead there were two or three stars still visible, faded and nearly gone. The beach was empty except for a flock of seagulls, a hundred or so that stood facing the west on the ocean side of the fire pits as if they were waiting for the sun, or for some long-anticipated seagull god to crawl up from out of the ocean.

At the top of the beach were sections of low barrier walls built of concrete blocks along the edge of the empty parking lots—county park renovations of more recent years. Beach sand had drifted up against the walls in shallow dunes, spilling out from between the sections onto an asphalt access road that ran the length of the beach, from beyond Brookhurst Street all the way to the pier. In the summer the road would be full of tourists crossing the access road from the crowded parking lots, dodging a steady procession of in-line skaters and cyclists. The old wooden concession stands were long gone, along with the ice plant and the rusted chain link and the railroad flotsam, all of it bulldozed years ago, the concession stands replaced with concrete block buildings, with picnic tables and drinking fountains and showers.

The beach itself hadn't changed. Ten million waves had broken along it in the past fifteen years, and those waves had shifted millions of tons of sand and seashells and rocks, scouring the ocean bottom, cutting channels and filling them in again, the sandbars drifting with the seasons and the changing swell, all of the movement and change hidden beneath a few feet of enigmatic ocean. By some trick of tide or of dawn light, the ocean seemed to be strangely elevated now, as if Dave were looking up at it from where he sat at the crest of the slope that angled down into the water, as if at any moment a wave might simply surge forward and inundate the beach.

Casey handed him the doughnut bag, and he took out a plain cake doughnut and dipped it into his coffee, watching as a lone surfer jumped to his feet at the top of a wave and dropped across the wave's face. In his black wetsuit the surfer was nearly invisible against the dark ocean, although the front half of his white board traced a ghostly path along the wave, angling upward until it thrust through the crest of the wave and was silhouetted against the early-morning sky and then slashing downward and driving into the trough, where the surfer disappeared suddenly, hidden by a wave breaking farther inshore, and then reappeared down the beach, flying across a dark, dawn-lit section that seemed to defy gravity in its steep vertical rush.

"It's not going to get any better than this," Casey said, crumpling up the empty paper sack. "I hate to say it, but this spot hasn't broken this good in I don't know how long. So if this burning news of yours is *too* long and weird, how about saving it until we're out in the water? It's going to be serious daylight in about ten minutes."

Dave looked at him for a long moment and then said, "Your brother's stealing money from your father, basically. Stealing properties. I don't know what he's doing with them. Selling them, I guess."

Casey nodded slowly. "Where'd you come up with this information?"

"From this old homeless guy named Mayhew. You'd recognize him if you saw him. I was working late and he came around looking for your brother who, this guy said, owed him money for some work. What he said was that he had posed as your father."

"*Posed* as him?"

"At a notary public up Beach Boulevard near Talbert. Apparently Edmund brought this guy in carrying your father's driver's license. They look enough alike to fool somebody who's not paying too much attention. Anyway, this old guy signed a quitclaim deed, then your brother gave him twenty bucks and sent him on his way."

"For what? What was the deed?"

"I honestly don't know."

"And this was when the Earl was out of town?"

"Might have been. I don't know how long ago it was. I get the impression it was a couple of weeks ago, maybe less."

"Well, probably it was just some routine business, and Edmund didn't want to wait for the Earl to get home, so he managed it his own way. You've got to quit working this thing against my brother, man. Not that he doesn't deserve it, but it's not doing *you* any damned good at all. You're getting obsessed."

Dave stared at him. "Are you kidding, or just self-deluded in some amazing new way?"

"Why should I be either one?"

"Because what you just said is completely nuts. *Busi-*

ness? Committing fraud just because it's more convenient than waiting a day or two? Nobody would do that. This doesn't look like business, Case, it looks like theft.''

"So this Mayhew character *told* you this, that he signed a quitclaim deed?"

"No, all he told me was that he 'simulated' your father. That was the way he put it. The quitclaim was my idea, since I couldn't think of any other reason that Edmund would need a notary and a fake signature."

"So this is speculation on your part?"

"No, I don't think it is. I think I'm right."

"And you *think* it's a piece of property?"

"What else would it be? The Earl's car's a bigger joke than Collier's was. What else has he got that your brother would want to put his hands on?"

"Nothing," Casey said after a moment. "If you're right, then it probably *is* a piece of property. He could shift a dozen of them into his name, and I'd never know anything about it. I'm easy that way."

"You're *too* easy that way." Dave poured the rest of his coffee into the sand. It was gray daylight now, and there were half a dozen surfers in the water. The stars and the moon were gone, and the tip of the sun had risen above the mountains. Casey kneeled next to his surfboard and methodically rubbed wax across the deck. "I drove over to the notary," Dave said.

"Why the hell did you do that?" Casey didn't look up, but worked at the wax, layering it up. His voice was flat, as close as it came to anger.

"Curiosity."

"I wish you would have called me first. You know what they say about the cat, man."

"I didn't tell him who I was or what I knew except for one thing—that there's a brother in the picture, meaning you. This notary, as far as I can make out, had no idea that Edmund had a brother or that old Mayhew was a fake. Now he knows. The truth never hurt anybody, except maybe Edmund, in this case."

"Now *that's* a truly naive idea. The truth can do a hell of a lot of damage when it gets loose. I just wish you'd have told me first and let me take care of it.''

"What would you have done?''

"Done?'' Casey stood up and looked toward the ocean. He turned around and shook his head. "I wouldn't have done anything. But that's my call, isn't it?''

"You'd have let him go on with it?''

"That's right. I just don't care, bro. It just doesn't compute.''

"It's a *lot* of money.''

"I've *got* a lot of money. The Earl put a ton of it in trust years ago. I don't have to work. I never will. I'm a privately financed derelict. Nancy works because she wants to. We traveled so much last year I got sick of it. We can eat out every night of the week, but we don't want to. I can smoke Cuban cigars, except I don't smoke. Now that I don't drink, my only expensive vice is surfboards, and I don't break that many. And speaking of surfing, now that you've had your say, I'm going to hold you to your part of the deal.'' He tossed Dave the bar of wax and picked up his board.

"Okay, never mind the money,'' Dave said. "To hell with the money. Doesn't it bother you just a little bit that you're being cheated?''

"Nope.''

"Well, it bothers me. But to you it's just like that kite in the wind, or whatever the hell it was; you just let it go.''

"I just let it go. My brother is who he is, like I said. The clothes, the car, the country club. All of that shit just bores the hell out of me. The *last* thing I give a damn about is getting my share of it. Let him have the damned properties. I won't waste ten seconds on him, Dave. And that goes double as long as my father's alive. You know what the Earl thinks about Edmund. The Earl doesn't remember anything but what he wants to remember. The past is just dust to him. Edmund's the success. Edmund's the shining star. Edmund came into the family business with all his expertise, and the Earl went into semiretirement. He can spend all his time horsing around with Collier.''

"All what expertise?''

"*I* don't know what the hell kind of expertise. Edmund's *family*, Dave. He's my mother's son. He's nearly respectable. You know, to tell you the truth, I don't have any damned idea what my father *really* thinks about Edmund. All I know is that he won't listen to you if you say anything against him. He won't even hear you. He certainly never heard me, so I just shut up finally. I found out I was happier when I shut up.''

"He's stealing from your old man like a fox in the god-damn henhouse.''

"It's a *big* henhouse. Plenty of chickens to go around. The only thing the Earl doesn't have plenty of is *time*. What the hell good is the truth to a man whose heart's on the ropes? When you're that close to the graveyard, you stop giving a damn about the henhouse. Why the hell would you want to tell him that his number-one son is a liar and a thief? You think it would make him happier? That he'd shake your hand? Check it out: I don't *care* about proper-ties, and neither does the Earl. All I give a damn for is moving this whole tired charade along from one day to the next without the old man getting hurt. I get a few waves on the side, keep Nancy happy, and I'm a satisfied man.''

"How about Collier? Do you care about Collier?''

"How is Collier involved in this?''

"Collier's certain that Edmund's going to evict him from the bungalow and sell the property to the city for municipal parking.''

"Edmund wouldn't do that. He couldn't do that. He doesn't have the authority.''

"He doesn't have the authority to hire Mayhew to mas-querade as your father, either, but he did it.''

"That's entirely different. That's just money. What you're talking about is more than just money.''

"To whom? It's more than just money to *you*, maybe. Or to the Earl. To Edmund, though, it's just money. Every-thing's just money. Edmund's always thought Collier was a sponge. You've heard him go on about it—wasting thousands of dollars on goofball plays that don't earn a penny. You ought to see what Collier's got cooked up this time. Edmund's going to bleed from the ears when he finds out.''

Casey shrugged. "Okay, you're right. Edmund's got a

thing about Collier. That's fair enough. And now I'm warned. I'm ready for him. If he wants to take me on over Collier and the bungalow, I'll fight with him. Otherwise he can go to hell rich. Just promise me you won't go calling the cops or anything like that. I don't need it, the old man doesn't need it, nobody needs it. If something comes up, call *me*. Keep it in the family."

"Whatever you say."

"That's what I say. And one more thing. I keep telling you to leave Edmund alone. It's bad for your karma, you know? Your chakras get all messed around, completely out of alignment."

"I guess I don't give nearly as much of a damn for my karma, or whatever the hell it is, as you do, Case. I just can't play make-believe all the time."

"I understand that, although I'm going to keep working on you. My brother's just smoke, man. Tinted glass. Try looking right through him."

"I really wish I could. I keep straining my eyes, you know?"

"Get a new pair of glasses, then. And one last thing," Casey said, swinging his board up under his arm. "There's more to Mr. Edmund than meets the eye. You know what I'm talking about? He's a jerk, but that doesn't make him a fool. He can actually be *very* dangerous. He has a *long* history. So don't even think about taking him on. It's just not worth it. Life's too short."

"You're right about that," Dave told him.

Casey stood looking at him for a moment. "All right," he said at last. "I'll say something to Edmund, at least about Collier. We'll leave the money issue alone, though."

"Fair enough," Dave said.

35

EDMUND LEFT HIS CAR PARKED ON 8TH STREET AND walked the two blocks to the Earl's through the early-morning darkness. He wore a sweat suit over his jogging togs, and he had put on his Nike running shoes. From the look of it, he was just another early-morning jogger burning up a couple of miles of pavement before the day started. He felt good—alert and rested. Last night he had taken a couple of pills and made a point of sleeping. It was a matter of control more than anything else. The day before, he had lain in bed all day, hadn't even shaved. If he let himself degenerate that way . . .

A car cruised past, turning at the corner and disappearing, and he saw the roof of the Earl's over the housetops. There was no way Collier would be awake yet. The morning belonged to Edmund. He felt safe, nearly invisible. The world was waiting for him to make sense out of it. When he reached the west side of the theatre parking lot, he took one last hasty look up and down the street and cut across the lot, back into the shadow of the high theatre wall. Collier's house was dark.

Dave's car was parked in the lot near Collier's lawn, and Edmund stood watching it for a few moments. It would be fun to torch it, too. The car couldn't be seen from the street because of the theatre and the warehouse. While the morning darkness lasted, he could do anything to it that he wanted to do. His mind scurried around, thinking of flammable substances. The burned pallets had been cleared away, but there was a satisfying black smudge on the asphalt. A liquid that he could splash over the car would work better than the pallets, if only to burn the paint off before

somebody put the fire out. There was thinner and turpentine
in the Earl's, but if anyone—like Dave—was working
early, then going into the warehouse would wreck things
entirely. And anyway, it was best to stick with whatever he
could find lying around, just like a kid would do. Collier
probably wouldn't leave his lighter fluid next to his barbecue any more, not with his pyromaniac granddaughter on
a rampage. . . .

Another morning, perhaps. A car fire now would just
wreck his plans, since Jenny was in bed and couldn't be
blamed for starting it. He set out up the kitchen side of
Collier's bungalow, walking carefully through the grass,
making as little noise as possible and looking around carefully for something he could use. He stopped at Collier's
rusty old Weber barbecue, carefully lifting the lid high
enough to see underneath. There was half a bag of charcoal
briquettes under there along with a can of lighter fluid. The
old man had left it accessible after all! Apparently there
was no accounting for idiot faith. He took out the can, then
reached in and slid the bag out, too, set the lid down silently, and unrolled the top of the bag. Sure enough, there
was a matchbook lying on top of the charcoal. He pulled
the matches out, rerolled the bag, and put it back under the
lid, then wiped his sooty hands on the grass. He saw a little
Matchbox truck in the weeds along the wall then, and he
picked it up and put it into the shallow pocket of his sweat-
pants along with the matches, nearly laughing at how appropriate it all was.

And then it struck him that it was more than appropriate.
It was synchronicity, purely and simply. Artistic intuition.
Things were falling into place because he was *allowing*
them to fall into place by letting go, by trusting to his art,
by trusting himself.

How wonderful that he hadn't given it a second thought!
It had simply happened. Intuition and instinct had opened
the doors to perception. . . . He found a doll in the weeds
farther along, back near the vacant lot—a little dime-store
doll about six inches high. It must have had clothes at one
time, but they'd been removed, which was too bad, because
the clothes would have made it that much more flammable.

On the other hand, there was a certain purity in the doll's nakedness. He ran his fingers over her smooth plastic flesh, cleaning off the dirt, sweeping her hair back. Her hair, probably, would go up like a torch. She had moveable joints at the elbows and knees, and he moved her arms up and down, swiveled her legs, understanding the vision that was spinning together in his mind, the picture that was taking shape. This blonde doll with its idealized figure was a counterpoint to the Night Girl's dolls. It was all surface, the facade that the world was anxious to believe in but knew to be false. The nylon dolls were true on the deepest level. He was full of the fire of inspiration now, energized by finding the doll.

Clutching it, he went hurriedly around the back of the bungalow, where for a few seconds he was exposed to the eyes of people in cars on the Highway, but then he was safe again, hidden by the bushes that crowded up against a big eucalyptus tree near the corner of the yard. Around the tree, lying on the lawn, were papery sheets of bark that the tree had sloughed off. On impulse he picked up a half-dozen hand-sized pieces along with a bunch of leaves, and, having no place else to put them, he shoved them up under his sweatshirt and tucked the shirt into his pants. He headed back up the bedroom side of the house now, moving very quietly and carefully, looking into the high grass and wishing he had brought a penlight along with him.

A decorated lunch sack lay at the back edge of the porch, and he picked it up to have a look at it. It contained what appeared to be baseball cards, although when he picked one out and looked close, it turned out to be some sort of comic trading card—a mutant-looking child holding a bloody ax. The very idea of such a thing disgusted him. It was nothing but pornography for children—the kind of thing that the social worker should get a good look at. He picked out a handful of the cards, enough to share, and dumped the rest into the grass, then put the doll and the toy truck into the sack with the cards. This would be enough, this sack of miscellaneous articles. Art made from found things—the Japanese had a word for it. . . . He couldn't remember what it was.

The bungalow's front porch was a couple of feet high, the crawl space beneath it sided with lattice. An overgrown night-blooming jasmine hid the back corner of it, where it extended a couple of feet beyond the house itself. Years ago there had been an opening down there, where the lattice had fallen apart, an opening wide enough for a child to crawl through. Edmund crouched beside the jasmine, pushing the spindly limbs aside and peering past it. The hole was still there, virtually unchanged from the days of his childhood. Years ago, he himself had played under that old porch, sitting alone, hidden from the world in his own personal cave. He had buried cats and small animals down there—a gopher, he remembered, that a cat had half killed, and a pigeon that had hit the kitchen window and knocked itself out. He had lured Casey down there when Casey was three, and tied him with cotton rope to an exposed post, and then boarded up the entrance with junk, keeping him down there all day long and into the evening until the Earl had gotten home. He had sat all day on the porch above, knocking like hell on the floorboards with a broom handle every time Casey had started to shout.

Surely Collier's granddaughter played in that cave, too. Dark places were irresistible to children. . . .

He pushed in past the jasmine, shoving his head and shoulders into the darkness. He could smell the fine dust and the old wood of the floorboards, and the smells brought it all back to him, all the dim memories, the things he had done beneath the porch, the things that were buried there, the things that nobody but he knew about. He thought about the Night Girl suddenly, what they had done together in the darkness during the past nights, and he was suddenly anxious to reveal himself to her—and to Anne—more fully. . . .

ON THE WAY HOME HE SAW A DEAD POSSUM IN THE ROAD, its body nearly flattened. He stopped the car, got his knife out of the glove compartment, and climbed out of the car, quickly severing the possum's long tail. He got back into the car and drove the rest of the way home, whistling happily.

In his kitchen he turned the oven onto low, put the leaves and bark inside to dry out. Then he sorted through the playing cards, finding a half-dozen that were particularly offensive. He set those aside and then poured a cup of lighter fluid into a cereal bowl and floated the rest of the cards in it. He would leave them there while he took a shower, and then package them in a Ziploc storage bag to keep them damp.

❈ 36 ❈

AFTER AN HOUR'S CONSTANT PADDLING TO STAY IN THE break off Magnolia Street, Dave let himself drift south, leaving Casey and eight or ten other surfers behind. There were sandbars working everywhere down the beach, plenty of waves for everyone, and even if all of them weren't up to the standard of the waves they'd paddled into at dawn, Dave would rather find a wave of his own than continually jockey for position with younger and more aggressive surfers. And besides, he was tired. Whatever muscles he had been using over the past fifteen years apparently weren't the muscles he was using now, and his arms and shoulders ached from paddling.

It was a good ache, though, and it was good to be wet, and it was almost funny the way Casey had muscled him into going out this morning after all these years away from it. It would be a lie to say that he had forgotten any of it— the salt smell of the morning ocean, the particular smell and feel of a Santa Ana wind on his face, the instant response to the moving gray mass of a wave looming up out of deep water. The whole thing was like an old and instantly familiar friend back in his life after years away. It had only taken a couple of waves to get the timing back,

too, to read the wave's face as it drove in over the sandbar
and started to peak, to spin around and go when he felt the
gathering energy beneath him.

What had Anne said yesterday when he had talked about
things working out differently? . . . Things are never different. They're just what they are. He had let a lot of waves
go by over the past fifteen years, but the waves hadn't
missed his presence for a moment. *Bygones*, he thought. It
was time to do it again—past time.

Alone now, he paddled even farther outside, just at the
far edge of the break, so that the long swells rolled under
him and he could sit in peace, listening to the sound of the
gulls and letting the offshore breeze blow against his face.
He watched the backs of the waves as they pushed in toward shore, spindrift flying backward on the wind. The
back of a wave never looked the same as the front: it looked
smaller, and it never really steepened and threw itself forward, but hid the violence of the wave's breaking and simply seemed to disappear into the sea again when its energy
was spent. The water had settled quickly after the storm
surf, and was deep green and clear, with sunlight glinting
from the diamond ripples on the surface. He could see a
school of dark fish swimming in the swell, reappearing
within successive waves, rising above the level of the ocean
toward the wave's crest, then disappearing suddenly before
the wave broke, back down into the depths.

It was nearly impossible to keep his mind off the shadows that shifted beneath the surface, the slowly darkening
depths when a wave passed beneath him or a scrap of
cloud-drift crossed the sun. A tangle of brown kelp drifted
past, buoyed up by air bladders, a long tendril dragging
across his calf like a languorous human touch, coiling
around his ankle. He stared at it, into the tangled brown
stalks and leaves, and he imagined that the kelp holdfasts
clung like fingers to a scrap of human bone. He forced
himself to recall the dream that recurred in late winter, to
recollect her face in that instant before she was snatched
away, her dark hair swirling, her eyes full of terror.

He still had no idea whether they had ever found her
body. Maybe he should have asked Anne last night, just in

order to know. He had always imagined that she was still out here, that she had drifted into deep water on winter currents, settling into the quiet darkness of the seabed, and his dreams had always included bones entangled in water weeds, kelp-filtered shafts of watery sunlight illuminating an ivory rib cage that tumbled over the ocean floor in a slow current. Somehow the image didn't hold any horror for him this morning. The cold salt water had washed it out of his head.

His board rose steeply over a passing swell, and he realized that he had drifted shoreward. He kicked around parallel with the beach now, watching the dark line of a wave roll toward him, pushing up out of the ocean as it felt the bottom, steepening perceptibly twenty yards to the north. He dug his hands into the water, paddling hard toward the wave's peak, and, in the instant before it reached him, spun around and took one last deep stroke, jumped to his feet, and dropped down the wave's face, stalling the board halfway down and ducking beneath the lip of the wave as it threw itself forward. He trailed his left hand across the long glass wall as the wave steepened in front of him. He hunkered down, feeling the board and the wave gather momentum, and he shifted his weight backward, the crest of the wave cascading over his head. He passed into its shadow, watching the sheet of falling water, the distant beach. And then he found himself in sunlight again, driving across the sun-glinting face of the wave, angling up toward the crest and flying up through the feathering lip as a long section of the wave closed out in front of him. Suddenly he was flying. His board, airborne, snapped tight at the end of its leash, and he fell backward into the now-still water, the wave having passed on, his board plunging down a few feet away. He let himself sink beneath the surface until, buoyant in his wetsuit, he floated upward again into the sunlight.

⊰37⊱

"HONESTLY," ANNE SAID. "I DIDN'T FIND ANY NOTE."

"It was taped to the outside of your door."

"Downstairs? On the street?"

"No. Upstairs. I let myself in with the key you gave me and taped the note to the apartment door. It was about five in the morning. I didn't want to wake you up." Anne had finished the four baby heads, which were stacked against the wall now, and was half through airbrushing the detail onto the Duke of Albany's palace, which was moved back under the balcony, out of the way of falling tikis.

"You didn't want to wake me up, but you wanted to tell me that you'd be late for work?"

He shrugged. "It seemed like the right thing to do at the time. The gentlemanly thing. I mean, I was sticking you with all the work, and it was only your second day on the job. And besides, I said I'd be here."

She grinned at him and nodded broadly. "Did you ride the big kahunas this morning?"

"Well, I guess I did. A couple of big kahunas anyway. It felt good to get wet again."

"I bet it did. Some day I want to go with you. I want to get wet, too."

"That's always the beginning of the end, when a surfer starts taking his girlfriend to the beach with him."

"Now I'm your girlfriend?"

"I didn't mean it *that* way. I was just pointing out that . . ." He shrugged. "Okay, I *did* mean it that way. What do you think?"

"What do I think? I think I haven't been a girlfriend in three years. My last boyfriend . . ."

"I don't want to hear about him," Dave said. "I already hate him."

"So do I, actually. I fell for his accent."

"Anyway," Dave said, "I left a note on the window. It was kind of a thank-you note, if you want to know the truth."

"What for?"

"For last night. There were a few things I needed to hear, and you said them."

"I wish I would have got the note."

"It's probably lying on the carpet."

"Probably," she said. "Except I think I would have seen it. I think maybe you're making all this note talk up. Next thing you'll tell me that the check's in the mail."

"Why would I tell you that?" Dave asked, opening his toolbox and taking out the top tray. "Do I owe you money?" He took out his Makita drill and a box of bits and screwdriver heads, then started to close the lid. He saw a scrap of paper, though, lying in the tray below, underneath a scattering of spade bits and punches and old pencils. Instantly recognizing it, he pinched up the corner of the paper and pulled it out, turning it over in his hand. It was the letter he had written to Anne, the one that he'd taped to her door that morning.

"What's that?" Anne asked. "Treasure map? Fan mail from some flounder?"

"It's the note."

"Which note would that be, now?" She saw his face then. "What's wrong?"

"It's the note I taped to your door this morning." Baffled, he handed it to her, and she read it.

"You're sweet," she said. "But I was actually kind of a clod last night. I never can think of the right thing to say until it's too late."

"That's . . . You're wrong, of course. But I taped this to your window at five o'clock this morning. What's it doing here?" The piece of tape was still attached to it, folded neatly back so that it was stuck entirely to the paper. "You see what I'm saying?"

Anne stepped back and looked appraisingly at the castle

for a moment, then sorted through bottles of colored paint. "Maybe you *thought* you taped it to the door, but really you taped it to the bottom of your toolbox. I did that once. I thought I put the checkbook in the drawer, but really I put it in the refrigerator. I found it there the next morning."

"I've done that kind of thing too. But when did I have a chance to put the note in here? I just got here. And it's underneath stuff, too. It's not just dropped in here."

She screwed a jar to the bottom of the airbrush and shot a test spray of paint onto a piece of cardboard, then started shading the stones of the castle. The compressor kicked on, and then after a few moments fell silent again. "Have you considered that maybe you're crazy?" she asked. "That's always an option, you know."

He watched her for a moment, and then a thought came to him. "*You* put it there," he said to her.

"I didn't either."

"You got mad because I left you to finish Collier's baby heads, and you hid this in the toolbox in order to blow my mind. Go ahead, deny it."

"Okay, I deny it."

"Do you *really* deny it?"

She nodded at him, quitting the work with the airbrush. "I didn't put the note in the toolbox, Dave."

"Okay, you didn't put it there. *I* didn't put it there. . . ." Suddenly the answer was apparent to him. Nothing about it was funny any more. He knew Anne saw it too.

"Edmund?" she asked doubtfully. She grimaced at him and pushed a lock of hair away from her forehead.

He glanced up at the offices, and Edmund's light was on. "Has he been here all morning?"

"I guess so," she said, "although he hasn't come out. He easily could have put it in the box before I came in."

Keeping his voice down, Dave told her then about Edmund's being parked on the street last night. "It was creepy," he said. "What the hell was he doing there?"

"I think he was sitting around being jealous," Anne said, and she told him about the gallery in Laguna, and Edmund's buying all the paintings. "He's apparently already gotten a little obsessive."

"A little," Dave said.

"I can't believe he would have taken the note off the door this morning, though. Why would he do that? What difference did it make?"

"Like you said, maybe he's just crazy. That's always an option. What time did you leave the apartment?"

"Nearly nine."

"And I left the note there at about five. That gave him four hours. He didn't knock or anything? You didn't hear him out there?"

"No, but I didn't wake up until nearly seven-thirty, and then I took a shower. There's no doorbell. I had the stereo going."

"What time do the other tenants show up?"

"Later, usually. The lawyer at the top of the hall gets there early sometimes, though."

"Was the street door locked when you came down at nine?"

"Yeah. I unlocked it to let myself out. And I didn't see that the lawyer was in, either. He might have been, but I didn't notice his lights on or anything. I didn't hear him."

"He *must* have been there. I bet that Edmund was hanging around outside, waiting for you to come out. The lawyer showed up, and Edmund talked him into letting him in. He knocked on your door, but you were in the shower. He read the note, it pissed him off, and so he took it with him, came down here, and put it into the toolbox."

"But why would he have done that? Put it in the box?"

Dave made his voice as light and matter-of-fact as he could, trying to keep things in proportion, at least for now. "He thinks it's funny."

"Funny?"

"Edmund's sense of humor works on levels that are hard for sane people to comprehend."

He glanced up at Edmund's office. If Anne weren't here right now, he would have had a little talk with Edmund. Casey's advice wasn't going to cut it. If Anne were involved, though—forced to take a side—then her job would instantly become a chaotic mess, and she'd probably run.

Dave didn't want her to run. And he surely didn't want to be the *cause* of her running.

Out of a sudden curiosity, he bent over and lifted the tray out of the center of the toolbox. He nearly dropped it again. Lying beneath it, like a dead gray snake, was the severed tail of some kind of ratlike animal—a possum, given the size of it. He started to lift it out; then he paused, glancing over at Anne. But she was airbrushing the castle again, concentrating on her work. He picked the tail out of the box and dumped it into the trash barrel, pulling wadded paper over the top of it to hide it.

EDMUND SAT IN HIS OFFICE, DRESSED IN A GRAY SUIT AND red tie, the suit fresh from the cleaners. Full of the intensity of waiting, he was too edgy for mundane work, and he leafed idly through a copy of *GQ*, glancing now and then through the office window, waiting for an opportunity. Edmund had been waiting half the morning for Collier to shift his fat tail off the porch and *do* something. Collier had been sitting there for two hours while his granddaughter ran around screaming and howling, dressed like a beggar girl. The old man stood up now and walked in through the screen door, letting it slam behind him. Edmund walked to the window to see if it was time. A few moments later, Collier came out again, waved at someone, and then Dave and Anne came into view, carrying the plywood heads for Collier's asinine play.

This was just about perfect—the whole gang out of the way. He lost sight of them when they rounded the corner of the warehouse, no doubt heading for the theatre to set the stage for the evening's rehearsal. He heard an office door shut—his father's, no doubt—and he opened his own door far enough to see out, watching as the Earl descended the stairs and went out the front door. Edmund went back to the window and waited until the Earl had rounded the corner of the building, too, apparently following the others.

He opened the desk drawer then and pulled out the pink lunch sack that he'd found that morning. Inside lay the fuel-soaked playing cards, the plastic doll and the toy truck, the matchbook, and the debris from the eucalyptus tree. He slid the cards out of their plastic bag and dumped them back into the sack, then tossed the Ziploc bag into the trash, opened the file cabinet, and took out one of the Night Girl's dolls, another female, the smallest of the four he had taken from the storage room. He went out through the office door and down the wooden stairs, stopping for a second in order to open Dave's toolbox. He took out the top tray and saw that the note was gone from where he'd put it early this morning. The possum tail was gone, too, along with the message he'd pinned to it. He grinned, put the tray back in, shut the lid, and then listened at the downstairs office door, where Jolene was working away at her keyboard.

He tiptoed outside and walked along the edge of the building before glancing back to make sure he was still in the clear. What he had in mind was probably going to wreck his suit, but the suit was part of his alibi, and he would cheerfully sacrifice it to put another nail in Collier's coffin. He hurried past the back of the warehouse, carrying the doll and the folded lunch sack crammed into his pants pockets, and angled across the edge of the vacant lot, covering the few steps to the shrubbery near the eucalyptus tree in seconds, where he slid into the shadows, crouching there out of sight while he caught his breath and looked around again.

So far, so good. He had never been in sight of the back of the theatre, where there was the sound of hammering now. They were hard at work, pissing away money, wasting time, putting on a "show" like Mickey Rooney and his crowd in some ridiculous old film. For people like Dave and Collier, that kind of screwing around passed for art, and they managed to buy groceries with the proceeds, en-

tirely at the Earl of Gloucester's expense. What Anne was
doing playing that game was hard to say, and it dawned on
him now that perhaps he had a calling to save her from
herself, to prevent the Daves and Colliers of the world
from using her the way they'd used the Earl over the years.

There was the sudden sound of the television set from
inside the bungalow, just now switched on—the theme
song to *Gilligan's Island*. Good. That would be Jenny,
safely inside. He looked east and saw that there were people
on the sidewalk, walking down toward the ocean, and so
he stayed put for a moment until they'd disappeared behind
the doughnut shop. Then he waited out three cars before
hunching out of the shrubbery and making his way across
ten feet of lawn to the back edge of the porch, where he
dropped to his hands and knees and crawled in behind the
night-blooming jasmine. He ducked his head under the
porch and squinted into the darkness, but the sun had been
too bright, and he could see nothing. He crawled a few feet
under and felt over his head, discovering that he could sit
up comfortably, the floor joists just skimming his head.

Sunlight shone through lattice at the front of the porch,
and he was already able to see things around him. He
looked around at the once-familiar space, at the cobwebs
and the soft dirt, the chunks of rock and the dead Bermuda
grass along the perimeter. He heard the muffled sounds of
a commercial on the television now, and realized that there
was someone walking in the house—he was surprised at
how loud it was—and then the screen door slammed, and
the footsteps scuffed on the porch over his head. Jenny
descended the steps and walked out onto the lawn. He could
see her standing there—the backs of her legs—and he wondered suddenly what he would do if Jenny chose that moment to come down into the hidey-hole with him. *That* was
something he hadn't anticipated.

Very carefully he shifted his legs out from under him
and crawled backward, pressing his back against the
wooden slats along the end of the porch, far enough back
into the shadows so that if she crawled in past the jasmine
she wouldn't see him until she was all the way in. She
would be facing away from him, too. He would let her

come in, all the way in, and then slip his hand over her mouth.

He looked around for a gag. Something to tie around her eyes, too. He didn't want to hit her. He didn't hit little girls. But she mustn't see him under there. She mustn't recognize him. She mustn't scream. He looked for her through the lattice again, but she wasn't there. He pressed himself against the wall, listening for her footsteps, for the sound of her pushing the limbs of the jasmine out of the way.

But then there was the scraping of shoes on the porch again, and the screen door banged shut. From inside the house came the sound of the television program, Gilligan and the Captain shouting at each other. He let out his breath, taking the paper sack out of his pocket with a shaking hand, and then bending forward to crawl through the dust again, deeper under the porch. He found a perfectly square patch of ground illuminated by a patch of sunlight. It happened that the illuminated area stood adjacent to an upright post—the same that he had tied Casey to all those years ago, when the dirt around it had been watered with his brother's tears. . . .

Carefully he built a card house, tilting two cards together as a foundation, and then adding cards at either end, finishing the wall at one end and leaving the other end open. The cards reeked of lighter fluid. He set the plastic doll on top of the house roof so that her back leaned against the wooden post, tilting her back so that she rested against it, the sunlight glowing on her silken hair. He studied her carefully for a moment, and then arranged her forearms so that they covered her breasts. Then he twisted her head to the side just a little, as if she were listening, as if she had been sunning herself in privacy, but had heard something, someone approaching perhaps. He ran the little Matchbox truck in through one open wall of the lower story, piling eucalyptus bark and leaves around it, resting more bark against the rough wood of the riser. Finally he laid the open, fuel-soaked lunch sack against the leaves and bark. With any luck the fire would climb the riser and ignite the porch, maybe burn the whole house down—instant eviction.

He realized then that the Night Girl's doll was hot in his

pocket, and he was struck with a sudden fear of its bursting into flame right there, igniting his clothing. . . . He fumbled it free, hurriedly setting it against the post, directly across from where Jenny's doll sat sunning itself. The two of them stared at each other, the card house neat and trim, the little truck just visible inside. Edmund took the bag away. It looked like trash sitting there. He crumpled it up, swept the twigs and leaves aside, pressed the crumpled sack against the post near the Night Girl's doll, and put the debris back around it. He took another appraising look, then rearranged it subtly.

It was perfect now, his little collage. The truck, of course, was Collier's truck. The card house was the bungalow. The doll on top . . . Well, it wasn't Anne entirely, not Anne the person. . . . It was *representative*, symbolic of the Day Girl aspect of Anne's persona. Both of them were present—the Day Girl and the Night Girl. The Night Girl's dark passion might at any moment ignite the entire collection, and it would consume the Day Girl with the flame of its own intense heat.

He saw now the totality of what it was he had created, and he was amazed at it. The entire thing was accidentally brilliant, stupefyingly brilliant. He had awakened early that morning with a mere compulsion—the vague urge to look around Collier's yard for something to use against him. And then, entirely by accident, he had found these odds and ends of junk and had taken them home, knowing they were *right* but not knowing why, bringing the nylon doll along with him, because it was right, too. And now he had fashioned this . . . this tableau; and out of nowhere this thing that he himself had fashioned had derived meaning. In effect he had summoned that meaning out of nowhere, just as he had summoned the Night Girl from that same realm.

It dawned on him then that perhaps *all* art was accidentally brilliant in just this same way. Certainly the greatest art was. An artist was simply *open* to the suggestion of meaning and form. Artistic genius was nothing more than a door, a door to which there was a secret key. He had unwittingly opened that door once again. He thought of the coming of the Night Girl, pictured the spirit door in the wall as it opened onto darkness. He breathed heavily, a little surprised at this sudden powerful insight coming at a time like this, in a place like this. It was a damned shame that he had to burn this little work of genius. But then he saw the inevitability of that, too. The fire of inspiration would become a literal fire—art fabricated out of nowhere, out of energy and passion, gone again into nowhere, and the world of these small people irrevocably changed by it.

He sat for a few more moments thinking, waiting for his mind to keep rolling, to develop the concept even further. He was onto something here, something immense, but he couldn't think any longer because of the insane chatter coming out of the television up in the house. The entire Gilligan's crew was shouting at once, and he could hear what sounded like the jabbering of monkeys and the Captain hollering for everyone to settle down, settle down, settle down. *Listen to him*, Edmund thought, and instantly there was peace on the television, as if they had responded not to the powerless and ineffective Captain, but to Edmund's command.

The wind suddenly ceased to blow outside, and as if he had been touched by an unseen hand, the hairs on his neck pricked up, and his heart leaped with an abrupt fear. He felt it again—the same presence he had felt in the storage room a couple of days ago, when he had rummaged through Anne's possessions, and out in the parking lot when he had burned Collier's truck. It was she, coming to him here! He listened for the telltale footsteps . . . and he heard them!— subtly now, like the beating of his own heart, the rushing of blood through his veins. *Step, step, step,* the leathery scrape of a nameless thing drawing closer to him, footsteps that doubtless only he could hear.

The space around him seemed abruptly close and restrictive, the small door almost infinitely far away. He realized that he was sweating, although the air beneath the porch had grown cooler, refrigerator cool. He felt claustrophobic, crushed by the pressure of the porch overhead. He took the matches out of his shirt pocket and pushed himself up onto his knees, hunching forward, leaning on his elbows to steady himself. He struck a match shakily, the head breaking off and flying away into the dirt like a tiny comet. And at that moment the Night Girl's doll, three feet away from the burning match head, ignited abruptly in an impossible whoosh of flame, singeing his arm and the side of his face. The flame seemed to roll out along the bottom of the porch floorboards like an angry wave, and he slapped at his smoking arm, smelling the stink of burning hair and choking on the sudden outpouring of smoke and fumes. Pulling his coat over his face and breathing through it, he backed away in fear and astonishment, watching as the flames engulfed the card house and the plastic doll, whose hair burned like sparklers. Her features stretched, melting in the heat. No longer strong enough to hold her arms across her breasts, she uncovered herself, exposing her flesh to the flame. Despite the heat, he watched her with avid concentration as she slowly tilted sideways and fell onto her side, turning her back to him. The card house collapsed in a low sheet of flame, the slips of bark and leaves burned higher, the flames shot up the dry wooden post. The Night Girl's doll was simply gone, consumed by the flames.

Edmund backed all the way out to the opening in the slats now, throwing the matchbook and the lighter fluid can back into the darkness and taking one last look at the collapsed and burning tableau.

He saw her then in the smoke—the girl who had helped him burn Collier's car. And he knew absolutely that she was the Night Girl herself; he could simply feel it—the presence of the same distilled emotion in the air, the dark passions, the terrible source of her desire, the sound of her footfalls as she walked through the hidden caverns of his own mind. She hovered in the air, illuminated by flame, made impossibly solid by the smoke itself. Her eyes stared straight through him, as if in that instant she had assessed his worthiness, and he was possessed with the sudden urge to bow down before her, to adore her. . . .

In his fascination he inadvertently breathed in a lungful of smoke. He lurched forward, retching and coughing, his eyes watering. In a sudden panic he pushed himself backward, cracking his head on the framing of the porch, fighting to wedge himself out through the secret entrance. Something jerked him to a stop, caught him, held him. He whimpered out loud, coughing, flailing with his arm, watching the still-hovering face of the girl in the smoke, the flames running out along the porch beams, darting toward him, dying back, springing up again.

His coat ripped, and suddenly he was free, crawling out in the open air again, only to find himself entangled in the jasmine branches. He fought his way clear and reeled wildly into the side yard, where he steadied himself against the wall of the house, shading his eyes against the glare of the sun.

⊰ 39 ⊱

THE INTERIOR OF THE OCEAN THEATRE WAS DIM, EVEN with the house lights and stage lights on. The windows were painted black to darken the theatre during matinees, and draperies of heavy black velvet cast broad areas of the black-painted wooden stage into even further shadow. To Anne, the old, decrepit theatre was just about perfect. The tattered curtains were heavy with the ghosts of hundreds of shows, and that ghostly magic echoed in the sound of the footsteps on the boards of the stage and hovered in the still air of the empty house and in the hot and dusty smell of the stage lights. She remembered dozens of trips to the theatre with her mother after Elinor's death, and what she remembered most was the enchanted moment of anticipation right before the play began, when the house lights dimmed, the music rose, and the stage lights were visible as a golden line beneath the hem of the curtains.

Just over the past few days she'd found that she had fallen instantly and comfortably into the world of this

strange little beach city theatre, as if *that's* what she had
been pursuing in her long drive south from British Columbia. And now, absurdly, it struck her as the most natural
thing in the world that she was tying two half hitches into
a rope that secured the head of a cloud-faced baby to an
overhead pulley. She yanked the knot tight and then waved
at Dave, who hauled the head into the air.

"Higher!" Collier shouted from a seat in the middle of
the house. The four-hundred-seat theatre was lined with old
cushionless mahogany seats with wire hat racks underneath
each one, relics of a bygone age. A double aisle led back
through a pair of heavy doors to a narrow lobby. Collier
waved his hand toward the ceiling, and Dave pulled on the
rope, the baby's face lifting another couple of feet into the
air.

Anne walked to the edge of the stage, near the open door
of the side entrance to the theatre, where a woman with
gray hair had just come in from outside.

"Hi," Anne said to her. "I'm Anne Morris."

"Lydia Nyles," the woman said. "I'm glad to meet
you."

"Are you in the play?" Anne asked. "An actor . . . ?"
She still had met only a few members of the cast.

"No, I'm afraid not. I'm just here on business, to talk
to Mr. Collier."

"Isn't he absolutely the best?" Anne asked. "He and
Earl Dalton are such a pair when they get going. And
Jenny's tops, too. She's lucky to have a grandfather like
Collier. He has *so* much enthusiasm. You should hear Jenny
do the scene where Cordelia and Lear have their big fight.
Collier's taught her nearly all of Cordelia's part, word for
word. It's unbelievable. I think she even understands most
of it, you know—she's not just parroting the lines."

"That's remarkable," Mrs. Nyles said. "It seems a little
unstable, though, doesn't it? Growing up in a theatre around
all these eccentric people?"

"I guess it depends on how you define stable. This place
is . . . It's got so much history and magic in it. And it's a
part of something really grand and colorful. Jenny's only
about five years old and already she's a part of something

that's understood all over the world. She's quoting Shakespeare, for God's sake, at *her* age. Maybe that's not stable like most people would mean stable, but I guess it's a kind of stable that I admire. And she's like Collier's shadow, too. They're a team. Maybe since I didn't have a father around when I grew up, I kind of envy that. And I guess I like eccentric people.''

Mrs. Nyles was silent for a moment, watching the work on the stage. "What's the point of these enormous heads?'' she asked finally.

"I'm a little hazy on it,'' Anne said. "Collier says they're a metaphor for the one-time innocence of Lear's three daughters. He also refers to them as 'spectacle.' He told me all about the theatrical value of 'spectacle.' ''

Mrs. Nyles nodded, as if she understood perfectly well.

Collier walked all the way to the back of the house now and sat down again in order to get another audience-eye view of the stage. "Another foot!'' he shouted, and Dave hauled on the line again, the head rising until it hung just below the bottom edge of the teaser curtain. "That's good!'' Collier shouted, and Dave tied the rope to a cleat and then climbed the ladder to put a stop on the rope so that the head would always descend to the same level, dead even with the other two heads.

Right then the Earl came up the stairs from the basement carrying a handful of colored gels for the lights. He shuffled through the plastic slips, finally holding one of them up and peering through it toward one of the house lights.

"Mrs. Nyles!'' he said, as if he was amazingly happy to see her.

She nodded pleasantly at him and shook his hand.

"Too much green, maybe,'' he said, waving the gel in her direction. "Give me a critical appraisal. Collier tells me you used to direct a play or two.''

"He's exaggerating,'' Mrs. Nyles said.

"We could use some help around here. Our man on the light board is threatening to go to Kansas for his daughter's wedding. You ever run a light board?''

"Not in years,'' Mrs. Nyles said. "Maybe some other

time. Really.'' She smiled at him in such a way as to put
an end to the idea.

''Bring it outside,'' Collier said to the Earl, coming up
onto the stage. ''You can see it more clearly in the sunshine. It's too damned dark in here. Well, Mrs. Nyles! What
a pleasure. I've asked her to take a part in *Lear*,'' he said
to Anne and the Earl, ''but she turned me down flat.''

''That's our loss,'' the Earl said. ''Won't reconsider?''

''Not this time,'' Mrs. Nyles said.

''Excuse us.'' The Earl nodded at Anne and Mrs. Nyles
both. ''We'll be back in a second.''

Anne watched as Collier went out through the parking
lot door. The Earl followed, but in the doorway he dropped
a half-dozen of the gels and then stooped to pick them up.
Anne started to speak to Mrs. Nyles again, but she was
interrupted by a sudden wild shout from outdoors, followed
by the sound of running footsteps and then another shout,
more distant.

⊁40⊰

EDMUND STRAIGHTENED UP, HIS COUGHING FIT OVER, AND
immediately he spotted Collier running straight toward him
across the theatre parking lot, shouting something incoher-
ent.

''Fire!'' Edmund yelled at him, and he waved his hands
over his head, as if he was purposefully trying to attract
Collier's attention. Collier was old and fat, and he almost
looked comical, coming along with his arm-swinging gait.
Edmund set out around the side of the porch at a run, shouting nonsensically now, ''Hey! Hey! Hey!'' and pointing
wildly at the house. Clearly Collier was insane with rage.
His face was a mask of anger.

"Inside!" Edmund screamed at him. "Jenny!" There was surprisingly little smoke, the freshening wind blowing most of it back in under the bungalow. Collier didn't know what the hell was going on. He had seen someone reeling out of the bushes, recognized who it was, and had gone crazy. . . .

"Dirty son-of-a-bitch!" Collier shouted at him, throwing a wild, windmilling punch, heaving himself around with the force of it, sprawling past Edmund, who easily ducked away.

"Fire! You crazy asshole!" Edmund screamed at him again. "Fire!" Other people were coming across the lot from the direction of the theatre now.

Collier spun around, understanding about the fire now, and Edmund backed away, holding his hands up defensively. Black smoke, thank God, had finally begun to billow out through the lattice, and the sight of it had stopped Collier dead. "The hose!" Edmund shouted at him, and then he turned around without another word and ran across the lawn and up the stairs. He yanked the screen door open and looked around the living room, which was empty. "Jenny!" Edmund shouted, kicking over a pole lamp for good measure as he headed straight on through toward the bedrooms.

The little girl appeared then, peering cautiously out through a half-open bedroom door. She looked curiously at him, not moving, putting a finger in her mouth. He grabbed her hand, drew her toward him, and picked her up, carrying her back out across the living room floor and out through the door, which he kicked open hard, hearing it bang against the house. Smoke was blowing back across the porch now, into the house, and he ran through the smoke, down the steps and out onto the lawn. Dave and Anne were just then arriving from the theatre. And here came the Earl, too, and an old woman in a dress, both of them following along. He heard a siren then. Someone had been bright enough to call the fire department!

Edmund set Jenny down safely at the edge of the lawn. "She's all right," he said to Anne, casting his voice a little deep. He looked briefly into Anne's face, struck suddenly with her almost supernatural similarity to the doll in his tableau beneath the porch, the way she tilted her head, just as the doll had tilted her own. For a moment he pictured Anne burning under there, looking back at him in wide wonder. . . .

He shook the image out of his head and yanked his ruined coat off, tossing it onto the grass, and then turned around and headed back toward where Collier was directing hose water through the lattice, or at least was trying to. Collier was down on his hands and knees, coughing in the smoke, the water glancing off the wooden slats and spraying him in the face. Edmund grasped the lattice with both hands and tore it entirely away, the old redwood laths splintering apart. "Here," he said, grabbing the hose away from Collier. He took a deep breath, held it, and then shoved his head in through the opening, closing his eyes against the smoke—which was mostly white now, the fire not burning nearly as savagely as he had thought it was when he was trapped beneath the porch.

Peering carefully into the flickering shadows, Edmund looked for the face in the smoke, trying to sense the presence of the child who had helped him with his task. But clearly she was gone, and most of the fire, it seemed, had gone with her.

He pointed the hose and sprayed the hell out of everything, pressing forward until his shoulders shoved through the gap, waving the hose up and down, inundating the dirt, flooding the bottom of the floorboards. The smoke cleared away, and he searched the burned debris with his eyes, trying to get a glimpse of the burned plastic doll. He felt his shirt rip, and the broken end of a piece of lath gouged him in the neck. With any luck it had cut him, and with even more luck, Collier would have managed to dampen the fire before the toys had been entirely burned so that the fire department would know that the whole thing was the work of a child, that Collier had been ignoring his pyromaniac daughter again. Water dripped onto his head and back. He saw the doll then, facing him now, her features withered, flesh charred. He had the sudden urge to take it, to keep it, to show it to the Night Girl when she came to him again tonight. He wondered how Anne would react to the sight of it.

But he controlled himself. Social Services would probably want it as evidence. All by itself, the burned doll could ruin Collier.

Edmund pushed back out of the hole, taking the hose with him. The smoke was sketchy and drifting now, clearing away. A fire truck had pulled into the theatre lot, and three helmeted firemen sprinted toward the porch, pushing past the onlookers. "I think I got it," Edmund said to them, tossing down the hose. One of the firemen kneeled in front of the hole, took a look, and then sprayed the hose under the porch again for a moment before being satisfied. Edmund walked back out into the middle of the lawn, smoothing his hair back, rolling up his sleeves. There were a dozen people standing around now—neighbors, a couple of kids. Two surfers were jogging across the vacant lot, carrying their boards under their arms, anxious to see what was going on.

"Everything's under control, folks," Edmund said, speaking to the crowd, and he bent down on one knee next to Jenny and asked, "Are you okay, darlin'?"

She nodded, clearly frightened out of her wits. Edmund looked at Anne and shook his head, trying to get the point across that this was the kind of trouble that none of them needed. He walked over to the Earl and in a low voice he said, "I'm sorry this had to happen, Dad. I saw smoke coming out through the front of the porch there and crawled underneath to have a look. The fire was already going. Lord knows how it started. Same as the car fire, I guess."

"You cut yourself," the Earl said tiredly.

Edmund wiped his neck, then looked at the blood smeared on his hand. "It's nothing."

Collier was stone-faced, staring dead ahead. Edmund wandered up to him next, searching for something to say that would irritate the old man without making him violent, something that, ideally, would sound innocent and helpful to a bystander. He folded his arms, clucking his tongue sympathetically. "It's better not to shoot water straight into a fire like that," he said. "It blows the embers around too much. What you want is a mist, a smothering mist.'' He worked his hands together in the air in order to illustrate. Collier looked at him blankly.

The fireman crawled out from under the porch and said something to the other two. One of them pried the lattice off the other side of the porch, and they sprayed the hose around under there, too, completely uselessly, from Edmund's point of view. Edmund bent down and looked underneath. The wooden post was charred, and the underside of the floorboards were smoky black, but there clearly wasn't any other damage. He saw that the fireman had brought out the doll, a couple of pieces of charred playing cards, and the lighter fluid can. One of them sniffed a card, then handed it to the other. Thank God Collier had knocked them apart with the hose before they were completely burned.

''I'm the one who spotted the fire,'' Edmund said to one of the firemen, who nodded and then ignored him. Collier headed up the side of the house. Had *he* seen the burned toys? Yes, he had. He was catching on. The old man lifted the barbecue lid, moved the charcoal sack, and then put the lid down again. He looked around, maybe hoping that he'd left the lighter fluid on the porch. Finally he turned and walked out toward the firemen.

''This is Mr. Collier,'' Edmund told them. ''He's my tenant. He and his granddaughter.''

''We've met,'' one of the firemen said.

''Of course,'' Edmund said. ''You were here the other night, when the truck burned. We were luckier this time. There doesn't look like much damage under there, although there was a hell of a lot of smoke. I saw it coming out through the lattice there and came down to check the situation out. When I saw what was burning, I summoned Mr. Collier and instructed him to get the garden hose while I went in after the little girl.''

''*Instructed!*'' Collier said, nearly spitting the word out. ''I don't need any goddamn instruction from you.''

''Hey, no harm meant,'' Edmund told him. ''I'm sorry. I guess we're all a little shook up.'' He wiped at the blood on his neck again, then made a point of staring at his bloodstained hand. Then he ran his hand over his forearm. "Singed the hair right off. I guess you don't feel the heat; you just do what you have to do. It's later on that the realization catches up to you."

"That does happen," the fireman said.

Edmund bent over and picked up his coat from where it still lay on the lawn. "Looks like something the cat dragged in," he said.

"You spotted the truck fire the other night, too, didn't you?" one of the firemen asked Edmund.

"Guilty as charged," he said. "I'm a little tired of it, too."

"Not half as tired as I am," Collier said.

"My father owns the warehouse here," Edmund told them. "I'm the general manager of it." He nodded at the Earl's. "That's my office window on the second floor. I was up there working when I glanced out and saw the smoke."

"Nobody else down here?" the first fireman asked.

"Not that I could see. I rushed straight down. Jenny— the little girl—had been out here playing a couple of minutes earlier, and I was afraid she was under there, under the porch. But I guess she went inside right before it started up. I had to move fast, I can tell you. No time to change out of my suit." He shook wet dirt out of the torn coat and folded it over his arm.

"Where were you, sir?" The fireman directed the question to Collier, who looked more lost than angry now.

"In the theatre," he said. "I sent Jenny inside to watch Gilligan, and I was heading over to check on her when I saw Edmund here crawling out from under the damn porch. I ran over to see what was up, and all of a sudden there's a fire broken out."

"Who's this Gilligan?" the fireman asked. "Some kind of pet?"

"The show," Collier said. "*Gilligan's Island.*"

The fireman nodded. "The girl was unsupervised, then?"

"For about a minute, like I said. I was right over there at the theatre, just long enough to get my sets people going, and then I intended to come back over. So let's cut the

crap.'' Edmund nearly laughed. The old man was getting
good and angry. ''Jenny didn't start this fire any more than
she started that fire the other night,'' he said. ''I'm about
sick of this kind of talk. When the hell did she have time
to light a fire? She wasn't alone longer than the blink of
an eye. And *no*body starts a house on fire and then goes
inside to watch the television. Even a four-year-old
wouldn't do a crazy damn thing like that.''

''I agree,'' Edmund said as if he meant it. ''That sounds
pretty crazy to me, too. I sure can't explain it.''

''No, I *bet* you can't,'' Collier said.

''I'm not sure I understand your implication,'' Edmund
said flatly. He looked back toward the parking lot and saw
that the crowd had pretty much gone away. Anne sat at the
edge of the lawn, playing some kind of hand jive game
with Jenny, and Dave stood talking to the Earl. The woman,
whoever she was, stood alone. ''Earl!'' Edmund hollered,
moving away from Collier and the fireman. The Earl strode
toward him, leaving Dave behind.

''Yeah,'' he said. ''What can I do?''

''Hang in here with Collier for a little while, will you?''
Edmund asked him. ''He's pretty shook up. This doesn't
look real good for Jenny, and he can see that. He's a little
defensive about it.'' Then to the fireman he said, ''Maybe
we can have a word in private.''

The fireman nodded, and they moved away, out of earshot of the others. ''I'm not happy to have to say this,''
Edmund told him, ''but Jenny's been in and out from under
that porch all morning. I know that doesn't necessarily
mean anything. But she was under there a couple of
minutes before I saw the smoke. Her grandfather doesn't
know that, because he was over in the theatre. He wasn't
over there that long, like he said, but she was under there
for . . . I don't know, five minutes anyway.'' He shook his
head sadly. ''I guess I don't know what to think. Like he
said, it doesn't make any sense, her going inside like that.
Maybe there was some kind of spontaneous combus-
tion. . . .''

''Mr. Collier asserts that you were under the porch too.''

''That's correct. I grew up around here. My father's

owned this place for nearly fifty years. I played under that porch myself when I was a kid. It's a private place. Kids love a private place. I'll tell you the truth—when I saw the smoke, I got suspicious. Like I said, I was a kid once myself."

"You started fires when you were a kid?"

The fireman looked straight at him, the dirty little bastard. Edmund fought down his anger. "I'll ignore that question," he said. "It's not the kind of thing I'd expect from a public servant."

"What did you see when you looked under there? Anything? Too smoky?"

"No, actually, the wind was blowing most of the smoke back under the house at first. I think that's why Mr. Collier didn't see any sign of it when he was coming back over from the theatre. Naturally he wondered what the hell I was doing under there. Anyway . . ." He paused and looked thoughtful, as if he had something tough to say. ". . . What I saw was a bunch of stuff burning. Looked like . . . I don't know, leaves and junk, wadded-up paper, toys, all set up against that post right about in the center of the porch. What got me was that there was a doll on fire, too, sitting in the middle of it all. I don't know why, but I guess it upset me a little bit. It was almost scary, you know? I can see now that it's not evidence of anything, maybe just kid stuff that got a little out of hand."

"But you didn't see anything that makes you *certain* that it was the little girl that started the fire? You didn't see her carry anything in or out of there?"

"Not a thing. No, sir. All I wanted to say was that she was under there. Her grandfather doesn't know that. He's telling you the absolute truth as far as he understands it."

"And there were no other children around?"

"Not a one."

"All right. Thanks for your help."

"Thank *you*. I wonder if I can say one more thing. I guess . . . I don't want it to sound like I'm accusing anybody here, but I'm not crazy about fires breaking out every other day, either. These old buildings . . ." He shook his head. "I've got employees working here, there's a play going up in a couple of weeks here in the theatre, and I've got my tenants to worry about. This could have been a tragedy today if I hadn't looked out the window when I did.''

"I appreciate that," the fireman said. "I couldn't agree with you more."

The fireman left him and walked toward Collier then, and Edmund drifted back to the porch and looked underneath. He pursed his lips and cocked his head, as if he were studying things out. The whole thing had gone unbelievably well. Not a hitch. This time nobody would buy any nonsense about imaginary friends. Collier's days were numbered.

Edmund turned around and headed back across the lawn in the direction of the warehouse. There was nothing more for him to do here, and his hanging around could easily set Collier off. The man was dangerously unstable, aside from being a loser and a welfare case. But he still had too much sympathy from the peanut gallery for Edmund to go *mano a mano* with him here. Today's activities would have to be a part of the tenderizing process. Later he could grill the old man over an open flame, literally, if he had to.

"Edmund!"

He heard the voice behind him and turned around, putting a quizzical look on his face. It was Dave, obviously full of baloney. Anne hadn't moved. They were out of earshot if they kept their voices down. "What's up?" Edmund asked, giving him a look of doubt, as if perhaps Dave were in some sort of immediate trouble and were asking for help.

Dave moved past him, blocking his way. "I just wanted to make a little something clear," he said.

"And what would that be?"

"I don't think it was Jenny who started this fire today. And it wasn't her who started the fire the other night, either."

"I agree entirely, Dave. She's a *very* misunderstood little girl. And I admire your stepping forward now, at a sensitive time like this. You're telling the wrong person, though. All I did was *rescue* her, Dave. You know what I mean? You and I don't always see eye to eye, but I can't imagine you're so small-minded as to have a problem with that. Maybe it's time you crawled out from under your past.''

Dave stared at him, and for a moment Edmund wondered if he'd gone too far. He braced himself, ready to block a punch.

''You want to explain that?''

''What's to explain? A little girl was in trouble, and I walked in and brought her out. People do that kind of thing all the time, Dave, and they don't make it into a lifetime issue. So now, if you're through, I'm late for about three meetings and I've got to run home and change suits and wash the blood off.'' He saw that Dave wasn't going to take a punch at him after all. He had gotten to the bastard, deflated him. He stepped aside and started off again, across the lot.

''I'll make it simple,'' Dave said to his back. ''Leave Collier alone. Leave Anne alone.''

Edmund turned toward him again and shook his head tiredly. ''My relationship with Anne is none of your business, Dave. Although I can understand why you're worried about it.''

''I'm making it my business. Stay out of her building. Don't hang around there.''

''Dave, I'm reminding you who signs your paycheck.''

''Makes no difference.''

''Really?''

''Not a bit.''

''Then you're fired. I can't have my employees threatening me. I'm sorry.''

''No, you're not sorry, and I'm not fired. The Earl hired me, and the Earl's got to fire me. Go ahead and ask him to. I don't think he will. What I think is that you've got your hand in the till, *Ed*. I think you're stealing from the Earl, and I think I can prove it.''

''Is *that* what you want to do?'' Edmund said, walking toward him and stopping a couple of feet away. ''You want to cause my father grief by making up a lot of slanderous crap? I'm a little surprised at that, Dave. I've always known you were emotional, but I didn't have any idea you were vicious.''

"Call it what you want. I'm ready to pull the plug. I'm not going to talk about this again. I'm serious."

"Not half as serious as I am, Dave."

"Then we understand each other."

Edmund smiled at him, giving the smile a moment to affect him. "I think we do," he said, and then walked away from him again, half expecting Dave to jump him from behind, to lose his sanity altogether. He half hoped he would. He could have him arrested for assault.

⊰ 41 ⊱

MAYHEW HAD BEEN HARD TO GET RID OF, ALTHOUGH IN the end he had taken Ray Mifflin's twenty-five dollars and two packs of cigarettes. He was dressed in the same faded yellow coat that he'd worn when he'd pretended to be Edmund Dalton's father, and with the same leisure suit, and true to form, he had headed next door to the liquor store to buy a morning bottle before walking away south again down Beach Boulevard.

Mifflin sat in his swivel chair now and stared out the window at the afternoon traffic, running through what he'd say to Dalton when the time came to bail out. Dalton wouldn't make it easy on him. But in the end—and Dalton *had* to know this—if one of them went down, they would both go down. Dalton's options were as limited as his own. And if push came absolutely to shove, Mifflin *could* simply turn him in. He could claim to have been hoaxed by the Mayhew fraud and then admit to relaxing the rules a couple of times afterward, not knowing that Dalton was up to any kind of real malarkey. The money that he had taken from Edmund had been cash. He hadn't signed any receipts. And so far he hadn't put a dime of it in the bank, so there were no big deposits to look suspicious to anyone snooping around.

So on the plus side of the ledger, he had made over fifteen thousand dollars in no time at all. No effort, no expenses, no trouble. He was on the edge of making more quick. Dalton had been right. Right Now Notary was pathetic. It was a living, but that's about all it was. Mifflin was sick of the trash-strewn strip mall, of the crush of petty business every winter, of the smell of stale coffee and the mountains of forms and the whole damned squalid thing that his life had become.

Thoughts of Mexico turned in his mind, and he doodled with a pencil on a piece of paper, adding up figures. What the hell would it take? The house in Punta Rioja needed work, but cheap labor was easy to find down there. A wife, for God's sake, was easy to find down there, or at least it was a hell of a lot easier down there than up here. Since he'd put on weight and his hairline had receded, his chances for companionship had fallen to absolute zip. He had even bought an issue of *Cherry Blossoms* in order to check out the possibility of buying a Filipino bride, but the next morning, when he had come out into the living room and seen the magazine on the table, he'd been so humiliated that he had tossed it into the trash.

He threw his pencil at the front door and pushed himself back from the desk. What was utterly clear to him was that Mayhew would soon favor him with another visit. And why not? Mifflin was easy money, and Mayhew knew it. Mayhew was an old drunk, but he wasn't a naive old drunk. He had been tolerably sober on the morning that he had impersonated Dalton's father, and he had taken a damn good look at the deed that he'd signed. Probably he knew that there was real money involved in the transaction. Mayhew was in a position to nickel-and-dime everyone involved until Hell froze over.

He hadn't been happy with the twenty-five bucks he'd gotten this morning, either. Dalton, the old man had told him, had given him fifty. And "that other guy" had given him twenty more. What the hell "other guy"? Mayhew wouldn't say. He had shaken his head shrewdly, as if he

wouldn't be outfoxed, as if he thought Mifflin himself
would start knocking people over for twenty-five bucks
himself, and wreck Mayhew's deal. *So who the hell was
the other guy?* Not Jimmy Stewart, unless he was paying
Mayhew for information. . . .

As much as he hated to talk to the man, Mifflin picked
up the phone and dialed Dalton's number. "We've got
more trouble," he said when Dalton answered.

42

THE FOG DRIFTED IN EARLY THAT EVENING, A MOVING
wall that came in off the ocean, drawn toward the warmth
of the coast. Anne and Dave watched it cross the Highway
from where they stood in front of Jack's Surf Shop at the
bottom of Main Street, and in moments it engulfed them.
They walked west along the sidewalk toward the doughnut
shop, cutting up the path through the vacant lot.

"Is it like this every spring?" Anne asked.

"Not really," Dave said. "I think it's foggy more often
in the early fall. It used to be worse, back when most of
Fountain Valley was agriculture. The fog would get so
thick that you had to drive with the door open, watching
the white line."

"Agriculture?" Anne asked. "How long ago?" They
passed the doughnut shop and turned up the path through
the foggy vacant lot.

"When I was a kid," Dave said. "Once it started to go,
though, it went fast, like the oil wells. It only took a couple
of years. The real estate was worth too much."

Anne stopped on the path and looked up at him. "What
did they grow," she asked softly, "hamsters?" The fog hid
them from the Highway and from 6th Street.

"A lot of hamsters," Dave said, nodding. "Hamsters and guinea pickles." He stood looking at her, his heart pounding. "Mostly they grew sugar beets."

"Sugar beets?"

"Looks like a sweet potato," Dave said. "They make sugar out of it."

"Why don't they call it a sugar potato?" she asked, looking at him doubtfully. "I think you're making all this up to impress me with your vast storehouse of knowledge."

"Why would I want to do that?"

"Because you're thinking that you want to kiss me, and you know I have high standards."

He hesitated, looking into her eyes.

"Yes, that was an invitation," she said. "Don't be hopeless."

He kissed her then, sliding his hands up under her jacket in order to hold her more closely.

"That was rather nice," she said after a moment. "I was afraid maybe you were waiting for a printed invitation."

"I'm slow that way," he said.

"Good," she told him. "I like slow men. Slow and goofy."

"Well," he said, "you found one. After all these years of searching."

"It seems like we're alone in the world, doesn't it?" Anne whispered. They listened to the slow creaking of the invisible oil well and to the sound of surf collapsing along the beach behind them. A dog barked somewhere in the distance, but it sounded as if it were a long way off, and after a moment another dog barked once, as if to answer it, and then both of them were silent. Dave kissed her again, uninvited this time, and then they set out again, walking past the chain-link fence toward the back of the Earl's.

The breeze died, the fog hung still in the air around them, and Dave was aware suddenly of a change in the atmosphere. The temperature seemed to decline at the moment that the breeze fell, and he could hear his own heart beating with remarkable clarity. Their own footfalls seemed to echo off the high wooden wall of the warehouse, and from somewhere out in the night, from some indefinable direction, there was the sound of someone else walking, matching them step for step, like an echo.

Anne's hand tightened over his, and she drew him to a sudden stop. The slow, scraping tread continued, and Dave could smell burning on the night air now, very faint, as if it came to them from miles and miles away.

"Do you hear it?" Anne said.

"The footsteps?"

"Yes." She looked around nervously. "Listen how they're not from any single direction. They're all around us."

"Maybe that's just a trick of the fog."

"It's *not* the fog," she said. "It's something else."

"*What* else?" he asked. "You're starting to spook the hell out of me."

"I don't know what else. . . . Look." She stopped again. The lights from Collier's front porch glowed to their left. The front door of the bungalow was open. Jenny stood on the porch dressed in a nightgown that dragged on the ground. She wore a feathered boa around her neck, and she stood staring out into the fog, toward the corner of the warehouse, near where the truck fire had broken out.

"Do you see her?" Anne whispered. She squeezed Dave's hand again, as if to compel his attention.

He *did* see her now—a red figure in the fog, standing still along the wall of the warehouse, her back turned toward them. It seemed to Dave, impossibly, that he could see the clapboards *through* her. He knew at once who, or what, he was looking at, knew that Anne was right about the odd sound of the footfalls. The figure wavered in the moving fog, now a nearly transparent red shadow, then something more solid, as if focused by the mist. Her hand moved across the gray clapboard, strobing in the light from the porch lamp, and there was a soft knocking and scraping, as if she were running her nails across the chalky old paint. Then she vanished, leaving a ghostly white patch of fog that faded into the gray of the surrounding night.

"That's her," Jenny said behind them, and Dave lurched in surprise at the sound of her voice. She had come down off the porch and stood behind them now.

"That's *who*?" Anne asked her softly.

Dave could see that there were marks on the wall—charcoal streaks, not in any pattern or picture, but feeble smears, utterly meaningless. A piece of charred wood lay on the ground, reminding Dave of the story that Anne had told him about her visit to Scotland.

"That's the *one*," Jenny said emphatically. "The one I said."

"Your imaginary friend?" Anne asked.

She shook her head hard.

"She's the one who started the fire," Dave said.

Jenny nodded, hugging herself now, as if she suddenly realized she was cold.

"What's her name?" Anne asked. "Do you know her name?"

"Elinor," Jenny said.

⊰43⊱

MORE TROUBLE ... THAT WAS RAY MIFFLIN'S CONSTANT complaint, and Edmund was tired of it. Edmund hated being tired of anything. Clearly it was time to do a little bit of housecleaning—throw some refuse into the trash bin. He turned left off the Highway, up Main Street into downtown Seal Beach. His rented Ford was charged to Ray Mifflin's Mastercard. Cheapskate Rent-a-car had an inventory of about eight cars and operated out of a building that was a remodeled gas station in Long Beach, on a bad block of Cherry Avenue. Hosing the kid at the counter had been easy—a false mustache, a bunch of mousse to slick his hair back, a suit and tie. Thank God he didn't look a *hell* of a lot like Ray Mifflin, just enough to rent a car with the man's I.D. He had even gotten the signature right.

Stealing Mifflin's Mastercard and driver's license had been even easier. Mifflin was in the habit of leaving his wallet on the desktop, because it was too incredibly fat to sit on. Slipping the credit card and license out of it had been the work of a moment, and Edmund was betting that Mifflin wouldn't look for either one of them tonight. After a long day's work, Mifflin would be heading home to an easy chair and a bottle of vin ordinaire; he wouldn't be out throwing the plastic around. And unless he was pulled over by a cop, the license wouldn't be an issue either. If he did discover them missing, he'd think he left them somewhere, and even if he reported the Mastercard missing or stolen now, so what? Tomorrow or the next day Edmund could shove it through the mail slot in the front door of Right Now Notary, and Mifflin would find it. Probably it would confuse the hell out of him.

It was past ten, and the shops in downtown Seal Beach were closed, although there were still a couple of bars open and a few scattered pedestrians on the sidewalks. The evening was foggy again, and Edmund switched on the wipers, watching the red glow of the traffic light at Central appear out of the mist. He had always hated fog, but it was just what the doctor ordered tonight. Just to be safe, on his way north he had pulled over in a parking lot in Sunset Beach and disconnected his license plate lamp, although he couldn't fix his mind on any real reason for having done so. Like so many other things, it fell into the category of inspiration.

Mifflin had been right, in his tiresome way. Mayhew was turning into a loose cannon, and it was time that Edmund defused him. Hiring him in the first place had been a mistake. He was apparently totally venal, no honor at all. Edmund turned left at Ocean Boulevard and slowed down, immediately spotting the old man standing near the foot of the pier. His clothes were disheveled and his hair was a frizzled mass in the wet air. Edmund lowered the passenger window, leaned across the seat, and whistled. Mayhew looked up as if he had been startled out of sleep, and then hurried across the fifteen feet of sidewalk, opened the car door, and climbed in.

A pair of foot travelers loomed out of the fog, heading across Ocean toward the pier, and Edmund accelerated slowly away from the curb, even before Mayhew's door was shut, in order to keep the rental car out of focus to them. *Just a ghost*, he thought, and the idea of it sent a thrill through him. He turned up 10th Street, through the neighborhood east of Main, where the streets were empty, the houses obscured by the fog, the car's wipers swishing back and forth at five second intervals. A cat darted out into the street from beneath a parked car, and Edmund swerved toward it, veering off at the last moment when he realized he couldn't hit it without running into an ivy-covered palm tree at the curb. The cat bounded up a driveway and disappeared.

"What the hell was that all about?" Mayhew asked him. The old man had an incredulous look on his face.

Edmund didn't say anything. He had a nearly over-whelming urge to spit on the old man, but he mastered it, and he swallowed heavily, sucking his mouth dry of saliva. He had spit on a woman in a supermarket parking lot yesterday when she had failed to move her shopping cart out of the way of his car. The act had turned her instantly into a screaming psychotic, and he had waited for her to see that he was laughing before driving calmly away. She had thrown a box of something at him, which had fallen piti-fully short, and that had made the whole thing even funnier, and it was all he could do not to circle the parking lot and spit on her again, maybe run her down right there on the spot.

He realized that Mayhew was still staring at him. After a moment the old man looked away, watching the shadowy houses slip past. At the Highway, Edmund turned right, heading back down through Surfside toward Sunset Beach again. He wasn't sure what their destination was yet. He would play this one entirely by ear, wait for the inspiration that he knew would come. The night would supply some-thing if only he opened his mind to it. The presence of the old man in the car congested him, though, interfered with his natural artistic impulses, him and his goddamn accu-satory staring.

Maybe he would play cat-and-mouse with old Mayhew—force him out of the car at gunpoint. Kick him in the knees and then make him crawl around a deserted parking lot while Edmund buzzed him in the rental car, closer and closer. He pictured the panic in the old man's eyes, the sound of the car glancing off a hip, bumping over a foot, old Mayhew limping along ahead of the bumper, the air wheezing out of his lungs. He'd *know* what the hell it was all about then. He wouldn't have to ask. Edmund would have to kill him finally, of course, but that would rid the world of one more piece of human trash. . . .

He fought to control his temper. If there was one thing that murdered artistic impulses, it was temper.

"What's the deal this time?" Mayhew asked him finally. He sounded tired out, the poor old thing.

"How are you feeling?" Edmund asked him, filling his voice with concern. "Have you eaten today? Have you had a chance to bathe?"

"What's the goddamn deal?"

"Which goddamn deal was that?"

The old man was silent for a moment. Then he said, "I shagged a ride up to the Glider Inn with a man I know, but I had to walk from there. The whole thing took me three hours, and then I stood there at the pier for two more. That's five hours I've got in this transaction so far."

"I honestly appreciate that."

"Well, that's good. Because you didn't appreciate it worth a damn last time. I keep wearing out shoe leather while you get fat. That's *got* to stop."

"I couldn't agree with you more, Mr. Mayhew." They cruised past Bolsa Chica Beach, along the dark Highway. So far the night was moonless, and the fog obscured any starlight. They might have been traveling in the middle of a desert.

"As an independent contractor," Mayhew said, "I've got to look out after myself."

"That's an attitude I can sympathize with. You're a man of business. You're an independent contractor. God, that sounds just right, doesn't it? A *con*tractor." Edmund considered the possibility of pulling over right here and cutting

Mayhew's tongue out as he had promised to do, but there was nowhere to park except on the Highway itself. It was past the beach curfew, and a lone parked car would draw too much attention to itself, rental or no rental. And besides that, he didn't have any quarters for the meter. He laughed out loud at the very idea of it. How many quarters would it take, at fifteen minutes a pop, to buy enough time to murder a man? One would do it.

Abruptly he made the decision to head farther south, to draw this out, whatever it was, while he waited for true inspiration. So far he was just jazzing around here. He couldn't see a clear structure yet, artistically speaking. He had loaded the trunk of the car with his tools, just as would any artist. But until you found your true subject, how did you know if you wanted oils or pastels, marble or wood or plaster of Paris? Something told him that this one would be a bigger undertaking than anything else so far, that he had been warming up to this, learning his craft. It was no time to be hasty.

"If we're heading back into Huntington anyway," Mayhew said, "then I can't see why the hell I killed the last five hours hauling myself up to Seal."

"You can't *see*."

"That's right. I could have stayed in town. All this folderol of yours is pure crap, if you ask me."

"You'll be compensated for your time, Mr. Mayhew."

"In what way? That's all I'm trying to find out here."

"What did you have in mind?" Edmund looked sharply at him. "If you're an independent contractor, make me a bid."

"Ten dollars an hour for the five hours I've already got in this, another fifty for my services, and ten an hour to get me back home again. And I don't mean to the Seal Beach Pier, either. I mean home. I don't mind a cab, but you pay for the cab, tip and all. I don't stiff a cab driver on a tip."

"Well . . . I don't think that's out of line at all."

"Good. Because if you *do*, you can let me off right up ahead, right here at Seventh Street, and I'll walk to my place."

Edmund drove through the green light at 7th, and then

made the light at Main, accelerating up the Highway toward Newport Beach. "That won't be necessary. I'm happy to pay you a fair price. Your services are invaluable to me."

"Your idea of a fair price and my idea are two different things. I hope you don't mind my saying that."

"I don't mind at all. But it seems to me that we've already exhausted the wage talk, Mr. Mayhew. We've got a ways to go, and I want to think something through. You wouldn't mind if I put on a little music?"

"Suit yourself."

"Thank you." Edmund pushed a cassette into the player and turned up the sound—a randomly chosen volume of "Melodies of the Masters." It was perfect mood music, all the great melodies, just the good parts, not drawn out so far that you got bored by them. He kept his eyes on the road, listening to the music and trying to put the old man out of his mind, which would have been more possible if he didn't stink so badly. He glanced at him again, but Mayhew was looking out of the window, and in that moment, with the highway lights glowing through the windshield, he was a dead ringer for the Earl. It wasn't just the way he looked, either, it was his whole attitude. It was a bum attitude. A lazy, shiftless, ignorant, lily-of-the-field attitude, and it made Edmund sick. The Earl had made some money by dumb luck, and then when his wife died—Edmund's mother—he just quit. It was as simple as that. He had given up, and had decided to act happy, and had surrounded himself with forty tons of weird juju crap.

Casey was the same way, of course, except he was a drunk. Their mother had died giving birth to Casey, which was the first and last piece of evidence Edmund needed that the world wasn't fair, that it didn't matter a damned bit who lived and who died. Casey was bound for a life in the streets, just like Mayhew, begging for money, lying, drunk without even trying to hide it. The worst part about that attitude was how damned *superior* they were about it despite the damage they did. They had the world all worked out. They wore their crappy rags like a coat of many colors, like any self-respecting man wore his three-piece suit, and they would tell you to your face that it was *your* suit that

was the problem, that it was *you*. Then they'd ask you for
ten dollars an hour, which they'd spend on bourbon and
canned pudding.

He couldn't remember a time that he hadn't been
ashamed of his father, of their crappy car, of his crappy
sack lunches and his Sears and Roebuck jeans. And they
were *rich*, too. He had read enough of Freud to understand
complexes. He knew that a man's desire to kill his own
father was simply the desire for freedom, the desire to rid
himself of influences that kept his own energies bound and
gagged, his spirit blocked. Patricide, according to Freud,
was simple freedom.

There were locked doors that had to be opened. Some
men had opened those doors and been overwhelmed by
what lay on the other side—their nighttime selves, shadows
of unimaginable things. But those shadows only hid the
secret colors of the world, a palette of deep hues that an
artist might borrow from—a daub here, a tint over there—
in order to paint his own way into wholeness and self-
actualization.

The fog rolled across the Highway now, and the late-
night lights of Corona del Mar slipped past, the town
asleep. Edmund recalled the painting he had seen in the
storeroom, the Night Girl's painting—the confusion of
leaves and insects, the shadows, the dark suggestion that
there was something hidden back in among the nightmare
trees, something waiting and watching, breathing from the
very brush strokes themselves, something that only the
strong and the truly curious would want to see. Perhaps
only the strong and the curious could *stand* to see it.

Whatever it was, it was something that Anne the Day
Girl blocked out of her world by day just as she blocked it
out of her paintings. Only by finding her way into the night
again would she find her way to the heart of it once more.
If you could look at truth squarely, without fear, without
judgment, you could see straight into the deep and hidden
realms of your mind, as into the depths of a suddenly still
tide pool. And there in that hidden realm lay true darkness,
the combination of all natural colors. . . .

He saw the shadow of a woman walking among the roadside trees in the very moment that the car sped past her, and in that instant, when he was consumed by the very image of darkness, he knew who she was—the Night Girl, her black hair swept back on the ocean wind, her flesh pale in the misty moonlight.

He braked hard, throwing Mayhew forward. The old man grunted, pressing his hands against the dash. The car bumped onto the shoulder, and there was the sound of flying gravel, a cloud of dust rising behind them, obscuring his vision in the rearview mirror. He threw the car into reverse and accelerated backward toward the fog-shrouded trees, a hundred yards behind him now, which bordered the entrance to a guarded, cliffside community. A car swerved past, honking wildly, and Edmund slowed down, searching the night with his eyes, the trees looming up at them out of the fog.

"Did you see her?" he asked, his voice husky. He licked his lips, stopping the car in front of the half-dozen trees—heavy-trunked camphor trees with long, ground-sweeping limbs.

"Who?"

"The woman. Did you see a woman walking?"

"When?"

"Just now, for God's sake. Right here."

But there was no one visible now. On beyond the trees stood a barbed wire fence that divided the scrub-covered bluffs from the Highway. There were lights mounted on the outside of the tiny guardhouse, which sat square in the middle of the entrance road, and the lights illuminated the road itself, which was empty of people. Fog drifted through the trees. Another car passed on the highway.

"I didn't see any damn woman," Mayhew said.

"No, you wouldn't have. Of course you wouldn't have." Edmund looked at him sharply, just now realizing the truth. Why *should* Mayhew have seen her? He didn't have the power to see her. He had lost his capacity to see anything at all beyond the label on a bottle. Edmund waited another moment, then accelerated slowly forward again, suddenly anxious to discover what the night would bring him. She was *with* him. That's why she had appeared to him. He recalled the dismembering of the spiders, the two of them crouched together on the carpet, breathing as one, his fingers capable of incredibly delicate work. . . .

And now he saw her again, walking in the fog, in the darkness. Again they passed her before he could slow down. He couldn't see her in the rearview mirror.

He slowed the car, although he knew he wouldn't go back this time. He wouldn't search for her. She would make herself known to him. He glanced at Mayhew, but the old man had clearly seen nothing, and when, a quarter mile farther on, she appeared again, Edmund said, "Take a look at that," and nodded hard at the side of the road.

"What?" Mayhew asked.

"Boo!" Edmund yelled at him, straight into his face.

Mayhew flinched, recoiling toward the window, his hand going for the door handle again. Edmund laughed. "Relax," he said. "We're nearly there. You didn't wet your pants, did you? These are leather seats."

The music tape came to an end just then, and the sudden silence was full of significance. They were just north of Laguna Beach now, along a deserted stretch of highway a mile up from Scotchman's Cove. There were empty foothills on the left; on the right lay vegetation-covered bluffs that stretched away toward the ocean. "The sounds of silence . . ." Edmund muttered, slowing down. He glanced again into the rearview mirror at the empty asphalt behind them, and then pulled off the road and onto the shoulder.

SUDDENLY AWARE OF A SWISH OF SOUND, ANNE SET HER brush down and listened. But now it had disappeared, as if her awareness of it had stopped it. There was the noise of traffic, of activity down on the street, but nothing more.

What she thought she'd heard had been closer, very close, like someone walking on the carpeted corridor outside. She glanced up at the door, which was bolted and chained, and then listened for another moment. There was nothing out there in the hallway, she told herself, and at the same time she knew that there was no way she was going to open the door and look.

She realized that she was spooked: probably the incident of the note on the door had done it to her, the idea that Edmund Dalton had been up here lurking around, and that she hadn't known it. It wouldn't be the first time that a man had paid her an unwanted visit, but in the past she had always managed to be firm enough to get the point across. Edmund Dalton was too weird to get the point. Not that she had tried very hard to drive him away. In fact, obviously this was something that she was going to have to live with until she came right out and told him that she didn't want him around, which she'd better do, or else stop complaining.

She shook off the distracting thoughts and focused on the painting that was taking shape on her canvas. Most of the canvas was still just covered with gesso, the soft ripples of white priming partly covered with blue-gray sky. The sky was too carefree still, too much a springtime sky. She wanted winter—more gray, something that would contrast fiercely with the white and iron-gray of storm clouds. She didn't like the painting yet, even though there wasn't enough of it yet to dislike. Sometimes when she started a piece there was something in it—or in her—that was so perfectly right that she knew the work was going to be good. That wasn't happening now.

Tonight she felt particularly nervous, as if something were pending, a thunderstorm waiting to break. She squeezed gray paint onto her palette, picked up a can of copal, and dripped the liquid into the paint, mixing it with the brush and then dripping more copal into it to get the consistency right. She swirled the brush in turpentine to clean it, the pine smell of the turpentine rising around her. Realizing abruptly that she was dizzy, she capped the turpentine jar. Her blood rushed in her ears, and she could

hear her own heart beating within the rush of blood. The
lights in the room were unnaturally dim, as if the power
had diminished, and she heard the sound of someone treading on carpet again, a languid swishing that matched her
heartbeat. The sound grew more insistent, louder, well defined, as if a sentry were pacing beyond the door. And
almost lost within the footfalls was a small ticking sound,
an insect sound, the sound of a fingernail tapping on a
window.

"Elinor?" Anne whispered the name. She waited, holding her breath, not daring to move.

There was a brief, acrid smell of musty burning, like
smoke on a sudden gust of wind. She looked back at the
windows, half expecting to see her sister's reflection in the
glass, and a wave of anger washed through her. She had
put up with Elinor's nasty games while her sister was alive,
and here, all these years later, she was still putting up with
them. "Elinor!" she said, louder now, in a voice that she
meant to be commanding, but which sounded small and
unconvincing to her. She was struck then with how cold
the room had grown, a refrigerator cold that had entered
the room like a presence.

The tapping and clicking emanated from near her foot.
She stepped away from her easel, full of the urge to run
into the bedroom and shut the door, just as she had run out
of the bookstore in Victoria, just as she had run from what
she'd seen on the pier. Then she saw what it was that was
rattling. A tube of red paint lay on the floor among a litter
of other half-empty tubes and laid-out brushes. The tube
rocked forward and backward, as if something small and
ineffectual were trying to move it. The tube rocked again
as she watched, the metal collar of the tube tap-tapping on
the wooden floor. The tube fell momentarily still. And then
slowly, almost imperceptibly at first, the cap on the tube
began to turn. The tube itself began to shake, vibrating in
the grip of a weak and unseen hand. The cap turned a quarter turn, and then, as if the focus of energy had exhausted
itself, it fell still once more, and the atmosphere in the room
seemed to hold its breath.

Anne knew, though, that it wasn't done; whatever had

come into the room was still present. The tube vibrated
again briefly, then was tossed a half inch into the air, clicking against the floor again, the cap turning slowly and
smoothly now, as if something were putting tremendous
effort into the struggle. She watched with horror and fascination, half tempted to stomp on the tube with her tennis
shoe as if it were an insect, a living thing. The tube lay
still now, but the cap continued to turn, abruptly falling off
the end of the tube and lying before it paint side up. She
realized that the footsteps had fallen silent, that the entire
night was silent, the street noise held outside by the tremendous, cold pressure in the room.

"Go away," Anne said, forcing a calmness into her
voice that she didn't feel.

The pressure in the room increased, and she swallowed
to clear her ears. "Elinor, go away," she said again.

And then slowly, as if something enormous leaned its
weight against it, the paint tube flattened along its entire
length, the red oil squeezing out onto the floor. The tube
itself vibrated urgently, slowly spinning counterclockwise,
smearing through the already squeezed-out paint, faster and
faster, dragging the paint in a whorl of patchy red across
the floor. Anne stepped away from it, holding her hands up
defensively. The tube spun like a top, then skittered away,
clacking against the door and lying still. The lights in the
room flared suddenly and then dimmed again, and the smell
of smoke, of burning wool and rat hide, nearly choked her.
The door shook on its hinges, clacking in its frame, the
loose old iron knob clattering, the chain lock rattling. She
stepped backward toward the bedroom, the pressure itself
forcing her back, an invisible wall of moving resistance.

The squeezed-out tube of paint levitated for a moment
above the floor. She turned and ran, pushing the bedroom
door open in front of her, feeling something hit her on the
leg in the moment that she was through it. The apartment
fell silent now. Almost instantaneously the burning smell
diminished in intensity until it was gone. She heard voices
from down on the street, the sound of passing cars, distant
music. She knew with utter certainty now that she was
alone in the apartment. Elinor had vanished again, although

certainly not because of any of Anne's feeble commands. She opened the bedroom door and peered out. The lights were their normal cheerful yellow color, and there was no hint of the chill air.

She picked up the sticky paint tube from the floor in front of the door and stepped out into the living room, dropping the tube into the wooden box that she kept her paints in. She hugged herself, licking her dry lips, wondering if the noise would start up again, if the temperature would drop.

Elinor. She thought the name. *Was* this Elinor? Or was this something else, some ghost in the wires of her own psyche that she herself infected with the recollected remnants of Elinor's dark and unhappy presence? Perhaps her own fear of Elinor's ghost gave the ghost life. She had dragged it with her from Vancouver Island, as if it were another piece of luggage.

In the living room she looked at the painting on the easel. There was a streak of red paint across the gray-green ocean. There was another smear of red paint on the back of her jeans where the tube had struck her.

She picked up a palette knife and carefully scraped the painting clean, thinking of her birthday cake, of the traces of chocolate frosting on the canvas and floor, far from where the cake had fallen. Elinor's destructive gestures struck her as feeble suddenly: all this ghostly energy expended, all the shaking and rattling and terrible pressure for the sake of some pitifully weak and infantile statement. *Elinor*, she thought, shaking her head, *get a life.*

Her laughter diminished when she thought of Elinor's paintings, and of the dolls, wrapped and boxed and stored in the warehouse. She hadn't looked at her dead sister's paintings when she'd wrapped them two months ago. She couldn't stand to. She quite simply hated and feared them in a way nearly equal to her hatred and fear of Elinor herself. And yet Anne had carted them along with her, those dolls and paintings—all that was left of her long-dead sister.

A chill ran through her, and she abruptly picked up the telephone and dialed Dave's number. But there was no answer at Dave's end.

❧ 45 ❧

EDMUND LEFT THE CAR ENGINE RUNNING. HE SAT STUDY-
ing Mayhew, ideas flitting in and out of his mind like bats.
He was hot, and his flesh tingled as if he were completely
wired.

"What the hell is this?" Mayhew asked him.

"We're meeting someone."

"Out here?"

Edmund saw that there was a dirt road ahead on the right,
leading out onto the bluffs. Synchronicity again—the music
dying just at the moment that the road had appeared. It was
all clicking, all coming together. What looked like coinci-
dence *always* turned out to be something more. He drove
forward slowly now and turned down the road, the car
bumping along over rocks and chuckholes, the Highway
disappearing behind them. Mayhew shifted uneasily in his
seat, clearly wide awake. He darted a glance toward the
door lock, and just to frost the cake, just to give him a
thrill, Edmund pushed the lock switch, and there was the
click of the doors locking. "Dangerous road," Edmund
told him.

"Damn straight it is," Mayhew said, looking uneasily
out the window. "You know, I got friends who know
where I am."

"Don't concern yourself with any of this," Edmund
said. "Mr. Mifflin, the man we worked with before, lives
down in Laguna. We're meeting him out here."

"Why?"

"He stables his horses near here. He's quite an avid
equestrian." There were, in fact, horse trails along the
bluffs, and Mayhew didn't contradict him. Edmund

switched off the headlights now, and the sudden darkness was so deep that he braked hard and stopped the car. There were black shadows around them—the outline of ragged shrubs against the grayer darkness of the foggy night sky, which barely glowed with moonlight. He switched the dashboard lights back on.

"If you had something to say, you didn't have to haul me way to hell and gone out here."

"On the contrary," Edmund told him. "That's just what I had to do."

"Okay. I guess I get it. I'm scared. Is that what you want? I'm scared as hell. Look, I'm shaking bad." He held his hand out.

Edmund glanced in the rearview mirror. The dust had settled, and the fog was impenetrable. The night was silent except for the whirring of the fan under the hood. From somewhere ahead of them there was the sound of waves breaking. He could hear the old man's breathing.

"If you were dissatisfied with what I paid you for your services last time, you should have spoken up," Edmund told him, "and not gone talking to my employees." He kept his expression flat and unreadable, as if he were merely making an observation.

"Is *that* what this is about? God almighty . . ."

"Now, Mr. Mayhew . . ." Edmund shook his head and smiled faintly. "*Why* was it necessary that my employees learn about our business transaction with Mr. Mifflin?"

"Necessary? It wasn't necessary. I came around looking for *you*. The man I spoke to loaned me enough money to see me through a couple of days, that's all. If you'd have *paid* me . . ."

"That can't be *all*, can it? I got a call from our friend Mr. Mifflin. He was *very* upset. The man you spoke to has tried to turn this to his advantage. I believe that you meant to turn it to your advantage, too."

"By God, I did *not*. Whatever this man did, I didn't mean for it to happen. All I wanted was another twenty lousy bucks."

"Did you mean for *this* to happen?" He took a .45 caliber derringer out from his inside coat pocket, and, with his trigger finger along the barrel, he held it palm up, pointed at the dashboard. He realized that he had known all along that he was going to show Mayhew the gun. He hadn't been conscious of it, but it had been inevitable.

Mayhew glared at the pistol and then at Edmund. "Shit," he said. "Don't threaten me, you little asshole. Punks like you . . ."

"Shut up!" Edmund shouted, his voice unnaturally high. He swiveled in the seat, aiming the pistol at the old man now, holding his forearm flat against his side to stop his hand from shaking. It was loaded with steel shot, which would screw up any chance of police learning anything from ballistics if they ever found the gun, which they wouldn't. And of course they wouldn't give a damn anyway, not about a dead bum. Mayhew was roadkill. The pistol grip felt huge in his hand, like holding onto a wooden golf ball. He had only shot the gun a few times before, and the recoil had nearly broken his wrist.

"The man you spoke to is off limits to you, Mr. Mayhew. From now on, if you want to talk to me, you can beep me. Do you know what a beeper is?"

Mayhew sat back carefully against the door. He grinned suddenly and nodded, still watching the gun. His attitude was different now that it was pointed at his face. "Yes, I do know what a beeper is. I'm . . . I'm fine with that."

"You are *not* fine, Mr. Mayhew. You're a piece of human trash. You'll keep a civil tongue in your head when you talk to me. You'll address me as *Mr.* Dalton from now on." The windshield was opaque with moisture now, and out the side windows the fog rolled through in waves that intermittently obscured the brush even a few yards from the car.

"That's fine," he said, nodding heavily. "I'll . . ."

"Do you *want* to be shot? Right here? Is this where you want to die? Because I *will* shoot you." He lifted his hand away from his side, and it shook nearly uncontrollably, so he grabbed his wrist with his left hand to steady it. Mayhew's eyes were wide now, focused on the gun barrel.

"No," the old man said weakly.

"What? Speak up. And once again, address me as *Mr.* Dalton."

"No, Mr. Dalton." Mayhew held his hands up in front of him, as if he were giving up, and then lurched suddenly forward, knocking Edmund's hand into the air. The pistol slammed against the low ceiling of the car, but Edmund held onto it, pushing his free hand under Mayhew's chin as the old man lunged for the door lock. The locks disengaged, Edmund shouldered him sideways into the dashboard, and Mayhew threw himself back against the seat again, punching at Edmund's face with his left hand as he snatched at the door handle. The car door flew open, and Mayhew propelled himself backward through it, sliding off the edge of the seat into the dirt of the roadway with a wild grunt. He was illuminated now by the dome light. Edmund threw himself prone on the seat, clutched a handful of the old man's tweed coat, and held on. Mayhew twisted away from him, jerking his arm out of the coat sleeve and simultaneously standing up and slamming the door. The door sprang back open, the latch jammed by the empty arm of the coat, and Edmund scrambled across the console as the door slammed shut again—on his arm now, smashing against his elbow. He whimpered in pain and clambered headfirst out onto the dirt, swinging the gun up as he crawled to his knees.

He yanked on the trigger without aiming. The recoil of the little .45 slammed his arm backward so hard that he hit himself in the face with the back of his hand. He staggered to his feet, deafened by the noise, and saw the old man rushing at him through the fog, swinging his loose coat around his head like a cowboy with a rope. Before Edmund could raise the pistol again, the loose coat flapped down over his head, and Mayhew smashed into him, pushing him over backward, his knee cracking into Edmund's chin. Edmund flailed at him as the old man snatched the coat away again, the dry bushes crackling under their feet.

Mayhew ran, waving the coat, and Edmund scrambled forward now, aiming the pistol, and saw the old man loping into the fog fifteen feet ahead, heading for the cliffs. Without thinking, Edmund squeezed the trigger, holding the gun two-handed, ready this time for the recoil. But the trigger, somehow, was jammed against the grip, and the gun didn't fire. He stumbled to his feet, cursing himself for having forgotten to cock it.

Mayhew was gone, disappeared in the fog. Edmund followed him, peering into the mist ahead, holding the pistol out in front of him and trying to cock it. The mechanism was stiff, and his wrist hurt like hell, sprained by the last recoil. He stopped and used both hands to cock the pistol, and then started out at a run again down the narrow trail. There was nowhere to go but straight on. Mayhew wouldn't elude him. Within moments the old man appeared again before him, loping slowly along with a heavy limp like some shadowy, hunched devil half hidden by the fog. Edmund ran right up on him, keeping pace easily, mimicking the old man's limp, wheezing wildly as if he were singing along. Mayhew looked over his shoulder at Edmund, clearly wild with fear, and Edmund stopped running, stood in place, and fired the pistol straight at the old man's back, his hands jerking skyward with the recoil. Mayhew vanished, lunging forward into the mist, and Edmund set out again, nearly stumbling over the old man where he lay in the dirt of the roadway.

He stood staring at Mayhew, at the bloodstained coat that he still clutched in his arms. *A hobo till the end*, Edmund thought, snickering with laughter. He would give up his life, but he wouldn't give up his damned stinking coat. It was poetic somehow.

This was what they had driven out here for, Edmund realized—the killing of Mr. Mayhew in the darkness and the fog, hidden from the day, separate from the world. This was why it had occurred to him like a bolt out of the blue to borrow Mifflin's credit card. This was why he had disconnected the license plate lamp, why he had thought to bring the gun and the video camera and the rest of the equipment in the trunk, why he had pulled over at the curb at just *exactly* the point where he had access to a dark and hidden place. Even the fog . . . he hadn't seen fog this heavy in twenty-five years. Why tonight, of all nights?

He was full of an energetic insight, of a keen apprecia-

tion of the degree to which all of this had almost been
choreographed up until now. He had trusted the deep places
in his own mind, and, once again, he hadn't let himself
down. Oil or pastel? Marble or alabaster? All the vital questions had been answered, and he knew now what lay ahead
of him. He thought of the Night Girl, of her paintings, of
her secret place in the woods. He knew that she was waiting
here in the fog, that she would come to him, that together
they would see to the final details. He turned around and
headed back down the trail toward the car, where his tools
waited for him in the trunk.

⊰ 46 ⊱

EDMUND THOUGHT OF THE PAY PHONE ON THE NORTHEAST
corner of Walnut and Main, near Anne's apartment, as his
"business phone." He used it especially when he was at
work and didn't want to be overheard making a sensitive
call from an office cubicle with thin wooden and glass
walls. There was a certain glamour in the pay phone calls,
too, whether he was calling Social Services to make up lies
on Collier or was talking to Ray Mifflin's old friend Hector,
who was doing time in Chino Prison for smuggling drugs
and aliens across the border. It had been Hector who had
led him to Mifflin in the first place. This morning Edmund
had put through a call to Hector's cousin, a man named
Fernando in East L.A., whom he had never met or spoken
to until yesterday.

Like in the old song about Alice's Restaurant, it was true
that you could get anything you want from a man in prison,
and usually it didn't cost you any more than a couple of
cartons of cigarettes that you sent over to the prison property room. Some sorts of information cost considerably

more than that, of course, but all Edmund had needed this time was information about purchasing false identification documents—a simple set, two authentic credit cards and a fake driver's license. Stealing and using Mifflin's cards had been easy, but perhaps wouldn't have been as easy if he had hit a bigger, more security-conscious car rental agency like Hertz or Avis. Anyway, working the same kind of hoax more than once was both dangerous and inartistic.

Things had evolved to the point where Edmund needed a *nom de plume*. There was certain work that an artist such as himself simply couldn't do under his own name, no matter how elegant the work. What had happened with Mayhew was that sort of work. He wished that he could choose the name himself, but he probably wouldn't be able to, not on short notice. He was anxious to give Mifflin his cards back, if only to see how the man would react when he discovered that once again he was a pawn, entirely at the mercy of forces he couldn't begin to comprehend. And who could blame him? Mifflin no doubt thought by now that he was the means to an end; that Edmund was simply using him to make a quick bundle of money. There was no way that he could guess that the means and the end were the same, that he was as much the centerpiece of Edmund's elaborate table setting as Mayhew had been. Mifflin's fate was still hidden from Edmund, but by and by it would be revealed, and then Edmund would reveal it to Mifflin. . . .

Edmund could hear music over the phone now, some kind of salsa music, and the sound of pots and pans clanging around, as if Fernando had uncradled a phone in the kitchen of a restaurant. He had the feeling that the man was making him wait just for the hell of it, maybe to get a psychological upper hand on him. But of course he had to put up with that kind of moronic behavior. He wasn't in a position right now to do anything about it.

"What?" Edmund asked. The sudden voice on the other end had taken him by surprise.

"Okay. You said you need this quick?"

"The quicker the better."

"Quick's more expensive."

"We were talking about twelve hundred dollars," Edmund told him.

"Fifteen hundred is quicker."

Edmund was silent for a moment. Obviously he was being screwed out of three hundred dollars. And if there was one thing he couldn't tolerate, it was somebody weaseling his money, although he didn't give much of a damn for the money itself.

"I can do it for twelve hundred," Fernando said, "but it's going to take another couple of days."

"Let's do it now," Edmund told him.

"All right. Now what about the credit cards?"

"Visa and American Express."

"Yeah, but what quality? For the money we're talking you get stolen cards; they'll be good maybe forty-eight, seventy-two hours max before they're reported. You've got to move pretty fast."

"So what are you telling me?"

"There's better product, you know what I mean?"

"Okay."

"For another five hundred we can find cards with a longer life span."

"How long?"

"Two or three weeks."

"What's the deal with that? What's the difference?"

"The good cards come from old folks, say in a convalescent hospital. Or dead people. Whatever kind of people aren't paying attention very hard. Nobody figures it out till the bill comes at the end of the month."

"These come with some kind of guarantee, then? If they kill the card number in four days, I get some money back?"

"No guarantees, my friend. They'll be good, though."

"How much do you want? You know damned well that you're nickel-and-diming me here. Why don't you give me a total—one price for the whole package?"

"Twenty-eight hundred."

"Fine. Twenty-eight hundred."

"I need some details. What was the name of the hotel. The one you told me yesterday?"

"Huntington Towers. It's on the Coast Highway south

of Beach Boulevard. Six stories high, pink and green—you
can't miss it.''

"Listen, then. Here's the drill, my friend. You put the
cash in an envelope along with a passport photo and leave
it for a Mr. Johnson. You got that?''

"Mr. Johnson.''

"Do it right away. Within the hour. Tomorrow morning
you pick up the documents the same way.''

"What name do I use when I pick them up? I don't want
to use my own name at all, not around town here.''

"Call in the morning and we'll tell you.'' The phone
was hung up then, and for a moment Edmund thought
they'd been cut off. Then he realized that the conversation
was simply over.

"Asshole,'' Edmund said into the dead receiver. He
hung up the phone.

Edmund looked at his watch. Anne still hadn't come out
of her apartment, although she was only a couple of
minutes behind the schedule she'd kept for the last couple
of days. Edmund was wearing his jogging togs, and he set
out north now, jogging toward Olive Street, where he
headed east for half a block before ducking into an alley
and starting back down toward Walnut again. As he
rounded the corner onto Main, he saw that Anne was
crossing the street toward Starbucks. He spotted a break in
traffic and jogged across, waving happily at her, as if he
were surprised to see her. She smiled back at him, and
waited while he caught up to her.

"Out jogging?'' she said.

"Four miles every morning before work. Can I join
you?''

She looked at him blankly for a moment before saying,
"Yeah, sure. I'm just chasing a cup of coffee.''

"I need something cold. You want to grab a table? What
do you want? A cappuccino? It's on me.''

"Really, you don't have to,'' she said.

"It's my pleasure, Anne.''

"Then just a simple coffee. Whatever they've got today.''

He went inside and ordered, watching her through the

window. He had strong feelings about her this morning. She was clearly impressed with his physical fitness, with the jogging. Women were attracted to a package, to the whole picture, and anybody who said they weren't was crazy. There wasn't much room for improvement in his package, if he did say so himself: money, looks, health—he had all that wired. As for his artistic talent and his intellect, she'd know all about that if only she'd give him a chance here—which she would.

Her attraction to Dave had come very near to spoiling everything. He was so obviously beneath her. A woman worthy of Edmund Dalton wouldn't descend to that level unless she had been fooled. And if she had been fooled, then he had to be fair. He had to give her a chance. He understood the Night Girl well enough, since he was largely responsible for her—for her shape, her passions, her being. He knew absolutely that he was the literally creative link between the Day Girl and the Night Girl. Without him, the Night Girl would not have come into existence at all, and Anne would have forever denied half of her being. But Anne herself, the Day Girl, was largely a mystery to him. She was a little bit like a sprightly, forward child, and it was only fair that he had to lead her a little bit—show her the way. Their drinks were up, and he brought Anne's coffee and his own more healthful fruit drink outside and sat down.

"So how do you like work so far?" Edmund asked. "Everything satisfactory? Nobody bothering you?"

"I'm fine," Anne said.

"Good. That's good." He sipped his drink and smiled at her. It occurred to him that her manner was a little brisk—which was rude, considering that he was her superior and that he'd just bought her a cup of coffee. He had gotten this same treatment at the gallery the other night. It didn't become her. "I've got a little proposition for you," he said, getting right down to the point.

She nodded at him, still not smiling quite enough to suit him.

"You remember when we talked about you and I going down to Mexico together? To Club Mex, near San Felipe?"

"*Together?*" she asked.

"Well, I think I mentioned it to you, yes. In the parking garage, in Laguna the other night."

"You mentioned you were going to Mexico, I think, but I don't remember that you asked me to go along."

He smiled winningly at her. "Then I guess I'm asking you now."

She started to say something, but he waved her quiet. "Wait," he said. "Look at this." He opened his belt pack and took out a pair of plane tickets and the Club Mex resort brochure. "I took a chance on you," he said, pointing to her name on one of the tickets. "One thing that you don't know about me is that I love the way fate works. Sometimes you just have to trust it."

"You were carrying these around with you while you were jogging?"

Her tone sounded snide to him, but he didn't let it get to him. "The travel agent's down on Acacia Street," he said. "I stopped by just now, then I headed back downtown on the off chance I'd see you. What do you say? Wait. Don't say anything until you know what I'm talking about. Take a look at this."

He opened the brochure onto the tabletop and gestured at the photos. Club Mex was a first-rate vacation spot— water sports, tennis, a four-star restaurant; the place had it all. "I've booked separate rooms, of course. I'm not suggesting anything out of line here."

"I think it's a little bit out of line to show me any of this," she said.

He was baffled at first. "I'm not sure I understand," he said.

"We hardly know each other, Edmund. You honestly don't think I'd run off to Mexico with a man I don't know?"

"Oh, I think we know each other better than you're willing to admit."

"I don't follow you. We've talked with each other a total of about four times. I don't mean to be rude or anything, but I guess I'm not that easy."

"Well, let's just say that I know something about you,

then, about . . . the darker side of your work. You won't deny that there is one?''

''Deny it? What are you talking about? Why would I want to deny anything to you? You've made some kind of mistake, Edmund. I don't know why you bought so many of my paintings, and I don't know why you bought these plane tickets, but it's all part of the same mistake. And it's really got to stop right now.''

''I'm asking you to think about it, Anne. How is that a mistake? Listen to what I'm saying. I'm *very* much attracted to you, on an intellectual and artistic level.'' He gestured at the brochure. ''And I can certainly vouch for the quality of the resort.'' He broadened his smile, although he wasn't smiling at all inside. She was acting like he was asking her for some kind of favor. Here she was locked up in her goddamn Mary Poppins world of pretty pictures, obstinately letting the fire in her soul burn out. All he wanted to do was fan it back into flame. He knew the way to that fire, but she wouldn't let him take her there. What the hell did she want from him? ''Listen to me,'' he said, lowering his voice and leaning forward. It was time to level with her. ''What do you know about the astral plane?''

''Is that what you're taking to Mexico?''

He stared at her, not quite comprehending . . . Then he knew that she was joking. He picked up the Club Mex brochure and held it out. He would give it one more try. ''I'm talking about all expenses *paid*,'' he said.

There was a long moment of silence. ''Do I look like a prostitute to you, Edmund?'' she asked finally.

''Whoa!'' He held out his hands. ''I didn't say *that*.''

''Of course you did. Really, this irritates the hell out of me. You have no right to make any assumptions about me at all. You wasted your money, Edmund, and you're wasting your time. If I'm fired, tell me right now. I suppose that's next.''

''Why should it be? Anne . . .'' He shook his head helplessly. ''On the surface we see this whole thing from such *different* points of view.''

''I guess we do.''

"But it's *under* the surface that we're so much alike." He sat back and winked at her.

"Thanks for the coffee." She stood up, turned around, and walked away up the street toward the Earl's.

He watched her go. No way in hell was he going to chase her. He really wasn't very surprised. She hadn't rejected him—he knew that. She hadn't understood him well enough to reject him. She was like a child rejecting some healthful food out of ignorance. She didn't know anything about nutritional value. What surprised him about it was not that *she* didn't measure up, because in his experience, people *never* really measured up. What surprised him was that he himself hadn't read her better. He had overestimated her, and that was a bad mistake.

Still, what had he offered her? A resort vacation in the sun. Maybe *that* was his mistake. He had wanted to appeal to something deep within her, and instead he had tried to entice her with something superficial. He had attempted to play the game by her rules, by navigating in her world, instead of inviting her into his own. . . .

He tore her plane ticket in two and dropped it into the trash. He had an intuitive suspicion that he might soon make good use of his own ticket, although he would have to save Club Mex for the fall. He wasn't going there after all. Not now.

⇥ 47 ⇤

RAY MIFFLIN PULLED INTO THE PARKING LOT AFTER A three-hour lunch. He bought a newspaper off the stack in the liquor store, then walked down to Right Now Notary and let himself in. He flipped the clock sign around and stood for a moment looking out at the parking lot. All day

long cars pulled in and cars pulled out. Either they stopped
for five minutes at the liquor store or for an hour at the
Laundromat. Now and then a Mexican alien came into his
office in order to wire money home. This time of year, that
was about it. Today no one at all had come into the office.
He might as well have stayed home. And now that he had
the deal going with Dalton, working was turning into a
farce, which made him nervous. Easy money always made
him nervous, and it turned out that *really* easy money made
him really nervous.

The day's mail lay in a pile under the slot, and he bent
over to pick it up. Beneath the mail, strangely, lay his
driver's license, face up. And a couple of feet away, as if
it had bounced, lay his Mastercard.

Puzzled, he took his wallet out of his back pocket. Despite what he saw on the floor, he was vaguely surprised
to find that they were missing from where he kept them in
the wallet, slipped in with his Visa card in a leather slot.
Had they slid out of the slot somehow? He couldn't recall
whether he'd had his wallet out of his pocket earlier in the
day—perhaps when he was going out the door to lunch.
. . . He was pretty sure he hadn't. It was more likely that
he had left them somewhere, and that some good Samaritan
had run his address down, shoving the cards through the
slot while he was gone to lunch. He tried to remember the
last time he'd used them both, but he couldn't. They might
have been missing for a week, two weeks.

He was too tired today for mysteries. The good news
was that he had gotten them back. Apparently there were
still honest people in the world.

He opened the newspaper, leaned back in the swivel
chair, and worked through the sports before he got onto the
local news, where he found a quarter-column article about
a murder—only the second murder in Laguna Beach this
year. He read the article through without really paying
much attention to it: a man's body found on the bluffs north
of Laguna Beach by two women on horseback. The victim
had been decapitated after he had been shot. The police
weren't making it clear how. The corpse's finger pointed
toward an open Gideon's Bible with an underlined passage.

There was a reference in the newspaper article to a satanic cult murder a decade past, but the police insisted that there was no real reason to believe this was any such thing.

Mifflin nearly stopped reading in disgust. He had no kind of fascination with cult murders, if that was what this was. They were evidence that the world was full of the worst kind of idiots, and that was about all. He read the last paragraph, though: the night, according to the police, had been densely foggy, and there were no reports of gunfire or suspicious activity. The victim hadn't been identified, but given the condition of his clothes he was quite possibly a homeless man. There was a brief description of his faded yellow coat, a worn brown leisure suit. . . .

His hands shaking now, Mifflin set the paper down on his desk and took out another cigarette. He picked up the paper and read the entire column again. The dead man was old Mayhew. It had to be. Mifflin slowly felt a general relief, which he was only momentarily ashamed of. If he were a good citizen, he would call the Laguna Beach police and identify the body, at least anonymously. But he wasn't a good citizen—not any longer. He was up to his neck in fraud, and he was dangerously closely connected to the victim. It was a tough way for old Mayhew to check out, but all that aside, at least the man was no longer a threat.

Had *Dalton* killed him? The idea paralyzed him. Of course not. It was impossible. Mayhew was a pain in the neck, but he was cheap. You didn't kill a man if you could buy him for a carton of cigarettes and a pint of Jack Daniels. And although Dalton was squirrelly as a hollow tree, he couldn't be as stupid as *that*. Not with a million easy dollars in the picture. Not even if Mayhew had threatened him with real trouble. It just wasn't worth it. And mutilating the body . . .

He tossed the newspaper down and sat smoking, watching the cars out on Beach Boulevard. He realized that he knew absolutely nothing about Edmund Dalton. Half of what Dalton had told him had turned out to be lies. Why *shouldn't* he be a murderer? Why shouldn't he be any damned thing at all, including the worst kind of crazy man?

He dug out the white pages, found the 800 number for

Mastercard and punched it into the phone, then punched in the digit for account information. A woman came on the line and asked for his name and card number. "What can I help you with?" she asked finally.

"I recently lost my card," he said. "I hope it's not stolen. Can you tell me if it's been used within the past couple of days?"

He gave her his name, and there was the sound of a keyboard momentarily. "Day before yesterday," the woman said. "A car rental agency in Long Beach, called . . . I guess it's Cheapskate Rent-a-car."

"Of course!" Ray said. "Cheapskate! That's a relief."

"Do you want to report the card stolen?"

"No. I guess I was mistaken. I think I left it on the counter down there. I'll swing past and pick it up. Goodbye." He hung up, his head spinning. Someone had rented a car using his stolen Mastercard. Dalton. It had to be Dalton. The bastard had stolen the card and license out of his wallet when he'd been in the office day before yesterday. He had rented a car for the purpose of murdering a man, and then come back around in his own good time to dump the cards back through the mail slot. He probably thought it was funny. Dalton had killed Mayhew and then mutilated his body, and the whole thing was a joke to him.

He found the directory for the Long Beach area and looked up Cheapskate Rent-a-car. He ripped the page out of the book, took fifty-odd dollars in petty cash out of the office drawer, locked the place up, and climbed into his car. Long Beach was thirty minutes away, and it suddenly seemed to him that time was short.

MIFFLIN CIRCLED THE 800 BLOCK OF NORTH CHERRY, PASSing Cheapskate Rent-a-car the first time in order to look the place over. He half expected to see police cars, but there weren't any, just a dumpy stucco building in front of a gated yard with several rentals parked in back and a tired curb tree in front. He drove carefully, signaling a hundred feet before turning, checking the rearview mirror every twenty seconds or so. It was the kind of excessive care he took in driving when he'd had too many drinks, when it was absolutely paramount that he didn't get pulled over.

When he approached the building for the second time, he parked on the street, well out of sight of the front window, just to play it safe. He had a couple of half-baked routines worked out, depending on whether the clerk recognized his name or not. He thought about the Jimmy Stewart–Jones character again, about his nervous, turnip-truck detective work. The poor bastard apparently didn't have a clue about what kind of monster he was dealing with in Edmund Dalton. Whatever else happened, Mifflin decided, he at least owed the man Jones a phone call.

He pushed in through the front door of the rental agency and smiled at the man behind the counter.

"Need a car?" the man asked him.

"I just brought one back."

The man simply nodded. "When was that?"

"This morning."

"Problem of some sort?"

"That's right," Mifflin said. "I bought a gift for my wife, and I think I left it in the car."

"Small package?" The man looked through a bin of carbon-copy receipts.

"A pair of diamond earrings, in a small box. I'm not certain, but I think that maybe I left them in the trunk, or else maybe they got shoved under the seat." He gestured helplessly. "I did a lot of shopping, made a few stops. I *hope* to hell I left them in the car. Is the gentleman here who helped me before?" He was taking a chance with this one. The *last* thing he wanted to do now was talk with anyone who would know he *hadn't* rented a car night before last.

The clerk found a receipt in the bin and looked it over. "No, that's Ronnie. Ronnie went home at noon today. He doesn't work again until . . ." He looked at a schedule on the wall, tracing dates with his finger. "Thursday. He's got a couple days off."

"I was hoping maybe he'd found it. Would he have cleaned the car out?"

"Not very likely. I doubt anyone cleaned the car out,

since it only came back in this morning. It's out back. That
was the white Ford, wasn't it?''

"That's right," Mifflin told him.

"Well, if you left it in the car, it's still in the car. Take
a good long look." He picked through several rings of car
keys, found a Ford set, and handed them to Mifflin.

"Can I see the receipt for a second?" Mifflin asked.

"Sure." He handed that over, too. The phone rang, and
he nodded toward the yard in back before picking up the
receiver.

The signature on the receipt was apparently his signature.
Dalton had forged it like a pro. Mifflin laid the receipt on
the counter and went out through the side door and up the
asphalt drive. Four cars were parked in the back lot. Thank
God the man hadn't asked *him* what car he'd rented.
Straight off he saw that the Ford had been washed, if not
by Ronnie, then by Edmund Dalton. Why? Bloodstains?
He walked around it, taking a good look. There was no
dust on it at all, no flattened bugs. The windows were clean.
Even the chrome was polished. The car looked as if it had
been detailed. There was no indication that anyone had
driven it anywhere, let alone off-road. Dalton had evidently
kept it an extra day in order to clean it up.

Mifflin opened the trunk, but it was empty—no telltale
bloodstains, just an owner's manual. He looked back toward the office. There was a rear window, but it looked out
of a back room. No one could see him. As long as he was
quick, the man in the office probably wouldn't give a damn
about him.

He opened the passenger door and stuck his head in.
There was a faint odor just discernible beneath the car-wash
smell. He was no kind of detective, but it smelled to him
like Mayhew's crappy old sports coat—the urine and body
odor smell of a longtime drunk. He opened the glove box,
but there was nothing inside except a few papers. The car
had been vacuumed, and the dash was slick with vinyl polish. He glanced back toward the office again, then bent over
and sniffed the seat and seat back. Mayhew again. Goddamn Mayhew. That's where the smell was. He was
damned well certain of it. It occurred to him then that Ed-

mund might have cleaned the car up in order to get rid of
fingerprints, and he looked at his hands, abruptly aware that
he must be smearing his own damned prints all over everything. . . .

Leaving the door open, he moved around to the front of
the car and got down onto his hands and knees on the
asphalt. He looked under the chassis. There was dust and
oil, but who could say where the hell the dust had come
from? The answer occurred to him immediately: a police
lab.

He saw something then—vegetation of some sort caught
in the strap that held the muffler. He hurried around to the
rear of the car, crouched on the asphalt again, and reached
underneath, feeling around with his hand. He found it,
grabbed on tight, and yanked it out. It was a piece of a
bush, some kind of goddamn bush. And it was mostly
green, too. Some of it had been dried brown by the muffler
heat, but part of it was fresh. Someone had driven the car
through shrubbery, and recently, too. No good could come
from anyone else finding dried weeds tangled in the undercarriage of a murderer's car, not when Ray Mifflin's
credit card had rented it, not when he was taking a percentage of illegal money from the murderer himself.

"What the hell are you up to?" The man's voice startled
him, and he scuttled back out from under the car, still
clutching the weeds he'd first pulled clear of the muffler.

"I couldn't find it," Mifflin said lamely.

"*Under* the car?" The man hunkered down by the
bumper and looked underneath. Mifflin shoved the weeds
into his pocket. "What were you doing under there?"

"To tell you the truth," Mifflin said, "last night the
exhaust pipe or the muffler was banging around. I forgot
to say anything to Ronnie when I brought it back in."

The man reached under and pushed on the muffler.
"Feels tight."

"Yeah, to me too. I don't know."

"You say it was banging around?"

"Only for a half mile or so, when I got off the freeway."

"You ran over something. Probably dragged some piece
of junk for a ways and then dropped it."

"Sure. Of course."

"No earrings?"

"No. I guess I dropped them somewhere else."

"If they turn up, we'll call you. You want to leave a number?"

"Sure," Mifflin said. He followed the man back into the office and gave him a bogus phone number. He left immediately, got into his car, and headed back up toward the freeway. It was three o'clock, and traffic on the 405 past Signal Hill was thickening up. It would only get worse as he got into Orange County, but he couldn't help it. There was no use getting frustrated. He had places to go—a lot of places to go.

THE SUN WAS LOW IN THE SKY WHEN HE PULLED OFF THE road at Scotchman's Cove, near Laguna Beach. The parking lot was deserted, which wasn't surprising this late on a weekday afternoon, and the empty bluffs were lonesome and foreign. Strangely, it seemed to him that it had literally been years since he had driven this far east. Unless he was going somewhere on business, he rarely got more than a few miles from home. He hardly ever got down to Mexico any more, which was the only place he was even close to being happy. The depressing picture of his life owed more to desktop ashtrays and IRS forms and worn-out commercial carpeting than to anything suggested by this empty coastline and the sea wind.

He sat for another moment, listening to the silence, smelling the wind off the ocean and the wet vegetation, watching the evening fog bank that lay out over the horizon, drifting in on the onshore breezes. Finally he got out of the car, with the bits of weed still in his pocket, and walked down the trail toward the beach. Halfway down he stopped. There was no point in walking farther. The weeds in question were growing all over the place, thick and green with the fog and the spring rains. He turned around and headed back up to the car, mulling things over in his mind. He knew nearly everything that he needed to know.

Dalton's returning his Mastercard and license was interesting. He could as easily have thrown them away. It meant

simply that Dalton didn't care if he knew. He *wanted* him
to know. Dalton was up to something more than merely
stealing money from his brother. He was obviously acting
out some sort of twisted psychodrama that it would take a
team of psychologists to understand. And the theft of the
cards was meant to give Mifflin a bigger role in the man's
farce.

He was suddenly tired of playing Edmund Dalton's
games. He checked his watch: fifteen hours until his bank
opened. Plenty of time, if he played it right.

⊰48⊱

DAVE POLISHED THE CHROME ON THE KITCHEN FAUCETS
with a tea towel and then wiped down the counter before
going on to the cupboard doors. The last couple of years
of being single had gotten him used to putting in a lot of
time alone, sitting up late reading or working in the shop.
The few days that he'd known Anne, though, had wiped
all that out, and without her company he was restless and
marking time. He could remember a couple of times when
he had left a girlfriend alone on the beach while he put in
a three- or four-hour session out in the water. Now he had
a girlfriend who ditched *him* for a paintbrush. . . .

The phone rang, and he picked it up anxiously. But it
wasn't Anne's voice; it was the cigarette-stained voice of
the notary from down on Beach Boulevard, and he put the
wet tea towel down on the kitchen counter and concentrated.

"Is this Jim Jones?" the man asked.

"Yeah," Dave said. "In the flesh."

"I'll make this quick. What you were asking about? All
of it's true. You hit the nail on the head."

"Okay . . ." Dave said. "*All* of it?"

"Just what you thought was going on, that's what was going on. But listen to me; that turns out to be the tip of the goddamn iceberg. You seem like a nice enough guy, so I'm telling you this, but I'm only going to tell you once. My advice hasn't changed from when we talked last. What I'm telling you here is to keep the hell out of it entirely. You don't want to be anywhere near it. And if I were you, I wouldn't have anything to do with our mutual friend. You know who I'm talking about?"

"Sure. I already have something to do with him. You're not telling me much."

"I'm telling you that he's a very dangerous man. He's a first-class nut case. I had to be completely off my chump ever to talk to the man, and now I find myself talking to you, which is just about as bad. Anyway, that's the end of the conversation. Our hypothetical acquaintance with each other is through. Take my advice, and keep your nose out of a swinging door."

Dave was still listening when he realized that the man had hung up. He put the receiver down and stood looking through the kitchen window at the green foliage of his neighbor's banana trees. Was the phone call a threat? He decided that it wasn't. It was a man trying to fix something that he had helped to break. Like everyone else, by the time Ray Mifflin had figured out that Edmund Dalton was a spider, he was already tangled up in the man's webs.

49

MIFFLIN'S APARTMENT IN HUNTINGTON BEACH HAD BEEN furnished, which made getting out easy—a couple of quick trips to the Goodwill drop-off, half a dozen cardboard boxes taped up and ready to go to the post office in the morning, and some first-rate Pontiac trunk stuffing. He had left the rest of his junk for the apartment manager with a note to throw what he didn't want into the Dumpster. To hell with his cleaning deposit and half of his already-paid rent. Right Now Notary was locked up tight. He had mailed in rent for the next four months and closed the Levelors after cleaning out any papers and documents that he cared a damn about. Some time in the next four months, if something changed, he could blow back into town one last quick time and make any final business arrangements—in and out in a day.

It was still fairly early, nine o'clock in the evening. Mifflin had said a last good-bye to his apartment and business two hours ago and then grabbed a steak at the Sizzler on Beach Boulevard. He stood now at the pay phone in the lobby of the Embassy Suites hotel in Santa Ana. The hotel lobby was a jungle of potted plants beneath a soaring atrium ceiling. He would have liked to drink a beer in the lounge, just to take the edge off a long day, but it was far too risky. As soon as he hung up the phone, he had to leave. He had a room reserved at a Motel 6 down the freeway in Costa Mesa under the name of Marx. The room he had paid for here at the Embassy Suites was under the name of Frobisher. Making this phone call at all was a long shot, a dangerous long shot, but if he was going to take an early retirement, he had to push his little pile of chips into the middle of the table and play his hand. Edmund Dalton answered the phone on the second ring.

"Edmund, this is Ray," Mifflin said to him.

"It's good to hear your voice, Ray. What's up?"

"I've decided to retire, Edmund."

"Now that's not a bad idea. I've been thinking the same thing."

"That I ought to retire?"

"Something like that. Sometimes I think you're a little too nervous to be a real player. But so what? Who cares what I think? Tell me what you have in mind. You're talking business. Make me an offer. Let's not play word games here."

"All right," Ray said. "When this thing got off the

ground, you told me you'd buy me out any time I wanted to go. We settled on your paying me half of the balance that you still owed me. I think I called it three-quarters of a pie. The other day when I called and wanted out, you bull-shitted the idea away. I'm talking the same thing here. Only this time, like you said, no word games, no bullshit. You do remember our agreement?''

''I remember it perfectly. And what you're telling me now is that you want the famous pie?''

''That's most of what I'm telling you. I want the *whole* pie, though. I don't want three-quarters of it any more.''

''You disappoint me a little,'' Edmund told him after a couple of moments of silence. ''That's the kind of thing I expected out of a bum like Mayhew, but I'd have guessed you'd be happy with the deal you agreed to. And I'll admit that I'm a little surprised at your self-righteous tone, when it's you that's backing down on the deal after making easy money.''

''The deal we agreed to was always a myth, Edmund. The hippie brother who hates money was bad enough, but what I read in the newspaper today was worse, way worse.''

''I couldn't agree with you more. If there's another baseball strike, I'm turning in my Angels cap. I've had it with the sport.''

''Right. That's what I'm telling you. I've had it with the sport too. I agreed to stamp a few papers, Edmund. I didn't agree to being accessory to a capital crime. This whole thing is out of control.''

''I'd argue with that. Control is my strong suit, Ray.''

''You're not playing it that way.''

''Things have never been more entirely in control than they are right now.''

''Not from where I stand. And to tell you the truth, I no longer give much of a damn for anyone else's opinion, especially yours. So let me get back around to the point. I want you to honor our agreement and cash me out—a full hundred percent.''

''*Honor* the agreement? That's rich, Ray. What if I tell you to go to hell?''

"Take a wild guess. I told you I'm betting all the chips here, Edmund. You gave me the trump card when you killed Mayhew."

"That sounds almost like a threat."

"It's business. It's strictly business. And it's the last piece of business between us, Edmund. You can find another Ray Mifflin easy enough. You found *me* easy enough."

"Well, I hate to hear this. We were a good team. But go ahead and finish your story."

"It's a simple story. I want the rest of the cash—exactly the same amount you've already paid me. And I want advance money on the property you haven't sold yet. That way nothing's hanging fire. I want it tonight."

"Tonight? That's a tough one. The banks closed three hours ago."

"Don't treat me like a fool, Edmund. You can find the cash. If it costs you a few bucks to buy it from someone, I'll split the difference with you. Put it in a briefcase and leave it at the desk at the Embassy Suites hotel under the name Frobisher."

"That's it? You're not going to hold me up for an extra fifty K? You're not going to run me around from place to place like in the movies?"

"No running around. No getting greedy. No fuss, no bother. Just one last piece of business, like I said. It's a quarter past nine. I'd like for the money to be here by midnight. I've got a written statement about our business and about your relationship with Mayhew in a very safe, very accessible place. So good-bye, Edmund. Give my regards to your father. I hope he lives another thirty years."

He hung up before Edmund had a chance to say another word. Either he would bring the money or he wouldn't. If he didn't, then nothing would have changed. If he did, then retirement was that much greener.

Ray realized that his hands were shaking and he was sweating despite the cool air in the lobby. He walked into the lounge after all and ordered a double scotch on the rocks at the bar, then drank it in the time it took him to smoke another cigarette.

50

IT WAS NEARLY NINE IN THE MORNING WHEN ANNE GOT out of bed and showered. In the kitchen she put the teakettle on the burner, then walked back into the bedroom. She felt strangely happy, anxious to get to work, and for a moment she wondered why. Somehow it seemed as if something particularly nice were going on today, but as far as she could see it was just another Tuesday.

And then she remembered what it was: Edmund was on vacation for the week! She opened her closet and stepped inside to find something to wear, and in the semidarkness at the back of the closet she kicked one of the cardboard cartons of unpacked clothes that sat on the floor. She groped for the light chain and switched on the overhead bulb, then bent over to push the box out of the way, farther into the disused back corner. She stopped abruptly, though, and straightened up, backing slowly away from the box toward the open door. One of Elinor's dolls stared up at her from the top of the open box, its lizardlike eyes leering, its mouth slack. One of its clawed hands gripped the box edge; the other held her father's pocket watch between its legs. The doll's robe had been pulled up just far enough to expose Elinor's depraved obsession with sexual anatomy.

Elinor. Her first thought was of Elinor's presence in the apartment Sunday night. But what was she suggesting— that Elinor's ghost had brought the doll along with it?

*Some*body had. With forced calm, she picked the watch up and put it back in the box with her mother's junk jewelry, then shoved the doll farther down into the box and pulled clothes over it. She found a sweater and a pair of jeans and pulled them on, then picked out a pair of shoes

from the floor on the opposite side of the closet. She paused
momentarily, looking at the connecting door that led to the
law office. Cautiously, as if the door were a wound-up jack-
in-the-box, she turned the knob and pushed. The door was
locked.

She was aware now that the teakettle was whistling on
the stove, and she shut the closet door and went into the
kitchen, carrying her shoes. She poured hot water through
the coffee in the filter and sat down at the kitchen table.
So if Elinor hadn't left the doll for her to find, who had?
The answer, or at least a possible answer, stared her in the
face: Edmund.

Except how the hell had Edmund gotten into the apartment? The only person besides herself who had been in the
apartment was Dave, and the only other person who owned
a key was Mr. Hedgepeth. She recalled what Edmund had
told her about someone opening her boxes at the Earl's,
and suddenly it was plain as day—a simpleminded, Elinor-
type trick. Edmund had opened the boxes and then immediately told her they'd *been* opened in order to shift the
blame, knowing that she'd suspect him. He'd been doing
that all along, setting her up, bad-mouthing Dave at every
opportunity—his reference to Dave's obsession with the
drowning, his warning that Dave might be "out of line"
with her, his suggesting that Dave had some kind of criminal past. For most of it, Edmund might as well have been
describing himself. He had been deliberately setting Dave
up, setting *her* up, from the first time she'd spoken to him.

A knock on the door interrupted her thinking, and she
got up and went into the living room before it dawned on
her that she might not want to open it. She tiptoed across
the floor in her stocking feet and looked out through the
peephole. It was Dave.

She opened the door, and he said, "I thought maybe
you'd want to grab a cup of coffee."

"Maybe in a minute," she said. "Would you come in?
I want to show you something."

"Is something wrong?" he asked, stepping inside and
looking around.

"Yeah," she said. "Something's *real* wrong."

51

"I'M GLAD YOU DIDN'T THINK IT WAS ME WHO PUT IT here," Dave said. "Did you notice that it's got a . . ." He waved his hand helplessly, dripping soapy water on the kitchen counter. Anne was clearly shaken up, and Dave decided to try to lighten the atmosphere while they waited for the police.

"Yes, I did. That's what some people call a penis. Elinor made a bunch of these dolls after my mother taught her to sew. She did nearly nothing else for six months or more during the year before she drowned. She was obsessed with the details. Take my word for it. All of them are very nasty, very evil. You wouldn't think that an adolescent girl would have the skill to make them, let alone want to."

"She was obviously talented," Dave said. He picked up a glass from the kitchen counter and submerged it in dishwater. "I know you said you were jealous of her talent, but was she really as good as you back then?"

Anne waved the idea away. "I wasn't any good at all back then, not really. I drew horses and trees. It took years of work for me to paint what I paint now. Lots of wrecked canvas. Elinor didn't have to work for it. She was a prodigy from around eight years old, like those child math wizards. That was always an irritation, too. I couldn't see why it came so easy for her and so hard for me."

"Sibling envy," Dave said. He rinsed the glass and held it up to the light. "I read about that in some class in school. I never had a sibling, so I missed out on the fun."

"Yeah, envy," Anne said. "Don't be so obsessed with getting the dishes clean. I'm starting to get a complex."

"You're starting to get dishwashing envy," Dave said.

"I'm a very particular dish-doer. It's one of my faults. Anyway, you didn't have any reason to be jealous. I mean, you couldn't have been jealous of *that*." He waved the dish sponge in the general direction of the doll, which still sat out of sight in the closet.

"I wasn't. I hated her dolls. It was just effortless for her, that's all. And on top of that, she was obsessed with these awful subjects. She was just full of this weird darkness. I couldn't understand it then, and I can't understand it now. She grew up without a father from the time she was five, but so did I. She wasn't abused. She wasn't the victim of a satanic cult. She wasn't abducted by space aliens. She was just this sort of . . . *conductor* for all this evil stuff that surfaced in her art. God knows what she would have produced if she'd lived." She abruptly stopped talking.

"Go on," he said.

"I sound like I've gone mental."

"Probably you have. That's always an option. Didn't you tell me that? Here. Dry this glass."

"No," she said. "You read that in your horoscope. Anyway, I was always jealous of her. So you think it was Edmund that put the doll in the closet?"

"Yeah, of course it was Edmund. There's no telling *what* Edmund puts in people's closets. I just got a phone call from a man who knows him—one of his recent business partners, let's say. He warned me that Edmund's both crazy and dangerous, which is something that I've known for a long time. I just didn't know it was serious enough to worry about. I've always taken it personally, and I thought it was a weakness."

"I'm taking this a little bit personally myself."

"Edmund has this habit of leaving what he calls 'little gifts' for people," Dave said. "People he has a particular interest in. Sometimes it's a dead rat in your lunchbox; sometimes it's something more elaborate—two or three little goodies arranged like a display in a store window. He thinks he's artistic."

"He told me all about his art. And he wanted to tell me about the astral plane, but I wouldn't let him."

"He thinks you're some kind of soul mate. He's serious

about you, too. I imagine he's out of his mind that you and I are seeing each other. He'd take it as a blow to his ego, although he wouldn't let himself admit it. I should have known he'd get into the boxes you left at the Earl's.''

''The boxes would have been easy. The question is, how did he get into my apartment?''

''He probably just took the key out of your purse. He's had access to it nearly every day. You've spent a couple hours at a time in the theatre while your purse was in the warehouse.''

''You're telling me he'd steal my key and break into my apartment just to leave one of these 'gifts' of his?''

''Sounds crazy, but I wouldn't put it past him. He has no scruples, Anne. He doesn't look at these things like you or I would look at them. He's so completely egocentric that he's unaware that this might bother you. Either that or he *wants* to bother you. And either way, it's only Edmund's take on things that matters to him. There is no other point of view.''

''God, he reminds me of Elinor.''

''I'm sorry to hear that.''

''What will the police do?''

''Do? Nothing much, probably. Take a report.''

''I wish we hadn't even called them.''

''Had to. We've got to start doing something about Edmund.''

There was a knock at the door then, and Anne and Dave went to answer it together.

❧ 52 ❧

SOUTH OF SAN DIEGO THE FOG AND OVERCAST HAD started to thin, and the sun shone through the murk so that the misty, late-morning sky was a milky white. There was quite a bit of border traffic for a weekday morning, and in the time that Mifflin sat in his car, moving forward toward the crossing, the fog burned away entirely, and it grew abruptly hotter. He took off his coat, rolled the windows down, and lit a cigarette. There was something almost poetic about the weather clearing up like this, and he was tempted to whistle or sing. But he couldn't sing or whistle worth a damn anyway, so he watched the border approaching, closer and closer, utterly aware that he wasn't merely coming down here on vacation this time; he was coming for good. Crazy Edmund Dalton had actually done him a favor by closing the door on business as usual in Orange County. *Adiós* Huntington Beach; *hola*, Punta Rioja.

He was through the border in under fifteen minutes, and then slanting past Tijuana, skirting the border town for points south. His Mexican residency was enough to make him a solid citizen. The guard hadn't asked to look in his bags, which in fact held over a hundred thousand dollars in cash and traveler's checks along with gold jewelry and all the clothes that seemed worth taking. His .38 was loaded and available, hidden under the seat in a natural cubbyhole where the upholstery wrapped around the wire seat support.

He'd had the gun in his pocket when he picked up the briefcase full of money two and a half hours ago at the Embassy Suites. Actually carrying a loaded gun made him feel like some kind of cowboy, but if Edmund Dalton had decided to get nasty, then that meant that the English language had failed him, and in that case there was nothing that spoke more clearly than a gun. He hadn't needed it, though. He had cruised the parking lot looking for Dalton's car, and then had been in and out of the hotel in under five minutes, not looking into the briefcase until he was back in the car and heading south down the freeway. He had pulled over at a McDonald's in Encinitas for a late breakfast, where he had counted the money twice. Edmund had paid him every penny. The thought had occurred to him, and not for the first time, that he could have snaked even more money out of the man. Clearly he was anxious to close this whole thing down, no matter how smartass he had acted on the phone. But to hell with that. Blackmail wasn't in Mifflin's line of work.

Beyond Tijuana the countryside was open and green, and the third-world poverty was staggering—half-built shacks covered in old tar paper, women dipping water out of rusty, open-air oil drums. It was dead true that he had made a certain amount of money in the past facilitating illegal immigration. But for God's sake, if he lived here under these conditions, he'd get the hell out, too, any way he could. And the same goddamn U.S. citizens who were hot under the collar about it were happy enough to pay immigrants four dollars an hour to paint their houses and pour concrete. They said they wanted to deport people wholesale, but every last one of them wanted to wait until after the work got done. No, he had no regrets at all about that end of his business, and there was no reason that he couldn't go right on making a dollar or two along the same lines.

He passed the lobster restaurants at Puerto Nuevo and nearly pulled off the road for lunch, but he decided against it. It was better to get home and get the car unpacked and everything squared away. The house would be empty, and he would have to fend for himself tonight. On the way in, though, he'd stop in town and find a maid. She could start tomorrow morning.

The countryside flew past now, much of it empty, looking like southern California must have looked a hundred years ago. The road finally wound around the upper edge of a hillside shaded by a half-dozen big oak trees. When he was a child, and the drive down here seemed endlessly long, these old oaks were this same size, and over the years they had become his own personal landmark rooted in the Mexican earth. They seemed to have a home-at-last quality about them today, and he was surprised at his sentimentality. He watched almost anxiously for the coastline to open up, and soon the land fell away on the right, the rocky hillside flattening into grassy scrub that ran down to the edge of the cliffs. A sliver of blue-green ocean appeared over the cliff tops, broadened into a bay with an island in the dim distance, and he could see a scattering of houses spread out along the bluffs, maybe a quarter mile apart. There were two that he didn't recognize, which didn't make him happy: when it came to Mexico, he was a no-growth kind of guy. But like everywhere else, Punta Rioja was destined to go the way of the world. Right now it still looked pretty much like home to him.

He turned off the highway onto a dirt road that dipped through a streambed. Dragonflies rose out of the vegetation along the stream, and one bumped against the window, rose into the air, and disappeared. Through the open car window the air smelled hot, as if it were already summer in Mexico. The road angled upward, then found level ground, and there was the house, sitting there as always, the shutters drawn, the yard empty of cars. He shut off the motor and coasted to a stop, savoring the silence—nothing but the sound of locusts or cicadas or whatever the hell they were scraping away out in the brush. He climbed stiffly out of the Pontiac, retrieved his gun from under the seat, and then pulled one of the cash-filled suitcases from the back trunk, opened it up, and put the gun inside. He found the house key hanging under the garden bench just like always, and he let himself into the house, squinting into the darkness, navigating mostly by memory. He set the suitcase on the floor and stood for a moment letting his eyes adjust.

The place was cool and dusty, the furniture covered with white sheets. He slapped the back of the couch, and a cloud of dust rose above it, hanging in the still air. Immediately he sneezed twice, then blessed himself out loud. He heard at that same moment what sounded like movement, a muted

shuffling from somewhere back in the house. He stood still,
listening hard, but there was only silence now, the absolute
silence of the deserted bluffs. It would take him a few days
to get used to the silence, to the absence of traffic noise, to
the sound of the ocean at night, of coyotes and seabirds.
He saw that there were dust-covered cobwebs everywhere—
hanging from the plaster in the corners of the room, draped
from the wrought iron chandelier and the wooden shutters.
The whole place needed to be vacuumed out, the furniture
polished. Right now it was about as homey as a crypt.

He moved on across the living room and into the back
of the house. The air was heavy with the faint odor of decay
in the rear hallway. Something had probably gotten under
the sleeping porch and died—most likely a possum. It
wouldn't be the first time. The bluffs were full of coyotes
and rabbits and wood rats and possums, and dead animals
were common. There were turkey vultures circling in the
sky virtually every afternoon.

The big bedroom that stood at the back of the house had
been his parents' bedroom years ago. The door to the room
was shut now, and he waved his hand and arm in front of
his face in the gloomy hallway, clearing away cobwebs. He
had put off the job of clearing his parents' stuff out of the
room, partly out of sentimentality, partly out of laziness.
The last time he was here he had nearly finished the job,
but sorting and packing had taken more time than he had
thought it would, and when he pushed open the door and
walked in now, he saw the half-dozen boxes he had left
behind sitting around an immense old steamer trunk that
would probably be worth a couple hundred bucks in an
antiques store in southern California. He would give the
whole works to the maid when she showed up in the morning. That would buy her.

The odor was worse in the bedroom, fetid and almost
sweet, and he wondered if there was something in the toi-
letries shoved into one of the boxes, some kind of organic
soap, maybe, that had gone bad. He opened the shutters to
let in sunlight, then searched behind the boxes for a dead
rat. The boxes themselves were tied with twine, and clearly
hadn't been chewed open. He sat down on the four-poster

bed, shoving the bed drape all the way up to the head end.
He couldn't sleep in here along with the smell. He had to
find it.

He saw then that the trunk lid was not closed all the way,
so that a half inch of interior darkness was visible beneath
the boxy edge of the lid, and the thought occurred to him
that rats had gotten into the trunk, although the odor didn't
really have the musky urine smell of a rat's nest. He must
have shut the trunk when he'd packed it two years ago. It
had four spring latches, all of which were open. Hell, had
the house been broken into? Curious now, his senses suddenly alert, he stood up from the bed, and the movement
of the mattress caused one of the pillows to shift oddly, as
if something heavy had been balanced under the bedcovers.

He grasped the bedspread and pulled it back, and there,
nestled between two down pillows, lay a severed human
head, staring up at the ceiling through sunken milky eyes.

Mifflin reeled backward, stumbling against the edge of
the steamer trunk, grabbing the corner post of the bed to
keep himself from falling. There was the creaking sound of
disused hinges, of the trunk lid opening. He turned, throwing his hands in front of him defensively. Edmund Dalton
stood up from inside the trunk, a wide grin on his face, his
head nodding rapidly as if he had some kind of palsy.
''Boo!'' he said, and then started to laugh.

Mifflin rolled backward across the bed, landing heavily
on the floor and scrambling at once to his feet. Without a
backward glance he sprinted for the door, and Dalton followed him, taking his time, aiming his pistol. When Mifflin
was halfway down the hall, with no place to run but straight
ahead, Dalton shot him.

⊰53⊱

RED MAYHEW'S HEAD SAT IN A SHALLOW BAKING PAN ON the living room coffee table. The head wouldn't stand up on its own, so Edmund had propped it up with rocks out of the yard out front. Mifflin didn't seem to want to look at it. He didn't want to look at the can of lamp oil on the table, either. He was in a terrible state—frayed nerves, tied hand and foot to the couch, shot full of holes. "Ray Mifflin is alive, but not kicking," Edmund announced, deepening his voice like a sportscaster and then laughing out loud. He panned the room with the video camera, closing in on Mifflin, wide-eyed and sweating, then swung in for a close-up of Mayhew's rotten face. He shut the camera off, screwed it onto its tripod, turned it back on, and got down to business.

Next to the head in the pan he set a fist-sized candle fashioned like a multicolored Thanksgiving turkey. He had bought it on impulse at one of the so-called 99 cent stores that were spreading like a disease through southern California. Next to the turkey he laid five twenty-dollar bills that he had retrieved from Mifflin's luggage, fanning the bills out like a hand of cards. And behind those three elements of the piece, he set a heavy old windup alarm clock that had been in the steamer trunk in the bedroom. It ticked loudly now, filling the room with the sound of time flying by. He stepped back a couple of feet to admire the arrangement. It was good, very good. There was humor in it, what with the turkey sitting in a baking dish and all, ready to offer itself up to potential lamp oil flames. There was a message in the money aspect of the piece, too, a symbolic treatise on the dangers of greed. He angled the turkey a little bit more, so that it seemed to be looking at both Mifflin and Mayhew, two men who, depending upon chance and inspiration, might well end up companions in death. "Bring me the head of Red Mayhew," he said in the announcer's voice, then laughed again.

Mifflin was apparently in no mood to join in the laughter. In the hallway, Edmund had shot him through the right shoulder. The slug had a full metal jacket to minimize damage, something which Mifflin probably didn't appreciate as much as he should. Mifflin had passed out there in the hall, which had made it all that much easier to tie him to the couch. He wasn't in much danger of dying—not from the bullet wound, anyway. There wasn't enough blood leaking out of him to do anything more than stain the couch cover. And he was very much awake now. His eyes were glazed with pain and fear. There was no need to gag him, since it was unlikely that a neighbor would come calling.

"This turkey candle is a cheapie, Ray. It's meant as decoration, not as illumination. The lamp oil will provide the illumination. To an artist, there's a *big* difference between illumination and decoration. Now, the thing about this sort of candle is that it sputters and flares—burns down *really* fast—so fast that I might easily see hacienda smoke in my rearview mirror before I'm a half mile down the road. Frankly, I'd rather not. I'd rather be a bit closer to the border when this place goes up. That's the chance *I'm* willing to take, Ray. Of course, maybe the wick won't burn down far enough to light the oil at all, in which case the candle will fizzle out like bad fireworks. Or—here's another one—it could be that the house fills up with vapor from the lamp oil and simply explodes. Any authority on the subject will tell you that a vapor is *much* more explosive than a liquid. What I'm saying is that I can't be expected to know exactly what fate lies in store for Ray Mifflin. That's the entire point. I *love* that element of chance, Ray. Chance and intuition point the artist's way to inspiration."

Mifflin gaped at him. Terror apparently made him a good audience. He listened with perfect patience now as Edmund told him the story of the last couple of days—how he had come up out of nowhere with the idea of renting the car using the stolen credit card, how that had led him to the idea of killing Mayhew, and how he had borrowed a false mustache and makeup from the costume room at the Earl's, so as to pass himself off as one Ray Mifflin, businessman.

"The stolen driver's license is an unbelievably workable scam," he said. "I found that out weeks ago when I brought Mayhew in to impersonate my father. The truth is, Ray, there's a vast power in the world, a life force, waiting to be tapped. It's like solar power. It's free. It's unlimited. But the thing is, without inspiration, you can't see it and you can't access it. You don't have the right credit card. You look up in the sky, and there's the sun, way out there in space, ninety-three million miles away. A science book will tell you that what almost nobody realized until recently was that the sun's light was all around them—it was a force, like I said, an invisible force. Those rays could burn us up, Ray, or they could light our mind. The energy of artistic inspiration is the same damned thing. Artistic inspiration gives a man the kind of vision it takes to see the energy around him, and to know how to access it. Do you follow me?"

Mifflin nodded his head, letting it thump against the sheet-covered couch.

"I don't think you do, Ray. You're trying too hard. And anything you have to try hard at, you're not catching on to. But listen to this. Try to grasp the basic concept. There are some objects that are potential energy batteries. Like what, you're wondering. Take a clipboard, for instance. A man with a clipboard can get away with murder, Ray. He automatically becomes *official*, if you follow me. His line of baloney is suddenly gospel, because he's carrying a clipboard. Maybe he's got a pencil behind his ear. He has people sign their name. His clipboard and his pencil give him *power*.

"Believe it or not, a uniform works the same way. And I'm not talking about a policeman's uniform, either. It's got plenty of power, but it's dangerous power—too apparent. I'm talking about *any* uniform. A milkman's uniform, for God's sake. Have you ever been a Boy Scout leader?"

Mifflin shook his head. He looked confused, which was

natural. Probably he had never actually *thought* about anything before. Ray Mifflin was no intellectual.

"Neither have I," Edmund told him. "But just for fun I bought a scout leader's uniform once—bought the badges, the epaulets for the shoulder, the belt and buckle, the whole works. I'll tell you something, Ray, women fell all over me, especially the single moms, and the housewives whose husbands were too weak to keep them happy. A woman will do *anything* you ask her to do if you've got a scout leader's uniform on. That's a fact, Ray. Somebody probably should have told you this years ago, when it could have done you some good. She'll climb right into your car, if you want her to. Hell, into your *bed*. Now, some men will tell you that a set of Porsche keys, say, will give you that same kind of power, and that's not a lie by any means. Porsche keys will kindle her interest. But there's one thing Porsche keys won't kindle, and that's a woman's trust. A scout uniform will kindle her trust. And once you have a woman's trust . . .

"Well, let's just say that once she's given you her trust, you can pretty much have her life along with it. Does that appall you, Ray, that kind of talk? Do you begin to understand me?"

Mifflin stared at him.

Edmund shook his head. He was wasting his breath here, talking to a man like Mifflin. His eyes were closed now. Probably his mind was a mile away. Well, you could lead a horse to water, but talking to him wasn't going to make him drink.

"Listen to that clock ticking, Ray. It says a lot, doesn't it? Everyone understands the language of time. So tell me something, Ray: it looks like you've been carrying around Dave Quinn's telephone number—the number of the elusive Mr. Jim Jones. Why?" He showed him the number, which he'd found stuffed into Mifflin's wallet.

"No reason," Mifflin said weakly, opening his eyes and swallowing hard.

"*No* reason? That's a *good* reason to be carrying it around. Did you call him yesterday?"

"No."

''Today?''

''*No.*''

''Are you lying to me, Ray? I think you are.''

''No, hell no,'' Mifflin said.

''Because if you are, Ray, I'm going to light this couch on fire right now. I'm going to soak the couch with lamp oil and light it on fire. We'll have Mifflin on the barby.''

''I didn't say anything to anybody,'' Mifflin gasped. ''I just got the hell out. I found out about the car and Mayhew and got out. I just wanted out.''

''I get the point, Ray. You wanted out.'' Dalton laughed out loud. He crumpled up the paper with the phone number on it and threw it on the floor. ''That was my little IQ test, by the way—giving you the Mastercard and the driver's license back. I had a *great* deal of fun with that. I followed you all over town, Ray, out to Long Beach, down to Laguna. You were putting the pieces together, puzzling things out like a private eye. You were a busy man, Ray, a *busy* man, you and your handful of weeds. I'll admit, though, your phone call last night took me by surprise. I had actually come to believe that you were an honest man, and then the phone rang, and there you were trying to extort an extra ten thousand out of me. I said to myself, '*This* is not the Ray Mifflin I know.' Greed had worked its magic on you, and I determined right then to plan out a way to undo the damage that the easy money had done.

''Anyway, when you hit the bank this morning, I knew for certain what Ray Mifflin was up to. 'Ray Mifflin is running,' I told myself, and I drove right on down here to the Mifflin hacienda to prepare my little surprise. You didn't give me much time, either. You've got a *hell* of a lead foot. I got down here about a half hour earlier than you did. I walked in through the garage and—wham!— something wonderful happened: in the darkness I kicked this full can of lamp oil. I've already told you about chance and intuition, Ray. Things come to us out of the darkness when we leave ourselves open to them, and this can of lamp oil was like that. It *spoke* to me, Ray. I had a mental image of a man in flames, and I knew that man was you, and that the flames were in this red-and-white can.

"What I didn't know was what I was going to do with
Mr. Mayhew's head, which was in need of immediate attention. Mr. Mayhew, as you yourself know, smells even
worse dead than alive. Should I put the head in the steamer
trunk and hide myself under the bed? Or should I put the
head in the bed and hide myself in the trunk? Now, all else
being equal, I would favor putting the head in the trunk,
because I've always liked the idea of leaving little *gifts* for
people in clever little ways, and the trunk suggests itself
for that, don't you think? A gift box for Ray Mifflin?"

Mifflin had closed his eyes again, and he had started to
sweat profusely. "Nod your head if you're listening, Ray!
Good!" he said, when Mifflin nodded. "Anyway, there you
were, coming through the door, and I had to make my decision quick. 'Head in the bed,' I thought, and I realized it
rhymed. It was just like kicking that can in the dark garage.
It was *right*. It was artistically copacetic. So I decided that
in your case *I'd* be the little gift, Ray. I'm proud of that
decision, too. It was extremely effective, I think. Very artistic, the way it was timed. How about you? Did you find
it artistic?"

He bent down and flicked Mifflin's ear hard enough to
make the man's eyes shoot open. Suddenly Mifflin went
rigid, arching his back, putting all of his strength into
breaking free of the cords that tied him to the couch. The
pain in his shoulder contorted his face. Clearly he wasn't
up to breaking anything. Given a little time he might wiggle
his way loose, if he had the backbone to see it through.

"By the way, I found out where they buried Hoffa,"
Edmund told him, making another slight adjustment to the
turkey candle. "It was in New York, in Giants Stadium,
under the goal posts. Do you know what they did to him,
Ray? What they did to Hoffa?"

He waited patiently now for Mifflin to shake his head.
"They cut him into pieces with a chain saw and carried
him away in suitcases. Those suitcases became his coffin.
This house, quite frankly, might well be *your* coffin, Ray.
Before the hour is through, you stand a chance of being
consumed by your own birthright. But just between you
and me, I haven't made up my mind about that yet. I

haven't thought that part through yet. Think of it: your life hangs in the delicate balance at this very moment.''

In the relative silence that followed, the ticking of the clock reminded Edmund that it was getting on toward dusk. The living room was even heavier with gloom now that evening was falling, and in another hour, out here on these lonely bluffs, the interior of the house would be utterly dark. The white sheets draped over the furniture already shone in the waning daylight like pale, hovering ghosts. Edmund felt something uncanny in the still air of the room, and he blinked his eyes slowly, concentrating, focusing. He moved slowly to the camera on the tripod. There was something . . . a presence in the room, a familiar presence.

He studied the dim room. It seemed to him that there were moth-flutters of movement in the deeper shadows, back amid the heavy wooden furniture, and he moved the camera lens toward it, backing the zoom away to open the lens up full. From the corner of his eye he saw what looked like the brief tremble of a veil blowing across a dark doorway. He tilted his head, searching the edge of his vision, sweeping his mind clear almost without effort now, holding himself utterly still and calling her to him across the infinite dimension of darkness. There was a shimmering motion, almost like falling glitter, near a shuttered window, and then, for a moment, for just the blink of an eye, she moved in the darkness near the fireplace—the Night Girl's shadowy silhouette against the heavy white plaster of the hearth. He aimed the camera at her, not daring to look through the viewfinder.

He closed his eyes and pictured her face, the curve of her shoulders, her black hair. She was with him again at last, a collaborator, as she had been with him when he had worked with the man who had been Mayhew, who had impersonated his own father. ''Yes,'' he said out loud, affirming his faith in her, in the two of them. ''Come with me . . .'' It was time to decide Ray Mifflin's fate, time to bring this to a close. He angled the camera toward the couch again, then picked up a book of matches from a ceramic dish on the mantel. The face of the cardboard matchbook was blank; it told him nothing. He looked around, searching for guidance in the room—a sign, a symbol.

Mifflin was staring at him wide-eyed, shaking his head. Without speaking, Edmund picked up the can of lamp oil and carefully doused the couch and the area rug that the table sat on, then poured a pool of the liquid in the baking dish, dribbling it out onto the coffee table before setting the can down again. The lamp oil had a lemon and kerosene smell that masked the corrupt smell of Mayhew's head. The five twenties floated on the surface of the oil, miraculously maintaining the precise symmetry of their arrangement. The wick of the candle thrust up out of the middle of the turkey's back, waiting for the touch of a match. The clock ticked, the minute hand turning toward six o'clock, the day almost exactly three-quarters gone. Edmund Dalton breathed rhythmically, trancelike, clearing his mind of mental debris, feeling the nearness of the Night Girl, her spirit seeping into him, filling him.

"How old are you, Ray Mifflin?" He asked the question in a monotone, careful not to break the springlike tension in the air, staring straight before him, the room having lost dimension, the sound of the clock shutting out all other sound.

He knew that Mifflin was watching him, that the man was lost and waiting, but he didn't meet Mifflin's terror-filled eyes. And he wouldn't meet them—he wanted no distraction, not until he had determined the man's fate.

He repeated his question—that evening's key to the puzzle of life and death. "How old are you, Ray Mifflin?"

"Sixty," Mifflin whispered, heaving an impossibly deep breath.

Sixty. The word was inevitable. Dalton had sensed it. Somehow it had come to him a moment ago, hidden in the ticking of the clock. He focused again on the clock face. The minute hand touched the twelve now; the hour hand rested solidly on the six. So just as three-quarters of the day had passed, three-quarters of Mifflin's life had gone the same way. There was a perfect parallel, a true synchronicity.

Yes.

He heard the affirming voice in his mind, like the wind whispering.

As the last sibilant fragments of the word faded into the darkness, he stood up slowly, shrugging his shoulders, shaking the trance out of his head. He breathed deeply, looking at Mifflin. Sometimes there was more power in letting a weak man live than in killing a strong man. He held up the matchbook so that Mifflin could see it, and then tossed it down onto the five twenties floating in the tray. The bills drifted apart. The minute hand of the clock jumped forward, time running on into the close of day.

"*Bon voyage*, Ray. I wish you a good life down here in Mexico. I think you should stay here. I'm going to let you keep most of your money, by the way, and I'm going to let you keep Mr. Mayhew's head. It's served its purpose, and I can't stand the smell of it. I truly believe that you did not call Mr. Davey Jones. And that means that you didn't try to betray me, although you could have. You kept the faith, and I appreciate that; I truly do. I appreciate it so much that I'm going to forgive you for trying to take more than your share of the pie. It was a *big* piece of pie, Ray, for a little man like you. But I'm a man of my word. I'm going to let you keep it. I'm not even going to charge you a fee for driving down here, because it really has been fun. And let me tell you one last thing. Money is not the issue with me, Ray. It never has been. I'm an artist. Some artists work on canvas or clay; I work on people. I reshape their lives. Sometimes I reshape their physical forms. You might say that my audience is my medium. It's the purest form of art, Ray, and you've been a part of it."

He looked around one last time, realizing that the Night Girl was gone. He was through here. He stared out through the shutters at the empty evening. There were lights on in the neighboring house, but it was a quarter mile away; nobody would see him leave. He realized that he felt very damned good, very fit and sharp. The dark shrubbery stood out in perfect clarity beyond the window, and he perceived every leaf and twig and branch as if he were studying an artist's rendering, as if finally he could truly *see*. The distant lights along the bluffs shone like personal beacons, and he

was brimming with inspiration, with the essential *rightness*
that had come into his world. He looked down on Mifflin
now as if from an eminence, a height that he had been
ascending these last few weeks. He knew that he was
nearly, but not quite, to the peak.

Suddenly he thought about the long drive home in the
rented car. He had the false I.D. and credit cards in his
wallet, and he saw himself driving back up the freeway into
southern California, basking in the utter and complete freedom of a man with an assumed identity. He picked up the
camera and the tripod and went out through the front door,
leaving Ray Mifflin once again the master of his own forever altered fate.

⊰54⊱

EDMUND'S ROOM AT THE MT. PLEASANT MOTOR HOTEL
on Beach Boulevard was only a block down from Right
Now Notary. It had obviously been furnished twenty or
thirty years ago. The rust-orange shag carpet had been vacuumed, but the vacuuming hadn't helped, and the seascape
painting on the wall was straight out of a thrift store. When
he had arrived two mornings ago, he had moved the painting into the closet and then had slid the dresser aside in
order to expose the white-painted wall. The fleabag rooms
were semidetached and rentable by the month—not the sort
of place a tourist would check into. Unlike an authentic
motel, there were no maids wheeling carts up and down
outside the room, and he had made it clear to the manage-
ment that he didn't want to be disturbed. Best of all, the
Mt. Pleasant was a place where tenants had long ago put a
lid on their curiosity.

His relationship with the Night Girl was stronger than

ever since he had dealt with Mayhew and Mifflin, and what he needed now was to be left alone with her when he chose to be alone. He had been fairly successful in capturing her image on film, although the results were shadowy and indistinct. He had read that primitive people feared that a photograph would steal a man's soul, and he was convinced that under the right conditions there might be a certain truth in the idea. Voodoo priests, certainly, saw a similar magic in a photographic image and the image represented by a cloth doll. A photograph of the Night Girl, at the very least, demonstrated that something increasingly permanent had come into existence at his bidding. And yet she was still merely a figment of his passions. Something prevented her from being fully realized, from having existence beyond his own desires, and he knew what that something was.

The Day Girl and the Night Girl were meant to be one, not two. Anne's stubborn attachment to the Day Girl persona was a closed door. What to do to open that door, or simply to obliterate it: that was the very interesting problem.

In the time since his return from Mexico he'd had a vague sense of impending trouble. There was something in the air, and he had sensed it right away when he had passed into Orange County. The elevated mood provided by his successes with Mayhew and Mifflin had evaporated like the foggy spring weather. He felt slightly edgy now, and he found himself constantly checking the street past the heavy window curtains, half expecting to see a police car slowing down to turn into the tree-shaded lot. What he wanted now was a clarity of focus, but despite reading and meditation, he couldn't quite maintain it.

He also wanted to clean out the condo, especially to dismantle the darkroom and retrieve the stuff from the library. That was something he should have done before driving down to Mexico. He found these days that he quickly lost interest in his own films and photos; the thrill was in the *process*, as it was for any artist; and when the process was complete, his eyes were on the next piece, figuratively speaking. His collected work, like the work of any artist, was meant to affect an audience, but as the creator of a piece, he couldn't also be an audience to it. One way or another, he shouldn't have left the films lying around in his apartment. It was simply incriminating, and the sooner he found a market for them, the better. The next couple of days were going to be busy.

He gathered up the odds and ends on the table in order to put them into the trunk of his rented car: an extension cord, a cheap plastic drop cloth, a ten-dollar lamp timer from the dime store, a light-bulb socket with a cord, and a hundred-watt bulb with a hole punched into the top of it to expose the intact filament, which would heat up to over a thousand degrees when the bulb was screwed into the socket and plugged in. All together the cheap collection would make a simple incendiary timer, and out of that simplicity would come a complication of priceless results.

When he left the room, locking the door behind him, it was still two hours before dawn.

AFTER TWO DAYS OF CLEAR, WINDBLOWN SKIES, THE warm inland temperatures drew moisture in off the ocean again, and the coast was once more gray with fog in the early-morning darkness. Edmund was forced to follow closely behind Casey's truck, south through Surfside and into Sunset Beach, keeping the old bullet-shaped tail lights in view. When the truck angled toward the edge of the Highway and slowed down, Edmund turned left and circled the block, parking on 23rd Street where he could see, dimly through the fog, the front end of the parked truck. There was an Arco station open on the corner, and a motorist stood at the pumps. Another drove into the lot now and got out of his car, heading in to pay in advance for his gas.

This spot was *way* too busy, Edmund told himself, no place to kill your brother. He laughed a little bit, hunkering down in the seat, eating almonds out of a Baggie and waiting for Casey to come back. His brother's early-morning routine was virtually always the same: three or four pre-dawn stops to check out the surf along the several miles of beach break between Seal Beach and Newport, and then straight back to whatever beach looked good to him.

Casey reappeared from between two rows of apartment houses. He climbed straight back into the truck and fired up the engine, then rolled away again, south toward Huntington, and Edmund let him get far out of sight before swinging away from the curb and following. He reached over and repositioned the video camera on the passenger seat, making sure again that it hadn't shut itself off.

It had first dawned on him down in Mexico that Casey was the problem. Casey had *always* been the problem. His hatred of his little brother was the first thing he remembered about childhood. He couldn't pin that hatred on any particular incident, either. It seemed to have no reason except the existence of Casey himself, and yet it was a very *real* hatred, an authentic hatred, not something that Edmund had made up out of jealousy or some other petty emotion. After all, there was nothing about Casey to be jealous about.

He spotted the truck's taillights ahead at an intersection, and he pulled over to wait again. If Casey recognized him, the morning would be wasted. Perhaps if his brother had amounted to something, if he had made any effort at all to carry his own weight, things would have been different. But Casey had never made any such effort. He had adapted perfectly to some kind of moron sixties hippie surfer philosophy, and had spent his life playing while other people worked. He was an uneducated bum, just as much as Mayhew had been a bum—a waste of the life force, a drain of cosmic energy like a leaky toilet. Somewhere Edmund had heard that a toilet can leak thousands of gallons of precious water a year, one drop at a time. Multiply that by thousands of leaky toilets, and you could fill a reservoir.

Last night Casey had called him on the telephone! He had asked Edmund to ''back off'' on Collier and to give

Anne "some space." Not only had Edmund held onto his temper, he had agreed wholeheartedly. Yes, indeed. He had pretended to be schooled by his little brother, his infantile, no account, do-nothing, beach bum little brother, who obviously was parroting something that he'd heard from Dave the lionheart, the proud bird with the golden hammer. "Lots of leaky toilets," Edmund muttered. Giving *him* advice! This morning he was going after one of those leaks with his plumber's helpers: a gallon of alcohol and a hell of a big spark. Lately he had extended his study of the fine art of fire, and he was anxious to witness the visual effect of the cool blue flame of burning alcohol. . . .

He slowed down when he passed Goldenwest Street, since Casey nearly always stopped for a wave check north of the pier. Sure enough, there was the truck, parked along the side of the Highway. Edmund moved into the left lane and drove on past, turned left at 7th Street, and pulled into the liquor store parking lot, where he cut his lights and waited, letting the engine idle. There were no other cars parked at the curb, but with dawn approaching, there soon would be. Next stop was Magnolia Street, where Casey would pull off into the turnaround by the lifeguard headquarters—no place to commit a murder. After that he'd either turn around or head south to Newport; either way it would be too late for any action. It was now or never.

He watched his brother get out of the truck and walk past the parking meter and across the grass toward the ocean. Because of the fog and the darkness, he would have to climb the stairs to the beach and walk nearly to the water's edge to check the waves, which ought to give Edmund plenty of time. He shut off the engine and climbed out of the car, wearing a pair of surgical gloves and carrying a gas can and a nearly empty vodka bottle—a quart that he'd bought two days ago at the supermarket. He had poured it into the empty gas can along with a second quart of vodka, then topped the can off with a half gallon of pure ethanol.

Predictably, his brother left his surfboard in the bed of the truck. If he decided to stay and surf, he'd return for his board and wetsuit, and the truck would sit here on the roadside for the next three or four hours. The alcohol would evaporate, and Edmund's plan would remain merely a good idea.

But if Casey decided to drive on, to check out one more spot . . .

Edmund loped across the empty Highway, carrying the gas can, which he set on the curb in front of the truck. Then, hurriedly, he followed the path his brother had taken to the stairs. There was no sign of him. Obviously he had gone on down to the beach. Edmund returned to the truck and raised the hood, then leaned in underneath and found the distributor cap and the wire that ran from the distributor to the coil, just like in the photo illustration from the repair manual that he'd bought at Pep Boys. He gripped the wire at its base, tugged and wiggled it halfway out of the coil, and then sloshed vodka and alcohol on it out of the can, pooling up the alcohol on the manifold. He splashed the liquid everywhere over the engine, dumping it through the open cable holes in the firewall. Then he shut the hood carefully, leaning hard on it to latch it. He spent five seconds listening hard for the slap of Casey's bare feet on the stairs, but he heard nothing but the sound of the ocean and the rumble of a car as it passed.

He dumped alcohol on the hood for good measure, pouring it along the base of the windshield. The fog was with him once again: the dewy truck would mask the wetness of the alcohol, and the alcohol, of course, would burn even when it was diluted with water. He opened the driver's side door, lifted the beach towel that covered the torn seat upholstery, and soaked the exposed foam seat cushion. He splashed it on the door panel and poured it under the wetsuit and the trash that littered the floor, splashing more across the top of the trash before flicking liquid up under the dash. He emptied the rest of the can, finally, shaking out the last drops, then shoved the vodka bottle back underneath the seat where his brother wouldn't see it when he climbed in. He shut the door carefully, and without a backward glance ran back across the highway, opened the trunk of his car and tossed in the gas can and the gloves, and then climbed into his car again, where he waited with the engine running.

He took a deep breath and settled down for the show. It would be safer to drive away, of course. But he *had* to watch it happen; he had to get it on film, the only permanent record of performance art. He pictured his brother climbing into the car, cranking the engine, the first creeping blue alcohol flames when the spark from the half-disengaged coil wire ignited the fuel. . . .

"A surefire thing," Edmund muttered in a cowpoke accent, then laughed at his own joke. The whole thing had been *per*fect. Casey had set himself up with his piglike truck knee-deep in garbage. The old broken-down seats and the wetsuit and the trash could have soaked up *two* gallons of alcohol, just like Casey himself. A man's car was an absolute reflection of his personality, after all, and . . .

Casey appeared right then, a shadow in the fog. He came straight around the front of the truck, opened the door, and stood for a moment in the street as if he were making up his mind about something. He looked at his watch. *Get in*, Edmund commanded silently, and abruptly Casey *did* get in. Edmund heard the old engine roar into life, and he half expected a big whoosh of flame, the truck going up like a funeral pyre.

Nothing apparently happened. Casey sat there for a moment or two with the engine idling, looking through the windshield at the fog. Then the truck moved slowly forward. Edmund prepared to follow him. He put one hand on the video camera, switching it on, and drove out toward the street, watching the truck pick up speed. He couldn't afford to fall behind now, not if he wanted this on film.

He saw something now! Flames, flickering up along the rear edge of the hood, dancing blue flames in a skirt along the base of the window. "Yes," he muttered, slapping his hand against the steering wheel. "Burn." The truck accelerated, heading south, and Edmund followed, running the light at 7th and looping around behind the truck, which was swerving erratically now, fifty yards ahead. Edmund grappled one-handed with the video camera, pressing the record button and steadying it against the dashboard.

There was fire inside the cab now, not the blue of an alcohol fire, but the yellow flames of the trash going up, the seat cushions burning. A reek of black smoke poured out of the rolled-down window, and the truck veered sharply across two lanes, angled across the intersection at Main, jumped the curb and sidewalk, and crashed into a stand of queen palms in front of Maxwell's, the old boarded-up pierside restaurant. The truck stopped dead, and both doors flew open with the impact.

Edmund slowed way down, craning his neck, desperate to see what would happen, aiming the camera as well as he could, but still moving. He whooped out loud, the sound of his voice mingling with the sudden howl of a police siren, right behind him. Shocked by the siren, he dropped the camera to the seat and looked into the rearview mirror, which reflected the flashing blue lights of a patrol car. He accelerated—not running, but as if anxious to get out of the way.

The cop pulled over to the curb and leaped out of the car, and Edmund kept going, moving the camera to the floor and dropping his coat over it. Watching the review mirror for any kind of pursuit, he drove south to the Huntington Towers before turning off the highway.

≈ 56 ≈

"A CAR FIRE?" DAVE SAID. "DID HE GET BURNED? WHAT the hell happened?" The waiting room at Humana Hospital was mostly empty and smelled of fresh paint and upholstery. Nancy's eyes were red from crying, but she was composed now. Her long blonde hair was pulled back in a heavy ponytail. She'd just been walking out the door to go to work when the phone had rung with the news of Casey's accident. She'd called Jolene, looking for the Earl, and Jolene had given the news to Dave when he showed up for work.

"The burns aren't bad," she told him. "He hit the windshield hard, though, and the doctors think he's got a subdural hematoma, that he's bleeding in the brain. They did a CAT scan, and I guess they're going to open him up to relieve the pressure."

"Open him up?"

"Drill a hole in his skull. That's how I understand it. The doctor acts like it's no big deal, but . . ."

Dave realized that she wasn't going to finish the sentence, that she was crying again. "I don't think it's all that uncommon, Nance. The brain works itself out. It's a weird organ."

"Uh-huh," she said after a moment. "Anyway, he has some burns on his legs and arms, but nothing worse than second degree. A cop was right there when the truck hit the tree, and he got the flames out as quick as he could. Casey had got out of the truck and made it down onto the beach. I guess he was trying to reach the water."

"He still wanted to get some waves," Dave said. Nancy didn't laugh. "How'd he get out of the car if he hit his head that hard? Maybe the injury's not that bad."

"Adrenaline. That's what the doctor said. When he was fighting to get out of the truck and put out the fire, the adrenaline blocked the bleeding. Then when the adrenaline backed off, he started bleeding again. He's been on and off, you know. First he's dingy and then he's okay. It's scary."

"He'll be all right, Nance."

"Yeah," she said flatly. There was relative silence in the waiting room now, the brief sound of a bell from up the hallway, the elevator doors opening and shutting.

"What did you mean about him getting cited? Earlier, over the phone. Did they arrest him? What did they charge him with, hitting a tree?"

"An open container in the car."

"I don't believe it."

Nancy stared at him, as if he'd said something utterly idiotic. "Well, Dave, it's true," she said. "You know how much he drank. You and I have talked about it more than once. So don't act like it's a shock. He's a big boy. You don't have to stick up for him.''

''And you *do* know he quit?''

''He's quit about ten times, Dave. There was an empty quart of vodka in the truck. It looks like he spilled it all over the place when the fire broke out. The alcohol apparently flared up. According to the police, it's easy to test for vodka residue in the upholstery and floor carpet. Even his wetsuit burned. You're not allowed to burn your own car up and run into a tree like that. Turns out it's against the law.''

''*Vodka*,'' Dave said flatly.

''That's what it was. A vodka bottle. They're not lying, Dave. The cop didn't rescue him and then plant a bottle in the truck.''

''Of course not. But did you *ever* see him drink vodka? I mean aside from in a bloody Mary or something?''

''That's the liquor of choice for the alcoholic who's hiding it. I'm not all that naive, Dave. I watched my father go down that same road, morning till night. Casey stayed up late and kept himself company. He left in the morning with a thermos full of coffee. Who knows what he put in his coffee? If you haven't lived with an alcoholic, you can't imagine.''

''I'm sorry,'' Dave said. ''I guess I can't imagine. If you told me that they found a can of Budweiser, *then* I could imagine. This was at five this morning?''

''Yeah, about.''

''Then he was on his way to the beach.''

''Of course he was. Casey was always on his way to the beach.''

''Well I can tell you that he never drank before he surfed, Nance. He just didn't. Alcohol doesn't go with the vibe, if you know what I mean. It kills your reaction time. It makes you stodgy. When you drink you don't want to surf, you want to drink. And when you drink, what you want is another drink. You want to keep the buzz. If you're out in the water for three hours, the buzz is going to die and leave you feeling stupid. I'm telling you the truth; he wouldn't have been drinking at all before he surfed, not even beer, and he certainly wouldn't have been drinking vodka out of the goddamn bottle.''

''Don't lecture at me, Dave. *I* didn't find the bottle in his truck; the cop did. I've been living with Casey's drinking for years, putting a smile on my face, pretending there was no problem. I've always been afraid of this kind of thing. All those years and he never even got a DUI. All I can tell you is that if he'd hit another car instead of a palm tree, he'd be in a hell of a lot more trouble.''

''Yeah,'' Dave said, lowering his voice. ''You're right. I don't mean to be arguing with you. It's just that . . . I don't know. I mean, I can buy there was a fire and all, but there's something dead wrong about the vodka bottle. And not only that, but he and I talked this out just a couple of days ago. Casey and I made a sort of deal, I guess you can say. He might have fallen off the wagon, Nance. All kinds of people do that every day—better people than me. But he would have told me if he did. I know he would have told me.''

''It was early. Maybe you weren't up yet,'' Nancy said.

Dave stared at her. She was shook up. There was no point in arguing this now. ''When can I see him?''

''I don't know. They chased me out. The Earl was here, but he left. He's coming back in a little bit.''

''How is he?''

''The Earl? He looks like hell. He's coping, though, or at least he seems to be. The doctors are pumping him full of positive statistics. You know how he is. It's like Casey's got tonsillitis or something. The Earl's not into negativity.''

''You'll give me a call when he can have visitors?''

''Right away. And I'm sorry I'm bad company. Thanks for having some faith in Casey. But he needs a reality check, Dave. We all need a reality check.''

''That's the truth,'' Dave said. He stood up and tried to smile at her. ''I'll be at the warehouse most of the time. Call me.'' She nodded, and he left, heading out through the glass doors and walking through the parking lot under a dreary sky.

"THAT WAS THE GIST OF IT," DAVE SAID TO ANNE. "Nancy's pretty upset. You haven't met Nancy?"

Anne sprayed dark gray shading onto the edges of the etched Styrofoam blocks of the palace. The compressor grumbled into life, pressurizing the sprayer, and Anne waited until it fell silent again before she answered. "No. I only met Casey once. Seemed like a nice guy. Edmund had a little bit of contempt for him. He called him a beach bum, I think."

"Well, I guess he is. He's an interesting guy. Drinks too much, or at least he used to. He happens to be my best friend."

"So I've gathered."

"Well, it looks like he might have been drinking before he drove the truck into the tree."

"Anybody else hurt?"

"Just him. He's got some sort of brain hemorrhage. They're going to operate to relieve the pressure."

"Well, he's a little bit lucky anyway. He'd be in trouble if he'd hurt anybody else."

"He's lucky. You're right about that. He also happens to be absolutely honest, at least outside of the drinking. And as far as I know, he's even been honest about that. He never hid it from me."

"He didn't have to. There's lots of stuff you don't have to hide from your friends. You hide things from your family. Sometimes it's the people you love the most who you hide things from." Anne switched paint jars, cleared the gray paint out of the spray tip, and misted the base of the stones with moss green, then stood back to take a look.

"I can't argue with that," Dave said. "And there's a *lot* of really complicated family politics in the Earl's case, a lot of trouble over the years that's been overlooked. The Earl's got a pair of rose-colored glasses that would fit Godzilla. Sometimes I wish I could borrow them."

"It's a little late for him to take them off now."

"I wouldn't want him to. But I'm really having a hard time with the cop finding an open container in Casey's truck. I just don't believe it. Casey was on the wagon. And not only that, but in all the years I've known him, he never drank before he surfed. It was maybe the only good reason he had *not* to drink, except Nancy, of course."

"Yeah, but drinking's a kind of a downhill slide, isn't it? Sooner or later it gets the upper hand. I'm sorry to talk in clichés, but it's true. He might have different habits now than he had ten years ago."

"If he does, he's kept them a secret from me. And he wasn't the kind of guy to keep secrets."

"So what are you saying, exactly?"

"I'm saying that something's wrong. They found an open bottle in his car. I don't think he put it there."

"Who did?" She brushed a strand of hair out of her eyes and looked at him, setting her airbrush down on a keg.

Dave waited for a moment before he responded. He felt as if he were crossing a line, committing himself to a course of action that he couldn't quite imagine, but that would change things irreversibly. "I think Edmund put it there. I shouldn't even tell you this, but Edmund's been stealing property from the Earl. He's been quitclaiming real estate into his own name and probably selling it. I talked to a tax accountant who I think was notarizing the deeds. I told Casey about it the other morning, and it didn't surprise him at all."

"What did he say he was going to do about it?"

"Nothing. He's a beach bum. He doesn't give a flying damn about his brother's greed. And what Edmund's stealing is just a piece of what the Earl owns."

"But with Casey dead, Edmund gets the whole thing, not just pieces."

"That's how I read it. The Earl's heart is a basket case.

He could be in more trouble over Casey's accident than Casey is.''

"*How* did he do it?''

"Who?''

"Edmund. You're telling me that he lit the truck on fire, planted the bottle, and ran the truck into a tree with Casey in it?''

Dave looked at her. "That's just what I'm saying. There's way too many fires breaking out around here. I think Edmund's lighting them. Every damned one. He's completely screwed in the head.''

"He's in Mexico, remember? He wanted me to go with him. I saw the plane tickets.''

"That doesn't change my mind. He could hire someone to do it easily enough. And maybe he's *not* in Mexico. Maybe he just *told* everyone he was going to Mexico. We didn't check.''

"How do you check?''

"I have no idea, but I'm going to find out. And in the meantime, I think we better change the locks on your apartment.''

"Today. I'll call Mr. Hedgepeth.''

"Forget Mr. Hedgepeth. I'll change them, and then you'll know you have every copy of the key. We'll bolt that connecting door, too, from your side.''

It occurred to Dave then that both of the warehouse trucks had long ago pulled away from the loading dock. Jolene was working away in her office. The Earl was at the hospital. Except for Dave and Anne, the warehouse was empty. He looked at Anne. "You know what I'm going to do?''

"What?''

"I'm going to break into the bastard's office.''

"What do you think is in there?''

"I don't really care. I've had it. I love this place, and I could work here till I drop dead, but unless something gets done right now, this place isn't going to be this place very much longer.''

"I'm going to break in, too,'' Anne said. "Turnabout's

fair play. If he can break into my apartment, I can break into his office.''

"I don't think so. It's illegal as hell. Even if we do find something in there, we probably can't use it against him, not legally. Even if we were cops, we couldn't use it against him.''

"Right, but I want to know. Right now I don't care about using it against him. I want to know, absolutely, that the creep was in my apartment. I'm the one with the big complaint against him, aren't I? He bad-mouths you, but he breaks into my apartment. There's no way you're doing this without me.''

"If Edmund finds out that we were in his office, he'll press charges against us for breaking and entering. He's liable to say anything—that we stole something, whatever he can dream up to cause us trouble. And if we *do* find anything interesting in there, it'll just make it worse.''

"He'll never know. All we have to do is climb over the wall, right? How hard could it be?''

Dave carried an extension ladder up the stairs and tilted it against the wall beside the door to Edmund's office cubicle. He climbed the ladder and looked in, but as always, there wasn't anything to see. It was the emptiest possible office, the office of a man who had nothing to do. He pulled himself up onto the wall, swung his legs over, and dropped down onto the top of the desk. He threw the bolt, stepped out on to the balcony and laid the extension ladder down so that it wouldn't be visible from below, and then followed Anne back into the office and shut the door.

"Two minutes and we're out of here,'' Anne said, wiping the footprint dust off the desktop. Immediately she looked beneath the desk itself, then opened the top desk drawer all the way and peered into the back of it, shutting it again almost at once. She opened another drawer and rifled through papers, and Dave pulled on one of the file cabinet drawers, which was locked.

"They're locked,'' he said. "All of them.''

"Of course they are,'' Anne said. She opened a third drawer, shifted the contents around carefully, and then reached up under it, feeling around on the inside walls of the desk and on the bottom of the drawer above. She opened another drawer and repeated the process, then stopped and seemed to be working at something. "Here's a key," she said, removing it from where it was hidden and peeling Scotch tape from it. She tossed it to Dave, who fit it into the lock at the top of the cabinet. He turned it, unlocking all the drawers at once. He pulled the top drawer open and looked inside. There was a litter of real estate pamphlets on the bottom along with a couple of ads for gyms and sports centers.

He opened the second drawer. It was empty except for one of Elinor's dolls, which lay in the bottom, staring upward out of eyes stitched out of black thread. Dave pulled his hand away from the metal drawer pull as if it were hot, then stepped back and gestured toward the drawer. Anne looked inside, started to pick up the doll, then let it lie there. Its face was nearly indistinguishable from the face on the doll in Anne's closet—the same slack mouth, the same demonic eyes, the same tumorous flesh from the lines of stitching pulled tight in the stuffed nylon. It was clearly a female doll, though, with long hair of stitched-in black thread and a tight black dress.

"Let's leave it," Anne said. "What's the point of taking it?"

Dave slid the drawer shut. She was right. They knew for certain what they'd already suspected, although even this wasn't enough to establish that Edmund had broken into Anne's apartment, only that he had gone through her boxes. Dave opened the third file drawer, which held a scattering of magazines and newspapers and two hardcover books. The newspapers were vending machine sex ads, one of which was folded open to a page displaying grainy-looking nude photos, some of them particularly obscene. Several telephone numbers had been crossed out with felt pen.

"Edmund's got a problem," Anne said, sitting down in the desk chair. "I just quit my detective job. I don't think it's worth it—whatever it was we're trying to find."

"When Collier's truck burned up, there was a bunch of this trash in the back end. The arsonist put it there to make

Collier look bad. Obviously he was hoping it would come to the notice of Social Services.''

''Where did he *buy* this stuff?''

''Porno shops, I guess,'' Dave said. ''I guess that's where he bought the magazines. You're asking the wrong guy, actually. These newspapers, though—you can find them in vending machines all over the place. Any kid with a handful of quarters can buy one.''

''You're kidding.''

''I'm not kidding. All this is legal, as far as I can see. If it was pedophile stuff, it wouldn't be legal. But it wouldn't matter to us anyway, because you can't break into someone's office or car or backpack or whatever looking for evidence. If we hauled this down to the police station, they'd arrest us for breaking and entering. Edmund would be the injured party.''

He picked up one of the books. It was titled simply *Sexual Magick*, and was illustrated with badly carved woodcut pictures of genitalia and sexual poses. Someone—Edmund, probably—had scribbled in the margins and underlined passages on nearly every page. The second book was the same kind of thing, even more thoroughly annotated and underlined. He laid the books back in the drawer and slid it shut.

''Edmund's sicker than I thought,'' he said. ''I thought he was just a common greedy, jealous creep, but he's worse. A lot worse. One more drawer.'' He opened the fourth drawer, which held untitled hanging file folders. He looked hurriedly into random files, but there was nothing evidently incriminating. He had no real notion what he was looking for. Simple bills of sale or real estate deeds meant nothing to him. None of them suggested anything particularly illegal.

''Anything interesting?'' Anne asked.

''No. I guess I can't tell. I've got a friend who's a cop, though. I'm going to call him.''

''A Huntington Beach cop?''

Dave shook his head. ''Laguna Beach. He graduated from Huntington Beach High the same year I did. My old friend Jim Hoover.''

''Are you going to mention breaking in like this?''

"Yeah," Dave said. "I guess I am. I can't just do nothing."

He shut the last drawer and relocked the cabinet, then tossed the key back to Anne.

"I've been doing nothing for a long time," he said, standing up. "I'm sick of it."

꤀ **58** ꤀

IN ANNE'S APARTMENT, DAVE PUT A TOP AND BOTTOM bolt on the connecting door in the closet, and then replaced the dead bolt on the front door. Jim Hoover, Dave's policeman friend, was off work at four, and at four-thirty Dave dialed the phone in Anne's kitchen for the third time, but there was still no answer.

"More iced tea?" Anne asked.

"No, thanks." Dave idly swirled the ice in his glass and then drank the tea-flavored water. "Even with these new locks, I'm not crazy about you staying here," he said.

"I'm not going to stay here."

The decisive sound of the statement surprised him. "Where are you going? I had a couple of ideas. . . ."

"Jane Potter asked me to stay with her. She lives in a part of Laguna called Bluebird Canyon. It's really very nice. Good view, a couple of really beautiful old sycamore trees. She's got a little rental cottage in back of her house that's empty right now. I've got to run some pictures up to the gallery anyway, so . . ." She shrugged.

"Okay," Dave said. "That's great."

"What were your ideas?"

"Nothing, really."

"Tell me."

"Just . . . I've got a guest room. That's all."

"And you were going to ask me to be a guest?"

Dave nodded. "You're welcome to."

"I know I am," she said, smiling at him. "Maybe it wouldn't be so bad, staying with you, except for your obsession with washing dishes."

"Then go ahead and stay."

"Do you have any other bad habits?"

"I'm obsessive about polishing the chrome on the faucets, too, but other than that I'm entirely sane."

"How often do you polish the chrome?"

"Six or seven times a day, but before I started with my analyst, I was up to fourteen times a day on weekends and ten on weekdays, so I've nearly got it under control."

"Maybe I should meet your analyst. Is he married?"

"No, but he wears Jello-filled rubber suits to bed. So what do you think?"

"It's a little kinky, but . . ."

"I mean about staying at my place."

She looked at him for a moment, and in that moment he knew that she wouldn't, that she was just trying to be funny and pleasant. He wasn't even sure what he himself was suggesting, but he was honest enough to know that he had more than her safety in mind. Probably she'd be safer out of town, staying with Jane Potter. The only thing he was certain of was his own awkwardness.

"What I was thinking," she said, "was that maybe we ought to get to know each other under conditions that aren't quite so screwy, you know what I mean?"

"I don't really polish chrome—not that often, anyway."

"What I mean is that our . . . relationship, whatever you want to call it, has been a little strange. We've got this weird past together, about thirty seconds of it on the beach one day long ago, but it's turned into fifteen years of our having this . . . connection, whatever you want to call it. Neither one of us has done very well with Elinor's death, Dave."

"I can't argue with that," Dave said. "Not for a second. But Casey likes to tell me that it's possible just to let things go. He says it's like cutting the string on a high-flying kite and watching the wind take it away."

"What if the kite comes crashing down? That's more likely, isn't it? A lot of broken sticks and paper?"

"I'm ready to take the chance. If there was a way to cut Elinor loose, I'd let her go in an instant."

"It's not only Elinor, Dave; it's Edmund, too. You and I got thrown together because we're both trying to deal with the same fruitcake. Most of the time we've spent together has been because of Edmund. Right now we're sitting here trying to figure out what to do about Edmund. I want to get to know you better without this web of bad circumstances. Do you know what I'm talking about?"

"You mean, who's the real Dave Quinn?"

"And who's the real Anne Morris. I came down here partly to find out. I think I brought Elinor along with me, and that was a mistake, but it's a mistake I'm dealing with. When I ran into you, she flared up like I'd fed her oxygen. I want you to give me a little more time, okay?"

"Okay," Dave said after a moment. "How long will you be in Laguna?"

"I don't know."

"Are you giving this place up?"

"I don't know. No, I guess not. Right now it's . . . compromised, I guess I'd say. Even with the new locks, it doesn't quite feel safe, just like you said a few minutes ago. Elinor doesn't care about locks. Edmund doesn't care about locks."

"I guess I want you to tell me something right now, and I swear it won't affect our friendship."

"Anything."

"Is this the brush-off? Because if you mean what you say, then I'm going to keep trying."

"No, it's not the brush-off. Don't even begin to *think* it's the brush-off. I mean just what I say."

"Then I know some good restaurants in Laguna. There's a place on Cliff Drive with a view of Main Beach that'll knock you flat—especially this time of year with everything blooming. How about tomorrow night?"

"You're asking me out on a real date?"

"A real date."

"Okay," she said.

Dave picked up the phone receiver and punched in Jim Hoover's number again. After the fifth ring he was just about to hang up, when Hoover answered. "It's your dime," he said.

"Hoove, this is Dave Quinn."

"How do I know it's the true Dave Quinn? Maybe you're some guy pretending to be Dave Quinn. You'd better show me some I.D."

"I've got a serious question, Hoove."

"Sorry, go ahead. What's wrong?"

Dave sketched out the entire story, including the scam with the quitclaim deeds, the call from the notary, Casey's accident. He went into detail about Edmund's breaking into Anne's apartment and about Elinor's dolls and the fires at Collier's bungalow.

"Edmund Dalton?" Hoover said finally. "Why doesn't this surprise me? You know about his little problem—when was it? Six or eight years ago, I guess."

"No, I never heard about it. What problem?"

"He was associated with some characters who specialized in pornographic films using what you might call unwilling models, a lot of them underage. The films were made in Mexico, although they solicited runaways in San Diego and L.A."

"You're kidding. How come I didn't know anything about this?"

"I guess that was back when you were a respectable married man and lived out in the suburbs, before you crawled back into town single."

"Does Casey know?"

"I *guess* he does, although that was back when Casey was in his surf travel mode. He was gone most of the time, and when he wasn't gone, he probably wasn't in the mood to hear about his brother. Anyway, Edmund was arrested for buying from these creeps. I think he got away with a fine and probation even though he was probably guilty of a hell of a lot more than being a customer. It was Edmund's contention that he was involved in theatrical research. The whole thing involved big-time plea bargaining. I don't think the Earl ever really got the drift."

"Probably that's just as well. There's nothing he could have done about any of it."

"I don't know about that. Edmund's a goddamn rattlesnake, and sooner or later the old man was bound to get bit. Maybe he should have disowned the bastard. Anyway, I think you could say that Edmund's taste in sex is what you'd call nonstandard."

"Great. Edmund's a pervert on top of the rest."

"Besides that, what do you want? It sounds like you've got a whole bunch of nothing, legally speaking."

"I broke into Edmund's office this afternoon. He's out of town in Mexico for a couple of days, so I broke in and looked through his stuff."

"You broke in? Just like that?"

"That's right, Hoove. Just like that."

"Jesus, Dave. What do you have for brains? Breaking and entering is against the law, at least down here in Laguna."

"I smelled smoke, so I climbed over his office wall to see if something was on fire."

"Oh! That makes everything all right, then. Sure. The judge would *love* that one. You know, even if there was something incriminating in there, you probably killed any chance that it could ever be used as evidence. There's a certain protocol here, man. It doesn't matter now if you found a briefcase full of cocaine in there."

"Nothing that good. Just some dirty magazines and one of these dolls that I was telling you about."

"How about a corpse? If you found a corpse in his office, we can move on the guy. Otherwise, just give it up. Leave the man's stuff alone. And don't for God's sake call me and tell me about this kind of crap. I'm a cop, remember?"

"Well, how the hell far does it have to go before I call a cop?" Dave asked. "Edmund breaks into Anne's apartment and leaves this thing in her closet. He's supposed to get away with it?"

"That's a matter for the HB police, Dave."

"We already called them."

"Good. You did the right thing, although there's not a

hell of a lot they can do for you right now. But tell me something. What the hell did you say about this doll in her closet? It had a big *dick* on it? That's a little bit on the sick side. Your girlfriend's *sister* made these goddamn things?''

''Years ago. Sister's dead. The dolls were stored in boxes at the Earl's.''

''So this doll that was in her closet is actually something that she herself owns? How many people had access to the boxes?''

''Call it a dozen. Any of the Earl's employees.''

''You too, I guess.''

''Me too.''

''Dave, my man, what you've got is a lot of speculation. You're telling me that anybody could have stolen the doll, and that this notary called you up and made allegations but he didn't really say anything at all, and that Casey was drunk and drove into a tree.''

''Casey wasn't drunk.''

''Maybe you're right. Maybe this was one of the times that he wasn't drunk. But it sure as hell *looks* like he was drunk. Regardless of his blood alcohol, the open container and the vodka residue will incriminate him. It's not a big problem, though. Probably he'll lose his license for a while, wind up in AA for a few weeks.''

''It's not the charges I'm talking about, Hoove; it's the fire in the truck and the bottle under the seat. I *know* the man. Trust me on this one. Despite what anybody thinks, there's reasons that the bottle doesn't make any sense. Is it possible to rig something like that—the fire, the whole thing?''

''Sure it's possible. It's not only possible, it's easy. What's probably not possible is to nail Edmund for it, even if you think he's got some kind of motive. And from what you tell me, Edmund's down in Mexico. And also there were no witnesses to this quitclaim scam except this notary, and he's not talking?''

''Not only is he not talking, his office is locked up. I've driven past there three times since the phone call. It looks like he took a vacation the same time Edmund did.''

''You're racking up zeroes, Dave.''

"Okay, wait. There *was* one other guy. An old man who impersonated the Earl down at the notary's office and apparently signed at least one of the deeds. He lives on the street. I see him around town sometimes."

"And how do you know about him?"

"He came around to the Earl's in order to get some money out of Edmund. His name's Red Mayhew."

"What's he look like? Maybe I've seen him around, too."

"He looked something like the Earl—close enough to resemble the picture on the Earl's driver's license photo, anyway. That's why Edmund picked him up, I guess. He had a beard, walked with a stoop, drank a lot. He was always dressed in the same coat—an old yellow tweed jacket with torn-up leather patches on the elbows."

"Yellow tweed with patches?"

"Faded, but yellow."

"How about the rest?"

"Khaki leisure suit. Vinyl and nylon tennis shoes like you'd buy at the supermarket. One of them was broken open at the toe."

"Wide belt with an oval cowboy buckle, silver plated?"

"That's the guy," Dave said.

"Uh-huh. Dave, get in the car and come on down here. Bring your friend. What's her name again?"

"Anne," Dave said. "Anne Morris."

"Bring Anne Morris. I don't think we're going to see Edmund Dalton for a while. I think maybe he left for Mexico for a good reason."

"Why? What's going on?"

"The old man with the yellow coat was found dead on the bluffs down near Scotchman's Cove a few days ago. I.D.-ing him has been a little bit difficult, because whoever killed him cut his head off."

⇥59⇤

IT WAS MID-AFTERNOON WHEN EDMUND LOCKED THE HO-
tel door and drove into downtown Huntington Beach in the
rental car. He knew every street and alley in the city, but
something still felt off, so he cruised the neighborhood for
a few minutes, thinking things through, then parked a block
away and left the car door unlocked. He entered the condo
complex from what was essentially the back side, cutting
through the patio of a condo that had been empty for a
month. When he was certain there was nobody around, he
stepped out onto the narrow, shrubbery-crowded walk. He
left the gate to the patio slightly ajar, strolling down the
winding path past identical condos. Other paths branched
away on either side, and he took one to the right, and then
another to the left, which brought him out to the asphalt
driveway behind his garage. One of his neighbors was
washing a car, and the man saw him before he could reverse
course up the path again.

He didn't really know the man except to wave at, and
once he had loaned him the theatre section of the newspaper
on a Friday evening. He had the aggravating habit of wanting to be neighborly, but Edmund had killed that by refus-
ing to play along. The neighbor had doggedly stuck to the
ritual of waving, though, and so Edmund waved at the man
now. He grinned back, looked away, looked at Edmund
again, and then patiently turned off the water spigot and
put the hose down, even though his car was still half covered with suds. "Telephone!" he shouted at Edmund, and
made the thumb-and-pinkie-finger phone gesture at the side
of his face, and then hurried toward his open garden gate.

Edmund hadn't heard any telephone, and his neighbor's

response was unusual, especially the double take. What the hell had that meant? He stood for a moment, thinking about cutting this short and getting out, but then he moved forward again, hurrying across the driveway to his own back fence, taking the key to the lock out of his pocket and unlocking the gate. If something was happening, he had to know what it was, and he had to know now. Driving back to the Mt. Pleasant wouldn't solve any mysteries. He looked behind him at the now-empty driveway and then slipped through the gate, not quite closing it after him. Right inside the patio were a pair of tree ferns that nearly blocked the stepping-stone path, and he stood for a moment sheltered by the broad leaves of the fern, his feet in shadow, trying to see through the sliding glass door past the gap in the curtains. There was no apparent movement within, no noise. He waited another moment and then slipped toward the kitchen door along the stucco wall of the bedroom.

After waiting for another moment to listen, he unlocked the door, opened it, and stepped inside. Until he knew the house was untouched he was taking it slowly and quietly, and now he moved through the kitchen until he could look out through the dining area into the living room. It was then that he smelled cigarettes—not smoke, but the odor of someone who had smoke on his clothes. He stepped backward, onto the linoleum floor of the kitchen, at the same moment that he heard someone walking in the bedroom, and right then a man appeared in the bedroom door, sorting through photos—a cop in a suit. There was a simultaneous noise at the front door—the sound of someone turning the knob, people on the porch.

Edmund turned back through the kitchen at the same time that the man in the doorway looked up. He heard a grunt of surprise, but he was already out through the back door and into the garden, pulling the door shut after him, then out through the gate, the sound of running footsteps following. He heard someone yell as he ran across the driveway and up the path beyond, catching a quick glimpse of his neighbor, who stood stupidly by his half-washed car, craning his neck. The neighbor shouted a warning now, pointing and gesturing like a fool, and Edmund ducked left, down a path that led deeper into the condominium complex, then right again and then immediately left, heading due north toward the pool and clubhouse. On impulse he angled right at the first opportunity, slowing down now. He took a chance and stopped to listen. Miraculously, there was no sound of footsteps, no pursuit. He hurried on, coming to another driveway, where he stopped again, not crossing it until he was sure it was safe.

They had no idea what kind of car he was driving, and that was good. But if they saw him climb into the rental, he was done for; he'd have to ditch the car and try to get out of Huntington Beach on foot, maybe head toward Central Park.

He saw ahead of him the empty condo that he'd used to enter the complex, and he slowed down, anxious not to attract attention now. He walked toward it, catching his breath, hearing close by the sound of running feet again. One person? Two? He couldn't tell how many, and with the interwoven tiny paths, it was impossible to tell just where they were. He sprinted forward again, and right then he heard another shout. They'd seen him!

He looked back, surprised as hell to see his neighbor tearing toward him, carrying an aluminum baseball bat. There ahead of him was the unlocked gate, the street twenty feet beyond. He ran for it, pushing the gate open, stepping through, and stopping cold. He shifted his weight, pressing himself against the stucco wall, controlling his breathing, his focus. The gate swung open hard, and his neighbor flew through it, and Edmund swung his entire body around in a roundhouse kick to the man's stomach, connecting solidly. He heard a gasping choke as the neighbor's momentum spun him over, and the man sprawled forward onto his knees, fighting for breath and clutching his stomach, the baseball bat clattering away across the stepping stones and into the pea gravel of the weedy little garden. Instantly Edmund lunged for the bat, picked it up and swung it around, cracking the man on the side of the head and knocking him over sideways. He threw the bat away and pulled the front gate shut, suppressed the desire to kick his neighbor again as he lay there, and ran on instead, pushing

open the street gate and shutting it behind him, looking up
and down the sidewalk for cops. There were none. He ran
up the block toward the parked car, not giving a damn if
he was drawing attention from the locals now. It didn't
matter any more.

He yanked the door open and climbed in, fired the car
up, and swung a casual U-turn, heading toward Goldenwest
Street, where he could lose himself in evening commuter
traffic. He listened for pursuit, for the sound of police sirens. Two squad cars sped past him, heading back toward
town, but he didn't give them a second glance. His creep
neighbor! It was the irrepressible neighborly type who
would betray you first, the dirty bastard! Unlike the cop,
the neighbor had known the complex, and that had been
his downfall. He had gotten clever, and his cleverness had
cost him a fractured skull and, with any luck, a ruptured
spleen.

It had felt good to coldcock him with the bat! Yes, sir.
Edmund could use a couple more hits of that! He laughed
out loud at the pun. Goddamn! That was better than almost
anything he'd ever felt in his life, that egg-crushing smash
when the bat had connected, the solid power of it running
up into his hands and arms. And the roundhouse kick! That
was solid—double the impact with the man moving forward like that. He screamed twice, for two long six-counts,
to rid his system of the adrenaline rush that had fueled the
chase.

So he had intuited the danger correctly after all. He had
been sensitive to it. That would teach him not to question
himself. That was the absolute death of an artist, when he
started to question himself. He swung out into the evening
traffic of Goldenwest Street, thinking about this, about how
absolutely right things went when he trusted to instinct,
when he followed his vision. . . .

He suddenly saw something clearly. He saw that there
was nothing waiting for him back at the hotel. Things were
moving. *He* was moving. He himself had put the wheels
into relentless motion when he had met Anne Morris, and
those wheels had ground a few people in their cogs, people
who'd had no idea that when they stepped into the world

of Edmund Dalton, their lives would be irrevocably changed. And it wasn't over. That was as true as any of the rest of it. He had been working at something really big, really complex, and he was near the end of it. Very near the end of it. But he couldn't leave the picture unfinished—not out of fear, he couldn't.

Then he saw something that he hadn't understood clearly before—a way of looking at things, an angle that brought unclear things into focus. Anne, he knew suddenly, was a split personality in an authentic sense of the word. Anne the Day Girl simply didn't know about Anne the Night Girl. She had forgotten that part of her, hidden it away, wrapped it in paper and stuffed it into cardboard boxes. She hadn't been putting him off when he had approached the subject of the Night Girl that day on the sidewalk; she had simply repressed it. Surely on some very deep level she understood—that level where the fire burned, the fire in the dark woods. But it was a level that she could no longer access, not without help.

He turned right on Yorktown, heading east again, slipped his copy of *Melodies of the Masters* into the cassette player, and settled down to let the music sweep away the clank and clatter of the hectic afternoon.

"I'VE GOT SOME STUFF FOR YOU," HOOVER SAID WITHOUT any introduction when Dave answered the phone in his house.

"Good stuff?"

"Well, I don't know if it's all that good. Depends what you mean by good. Where's Anne?"

"She's staying with her friend just like we planned, al-

though we only got out of the Earl's about an hour ago.
She was going to run a couple of errands around town and
then drive down there. I'm just about to head in that direction myself. Why?''

"Because Edmund's back in town. He headed for his
condo and ran into a little surprise there.''

"But they didn't get him,'' Dave said. Through the front
window he could see the front porch ferns swaying in the
late afternoon onshore breeze.

"No, they didn't get him. Apparently he talked to a
neighbor on his way in, and he knew something was up.
Anyway, he's out there somewhere. If you've got any ideas
where he might go . . . ?''

"Not one. Edmund and I don't run in the same circles.
I think we can assume that he doesn't have any friends—
not like you and I would define friends.''

"Well, if I were him, I'd be long gone by now, maybe
back to Mexico. His Mercedes is in the garage, so we've
got no idea what he's driving. Anyway, I thought you and
Anne should know. How's Casey, by the way?''

"They drilled a hole in his head to bleed off the fluid.
They tell me he'll be okay.''

"You want to hear the rest?''

"Is the rest the good news or the bad news?''

"You be the judge. The D.A.'s agreed to grant you and
Anne immunity from prosecution because of your cooperation in the case.''

"Okay, that's good, I guess.''

"It's real good. You don't want a breaking and entering
charge brought against you by anyone, even Edmund. I
wish to hell I didn't have to say anything about you two
tossing his office, but I didn't have any choice. It was
bound to come out. You were the one who thought it was
a good idea to call the police and rat yourself out.''

"I know that. Don't worry about it. You did what you
had to do.''

"Here's what we did, just to catch you up. From what
you said, we had no evidence that there was anything in
Edmund's office at the Earl's to interest homicide, so we
couldn't ask for a warrant.''

"Wait a minute. I was at the Earl's when they opened up Edmund's office. *Somebody* had a warrant."

"Vice got the warrant. That's because of the porno stuff you reported seeing. That's what we used. Considering Edmund's habits and what you told us, we asked vice to ask the judge for the warrant, and they got it."

"This kind of thing doesn't take six weeks?"

"More like six hours, actually. Edmund's starting to look like a major-league creep, so there's *lots* of cooperation. We took another look at the bluffs out at Scotchman's Cove and found what appear to be tripod indentations in the dirt. It's possible that Edmund filmed the whole thing when he mutilated the old man. Anyway, when vice looked through his office at the Earl's, they found some fairly nasty black-and-white photos. You didn't come across these?"

"No, but then I was moving fast. I didn't go through the files much, because I didn't think they'd mean anything to me."

"Well, these photos would have meant something. You're lucky you didn't find them, though. He's a sick son of a bitch. A couple of the shots were taken in a garage that looked a lot like the garages in Edmund's condo, so vice used the photos to get the judge to extend the warrant to the condo, where they found all kinds of stuff in a hidey-hole under a bookcase—films, more photos. There was a darkroom, too, where he apparently did his black-and-white work."

"The same kind of thing that he was into a few years back?"

"Worse."

"And he did all the developing himself?"

"Not the color work. He paid for that."

"Where the hell did he go to get that kind of thing developed? You can't just walk into Sam's Club or K Mart or something and hand them the film."

"There's photo labs that do confidential work. In fact, the lab that did Edmund's photos does police work, too. Lots of confidential labs do. They'll do glamour shots of your wife, whatever the hell you want. Some of them draw the line at kiddy porn, but plenty of them don't. Edmund's line of baloney was the same as before, that he was in the theatrical business. He told them that the photos were staged, blood and all. The lab didn't ask any questions.''

''But it wasn't staged.''

''Not the recent stuff. We don't have any real proof yet, but we're running down a couple of possibilities. I think Edmund's goose is cooked. Anyway, what happened, to finish what I was saying, was that when Edmund came home, a vice detective was inside the condo, and Edmund walked into it. He ditched the detective in the condos, which are a complete goddamn maze, and now the man is at large, as we say. Anyway, go ahead on down to Laguna. Take Anne out someplace nice for a change, instead of the usual taquería. And keep an eye on her, Dave—phone checks, whatever it takes. Edmund's out there somewhere right now, driving around. Like I said, though, if I were Edmund, I'd head for the border again.''

''You're not Edmund,'' Dave said. ''Edmund's one of a kind. He's a very committed man.''

⊰ 61 ⊱

ANNE FED TWO QUARTERS INTO THE METER AND LEFT HER car on the street in a luckily empty space right in front of the street door to her apartment on Main Street. The door itself was locked, since it was after hours, and she let herself in with the key and climbed the stairs to the corridor for the second time that afternoon. Right after work she had stopped in to retrieve her phone messages: there had been only one, from Jane Potter, who had sold two more of her paintings. Now there was gallery space for six or eight paintings altogether, depending on the size.

After listening to the phone message, Anne had run er-

rands, which had taken an hour longer than she'd anticipated, and she had stopped back into the apartment now to
grab a couple of pieces of clothing and load the car with
the paintings. She had called Dave to tell him, because she
would be late getting back down to Laguna Beach, but his
line had been busy, and when she'd called back later, he'd
been gone. Well, Jane Potter would take care of Dave until
Anne got back down to Laguna. It would be a good excuse
for Jane to stretch cocktail hour a little bit.

The corridor was dim with Mr. Hedgepeth's low-wattage
bulbs—a different place than it had been three hours ago
when there was still sunlight through the few windows and
when there were open doors and activity. Her apartment
door was bolted, just as she had left it, and she had left the
living room light on, too, so that she wouldn't have to walk
into a dark room. Leaving the door open, she stepped inside
and laid her purse down on the chair. Her eyes were drawn
to the patch of floor, newly cleaned with turpentine, where
Elinor had pressed the red paint out of the tube, and she
listened to the evening traffic and the silence of the closed-
up building, half expecting to hear something out of place—
the sound of ghostly footfalls, unidentifiable creaking from
some far corner of the apartment.

She turned on another light and then headed into the
bedroom to get a coat and a sweater out of the closet and
another pair of jeans our of her drawer. The paintings were
wrapped and waiting, leaning against the wall by the easel.
She would toss the clothes into a shopping bag and then
move the paintings downstairs. Three quick trips ought to
do it. The bedroom was dark, and she reached around the
corner and flipped the light switch on before walking in,
then went straight for the closet, opened the door, and
pulled the ceiling chain. In an instant she had her jacket in
her hand, and she backed out of the closet, reaching for the
chain again to turn the light off.

Her hand raised, she stopped and stared at a spot a couple
of feet from the floor, nearly at the bottom of the blouses
and sweaters that hung on the closet rod in front of the
connecting door. It took her a moment to focus on it clearly,
to separate the closet shadows from the clothing and from

the dark angular outline of the paneled door. Then she made it out: a jagged blackness, as if the panel itself had been kicked out and then shoved back in, the wood splintered around it.

She spun around, clutching her jacket to her chest, and saw, facing her across the room, a video camera on a tripod, a red light glowing on top of it. The sight of it sent a thrill of fear through her, and with both hands she threw her jacket at the camera, knocking it against the wall. The tripod balanced on one leg for a moment, and then crashed to the floor. Anne stepped hastily past the foot of the bed toward the open door, and it was then that Edmund stepped into the doorway and stood with his arms folded and his lips pursed, contemplating her as if sizing her up. She stared back at him, stepping back toward the closet, gauging the distance to the bedroom windows, which were closed, the street fifteen feet below, impossible to reach. Scream? She suppressed it. She waited for him to speak.

"I let myself in," he said.

"Most people knock first." She managed to get this out, and the act of speaking calmed her a little. She remembered then that the front door was open. If he had been hiding in the bathroom or kitchen, it still might be. He didn't have any apparent weapon, and she glanced around her, looking for something she could use against him but seeing nothing except a ceramic teapot. . . .

One of her paintings hung on what had been a bare wall, and the sight of it was instantly disconcerting to her. It was a painting of a northern California roadside store above the ocean. It had been smeared with paint, and the first thought that came into her mind was of Elinor. The smears weren't random, though. Someone—Edmund—had daubed red and black streaks on it as if trying to shadow or darken the sky and the grass and the silver gray of the redwood siding on the ramshackle store. The painting was wrecked, the childishly applied red paint looking like something out of a comic-book depiction of Hell.

"What exactly is wrong with you?" she asked him, her sudden anger pushing fear aside. He seemed to recoil a little bit, but then he smiled.

"I have something I have to ask you, and I want you to answer me absolutely truthfully. I want you to know that I'm here only to ask you this question." His voice had the monotonous tone of a sham guru, and she was struck again by his similarity to Elinor. His demeanor and tone were so obviously fake that even *he* had to know how insane he sounded.

"You came here to ask me a question, but you couldn't just knock on the door and ask me like any sane human being would do? You had to break in and screw up one of my paintings first?"

The muscles in his neck jerked, and his eyes were abruptly mean and bitter. He forced a smile, though, and then his face grew placid and empty again. "Will you answer?"

"I don't know. Go ahead and ask." He still hadn't moved out of the doorway, and she forced herself not to glance at it.

"But will you answer?"

"Just ask me the question, you crazy goddamn creep." She realized that she was close to the edge, and she fought to control herself.

Perhpas sensing it, he smiled again, wider now, as if he knew that his voice and his insane sense of purpose was pushing her. "What do you know about the fire that burns in the deep woods?" he asked.

She stared at him. Whatever she had expected, this wasn't it.

"Have you *been* to that fire?" He narrowed his eyes at her, as if he were particularly keen to hear the answer.

"I . . . God. *That's* your question?" She had expected something else—a trip to Club Mex, a proposal.

"That's my question."

"I don't know what the hell you're talking about. That's the craziest thing I've ever heard."

"And yet you painted a picture of that fire?"

"Me? I painted a fire in the woods?"

"In the dead woods—the insects, the leaves, the glow of firelight? Anne . . ." He shook his head, as if he were a little bit surprised at her. "I've *seen* the paintings. I've seen the dolls. I've seen the work of the Night Girl.''

"The dolls? Those were the work of my *sister*. My sister painted those pictures. My sister made those dolls.''

"I'm sure that's true,'' he said. "How very right of you to call her your sister. I've got a name for her. I call her the Night Girl, because we find each other in the darkness. Do you want to know what I call you?''

"No, Edmund, I don't.'' She tensed herself now. Edmund was completely out of his mind. If she was going to run, she would have to choose the moment carefully. Trying to string him along wasn't going to work. When the time came, she would have to hit him hard. . . .

"The Day Girl. I call you the Day Girl.''

"That's good,'' she said, nodding and smiling. "Do you want to know what I call you, Edmund?''

"No I don't, Anne. I no longer expect that you'll be civil with me, that you'll give me a chance. You're too far gone in denial, and I can't help you. I can only help the Night Girl. I only *want* to help the Night Girl now. The Day Girl has ceased to interest me. The Day Girl has become a hindrance. Are you aware, Anne, that a diamond is nothing more than a compressed lump of coal?''

"Since I was about five, I think.''

"People are like that.''

She shifted her weight, and he responded by squaring himself in the doorway, blocking it entirely.

"We're partly diamond and we're partly coal. We want to think we're all diamond, but we're not, Anne. Our deepest and most secret desires are coal. Our dreams are made of coal dust. A psychologist will tell you that we don't remember our dreams because we repress them. But I believe we should embrace them. For years now I've tried to capture those dreams on film, and believe me, I've done pretty well. Look at this . . .''

He took a photo out from under his coat and held it in the light. Immediately she looked away, remembering what Jim Hoover had told Dave about Edmund's fascination with pornography.

"Take a look,'' he said gently. "It's not what you think

it is. It's not what you've been told it might be. I'm giving you a chance, Anne. Let me help you.''

She continued to stare at the floor. She wouldn't look at his damned picture.

''Look at it!'' he yelled, and he bounded across the floor and grabbed her arm before she could react. She screamed now, and tried to pull away. He pushed her over backward so that she sprawled on the bed, and in the next instant he held a knife in his hand, a thin stiletto with a blade five inches long. He bent over her, his eyes wide and his mouth working as if he'd lost control of his facial muscles. He held the photo up, and she stared at it. It was nearly completely black, only the faintest light.

''Do you see?'' he asked.

She nodded her head.

''There!'' He pointed at the photo, at a patch of darkness slightly darker than the background, the vague shape of something that appeared to have been moving when it was photographed, like a time exposure of a woman walking.

''You see her. Of course you see her. Do you recognize yourself in her?''

She stared at him. There was nothing she could say.

She's the Night Girl, Anne. She's my soul mate in the late hours. She does my bidding as I do hers. So please, Anne. Don't tell me about your twin sister. I *know* your sister. The one thing that I don't know, and I'll tell you this truthfully, is how the Day Girl and the Night Girl can become one, just as they used to be. Because I'm afraid that the Day Girl simply doesn't interest me very much.''

He backed away from her now, still holding the knife, the blade glinting in the lamplight. She sat up and took a deep breath, trying to calm herself. The knife changed everything. ''I don't think you understand what I'm saying,'' she told him. ''The paintings and dolls in storage were made by my sister Elinor. She's my actual sister.''

''You haven't been listening to me.''

''I'm telling you the truth. I can introduce you to her. She lives in Victoria, but . . .''

''You haven't been *listening* to me,'' he said again.

"You're right," she said. "And anyway, my sister's dead."

"Now at least you're telling the truth. You killed her, Anne, and you can bring her back. You and I together can bring her back."

"I wouldn't want to."

"Because you're afraid of her."

Anne nodded.

"Fear is our most limiting factor. Getting rid of our fears is the liberation of our art. And I mean *all* our fears, Anne, including the fear of our own sexuality. Our sexuality, in all its manifestations, might be the most private matter of them all, Anne, but within the confines of that privacy, its energies need know no limitations. It was your dolls that made me realize that you would understand what I mean. I can easily imagine that there were dolls that even *you* hid away and looked at only in secret. Even you believed that sometimes you'd gone too far. I'd like very much to see your secret things, Anne, because I don't believe that we can go too far. I don't believe that there's any such thing. . . ."

She closed her hand over the bedspread, then lunged toward the door, whipping the bedspread around toward him and ducking past it at the same time, trying to throw it over his head. With the edge of her fist she hit him on the cheekbone, and he caught her wrist, sweeping the bedspread aside with the hand that held the knife. The cloth caught on the blade, and Anne kicked him hard in the groin, then slammed her heel down onto the toe of his shoe. He doubled up, but held onto her wrist, twisting her arm up and away, trying to shake the bedspread off the knife. Pain lanced through her wrist and forearm, and she stood on tiptoe trying to relieve the pressure and grasping for the teapot on the dresser. Her hand closed over the handle, and she smashed it down on his head with her free hand, jerking her other hand from his suddenly weakened grasp and turning toward the door, grabbing the knob and dragging it shut after her. There was a grunt, and the door slammed against something, and in that moment he grabbed her ankle and she flew forward onto the floorboards, slamming down hard enough to take the breath out of her.

Immediately she threw herself over and tried to scramble to her feet, but he held on, stretched on the floor in the doorway, his chin pressed to the ground. Blood trickled out of his hair from where she'd hit him with the teapot, and his wild face was twisted and inhuman, his mouth open and panting. His grip on her ankle tightened as he used her weight to lever himself forward. He shook his right hand loose of the bedspread now and held the knife in the air as if he would plunge it into her leg. She shook her head at him and held her hands up. She saw then that the front door was locked, the chain fastened, and she felt absolutely trapped. The blinds were drawn on the windows, too. Edmund had seen to all of it as soon as she was safely in the apartment.

He stood up carefully, still holding onto her ankle, bending over and pointing the knife at her chest. "Up," he said.

She stood up, and he took her wrist in his free hand.

He composed himself, contorting his face as if stretching all the muscles, relieving the strain. "Do I bore you?" he asked.

She shook her head, still watching the knife.

"Good, because I have *much* more to say to you. Much more. It's time we got started." He pulled her toward the bedroom. "Come on," he said. ".We have a long journey ahead of us." He closed the bedroom door and then pulled the dresser in front of it, kicking the shards of teapot aside. Watching her out of the corner of his eye, he stepped beside the bed, then bent over and righted the camera, angling the wide lens toward her. "Takes a licking and keeps on ticking," he said, sighting through the eyepiece. He was six feet away from her.

She ran again, straight at the open closet door, ducking inside and pulling the door shut behind her, instinctively finding the knob on the connecting door and twisting it, picturing the bolts that Dave had so helpfully installed top and bottom. . . .

The door opened, stopping against the hanging clothes just as the door behind her wrenched open, too, the knob torn from her hand. She ducked forward, feeling his hand on her wrist again, twisting it away so hard that her elbow flew back and cracked on the door frame as she slipped through it, pulling the door shut behind her and throwing herself through the next, slamming it shut even as she heard him scrambling into the closet. There was no way to stop him, to lock the door. She looked around wildly, grabbing the edge of the lawyer's desk and pulling it toward the door, which flew open then, hitting her in the back. She grabbed the rolling desk chair with both hands, picking it up and whirling it around as he came through the door, and the chair hit him square in the chest, two of its legs banging the closet door, Edmund stumbling backward, going down, sweeping the chair away. Anne threw the bolt on the door and ran out into the hallway without looking back, bolting for the stairs. For a moment she ran in near silence down the carpeted corridor, hearing him stumbling along behind her. He was close. . . . She darted a glance over her shoulder and gasped involuntarily when she saw how close, reaching toward her, his face intent, spittle flecking his chin.

There was noise ahead, the sound of a horn honking—muted, then strangely loud, and a light swept across the bottom of the stairs as she threw herself forward in an out-of-control rush, falling onto the stairs and rolling, the breath knocked out of her. There was a shout, and feet slamming past, and she realized that the street door was open, that someone had come in. She sat up, her heart slamming in her chest, and saw Edmund running back up the corridor. Dave bent over her, asking her how she was. She shook her head. "I'm all right," she said.

Dave leaped up the stairs, but at that same moment there was the sound of a door banging shut. The building shook with the force of it, and then there was silence. Anne crawled to her feet, stepped through the door into the open air, and leaned against the wall in the foyer. Momentarily she heard feet on the stairs again, and Dave reappeared, coming down two stairs at a time.

She was crying in the instant that he hugged her, and he continued to hold her until she stopped and wiped her eyes. Together they walked back up to her apartment and called the police.

⁓62⁒

IT WAS COOL AND DARK BENEATH THE STAGE IN THE closed-up theatre, and the flashlight beam was blocked in nearly every direction by interlacing wooden posts and beams and by dusty old cardboard cartons of junk. The area under the stage had apparently always been a convenient dumping place, and Edmund pushed his way through the accumulated trash of thirty years—long-abandoned paint cans and broken-down Christmas ornaments and rolled paper signs and pieces of costumes and broken props. The place was an absolute firetrap. Edmund had even found a quart of acetone lying on its side, its paper label chewed off by mice. A couple of weeks ago it would have been pleasant to call the fire marshal anonymously and report the whole mess, if only to give Collier a little something to do with his time, but when he thought about it now, that couple of weeks seemed to Edmund like a year ago, a different life. Everything had changed. He had bigger fish to fry.

He laughed out loud at his own joke and shined the flashlight at the far back wall, pulling himself along through the heavy layer of dust and grime between the low crossbraces, hauling with him a canvas book bag half full of the stuff he had taken out of his room at the Mt. Pleasant. He brought the old can of acetone along, too, favoring it over the gasoline he had thought he was going to use. Just like with Mifflin's lamp oil and Jenny's doll and trading cards, the more he let serendipity play along, the more interesting and profound the results.

A broken-down box of junk blocked his way again, and he took a moment to slide it aside, averting his face from the dust. He played the flashlight over the next section of

wall and saw what he was looking for—a duplex electrical
outlet, uselessly far back beneath the stage. He crawled to
it, then settled himself comfortably, propped up the flashlight, and emptied the bag carefully, removing the light
bulb with the hole chipped through the top. At the Mt.
Pleasant he had crisscrossed the glass globe with masking
tape before popping the hole through it with a spring-loaded
center punch. The tape still clung to the bulb, and he de-
bated for a moment whether to try to remove it. The torn
pieces of tape looked inartistic to him somehow. . . .

He decided to let it go. If he broke the bulb now, he would
have to crawl out from beneath the stage and find another
one, and he just wasn't up to going through the rigamarole.
He had broken three bulbs already, trying to get the whole
thing right. He plugged the light socket cord into the wall
and touched the two metal prongs of his tester wires to the
metal contact. The test bulb lit, so the old wall socket was
hot. Voilà! The rest was easy. He had pictured the process in
his mind a dozen times. He unfolded the plastic drop cloth
and tacked it to the beams overhead, letting the bulk of the
cellophane-thin plastic hang loosely around the edges. He
bunched the front side of it and tacked it up temporarily in
order to give himself air. Then, sitting beneath the tented
plastic, he set a pie pan on the floor and carefully poured the
acetone into it. He plugged the timer and the light bulb
socket together, then set the timer for 2100 hours before
plugging the timer into the wall. He wouldn't need the extension cord, so he pitched it away into the darkness and threw
the empty acetone can and the tester wire after it. Gingerly,
he screwed the bulb into the socket and tacked the cord to an
overhead beam so that the bulb dangled an inch over the pool
of acetone. And then for a time he sat in perfect silence, waiting for the timer dial to move perceptibly.

And that was it. He crawled out from under the tent,
leaving his bag and his tools behind, and untacked the
bunched plastic, arranging it around the acetone and the
bulb. The acetone fumes were already heavy in the air, and
he crawled away from the area hastily, suppressing the need
to cough, and crept out from beneath the stage into the

night-dark theatre. It was still an hour before dawn, and he was dead tired, having been up for what must have been two days. Haunting the theatre at night like the famous Phantom of the Opera had been perfectly safe. The police simply hadn't thought to *look* for him there. And why would they?

He went down the stairs into the basement, through the basement corridors and into the costume room, where he let himself out the basement door, locking it behind him and making his way through the dark alley between the theatre and the warehouse, carrying what was now the only remaining key to the basement door. He had dropped the other two keys down a gopher hole in the vacant lot an hour ago.

Collier had blocked the hole under the jasmine bush with a sheet of plywood, and Edmund slid the plywood out of its niche quietly now and crawled in under the porch, pulling the plywood back into place behind him. The lattice had already been replaced along the front of the porch, and he could smell both the freshly cut redwood and the charred post where the dolls had been consumed by the magical flames. He lay down on his sleeping bag, staring above him at the porch floor, communing silently with the darkness and cheered by the idea of Collier and Jenny sleeping obliviously just a few feet away. It would be a long day, lying there under the house, but he would sleep through most of it, and tonight would be more than mildly entertaining.

DAVE HAD DISCOVERED YEARS AGO THAT TECH WEEK IN the world of the theatre was always completely crazy, no matter how much you thought you were prepared. There was always one last prop or set piece that had to be built

although the show went up in two days. The director, even
Collier—perhaps *especially* Collier—wasn't happy unless
he was changing his mind one more time. On every night
of the week, getting out of the theatre early inevitably
turned into getting out at midnight, and midnight turned
into one and two and three o'clock in the morning, until it
began to look utterly hopeless that the show would open at
all on Friday night. But it was always like that, and yet the
show always opened. That's how this week was shaping
up. Although it was only Sunday night, and the play didn't
open until Friday, the impossible problems and complications were stacking up. Collier used Dave as a gopher, and
Dave found himself running back and forth between the
warehouse and the theatre, chasing tools and supplies.

It was only about eight o'clock now, and already he was
tired, having been at the Earl's since dawn. Anne was due
at any moment—in fact, she was past due—having run
back up to Laguna Beach earlier in the evening, something
about the gallery. He had figured on her returning sometime
in the last half hour, and as he crossed the theatre parking
lot toward the back of the warehouse, he thought about who
he would call if she didn't show up soon. Jane Potter? Jane
at least would know the time that Anne had left Laguna for
her drive back down the Highway. With the fog and the
late hour, she might not have started out at all.

It was socked in worse than it had been for weeks, and
although he could hear the creaking of the oil well out in
the lot, no more than thirty feet away, he couldn't see it.
The windows of Collier's bungalow glowed through the
fog, and he could make out the ghostly outline of the front
porch railing and misty light from the porch lamp, but the
house itself was merely an angular shadow. Fog like this
would kill the size of the house on opening night. He
rounded the corner, heading up the dirt path, the dark clapboard wall of the Earl's towering above him.

There had been no word of Edmund. Nobody had caught
him at the border. If he showed himself now, they would
nail him for Mayhew's murder and for trafficking in pornography. Probably they'd find evidence that he had murdered the women he'd filmed. They'd already found Mifflin

the notary, who had fled to Mexico, and so now they knew
enough about Edmund's real estate frauds to convict him
on that, too, although in the light of all the rest, the fraud
was hardly worth bothering about. And Mifflin, it turned
out, had dual citizenship. He had made it clear that he
wasn't coming back to the States to testify against anyone,
and there was no way he could be extradited for his part
in Edmund's schemes.

So far the Earl didn't know about any of it. In the last
few days he had been nearly crippled with angina, and he
was under observation in the same hospital where Casey
was recovering. Jolene was running the Earl's pretty much
single-handedly. Dave thought suddenly about how much
of the world had changed in the last couple of weeks, how
the Earl's safe little corner of things had been shaken apart,
how he and Anne had been thrown together, how so many
lives had been altered or destroyed. Like Humpty Dumpty,
none of it could be put back together again. Edmund was
a small-time megalomaniac, but he was every bit as possessed as a Hitler or a Stalin, and, in his small way, every
bit as successful. . . .

But the show was going up in under a week, and to hell
with how the world had changed. Car wrecks, murders,
arson, bad hearts—nothing got in the way of opening night
except the end of the world or a power failure.

Dave reached the end of the path and stepped over the
curb and up onto the asphalt. There was a car in the lot,
and even through the fog he could see that it was Anne's
Saturn. He picked up his pace, anxious to talk to her, to
have some company . . . to have some help. Collier needed
two sheets of luan painted black—"right now," he had
said, forgetting apparently that the paint took a couple of
hours to dry. And there was a mushy spot in the stage, and
Jim Parsons, who was playing Lear, refused to act on a
stage that he might fall through, so Dave had to shore it up
tonight, just as soon as he'd put a coat of paint on the luan.

Dave opened the warehouse door and stepped inside. The
night lights were on, but none of the other lights, and there
was no sign of anyone in the dim interior. "Hello!" he
shouted.

There was no answer. The warehouse was silent. He listened to the scrabbling of mice behind the newspaper bin, and to the slow creaking of the oil well from the lot beyond the open window. Then he heard something else—the sound of voices, low and urgent, almost like a radio playing.

"Hello!" Again there was no answer. The voices rose in volume, or at least one of the voices did—a woman's voice. Her words were indistinct, but the tone sounded like pleading. It was suddenly silent, and then the man's voice erupted in laughter, fell silent, and the talking started up again.

It occurred to him that perhaps the talking came from outside somewhere, modulated by the fog. Maybe it was Collier's television. Except that Collier and Jenny were both in the theatre.

"Anne!" He shouted her name, but got no response. Clearly she had parked in the lot, found the warehouse empty, and headed around to the theatre by the front sidewalk at the same time that he was coming around the back. Momentarily relieved by the idea, he turned back toward the door, more anxious than ever to find her.

Then the woman's voice rose again against the backdrop of silence. She spoke in a breathy, trembling cry that sent a chill down his spine. The talking continued, slightly louder now, more adamant, and he knew absolutely that this was no television. The voices came from somewhere in the back of the warehouse. He was suddenly certain of it. He looked around for a weapon, and, thinking about his framing hammer, he turned to where his toolbox stood open on the ground. He stepped toward it, but then instantly stopped dead, his heart suddenly slamming in his chest. One of Elinor's dolls sat in the open toolbox, its legs thrust out, its hands positioned on the edge as if it were holding on. Its clothes, if it had ever had any, had been removed, and someone had discolored its nylon flesh, its eyes and its breasts, with finger-painted lines of bloodred paint.

It had to be paint. He steeled himself, bent over, touched it. It was wet, fresh, his fingertips stained red.

He sniffed the red ooze, realizing that he was faint and sick.

Paint. It was just paint. He turned quickly around, wiping his hand on his jeans, and grabbed the wall phone, glancing at the listed numbers inked onto the wall and punching the first three buttons of the police substation number before he realized that the phone was dead.

The woman's voice rose in a shriek now, and Dave dropped the phone and headed toward the rear of the warehouse looking around, his eyes wide to see through the darkness, wishing to heaven that he had flipped on all the breakers in the switch box. No time to go back. The place was too damned dark, too full of shadows. He stepped quietly out into the aisle that ran around the under-loft storage, and walked up past a lumber of piled junk—stacked facades and staircases and polystyrene rocks. Recently returned circus props stood in disarray, spilling out into the aisle. There were a hundred places for a person to hide, and he glanced over his shoulder every couple of seconds, half expecting Edmund to step out from behind something, his face distorted by his trademark grin.

And all the time there was the continuing low murmur of the man's voice from somewhere up ahead, the woman's voice interjecting a moan or a brief gasping scream. An enormous clown's head blocked half the aisle, and Dave edged past it, searching the shadows with his eyes. On the floor dead ahead there was a splash of red, a trail of glistening drops. More paint. Edmund was fooling with him, luring him back there. Paint or blood, Dave would have to come. He would have to find Anne. Edmund knew it.

The talking stopped abruptly, and then after two long seconds of silence, the man's voice spat out the single word "bitch." There was rapid, heavy breathing, obviously magnified, followed by Edmund's unmistakable laughter. Dave could see a dim and dusty light shining from one of the tiny storeroom windows. It was Jolene's storage closet, full of boxed records and receipts dating back years, old paper junk that the Earl had decided to keep forever. A pile of debris stood at Dave's left, broken pieces of wood and metal and trash that were splashed with more red paint. He stooped to grab up a foot-long length of galvanized iron pipe that lay on top of the litter, wiping the paint on his jeans.

He gripped the pipe tightly and held it at his side, edging forward toward the storage room door, which was cocked open. There was more red paint splashed on the wall, bloody handprints on the window glass, a pool of paint on the floor. Dave approached the door carefully, hefting the pipe in his hand, holding it ready. The sound of Edmund's voice came from within the room, droning along unceasingly now, as if he were making some kind of lunatic lecture to a child. Dave kicked the door open with his foot and stepped inside, holding his breath, ready to hit Edmund first and ask questions afterward.

But the room was empty of people—nothing but cardboard boxes and a cassette tape player that sat in the middle of the floor, the player's power light glowing red, the voice coming from the speaker.

"Hello, Dave."

Edmund's voice came from behind him now. Dave steeled himself, turned slowly, the truth dawning on him too late. Edmund stood grinning a foot or two beyond the doorway, his cheek smeared with red paint, more paint on his shirt. He held a pistol, which he pointed at Dave's chest.

"Put the pipe down," Edmund told him. He cocked the pistol.

Dave held onto the pipe. He had learned enough about Edmund in the last few days to know that Edmund would kill him, whether he put the pipe down or not. "You might as well shoot me," Dave said, but his voice was a nervous croak. His heart hammered.

Edmund winked at him. "You look frightened, Dave. Are you?"

Dave stared at him.

"Fear is one of the most potent emotions, Dave. You've only touched the surface of it here."

"Where's Anne?" Dave asked.

Edmund shook his head sadly. "Anne's safe," he said. "I haven't hurt her. I was just funnin' ya, with the red paint and all. *Very* theatrical, don't you think?" He grinned

widely. The pistol was rock-steady in his hand. Abruptly
he laughed out loud. "*Drop* the pipe," he said again. Dave
tried to stare him down, but there was nothing behind Edmund's eyes but a leaden emptiness. Edmund's cheek
twitched. He clamped his eyes shut and then opened them
wide. He was a mess, unshaven, his clothes dirty as if he'd
been sleeping in a ditch. "If you make me shoot you now,
Anne will be alone. Think about it."

Dave tossed the pipe to the floor and held up his hands
in resignation. *Mistake*, he thought immediately, listening
to the pipe clatter on the concrete floor.

"Good," Edmund told him. "You're going to have to
cooperate with me, Dave, if you want to help Anne. And I
know you do. We don't have much time. Nobody has much
time." His voice was scratchy and pitched high, as if he
were strung out by some terrible stress, as close as he could
come to the edge without snapping. "Walk on down the
aisle now, toward the deep woods. That's where I've got
Anne. She's bound with duct tape, but she's unhurt." He
gestured with the gun, hurrying Dave forward.

Someone—certainly Edmund—had cleared away a
broad area along the east wall of the warehouse near where
they stored what the Earl called Snow White's forest. Edmund had pulled the trees out into the cleared area and set
them around two and three deep in a rough circle, their
branches entangled. Anne sat on a piece of fake granite
built of wood and papier-mâché. She was apparently unhurt. Her wrists and ankles were bound with tape, and there
was a strip of tape over her mouth.

"Sorry," Dave said to her, and she shrugged and widened her eyes as if to say that she was taking it all in stride.
Dave watched Edmund. The man was stark staring crazy.
There was no question *if* Dave would make his move, only
a question of when. If he let Edmund tie him up with the
duct tape, it was over. It would be enormously better to be
shot dead trying than to give Edmund his way.

There were other rocks next to Anne, randomly positioned, and in among the rocks sat a dozen of Elinor's dolls,
carefully situated like an audience of deformed gnomes.
The largest doll, a female with trailing, coarse black hair,

sat next to Anne, dressed in a grossly oversized red coat.

Edmund waved, taking in the entire scene. "I give you the Day Girl and the Night Girl," he said, talking like a television announcer. "Or at least a facsimile of the Night Girl. The creature herself is nearby, awaiting my summons." Dave saw that there was a video camera set up on a tripod fifteen feet or so back, far enough away for the camera to capture the entire scene.

"It took me a little over an hour to set all of this up, although I'll admit that I spent some time in here last night working everything out, moving junk out of the way, getting things prepared so that we could move swiftly tonight. No one noticed a thing! Everybody's in the theatre working like busy little beavers, and so it was entirely simple for me to arrange my own little production right here. It's almost funny, how easy it was. It's always been easy. That's a mark of genius, Dave. The best work comes easy to a real artist. Effort is the mark of an amateur."

The lights dimmed just then, and there was the sound of an electrical buzzing. As if someone had opened a refrigerator door, the air in the old warehouse grew suddenly cool, and Dave could hear, way out on the edge of his consciousness, the dreamlike sound of slow pacing. Anne heard it too. He could see it in her eyes. She turned her head upward, looking at the lights. There was the smell of burning on the air, like the smoke from distant pruning fires carried on the wind. Elinor. He knew it was she. This time he simply was certain of it.

The lights went up again, and the sound of pacing stopped abruptly. Edmund stood with his head cocked, listening, a smile on his face. "Visitors," he said. "My guess is that she'll return. There might be fireworks tonight. Hold onto your hats and keep your arms and hands inside the car at all times." He waved his hand at the video camera. "Remote controlled," he said, and he pulled a remote box out of his pants pocket with his free hand, pointed it at the camera, and clicked it on. "I sometimes play a starring role in my films. Sadly, I won't be able to this time. I'll never even see the result of this one, not on film, anyway. Other people *will* see it, though—the police. A jury, maybe. A judge in his chambers. I wouldn't be surprised if copies got out. People pay a *lot* of money for the kind of thing I'm talking about, Dave—enough even to tempt a judge. You'd be surprised. And they'll get their money's worth, too. That judge will watch the film more than once in the privacy of his chambers, and then he'll come out into the courtroom and act as if he's positively outraged. During his lunch hour he'll watch it again. I'll change the quality of his dreams, Dave. How many artists can say that?''

Voices still sounded from the distant tape recorder, and now there was the sound of a woman's shriek, a sharp, high wail that was cut off in mid-voice. Again the tape fell silent. Anne shut her eyes, and Edmund laughed out loud. ''That, my friends, was the plaintive cry of the highway hippie, reacting to the bite of the nasty big spider who gave her a ride to his lair one sunny spring morning. I've got photos, which I unhappily won't be able to show you. I'd love to air the film for you, but the police confiscated it. I'm certain they enjoyed watching it nearly as much as I enjoyed making it.

''Sit,'' he said abruptly to Dave, nodding his head to underscore it. He gestured at a rock, and Dave stepped toward it, glancing at the pistol, hesitating for a split second. Edmund shook his head and grinned at him. ''*Bad* doggy,'' he said. ''Don't even think about it. You might find something entertaining in my little production anyway, Dave.'' He stood smiling for a moment, as if waiting for Dave to agree with him. Then he shook his head, as if he couldn't be fooled. ''Dave, Dave, Dave,'' he said. ''I know *exactly* what you're wondering, deep down in that dense head of yours. You're wondering what I'm going to do with Anne. What her fate will be. Whether it will be worth watching. I've piqued your interest with my tape recording. Your imagination's running with indelicate questions. There are shadows down there, Dave, and the shadows have shapes that you've never dared to look at, until now. You're really no different from me or from any other man. One man's perversions are another man's perversions, my friend. Priest or poet or postmaster, our deepest and darkest desires all take the same shapes.''

"You're wrong," Dave said.

"Oh, I don't think I am. I've often wondered what you did to that little girl before you drowned her. Why you *had* to drown her . . . My goodness!" He said with mock surprise. "Just *look* at your face. Why, I believe you're about to have a seizure." He laughed theatrically. "You are *so* damned easy, Dave. I believe I could talk you insane, if I wanted to. I managed it with Miss Hippie. You heard the tape. I don't have time, though, alas, and in fact your part in this little production is very brief. Hardly worth putting your name in the credits. I thought that we'd start the film with a close-up of the angry hero, who, once again, has failed miserably to help his lady love. And then the heroine will have her turn to watch the hero die. Just like that. Bang. Quick as a blink. She'll be terrified at the sight of it, and that's just what we want. Raw terror. Close-up of her eyes dilating with it. Or maybe not! Maybe we'll all be surprised at what happens, because I *always* leave room for the elements of chance, intuition, and visitations from the world beyond. Always. But one way or another, *fear* will be the controlling emotion here.

"But we have to hurry, don't we? At nine o'clock another show starts next door, tentatively titled 'The Fires of Hell,' and I'd like to have everything ready by then so that we can go on simultaneously."

The lights dimmed again suddenly, as if a switch had been thrown, and the warehouse fell into a sepia-tone shadow. Edmund glanced up at the lights, and a brief look of joy and confirmation crossed his face. The electrical buzzing that had accompanied the last brownout started up again, like a swarm of bees in a wall, and the sound of pacing rose around them as if it hovered on the fog beyond the old clapboard walls. Edmund stepped backward, looking around hastily, licking his lips. He whispered something, but Dave couldn't catch the words. Edmund seemed to *see* something, someone . . . and he cocked his head, squinting, and then darted a glance at Anne. Cool air rose around them again, as if it filtered up from beneath the floor, and there was the sharp smell of smoke and ash again, distinct and near, as if they stood inside a burned house.

The smoke smell was mingled with the stench of burned bone and hair.

Edmund laughed out loud with a shocking suddenness, and Dave threw his hands up defensively. The walls of the warehouse hummed with the sound of the pacing now, and the cloth leaves on the forest trees vibrated. Edmund stood still in the brown light, his eyes wide open, his tongue darting across his lips, the muscles in his cheeks jerking. He looked around, his eyes full of anticipation. He held the pistol on Dave as he bent over to pick up a roll of duct tape from a stack of piled wooden casks. He stepped forward, shifting the pistol so that it pointed at Anne.

"I'm going to ask you to turn around," he said to Dave. "I'll ask you to put your wrists together behind your back." With his teeth he yanked at a strip of tape, then ripped it loose. "You've got a couple of seconds left to pretend to act gallantly, Dave, before I tape your wrists. After that, it's all over except for the shouting and the fireworks. So if you're going to be heroic, you've *got* to hurry up. Any second now it'll be too late. *Don't* let another little girl drown, Dave. There's nothing in this pistol but a bullet. It's true that it's a .45 caliber bullet, which will blow a hole in you that we could drive a gerbil through, but . . . hey! I might miss. I'm five feet away from you. Make your move, Dave. You heard Miss Hippie's bright voice on tape. You don't want Anne to sing those same songs, do you?"

Dave sat silently, watching the pistol, watching Edmund. The room hummed more loudly than ever, and there was the continual echo of footfalls and the lights dim and yellow. There was the sound of creaking, and the room seemed to pulsate with a throbbing heartbeat of slowly increasing pressure. There was a crackling noise then, like paper crumpling, and a thin line of smoke rose from the red-coated doll sitting next to Anne. Edmund glanced at it, his eyes widening in a mixture of triumph and wonder. He started to speak, but just then, as if someone had put a match to it, the doll ignited. The collar of its coat caught fire, the flames running down the arms and out across the chest, the big plastic buttons warping and folding. A doll across from it exploded, spewing out a pinwheel of flaming bits of cotton wadding. The doll next to it went up, too, and then another, and in moments all of the dolls burned with a wild fury that lit the warehouse like daylight.

Anne instinctively jerked away from the intense heat, turning her face aside, sliding off the rock and onto the ground, pushing herself away from the trees, away from the papier-mâché. One of the rocks began to burn, and smoke poured out, spiraling upward toward the open skylights overhead. The smoke from the dolls rose straight into the air, too, drawn toward the ceiling like the funnel of a tornado. The room thrummed with footfalls, a heavy bass chord played over and over again, and the lights flickered, the power ebbing until they were like smoky yellow moons overhead.

There was a shout then, a man's hollering, coming from some distance away and nearly lost beneath the heartbeat sound of the heavy air around them. Edmund glanced behind him, back in the direction of the loading dock and the warehouse door, the pistol swinging momentarily wide, and in that moment Dave leaped up and threw himself forward at a dead run, kicking through the campfire sticks and launching himself into the air as Edmund whipped the gun around toward him. There was the deafening roar of the gun firing past his ear, and Dave felt the barrel glance off his forehead in the instant before he slammed into Edmund's chest, and the two of them tumbled backward into the litter of wooden casks.

The casks gave way like bowling pins, and Edmund grunted heavily as his head cracked against the floor. He clutched Dave's shirtfront and clubbed away at the back of his neck with the pistol. Dave levered his forearm across Edmund's throat and pushed himself up, still deafened by the gunfire. He hit Edmund as hard as he could in the face. Edmund's head snapped sideways, and Dave bent around and grabbed Edmund's gun hand by the wrist, standing up and twisting his forearm, levering Edmund's elbow against his own knee. There was the snap of a bone breaking, the pistol clattered to the floor, and Dave shoved it away with his foot, throwing himself off balance, the gun spinning, sliding in among the burning dolls. Edmund kicked him

then, arching his back and throwing his weight into the
kick, catching Dave on the hipbone. Dave stumbled backward, and Edmund turned over and scrambled to his feet,
looking around wildly, spotting a scrap of two-by-two lumber from the kicked-apart campfire. He snatched it up in
his right hand, his left arm dangling uselessly now. His face
was a mask of rage as he stepped forward, swinging the
club back and forth in front of him.

Even through the thickening smoke, Dave saw that the
lights were on now. Not just the night lights, but *all* the
lights. Someone had thrown the breakers. Edmund lunged
at him, cracking him on the forearm with the club, jerking
it back again and swinging it at Dave's head. Dave threw
his arm up again, but he tripped on the debris underfoot,
and felt the club hit him over the eye, heard the sound of
it cracking against his skull. He smashed backward through
the fallen casks, tripped, tumbled through broken barrel
staves. Frantically he turned over and scrambled away,
grabbing up one of the staves and standing up as Edmund
rushed toward him. Edmund held the wooden club over his
head, his mouth working insanely, his head shaking with a
lunatic's palsy. His eyes were slits, his mouth downturned,
mumbling incoherently as Dave stepped in toward him, up-
thrusting the broken stave into his chest, blocking the blow
of the two-by-two with his forearm again, and grabbing the
wrist of Edmund's broken arm, wrenching it around and
upward. Edmund screamed into his face, and Dave let go
of his wrist and grabbed his shirtfront, stepping into him,
pushing the stave into Edmund's throat now, tearing a gash
in the flesh of his neck. Edmund made a strangled noise
and went down onto his knees, dropping the club and
clutching his throat. Dave's vision blurred, and he wiped
his eyes with his hand, surprised at the wash of blood from
the cut on his forehead. He tossed down the stave and
picked up Edmund's two-by-two as Edmund staggered to
his feet, still holding his throat, blood running out through
his fingers. Anne had managed to crawl away from the fires
now—a dozen of them, the rocks and dolls burning
brightly.

In that moment there was a wild banging and clattering

behind Dave, and he half spun around, raising the club in surprise. It was Collier pushing through the piled sets and props, lunging heavily toward them with a heavy metal fire extinguisher in his hand. Edmund shrieked incoherently and stepped toward him, his face absolutely wild with loathing. Collier swung the extinguisher, holding it by the broad steel valve on top, the force of the swing spinning him half around. The bottom edge of the canister caught Edmund square on the side of his head, and he slammed straight to the floor and lay there, knocked senseless or dead. Dave leaped forward and caught Collier before he fell too, and then turned and ran back through the burning debris to where Anne sat against the warehouse wall. He pulled the tape loose from her wrists and ankles. She yanked the strip from her mouth, wincing with the sharp pain, and then rubbed her mouth with the back of her hand. Dave put his arms around her and held her. "I'm sorry," he whispered, realizing then that he was shaking, and she hugged him back, then pushed him away and looked at his forehead. Collier stormed back and forth with the fire extinguisher, spraying down the dolls and the burning rocks, which were skeleton hulks of chicken wire and charred wood.

"You're hurt," Anne said.

Dave blotted the cut with the sleeve of his shirt. "I'm all right," he said. "It's superficial."

The doll's red coat lay on the floor, still flickering with a slow fire that smoldered along a blackened edge of the collar. Anne stood up and stomped the fire out, then kicked the burned coat back into the shadows along the wall. The doll was completely gone, consumed by the flames. Only one doll remained unburned—a male doll, its nylon flesh and its black robes miraculously intact. Still holding the spent canister, Collier stood looking at the doll, his face full of disbelief.

"What the hell kind of sick crap . . . ?"

"Edmund's idea of a party," Dave told him. "Turns out he liked to play with dolls."

Collier bent over and lifted the hem of the doll's robes, daintily, with his fingers. He squinted for a moment and then dropped the robe again, shaking his head. "You know what?'' he said. ''I guess this doesn't surprise me. That's the stone truth. You find out that Edmund plays with obscene dolls, and all you can say about it is that it stands to reason. You okay, honey?'' he asked Anne.

''Yeah,'' she said. ''I guess I am. But it's lucky he liked to hear himself talk. I think we better call an ambulance for him.''

''Phone's down,'' Dave said.

''We can use the phone at my place,'' Collier told him.

Dave cranked open a window in the nearby wall of the warehouse, letting in the foggy night breeze. There was still a reek of smoke on the air, but the smoke itself hovered far overhead, still drifting out through the skylights. They walked across to where Edmund lay on the floor. The raw wound in his neck had quit oozing blood. His mouth was half open, his jaw slack. Collier reached down and felt for a pulse.

''He's alive,'' he said. ''But he's not sprightly.'' He kicked Edmund's leg a couple of times. ''I wish the bastard would get up, so I could hit him again.'' He pointed the fire extinguisher nozzle at him and cranked it on, hosing Edmund down with white powder so that he looked as if he had fallen into a flour barrel. ''Just in case he was on fire anywhere,'' Collier said to Dave and Anne. ''You can't be too safe.'' He laughed out loud and set the canister down onto the floor. Then he stopped, frowning, and said, ''What the hell's that?''

⹈64⹇

DAVE LISTENED INTENTLY, HEARING IN THE DISTANCE THE sounds of commotion, yelling, a sharp scream, voices shouting together.

''The theatre!'' Anne yelled. She turned and ran, Dave

and Collier following her, threading their way back through the props, past the storage room, past the spattered paint and out onto the loading dock. Dave recalled Edmund's crazy chatter, his reference to the "show" going up at nine in the theatre.

He passed Collier, following Anne along the back of the theatre, running blindly through the fog, past the shadows of cars in the parking lot toward the cloudy glow of the lamps on the outside wall of the theatre. There were people ahead, reeling out through the open side door. He saw old Parsons in his Lear robes, pulling off his false beard, doubled over coughing. The theatre was on fire inside. He could see flames through the door, up past the stage—the curtains burning. Thank God it was only a dress rehearsal. If the theatre had been full . . .

Collier shouted hoarsely at his back, and he turned momentarily to listen to him. "Jenny!" the old man cried, and pointed at the theatre. Dave waved at him, pushing past people in the parking lot. He saw Anne stop to help old Mrs. deShane, who had the role of Cordelia's attendant, and who sat on the pavement now, her hand pressed to her forehead. There was no sign of Jenny in the lot. Collier faded into the fog, running to check the bungalow. Jenny *might* be at home and not in the theatre at all. Collier wouldn't have known it if she'd left the theatre in the last ten or fifteen minutes.

Dave looked in through the theatre door, keeping below the smoke that roiled out from inside now. The fire sprinklers were on, and water was pattering down in virtually useless trickles. The fire was already too savage, too instantly out of control. He could see nobody else in the theatre itself. Nobody else was trying to get out.

"Was Jenny inside?" Dave shouted at Parsons's nephew, who was playing the Duke of Cornwall.

The boy shrugged at him and held his hands out hopelessly. "Earlier," he gasped, "she was downstairs, playing in the costume room. I don't know. . . ." He broke out in a fit of retching and doubled over. Dave thought instantly of Elinor swept out in the rip, how she had disappeared into the open ocean so quickly, virtually within moments.

He turned away and hunched in through the open door, ducking beneath the head-high haze of smoke that hung overhead like a lowering cloud.

He shaded his eyes with his hand and crouched on the floor, watching flames run up the heavy leg curtains at the left of the stage. The old velvet material went up like tinder, whooshing like wind through a door, and he heard the crackling of wood burning. The stage was on fire, flames flickering from beneath it along the front apron. The canvas backdrop for Lear's scene on the heath smoked and smoldered, and the Duke's Styrofoam palace poured out a poisonous reek of smoke.

He set out toward the stairs down to the basement, keeping low, thankful for the little bit of water from the ceiling sprinklers and breathing through his shirt even though he knew it was probably a useless precaution. Near the top of the stairs he turned to glance back at the door, hoping that they'd found Jenny in the bungalow, that someone would wave him back out of there. The doorway was empty. Beyond it were the moving shadows of people milling in the lot. There was the sound of the burned-through leg curtain whumping down onto the stage in a cascade of fire and sparks and smoke, and the air around them was filled with the uncanny noise of the fire and the sound of distant sirens out in the night.

Hurry up, Dave thought, hearing the sirens, but he pushed on, forced by the smoke and the heat toward the stairs to the basement, shading his face from the heat coming off the burning curtains. He descended the stairs into relative coolness, the basement still preserved from the smoke and flame. There were nearly a dozen basement rooms and corridors—bathrooms, prop room, dressing rooms, costume room. Jenny might be in any of them. She loved the costume room most, but it was at the far end. There was a basement exit in the costume room, and for a moment he was full of hope that she would have gone out the basement door and escaped through the alley that ran between the warehouse and the theatre. *He* would certainly have to go out that way; there would be no going back through the theatre itself. He thought about the basement door, which was almost always kept locked unless someone was hauling costumes in and out. He couldn't recall that anybody had been. Not tonight.

He threw open both bathroom doors and switched on the lights. The rooms were empty. He went on, down the first corridor toward the props room, listening to the low rumble and roar of the fire, things falling above, and he felt the heat from overhead now, from the burning stage above him. "Jenny!" he shouted, continuing to shout as he opened the prop room door, stepping inside, finding the light, realizing at that moment that he would be dead blind if the electricity went out.

"Jenny!" He overturned a prop table, pushed in behind boxes of junk. "Jenny!" There was no answer. She wasn't there. She wouldn't be playing any games; she'd be scared senseless. He went out, still calling her name, down to the end of the corridor where another door was closed in front of him. Surely if she were down here, she could hear the noise of the fire overhead, feel the heat, smell the smoke that now filtered like ghosts through the broken plaster of the ceiling. A patch of ceiling gave way just then, falling to the corridor floor in a dusty explosion. He kicked through it, opening the door, looking into the dressing rooms. They were littered with makeup boxes, hair dryers, scattered stools, the mirror lights glowing. He saw his own wild reflection in the lighted mirrors, and was shocked at his bloody forehead, at the blood on his shirtfront.

"Jenny!" He called her name once as he ran out. Again she wasn't there, and it was clear in a moment that she wasn't in the adjacent dressing room either. He slammed the door shut behind him and set out down the last stretch of corridor toward the costume room. The air smelled of burning, and the theatre shook with noise, as if a storm were raging above. But even in his haste, barely masked by the creaking and roaring and crashing, he heard something that made him pause—a steady, slow drumming and scraping, the too-familiar sound of footfalls on concrete. Instantly it recalled to him the slow rhythmic crashing of surf in his nightmares, and he felt on the heated air of the basement the unmistakable presence of Elinor's ghost.

"No," he said out loud, but the sound of pacing increased in intensity in that moment, as if the thrill of fear that ran through him now had intensified it, as if the sound itself came from somewhere deep within him, from a place of dreams and doubt.

There was a wild rending and tearing sound behind him, the sound of nails prying out of lumber, of wood splitting and splintering, and he spun around and ducked away in time to see a broad patch of ceiling come down in a crashing, flaming roar, smashing open the door to the dressing rooms, burning debris littering the corridor floor. Smoke billowed toward him, filling the corridor, and instinctively he yanked his shirt over his mouth and nose and ran toward the door ahead. The door wouldn't hold the fire out, but it might slow down the spread of smoke. The smoke would kill him.

He slipped through the door, shutting it behind him. The ceiling was hot, and he could hear the fire burning over his head. He kept moving, into the costume room, shouting Jenny's name at the top of his voice. Immediately he saw her, huddled beneath a rack of clothing, looking at him in stark terror. The exit door was shut. He leaped across and tried it. Locked. The key was gone from the bolt. He kicked the door, slammed at it with the heel of his shoe, listening to the ominous creaking in the timbers overhead, the backdrop of incessant, heavy pacing. He heard something then— a noise beyond the door, perhaps the sound of shoes scraping on the concrete landing.

Somebody was out there.

He pounded on the door panel, shouted at it, then turned around for Jenny. Smoke seeped through the ceiling now, drifted in under the corridor door.

Then something in the room changed. The pacing stopped. He could feel a growing pressure in his ears, as if he had just dived into deep water. Something, some energy, occupied space that had been empty a moment before, and he saw the door to the corridor bulge outward, smoke pouring in around it, flames visible just beyond. The doorknob rattled, the walls vibrated. The clothing racks shook. He caught a glimpse of something moving in the room, a milky blur in the smoke.

"Jenny!" he said, his voice tense and thin. He held out his hand and stepped across to where she still huddled under the costume racks. She put her hand out timidly, and he helped her stand, putting his arm around her waist and picking her up. She clung to him, her eyes wide with fear.

"Elinor," she whispered, looking past him.

Elinor, Elinor's ghost, stood before them in a swirling mass of smoke. He knew it was her absolutely, even before his eyes confirmed his knowledge. Her features grew solid and sharp in the smoke as she stood unmoving, staring at him, through him. She seemed to wear a red coat spun out of smoke, a misty facsimile of the coat with black buttons that Edmund had dressed the doll in, that had burned in the fire in the warehouse.

For a moment Dave heard nothing but the rushing of his own blood in his head, like the hiss of broken waves running up a steep beach. The air in the room was suddenly cool, and smelled like salt spray from a winter ocean, and the hanging costumes around him wavered and rippled on their racks like surge-washed kelp. He envisioned the bracelet in the desk drawer at home, wished that he had it with him, that he could return it to her, as if it were an offering. He had the deep urge, the need, to apologize to her, to explain the ocean's shifting tides, to explain the wave that had drowned her.

Jenny yanked on his neck then, recalling him to the smoky room, to the fire raging overhead, and in that instant he understood the futility of his lingering guilt. He couldn't explain away what had happened; it had simply happened. Anne, of course had been right. There was no blame. That was simply true, for all of them. Sometimes the world couldn't be counted on always to work out for the best. A couple of seconds one way or another—a missed turn, a broken alarm clock—and everything changes in a moment. Elinor, what Elinor was to him, was a figment.

Dave carried Jenny toward the door. Elinor's image wavered as they walked through her. She was a thing of smoke and fog, of night air and imagination, a murky transparency, her feet not quite touching the concrete floor.

The basement door swung open before them, and Edmund crouched through it, peering in at them through the reek, his clothes and face streaked with blood and white dust, his broken arm hanging limp. He held his head canted stiffly downward, so that he gaped up past his eyebrows. In his hand he held the key to the basement door, still grasped between his thumb and forefinger, as if he had more doors to open.

Cool night air pushed into the room, swirling the smoke aside, and right then the door to the corridor burst into flame, fed by the draft of oxygen. The clothes racks near the door ignited. Edmund stepped eagerly into the room, oblivious to the heat and smoke, and began to speak, although it was instantly clear that he wasn't speaking to Dave. He looked right past Dave and Jenny, a tight smile on his face, staring toward where Elinor's image still hung on the air. Dave pulled Jenny out through the door and set her down, sheltering Jenny with his body and ready to knock Edmund down if he had to. Jenny ran up the stairs into the lamplit brightness of the alley, but Dave lingered one more moment. Elinor's image seemed to him to be growing smaller, receding, as if the costume room were infinitely large and she were moving away along an invisible highway toward some unseen and distant horizon.

Edmund shuffled forward, deeper into the burning room, holding out his good arm, still grasping the key. "Edmund!" Dave shouted, but Edmund didn't turn around. Elinor's ghost, as tiny now as one of her own dolls, hovered in the smoke and flame. Edmund lurched forward, drawn toward the image, muttering unintelligibly. Dave stepped into the room again, reaching out to grab Edmund's shirt, but he was checked by the sound of something falling in the theatre above, a heavy crashing and splitting, and he turned and jumped back out through the door as plaster chunks rained down over the burning costumes, around Edmund's head and shoulders, and a half-dozen floor joists smashed downward as the entire ceiling collapsed, yanking itself to pieces, fire showering around them, knocking Edmund forward into the blazing costume racks and half burying him beneath burning debris. Elinor's ghost shimmered momentarily like a desert mirage and then blinked away. Edmund screamed, futilely trying to claw his way one-handed out from under the fallen beams and the clumps of flaming costumes, his clothing on fire now.

Dave ran up the stairs into the alley, into the heavy, drenching mist of a fire hose. There was the sound of shouting, a hand on his arm guiding him down the alley through the water that poured down around them, deflected from the wall of the buildings on either side and raining down from the roof of the theatre. Dave sheltered his face, spotting Anne standing at the top of the alley in the mercury vapor lamplight that glared from behind the bumper of a hook and ladder truck. She held Jenny's hand. Collier stood behind the two of them. Collier apparently saw Dave then, appearing out of the mist and tumult, and he waved both hands over his head, bent over and said something to Jenny. There was a heavy, echoing crash behind Dave then, the sound of what might have been the stage itself collapsing, perhaps the roof caving in. He caught a glimpse of the flames that edged the basement doorway now, but immediately the fire and the doorway disappeared behind a cone of water spraying from the nozzle of the fire hose, as the firemen moved into the building, white smoke pouring out around them.

THE EARL OF GLOUCESTER WAS HALF CLEARED OUT TO make room for a hastily assembled raked floor that was wide and deep enough to seat two hundred people in rented theatre seats. The temporary floor and outdoor-type stage had been shipped across town in pieces two days ago from the Light Opera in Fullerton, along with travelers and painted drops to take the place of the burned castle and the other set pieces that had gone up in the fire. Two of the baby faces had miraculously survived, and Dave and Anne had built and painted a third, and the faces hung from the ceiling of the Earl's now like a trio of watchful moon men. Dave and Anne were both running on three or four hours of sleep a night, but so was Collier, who didn't show any signs of slowing down, and who had been working with a tireless sense of purpose, as if it wasn't only the play he was trying to save, but the entire fallen world of the Earl of Gloucester, putting its broken-eggshell pieces back together with superglue and raw determination.

The show was going up after all—sold out opening night and for two nights after. Tickets for the matinee show were going fast. Collier was already putting together a plan for rebuilding the old Ocean Theatre, restoring it to its original grandeur, just as the old pier had been rebuilt after the winter storm in '88. And now that Collier was no longer under observation by Social Services, Mrs. Nyles had finally been drawn into the theatre's orbit, taking over the role of Cordelia's attendant from Mrs. deShane, who was the only member of the cast who had quit after the fire.

Even the Earl himself was back in action. After they released him from hospital observation, he had spent a couple of days resting at Casey's house on doctor's orders. He couldn't stand the solitude, though, and he stood along the edge of the raised floor now, directing the building of a temporary railing around the floor's perimeter, searching through a big can of carriage bolts and nuts and washers, pointing at something with a carved walking stick that he had gotten out of props. He had Benny Goodman on the stereo and had spent most of the morning making phone calls to theatre companies as far away as Santa Barbara and San Diego in order to call in favors—borrowing costumes, cutting deals.

Casey's head was shaved, and there was a hole in his skull, the skin over the top stitched up. As soon as the doctor had drained the fluid off, Casey had been wide awake and ready to go, as if a light bulb had gone on inside and the darkness swept away. In fact, he was *so* ready to go that the doctor had told him he could return to full activity within a few days. As soon as his scalp healed, he could even surf, as long as he didn't get hit in the head again. This morning he had been at the pier early, watching a new south swell and hooting at the locals out in the water at dawn, whistling advance notice of waves from the superior height of the pier. Nancy was still shaky about Casey's recovering so fast. Just a few days ago they had drilled through his skull with a fancy surgical router, and already he was talking about a trip to Puerto Escondido.

But Nancy had been out on the pier with Casey this morning, and she and Anne had even been talking about Dave and Casey teaching *them* how to surf, which was an idea that was going to take some getting used to, like Fred Mertz and Ricky Ricardo teaching Lucy and Ethel to shoot golf. Dave, unfortunately, had made that comparison out loud about an hour ago, which had been an incredibly witless mistake.

Dave watched the Earl work. The old man's face was furrowed with concentration, but there was no sign of anything wrong, no sign that what they were all doing right now was connected with Edmund's falling apart. Edmund's charred bones had only been hauled away a couple of days ago, his identity verified by the coroner and a set of dental records. But for the Earl, Edmund was apparently dead and buried in more ways than one. Dave could easily imagine the old man's never mentioning Edmund's name again, as if Edmund had gone out of the world like a bad spirit, as if he had simply never existed. Perhaps this was denial on some grand new scale. Or perhaps the Earl was fueled by the pure joy that he derived from Casey's recovery. He seemed to have taken Casey's return absolutely in stride, as if there had never been any question about it, as if one more hole in the head didn't make a damned bit of difference. The Earl, Dave decided, was simply too deep to fathom. He himself had spent a lot of years uselessly dwelling on the past. The Earl seemed to have buried it instantly.

The old man was shouting something now, gesturing at the ceiling with his stick, saying something about the light grid, which had just been hung that day. At the Earl of Gloucester it was business as usual, the beach washed clean by the outgoing tide, the darkness turning toward the morning.

⊰ 66 ⊱

EVEN THOUGH IT WAS LATE IN THE SPRING NOW, THERE had been a storm last night, and the afternoon sky was still black with clouds, the wind out of the west. Every once in a while rain fell, and the ocean danced with raindrops, and the water grew gray and ominous. The beach was empty in the bad weather, the sand wet, the concession stands closed down. Even the seagulls huddled together near the disused fire pits, as if waiting for the sky to clear. Dave was alone in the water, which was winter-cold with the new swell, and he turned around and paddled into a shifting peak that surged up out of nowhere, but then fell away again and disappeared before he could catch it.

The waves were knocked apart by the storm and were breaking haphazardly in chunky peaks, the entire surface of the ocean rising and falling in pieces, like water in a washing machine. Still, he had managed to paddle into a few of those peaks—a steep drop and a quick sprint for the shoulder, and about half the time a treacherous ledge or a collapsing section that dumped him into the white water and worked him a little before the wave lost its energy and faded.

THERE WAS A LULL NOW, AND HE DRIFTED SOUTH WITH the current, idly spinning around and watching the shore, recalling the plume of smoke in the sky on that long-ago day, the burning surfboard in the fire pit, the small dark figures of Anne and her mother pacing them down the strand. Right now, at least, the world and everything in it was muted and distant, veiled by the beach and by the Highway beyond, by the rainy weather and cloud shadow and the sound of breaking waves.

He reached into the sleeve of his wetsuit and took out Elinor's wristlet—the white beads that spelled out her name. He held it in the palm of his hand for a moment, not really looking at it, but looking into the ocean instead. They had never found Elinor's body. Anne had told him that when he had asked her finally. So she was still out here somewhere, maybe right below him—who could say?—her bones drifting on the tide.

The clouds parted then, and the sun shone through, instantly illuminating the surface of the ocean, throwing the depths into startling, bottle-green clarity. He turned his hand over and dropped the bracelet, which splashed into the water and swirled away downward, the porcelain beads catching the spring sunlight for a few moments until clouds covered the sun again, and the bracelet passed into shadow and disappeared.